ON
WINGS
OF
ASH
AND
DUST

ON
WINGS
OF
ASH
AND
DUST

BRITTANY WANG

FABLESONG BOOKS

To my wonderful husband, Ben,
who hates spoilers with a passion, but read every draft and helped me
brainstorm anyway. Thanks for always believing in me, even when I didn't.

Eldore

Shree

Vyndoria

THE FAERIE CLANS OF FAYLAN

GWYLLIONS
Dragon-like Wings

Mountains of Greymerrow

Etho of Strength

SYLPHS
Bird-like Wings

Sky City of Eldore

Etho of Knowledge

NYMPHS
Fin-like Wings

Waters of Isinglass

Etho of Beauty

DRYADS
Butterfly-like Wings

Forest of Vyndoria

Etho of Life

KOBOLDS
Bat-like Wings

Tunnels of Tartarus

Etho of Creativity

ON WINGS OF ASH AND DUST

EPISODE ORDER

WINGS OF
BETRAYAL

THE FAERIE REBEL

THE MYSTIC TOME

"Of all of Faylan's faerie clans,
Sylph knowledge none shall meet,
the beauty of the Nymphs unmatched,
the craft of Kobolds never sleeps,
Dryads nurture all of life,
Gwyllion strength no one can beat.
But darkness comes with no remorse.
All shall crumble at her feet."

FOUR YEARS AGO

I *have to get out of here.*

Fleeing down the cliffside streets of Greymerrow, I urge my dragon-like wings to quicken through the thick smog. Bladesmiths stoke their forges with early morning fire. Loud hammering and the whine of a sharpening wheel thrums through my body. My eyes sting from the smoke, but at least no one can see I've already rubbed them raw.

Blasted tears.

As a red sun rises, my vision blurs, and I crash into a display of swords. They clatter to the ground. Berating voices call after me for my carelessness. But I don't stop, speeding toward the beach below the mountain. The more the tears fall, the faster I fly as the Gwyllion mantra I claimed just the night before rings in my mind. Taunting me.

Gwyllions are strong as steel. They do not yield.

Magic is a crutch.

Laughter is frailty.

Tears are poison.

Collapsing on the beach, I cast my dagger into the sand, wrap my wings around me, and breathe in the cool, salty air. Steadily, the crashing waves drown out my raging thoughts and soothe the growing heat in my chest. The Silver Sea has always been my haven from the dreary, suffocating cliffs of Greymerrow. Out on the wide-open beach, I can finally breathe.

As the sun continues to rise, merchant ships come in and out of port, and it takes all my strength not to climb aboard one and never look back. To travel the rest of Faylan and find out if there's anywhere else in the five provinces I belong. I would even join the pirates if no other faerie clan would take me. A smile creeps onto my face as I imagine what it might be like to stow away on one of the Pirate Lord's ships, traveling Faylan's seas as part of his crew, far away from here.

"Quinn!"

My twin brother's voice brings me back. Gaius' training armor clangs as he lands in the sand beside me, stretching his own dragon like wings. Catching his breath, he runs a hand through his distinct white hair, highly unusual for a youngling of only thirteen.

Though Gaius is too kind to scold me for my tears, I rush to erase any evidence of them on my sleeve. Any evidence of weakness.

Still, I'm sure I'm a frightening sight: eyes ringed red, my brown nest of odd waves and curls in disarray. Never mind how my tears mix with the caked mud on my face from last night's battle sessions.

The sessions that decided our ranking in the Gwyllion Guard.

Gaius' pointed ears perk up as he turns to me. "Thought I'd find you here." He bumps me with his elbow. "You know, if we don't go back soon, we'll never be ready for the ceremony in time."

"You don't think I look presentable?" I try to joke, bumping him back.

It's not that I hate dressing up. In fact, I love it. I've always been theatrical, something our father never fails to reprimand me for. I just can't stand our clan's unimaginative affinity for furs with muted leathers and hide skins. Perfect for the cold mountain climate. Terribly dull on the eyes. I'm also not looking forward to being whispered about behind my back when everyone hears the news.

My smile falters. "It doesn't matter. I'm not going."

"Why not?" Gaius' tone drops, but I keep my gaze out to sea. It's always hard to deny him when the concern in his eyes tells me he's just trying to help. "Come on, you've become one of the most skilled among us. I know they didn't call your name first, but your ranking can't be that bad."

If only he knew.

Being selected for the Guard is a Gwyllion's highest honor. The ultimate sign of what our clan values most: *strength*. With our mountains surrounding all of Faylan, the Guard is its protector, defending its borders from invading giants and raiding dragons. Even against our traitorous brethren, the magic-wielding Mystics.

As Gwyllion Lord and general of our army, the ever-stoic Lord Feyden has overseen the training of all youngling aged fae for months. And after last night's exhausting duels and practice raids, he ushered in the new day by announcing to all recruits which of us made the cut.

Feyden has always favored Gaius, who is annoyingly good at everything he puts his hand to. But I've trained hard for a position too, quickly climbing the ranks, and I have the scars to prove it. Or so I thought.

"I wasn't chosen, Gaius. At all."

There, I said it.

Unsurprisingly, Gaius' name had been read first. The spot usually reserved for the youngling with the most promise. The one that would be trained to someday lead the entire Gwyllion army. Once they read his name, the Guard celebrated him with thundering stomps of their feet as Lord Feyden escorted him into the Victor's Hall.

I anxiously awaited my own moment as name after name sounded through the courtyard.

But that moment never came.

Later today, Lord Feyden himself will ceremonially present those that were selected for the Guard to the entire city. All will know of my failure.

With a sigh, Gaius puts a hand on my shoulder, and I allow my brother's attempt at comfort. If we weren't out in the open, he might have even put an arm around me. But we both know pity is not the Gwyllion way.

"It doesn't make sense." I hold back the quiver in my voice, trying to think of what I could have done wrong. "I mean, I know I have a different way of doing things…"

Gaius stifles a good-humored laugh. "You mean like barely ever listening to direction? Going off with your own plans, trying to wrangle the stragglers to join in your shenanigans?"

"Hey, that maneuver worked last night, didn't it?" I push back.

"I didn't say it was a bad idea," Gaius hedges. "Different isn't always bad."

I huff. "Well, I guess it doesn't work out for everyone, does it? Just look at what happened to the Mystics."

Banishment. That's what happened.

I swallow hard. "Maybe I'm just too different."

I run my fingers over the pattern of scars on my arms. No matter how sharp my blade, how hard I battle for the position, how skilled I become, it will never matter. Whatever the reason, I'll always be a weak little sprite in the Gwyllion Lord's eyes. Never strong enough.

Gaius sighs once more, heavy and reproachful. "Quinn…"

I shake my head. "If you want me there, you'll have to drag me kicking and screaming."

Gaius stays quiet as a warm breeze blows over the beach. While words usually pour from my mouth before I even know I'm thinking them, constantly getting me in trouble, Gaius always thinks carefully before he speaks.

"You know," he says finally, looking out to the sea. "I've seen you sneaking into the dungeons to hear stories from that pirate pixie. I bet you'd rather be out on the sea with her, having adventures."

I raise a brow. I shouldn't be surprised. Though we barely look like it, we are twins after all. Still, it's scary how well he knows me. Like he's inside my head, hearing my every thought.

He takes a slow breath, and I brace myself for the lecture I know is coming. "You can't just run away when things get hard, you know? You have to be—"

"Strong?" I cut him off with a huff. "Well, I guess I'm just not as strong as you are."

Gaius smiles. "Maybe not. But sometimes strength can be weakness, and weakness can be strength. You have a different kind of strength, I know it. Someday, you will too."

Frustrated by his riddles, I'm about to demand what in Faylan he's talking about when he unsheathes the dagger at his side and grabs mine from where I'd cast it into the sand. Putting the two mirrored halves together, they fit perfectly to form one blade. Our mother had commissioned the original weapon before we were born. Before she knew she was having twins. Before her death.

At our birth, she had it split in two, one for each of us. Our dual daggers. The first weapons we ever handled and used to train. Forever a reminder of our connection. Two edges of the same blade.

After swinging it through the air, Gaius splits the halves apart again. "I'm going to need that strength of yours, Quinn," he says gently, handing me my weapon. "I don't think I'd be as strong as I am if you weren't with me."

Holding the dagger, all my sharp edges soften.

"I'd never leave you," I promise, mustering an earnest smile. His face brightens, and he goes to speak again. This time, I'm the one who knows what *he's* thinking. "I'm still not going to the ceremony."

Gaius' shoulders slump, then shrug. "Can't say I didn't try." He stands, sighing dramatically. "I guess I'll just have to feast all by myself. Helene's been busy in the kitchen all night. I think she's even made a whole batch of lily tarts."

My head snaps up. "A whole batch?"

His eyes gleam. "Maybe even two."

He's not playing fair. If I had to live on only one food for the rest of my life, it would be Helene's lily tarts. My stomach grumbles, scolding me for even thinking about missing huge helpings of my favorite dessert.

I shoot to my feet. "You won't have anything left to eat if I beat you there!" Releasing my wings, I take off before he can respond.

"Ha!" Gaius lets out a short laugh and shoots into the air, following close behind.

As usual, Gaius gets what he wants. I make an appearance at the ceremony. But just long enough to sneak my way into the kitchen, snatch a whole plate of lily tarts, and take the servant's passageway down to the dungeons. At least the whispers of the other recruits can't reach me down here.

As always, a large tapestry greets me in the torchlight. It depicts a Gwyllion soldier viciously slaying a fire breathing dragon. The sudden sight of the dragon always sets me on edge. I shudder and quickly rush down the stairs.

"Another food delivery?" A guard meets me at the bottom and sniffs at my covered dish. "They sure keep you busy."

"All in a day's work." I hope he can't tell what deliciousness is hidden inside this time.

He narrows his eyes, but lets me pass. Breathing a sigh of relief, I make my way to where my pixie pirate friend is kept.

"Aren't you supposed to be at some party?" Whit's feathered wings

5

flex as she stirs in her cell, her horns glinting in the torchlight. Catching sight of the open platter in my hands, her mouth drops. "How did you get those?"

"I know my way around the kitchen. They're too busy flitting around up there to notice one platter missing." I bite into the warm pastry, and Whit licks her lips. I hold out the treats to her. "Trade you for the end of that story you started the other night?"

"You mean the one where we went pillaging in the Kobold tunnels and barely made it out alive?"

"Yes! And then Pirate Lord Maverick flew in at the last minute with the rest of the fleet."

"Ah, yes." Whit eyes my platter again, chewing her lip thoughtfully. "You pay so well. How can I refuse?"

As Whit spins her tales between bites of tart, I marvel at each of her stories. Though she isn't much older than me, she's already seen and done so much.

With the dessert platter licked clean and my head full of seafaring adventures, I realize I've lost track of time. Regretfully, I bid Whit farewell and climb back up the winding passageway, weighed down by a full stomach and a longing for more stories.

But opening the door to the kitchen, I come face to face with a very unhappy Gaius. It's so rare to see him with such a frown, I almost don't recognize him.

"Of course you're here. Have you been down there all this time?" he whispers crossly. Nudging me back into the stairway, he closes the door, cutting us off from the staff and hundreds of Gwyllion folk in the next room before anyone can notice us.

I sigh. He's only a minute older than me, yet he still acts like years separate us instead of seconds. "I was just visiting Whit," I try to defend myself. "She's all alone down there with all those criminals."

"*She*'s a criminal, Quinn."

"She stole because she was hungry, Gaius. Not because she's some diabolical lowlife."

"She's a pirate," he says firmly, struggling to keep the annoyance from his voice. "And while you've been off listening to stories, I've been making excuses for you for over an hour. Come on, I don't want you going down there anymore." He reaches for my hand.

"I'm not going." I pull away. I don't want to go anywhere with him while he's acting like this.

"Quinn, sometimes we have a responsibility to do things we don't want to do." He folds his arms, his tone threatening to rise.

"No." I grit my teeth, my fists growing clammy and hot. "You're the one with the responsibility. You're the one who's going to make something of himself, not me. Feyden has made that very clear."

"Quinn, stop it. You're not being fair."

"Fair?" My voice rises, echoing off the stone walls. "I'll tell you what's not fair." My blood blazes under my skin as I picture Lord Feyden's solemn face. "I'm not even worthy enough to be a guard in his ranks, Gaius. And you know why? Because I'm a screw-up! I know it. He knows it. But I won't give him the pleasure of seeing my face as he announces it to the world."

"Quinn." Gaius glances back at the door. "Keep your voice down. You don't understand."

"No, *you* don't understand!" I shriek, hot tears streaming down my cheeks. "No one understands!"

Gaius' face softens. He reaches toward me again, probably to extend an arm of comfort.

But I push him away, all the anguish in my heart rushing through my chest to my arms.

My hands are... *burning.*

I cry out in pain as a flash of heat and light release from them, a torrent of orange and red.

I reel back, watching in horror as flames shoot from my hands and fling Gaius back, his head smacking against the wall with a sickening *crack.* Just as quickly as the flames explode, they extinguish, and Gaius' body collapses to the ground. Smoke rises from his clothes and skin.

"Gaius!" I rush to his side. I reach out but pull my hands back, terrified of hurting him again. What in Faylan just happened? I rock back and forth, wrapping my hands around my body instead. "Gaius, please." My voice trembles and breaks.

His eyes don't open. He isn't moving. *This isn't happening.*

"Help! Somebody, help!"

In moments, the dungeon guard emerges from the stairway, and another appears from the kitchen. "What happened?" barks one, while the other stands with his mouth agape.

7

Before I can answer, Lord Feyden barges through the door. "What's going on here? How dare you leave your posts when I specifically commanded—"

His broad arms push the guards aside as if they're rag dolls, but the sight of Gaius on the ground silences him. His dark eyes ignite, the muscles in his neck straining with a panic I've never seen before. Turning to me, his ever-stern mouth opens, then twists with fury under his beard.

"I-I found him like this… just a moment ago," I stammer. But my youngling tongue has not yet mastered the art of lying. I try again. "I swear. I don't know what happened, Father!"

I shut my mouth. The general never likes when Gaius or I call him Father. Especially not in front of the other troops. But I don't need a general or the Gwyllion Lord right now. I need my father.

Feyden's eyes narrow, but not at the paternal title I've carelessly used.

They focus downward.

He's staring at my hands.

He can't know… can he?

He turns to the guards. "Don't just stand there. Get the prince to the infirmary!"

They spring into action, lifting Gaius' limp body just as he stirs and grabs for my arm. Relief washes over me, though the potent smell of smoke and the sight of his burns tell me it's going to be a long recovery.

"Quinn, it's okay… don't…" Gaius' voice is hoarse as he tries to speak. But as quickly as his eyes opened, they roll back into his head.

"Now!" Lord Feyden demands. "And send someone back who will guard their posts properly!"

They rush through the door, but my father remains, his face now blank.

I take a breath, ready to defend myself again, but no words come.

Feyden takes one last look at my hands. "I'll deal with you later," he snarls, then storms out the stone door, letting it slam.

Alone, I run my fingers over my palms. They're cool to the touch, not a singed spot on them. Though the pain was excruciating, the flames didn't leave a mark, as if it was…

Magic.

All the stories told to me as a little sprite about the magic-loving Mystics come rushing back. Stories of their ability to produce fire out of thin air, like the dragons they believed all Gwyllions to be descendants from.

I thought the tales were only myths, but my brother's burns are not my imagination.

My mind races.

What if Feyden knew I had this ability all along? Could that be why he rejected me from the Gwyllion Guard? Why I've been stifled all my life?

Maybe he wasn't trying to protect his daughter from the dangers of the world. He was trying to protect the world from *me*. To protect himself.

I'm not only a screw-up, and a continual disappointment. I'm dangerous.

I look at my hands. No wonder our clan hates magic. I hurt my own brother with it. The future captain of the Gwyllion army. The next Gwyllion Lord.

Who knows what Feyden will do to me now?

I curse. I can't go back to the celebration, and I can't stay here. Even if I somehow have the Mystics' fire abilities, the Mystics are long gone. And if it isn't that, what else can it be?

I look back at the stairway, and before I know it, I'm running. I run to the cell keys that always dangle on the far wall. It won't be long until a guard returns to the dungeon post.

"Back so soon? I hope you brought more food. These stories aren't cheap," Whit begins before she catches sight of my face. "What's wrong?"

"You still want to get out of here?" I whisper.

Whit lifts a brow. "Obviously. I'd also love to be the faerie queen, but that's never gonna happen—"

I jingle the keys in front of her. "Wanna bet?"

Whit's eyes widen, then narrow. "And how do you expect to get me out of here with the entire city gathered upstairs?"

I snort. "Look, I know this fortress like the back of my hand. There's a hidden passage through the kitchen that keeps the servants out of sight. We'll be on the other side of these walls and down to the beach before they even realize you're gone."

"Hidden passageways?" She crosses her arms. "You mean I've been down here for nearly two weeks and you knew this whole—"

"Whit! There isn't time," I cut her off. "Here's the deal. If I release you, you take me to your ship, and you don't tell anyone who I am."

Slowly, a grin tugs at her lips. "Are you sure? Once you turn pirate, there's no going back."

I give her the best smile I can muster despite the turmoil coiling in my chest. "That's exactly what I hoped you'd say."

Before stepping toward the cell, I touch the dagger at my side. This will break Gaius' heart, but he's better off without me. Besides, I'm not who he thinks I am. I never really belonged. It's time to disappear and become someone new. Some*thing* new.

Wiping any last trace of tears from my face, I put the key into the lock and turn hard.

I am changed.

There are no tears left.

CHAPTER 1

A lone at the bow of the Mad Minnow, sparks illuminate the fading daylight as I drag a whetstone down the edge of my dagger. I've been sharpening the blade for nearly an hour, trying to distract myself from the anxious twitching of my pointed ears, the way my wings beg to release and take flight.

Trying is the key word. It isn't working.

"Steady now," I warn my fidgety wings, keeping them tucked under the bones in my back.

It's just adrenaline. This is what I live for, after all. The chase. The challenge. No matter which faerie clan we're sent to plunder—snatching Kobold tech, pillaging Dryad moon festivals, crashing Nymph weddings where the faerie folk are too high on pixie dust to notice—it makes me feel alive.

But this is no ordinary assignment. This is the mission that could change everything. I can't lose my head before it's even begun.

I go over my objectives for the millionth time, punctuating each one with another rasp of the whetstone:

Capture the Sylph ship.

Bring home the chests of dust.

Become the youngest captain the Pirate Lord's fleet has ever seen.

Earn the freedom I've worked so hard for.

My thumb runs over the hilt of my dagger. Its intricate ridges of swirling patterns are usually calming to the touch. But as the sky's colors fade, an inner light awakens. A familiar, dangerous heat churns in my stomach, warming the dagger in my hand, betraying me to memories and regrets long past.

Gaius.

My fist tightens around the handle at the thought of my brother. It's been four years since I left home. Since I hurt him in more ways than one. Miles of sea between us, and I still can't escape him. As I've learned to do over the years, I swallow down the heat and force myself to breathe, letting the salty air calm the storm inside. But as the wind whistles past my ear, it's as if Gaius is standing right beside me, trying to tell me something I don't want to hear.

"Shade," a voice whispers my pirate name before I sense anyone there.

Startled, I whip around with my dagger drawn. Feathered wings flutter out of reach—familiar ones. It's just my first mate.

I sheathe my weapon with a curse, yanking off my hood. The same hood that usually shades my face, earning me my pirate name.

"Blast it, Whit! Don't you know it's dangerous sneaking up on me like that?" Honestly, I'm more surprised to see her at all. We haven't sailed too far from the Pirate cove. Manageable flying distance. But still, I didn't expect her to make it to us in time, not after the Pirate Lord sent her on a solo mission days ago. I bury the rise of jealousy under my relief in seeing her safe return.

"My, someone's jumpy tonight. I figured you'd want me to report for duty straight away, *Captain*." Whit gives me a dramatic bow, her stubby Dryad horns accentuating the motion.

She's teasing me with the premature title, but I smile at her use of it all the same. It's not without reason.

Though I'm just barely seventeen, my Gwyllion-born strength and unmatched skill with a blade have helped me climb the pirate ranks quicker than most. After catching the Pirate Lord's eye, he took me under his wing, grooming me for greatness like a proud father. Or at least, that's how I imagine fathers treat the sprites they actually love.

Despite his favor, however, I've still spent the last year proving myself worthy of promotion just like anyone else. Raising a crew. Completing a series of missions. We've done so well, most of my crew has been calling me Captain for months. But—

I shake my head. "I'm not officially captain of the Minnow yet," I remind Whit. And myself. "We've got one more job to do."

The ship shifts beneath our feet as I peer at the Silver Sea below. Since we set sail, it's been quiet. Too quiet. Like the sea herself has a secret she's trying to keep. But, like a lady scorned, the sea is never quiet for long. As the sun dips behind the distant mountains, its absence blankets us in a dense, black fog. I search for a celestial guide, but it seems the sea has convinced the clouds to snuff out the moons that are usually so kind to light our way.

Well played, I think to the sea with a smirk. *But you've only aided our cause.*

While I focus on the fact that we're now cloaked from our target, all Whit can seem to pay attention to is the thunder rumbling in the distance.

"Storm's a-brewin'," she says, squinting into the dark sky. As a rare half-breed of Dryad and Sylph heritage, Whit's Sylph-half shows not only through her feathered wings, but also in her words. Words of wisdom and warning—two things I seldom take easily to. "Won't be an easy raid with gallons of glowing moonrain pelting our backs."

"When was the last time you've actually seen it rain?" I challenge. "With how long this drought has carried on, I honestly don't know that we'll ever see moonrain again."

Lucky for us pirates. Not so lucky for Faylan's crops.

"Okay. Even if you're right, how do you expect to navigate like this? You couldn't spot a Leviathan in this fog."

Here we go again. I smile at the familiar scene. Since the day we met, Whit has always been cunning but perpetually cautious, constantly trying to keep me in check. It's my job, on the other hand, to push past her calculations, rally the crew, and get things done. It's been four years of barely ever agreeing, but somehow, it works.

"You worry too much, my friend." I place a hand on her shoulder. "Gather the crew. I've got an idea."

Whit hesitates for a moment, but soon the gentle call of a sparrow escapes her lips. Wind gusts through my curls as wings of all kinds flock to us. The wings of my crew. A beautifully dangerous sampling of Faylan's five clans.

Pirate Lord Maverick has always prided himself on collecting the strangest of the strange. Fae that refused or failed to fit their clan's beloved Etho: their highest value. Their culture's core and compass. Or, in my opinion, their twisted versions of perfection.

Whether Kobold, Dryad, Nymph, Gwyllion, or Sylph-born, Maverick has trained his recruits to terrorize the clans that despise them. Even forsaken half-breeds like Whit.

Tonight, I stare into the eyes of folk I've recruited the same way.

"What's the plan?" Zale asks with a crooked grin. The large puck cracks his knuckles as the gills on his neck pulse with anticipation. After being shunned by his fellow Nymphs for his hunched back and misshapen face, Zale is always ready for a fight, any additional wounds only adding to his unique appearance. But where his former clan had been repulsed at his lack of traditional beauty, I admire each new scar. It's part of his charm.

"Whatever it is, we're ready." Mira places a delicate hand on her brother's shoulder. Though her soft curves and luscious lips make her the epitome of the Nymphic ideal, Mira didn't think twice about leaving her clan when her brother wasn't accepted. Zale squeezes her hand, their bond an ever-comforting but stabbing reminder of what Gaius and I once had.

"Cannons are loaded and at the ready." Colt appears around Zale's large frame, brushing off cannon powder from his trousers and hooved feet. "Please tell me I get to blow something up tonight."

I smile. Colt's affinity for explosives might have gotten him banished from the life-protecting Dryads, but it's a gift that I value greatly here on the seas.

I search the gathering for our newest and smallest recruit. "Luna." I beckon her forward. Her Kobold eyes glow like the moons, illuminating her determined expression. Used to her former home underground, the darkness only strengthens Luna's sight—and her resolve to prove herself. She may not have lived up to the eccentric imaginations of her clanfolk, but she's as loyal as the day is long, ready to use her Kobold gifts for our cause.

"You're our eyes tonight." I motion toward the fog. "Find our prey."

"My pleasure, Captain." She flashes me a toothy grin.

I struggle to hold back a smile of my own. It isn't just the title of *Captain* on her lips that fills me with pride. Watching Luna, I see something else.

I see myself.

Though I left my clan of my own accord, we're all outcasts, whether by force or by choice. Misfits. Nomads. Desperately wanting somewhere to belong. The clans may have viciously named us *vagrants*, but this crew is our very own clan, this ship our ever-traveling home, and I, their leader. At least for now.

"They've come far in one short year," Whit comments quietly, nodding to the rest of the crew. They're as still as stars, their hands hovering over their weapons, awaiting my next command.

"They have indeed," I say. "To the rest of the pirate fleet's dismay, of course."

Whit snickers in agreement.

Anxious to see me fail, the more seasoned captains always snatched up the best recruits, leaving me the youngest and most inexperienced to choose from. But I've welcomed them with open arms. They're the hungriest. The most moldable. Whit and I also made sure to recruit many pixies like us. We were determined to show the male-dominated fleet that female fae are just as capable at fighting and swindling as pucks. And under my rigorous Gwyllion training, that's exactly what we've done.

"Did you see their particularly sour scowls at our last bounty?" Whit says. "Not bad for a bunch of younglings."

"Ah, yes, I don't think I'll ever tire of that. And that reminds me..." I move behind the helm, reaching for the sack I've stowed away.

Whit gives me a look, already guessing what's inside. "This again? Do you always need to bring along some elaborate costume?"

When my hood became too recognizable, I started creating a new disguise for each of our missions, hiding my face from all but Maverick's fleet. In my four years as a pirate, no one's been able to capture my true face—no one I left alive, at least. And I plan to keep it that way.

No one can learn who I truly am. What I can do. What I've done.

"Oh, come on, you know how much I love theatrics. And it's worked so far, hasn't it? Most fae are convinced Captain Shade is a puck, among other things..."

With a sly grin, I pull a folded piece of parchment out of my pocket and open it with a flick of my wrist, revealing a wanted poster. In the dark, my eyes have adjusted, and I can just make out the black fish-like eyes and long crooked nose of the culprit who stares back at us.

Whit spurts out a muffled laugh at the ridiculous sketch, but also at the name printed below it. "Captain Shade, Menace of the Five Provinces," she reads. "They've added to your title as of late. I can't believe Maverick hasn't said a word since these started popping up all over Faylan."

"He'd never say so, but I think he quite likes them." I smile at the thought. "I've only added to the fear Faylanians have for pirates, after all. Besides, it gives the crew something fun to do."

Ever since we came across my first wanted poster, the crew has made a game out of collecting and trading them. Each iteration seems to grow more bizarre and comical than the last, making for much needed nights of laughter.

"So, what disguise are you going with tonight?" Whit sighs.

"Tonight, I honor the one faerie who, at the end of all this, will finally call me captain." Opening up the sack, I pull out a lump of thick black fabric lined with silver trim. One of the iconic cloaks of Pirate Lord Maverick himself.

"How in Faylan did you get that?" Whit's eyes widen. In the dark, it's hard to tell if it's with admiration or terror at what Maverick might do if he finds out.

"I'm just borrowing it." Fastening the clasp around my neck, I imagine him announcing my new title to the entire fleet.

A title to replace the one I lost long ago.

"You're practically swimming in it." Whit tries not to laugh. "Don't you think it might impede your movements? Remember when you insisted on wearing those antlers? We were nearly captured by the Dryads when you got them caught in a tree branch."

"Captain!" Luna's voice snaps us to attention. She's pointing to a cluster of bouncing lights in the distance, cutting through the murky mist. A ship's foolishly lit lantern calls to us like a lighthouse beckoning its sailors home.

"Positions, mates!" I dart to the helm. "We have our heading."

The crew flies through the dark, to the deck and into the rigging. Blades, hooks, and maces are all in hand as lightning streaks the sky.

As usual, no moonrain comes. But even without it, the winds pick up and churn the sea until the Minnow rocks and creaks beneath my feet. With every inch we gain on our target, the waves grow larger, crashing onto the deck as if daring us to proceed.

Flurries of wings dart back and forth as the crew works to keep the storm from pulling our little ship apart.

"It's the work of the Numa!" some call over the increasing winds.

"They must not want us to capture this ship!"

"What if they've cursed it?"

I shake my head. They're my crew, but they're a superstitious rabble, the lot of them. And it doesn't help that Whit, our self-instituted storyteller, is constantly filling their heads with Dryad fables. Sure, the Silver Sea might act like she has a will of her own, but at least we can see her. The Numa are a different story.

"We're not turning back because of some mystical giants. Foolish faerietales to frighten sprites into obedience, they are! Do you know why they call them faerietales?" I relinquish the helm to Whit as they stare blankly. "Because faeries don't have tails!"

"Hey!" Zale calls from where he sits in the rigging. He shifts his legs into his Nymph fin-tail and waves it for all to see.

I point my sword in his direction. "Changelings don't count, Zale! Now get your team in the water and make sure none of your folk are down there stirring up trouble."

His shoulders sag, but he motions to Mira and the other Nymphs in our crew, and they dive into the water.

I scowl. It would be just like the Nymph clan to try and ruin my night. As we're constantly fighting for the sea's domain, they aren't exactly my biggest fans.

"Shade!" Whit struggles with the helm. "Numa or not, the Minnow is barely holding together and the battle hasn't even begun. Maybe we should turn back?"

I glare. She knows failure is not an option. "If we return empty-handed, we'll be back hoisting anchor on some other captain's ship. For good this time. Is that what you want? All our hard work lost to the wind?"

Not to mention my title. But I don't say that part out loud.

"Captain!" Colt's hooved feet sprint up the stairs as he pushes his drenched mane out of his face. "Cannons are secure, but not for long. What now?"

I follow Colt's gaze to my supposedly fearless crew on the lower decks. They've reverted to the fearful states in which I found many of them, huddling together with wide, frightened eyes. I cross my arms, ready to scold them like they're my own sprites, though my still-developing wings prove I'm not much older.

"Now, listen here. Like us, the Minnow is small, but she is fierce!" I pace, the wooden floorboards groaning beneath my feet. "And we all know Captain Maverick won't accept excuses of storms or mythical forces. Especially when it comes to pixie dust."

They grumble begrudging agreements. Usually, just mentioning the dust ignites their eyes with desire and determination. But it's as if their courage has washed away with the waves. Or perhaps my lust for captaincy is finally pushing me to the edge of recklessness. Unsure which is more likely, I fly down to them.

"Just imagine it. Success tonight means our next mission will be of our choosing. And half the plunder will be ours for whatever we wish. Before you know it, we'll be living more lavishly than the faerie queen herself! Who's with me?"

Though Luna shivers, fighting the cold and the fear of her first storm at sea, she steps forward. "I'm with you, Captain."

One by one, the others follow.

I smile. *We can do this.*

Lightning strikes. It illuminates our target as it cuts through the fog, only a few yards away.

Colt stands ready by a cannon. He nods, and I yank my cutlass from my waist and lift it with a shout.

"Fire!"

CHAPTER 2

Our first cannon booms, and my heart flutters as the blast lights up the dark sky like fireworks. The opposing vessel rocks from the impact, ship shards exploding into the air, and my crew charges with a terrifying cry.

"No fear, mates! We can't lose the dust on that ship!" My commands carry over the symphony of crashing waves, shouting faeries, and clanging swords. *Music to my ears.*

I fly to the lookout nest for a better vantage point and grip the rigging, the storm below threatening to engulf us.

As the fae on the opposing ship scramble for their weapons, the same crewmates who giggle over my wanted posters like little sprites ram into their targets. Just as I've trained them, they attack the ship like a well-oiled machine.

Even Luna is fighting a faerie twice her size. She disarms him with three swift thrusts of her blade, a move I taught her just last week.

I beam with pride.

Even as a wave attempts to knock me off my seafaring throne and drag me to the depths, I regain my footing and cackle wildly into the night, reveling in the sound much of Faylan has grown to fear.

If only they could put my laugh on the wanted posters.

The Sylph flag atop the opposing vessel, however, spoils my mood. The half-sun, half-moon symbol mockingly flaps in the breeze, and I spit in its direction.

The Sylphs may excel in intellect, but they're a bunch of spoiled socialites at best. Claiming to be the only clan fit to rule, they hoard heaps of pixie dust to sustain their precious floating city while the other clans suffer. No wonder whispers of uprising have spread through Faylan like the plague.

"Shade! A little help down here!" Whit calls from below.

Colt's white-knuckling the helm as Whit defends against a band of Sylph invaders.

How did they break through our ranks? I look for reinforcements, but those who aren't battling on the other ship are busy with the cannons.

No matter. I can handle this.

Unsheathing my cutlass, I dart below with a howl, landing at Whit's back.

She glances my way, and I give her a nod.

Just as we've done for years, we slice and bend like a whipping wind, anticipating each other's moves as we take down each feather-winged invader. Even with the tang of blood in my mouth and the salty wind stinging my eyes, my fervor only grows with each bone-jarring rattle of sword hitting sword.

My chest heaves as I cut down the last of them, only to see a stocky Sylph leading another battalion toward our ship through the harsh winds.

"I don't know how much longer I can keep this up," Whit says between labored breaths. She thrusts her horns toward the lack of cannon fire. "And it sounds like we're running out of ammo."

No. I shake my head. *We're not going home without that dust.*

"Whit, what does Maverick always say?" I ask.

She hesitates, frowning at the impish grin on my face. "When at first you don't succeed, sail far, far away?"

I roll my eyes and start to correct her, but stop.

The same stocky Sylph breaks through the fog with his crew. He's heading straight toward Whit, his broadsword drawn.

Pulling the hood of Maverick's cloak farther over my face, I knock Whit out of range and leap off the ship. The bones in my back lift as I release my dragon-like wings into a glide, meeting the guard in the air.

Our blades collide in an explosion of sparks.

He's not any more skilled than the others, but he's strong for a Sylph. His strikes hit hard.

I match them blow for blow, but my wings falter. I gasp for breath. Maverick's cloak is heavier than I thought, and I haven't recovered from the last fight.

Okay, no more playing around.

As our swords clash again, I pull out my hidden dagger. I swipe up, feeling resistance.

My blade cuts through skin.

The Sylph juts back and cries out, reaching for his face.

I release my menacing cackle.

"Captain Shade," he snarls, struggling to stay airborne. "The faerie queen will reward me well for bringing in the likes of you."

As he launches at me again, another cannon fires, lighting up his blood-spattered face.

A fresh crescent-shaped slash runs down his cheek.

But he halts, his expression shifting from loathing to shock.

He's staring at my face.

I reach for Maverick's hood, but my fingers encounter bare hair. The hood must have fallen off during the fight.

"You're a... a pixie?" he sputters.

"Yes, yes." I roll my eyes, flashing him a wicked grin. "And now, you're done for."

He charges me, fire in his eyes, but I dash to the left and plunge my dagger into his side. I yank it out.

The Sylph takes one more look at me before going limp. He plummets to the sea below and the waves swallow him up.

He isn't surfacing. I can't wait around any longer to make sure he doesn't, nor do I want to. Killing has never been an easy part of this pirate life, but neither is survival—or keeping myself hidden.

I replace my hood and look back to the Minnow. Whit is safely on deck, having wrangled enough of our crew to take on the rest of the brutes.

I call back to her with another laugh, answering my earlier question in my best Maverick impression, "A pirate never retreats!"

I turn to the Sylph ship, where the rest of our crew is just barely holding on. My folk are skilled, but we're definitely outnumbered. We only have one option left to get that dust.

I scan the fray until I spot the Sylph captain bellowing orders from the safety of the upper deck as his crew keeps mine busy.

He stands alone. Vulnerable. I must have disposed of his last personal defense.

I roll my shoulders back.

Time to finish this.

Zale and Mira appear in the waters below. Locking eyes with them, I scoop one hand under the other to signal a maneuver they know all too well. In seconds, they disappear again under the waves.

I fly straight toward the Sylph captain, my dragon-like wings casting an ominous shadow.

He looks up just as I pounce and kick him as hard as I can to the starboard side.

I point my cutlass at his heaving chest.

"I think it's time you surrender," I say in a low tone.

Though he's against the railing, struggling to stand, he lifts his sword to meet mine. The captain has the audacity to laugh. "Really? And pray tell, why is that? Just because you got a cheap shot in doesn't mean your crew can handle our numbers."

I shrug and point behind him. "You should probably ask them."

Appearing over the side of the ship, Zale brings his muscled arm down against the captain's, causing his cutlass to clatter to the deck.

Before the Sylph captain can react, Mira is at his throat with her knife.

After swimming under the ship and climbing up the other side, they were able to board with no one the wiser.

"My friends won't be asking you twice," I warn him.

Mira pulls the knife close enough to draw blood. Zale sneers.

Eyes wide, the Sylph's throat bobs. "S-stand down!" he calls to his crew. "We surrender!"

~

As day breaks, my crew is spent, and the Minnow is a mess. But we've won. And our prize will make it all worth it.

Even the once raging sea admits defeat as a gentle breeze blows across the stilled waters and caresses my cheek like a kiss. A satisfied sigh escapes my lips. Yes, for all its dangers, I'd still choose a life on the sea over anywhere on land.

Standing on the Minnow, I watch my crew tie up the surrendered Sylphs around their ship's mast, making sure to gag them tightly. The faerie queen's guards have been bested by a bunch of younglings. I smirk. The royal army has nothing on the crews of the great Pirate Lord, especially *my* crew. They were trained by me, of course.

Colt appears at my side. "Whit's helping secure the rabble, but here's her report."

"Damage?"

"Some torn sails and holes on the port side. A few banged up wings, some arms in slings, but we didn't lose one buccaneer."

Relief and pride wash over me as the rest of our lot brings aboard the chests of sparkling pixie dust. Its alluring scent wafts into my nose, a sugary aroma of all things sweet and tempting, yet light as air itself.

"It's the pure stuff!" Luna scoops up a handful of the powdered crystals and takes a deep whiff, her body starting to float without the use of her wings. "Really pure!"

Luna would know. Mined in the dark depths of the Kobold tunnels, there's nothing like smoking a pipe of fresh dust as the rush and soothing calm takes over. Once the greatest source of trade, Faylan depends on it for fuel, medicines, incantations, and more. Growing rarer and more valuable by the day, clans fight over and hoard it as black market biddings shoot sky-high. These days, acquiring any of it is a victory.

"Don't hog it all!" Zale pushes Luna aside, readying for a whiff.

"Pass it around!" others shout.

"No one's getting any until it's delivered to Maverick," I command. "Now, let's make sure those Sylphs are packaged up tightly for Her Majesty to find after we're long gone. Whit?"

She's close by, but her gaze is blank and far off.

"Whit?" I wave my hand in her face.

She snaps to attention. "Captain?"

"What's wrong?"

She shakes her head, her winning smile returning. "Nothing. I'll ensure the crew secures the ship."

Whit is a skilled liar, although she prefers the term *storyteller*. A skill that's often been the difference between life and death. But I know her better than anyone. Her eyes don't quite match her smile.

I pull her aside. "Look, whatever you're hiding, you can tell me."

"This isn't *my* secret." Whit looks down, fumbling with the switchblade in her hands.

I nod her on.

"When I was interrogating one of the guards, I asked where they were taking the dust. After much *convincing*..." She wipes off some blood from the weapon. "He admitted where they were bringing it."

I watch her squirm. This isn't like her at all, and it makes my stomach clench.

"Blast it, Whit." I pound my fist on the railing. "You know I don't have a drop of patience in my blood. If it's not a secret of yours, spit it out!"

Whit meets my eyes, her ashen face silencing me. "The Sylph vessel... It was heading to Gwyllion territory." She speaks slowly, as if any wrong word might cause me to crumble. "They were bringing the dust as a funeral tribute."

I freeze, an icy chill rushing through my entire body.

"Gaius is dead."

CHAPTER 3

G aius is dead.

Whit's words slam into me like a wave, and I stumble back into the railing, gripping it hard. I command myself to breathe, trying to picture my brother's vibrant face. The sound of his reassuring voice.

I wait for his whispers on the wind, but the air is stale.

I grab for my dagger, the only lifeline I have left to my twin. It's ice in my hand.

I shake my head. *No. This isn't real.* It's just a fearful thought surfacing from my subconscious. A dream. A nightmare.

I squeeze my eyes shut, desperate to wake up to my own screams in a sweaty, tangled mess of sheets on the floor. But none of that happens. Instead, I feel the rush of battle dissipating, exhaustion taking its place. An exhaustion that proves I'm very much awake—in the worst nightmare of all.

My muscles lock, mouth dry, brain racing.

It can't be. I ran away from Greymerrow to keep Gaius safe. Safe from me, so he could do what he was always destined to do. Not just become Captain of the Guard, but eventually the next Gwyllion Lord, following in the footsteps of our father.

Lord Feyden.

As I picture the persistent glower that still haunts my dreams, a furious shudder runs down my spine.

Though I was a princess and equal heir with Gaius, Feyden would have never put me on the throne. Not only was I a disappointing soldier to him, but also a disappointing daughter. I'd thought I could at least gain his favor by earning the rank of Captain of the Guard. Gaius would rule, and I would be his right hand. But that would never come to pass, especially not after what I'd done to my brother. That, and the fact that months after my disappearance, I'd heard Feyden had declared me dead. But none of that matters now.

Is this how Gaius felt when he thought I was dead?

I shake off the thought and look at the Sylph ship, trying to make sense of it all.

The dust I've plundered isn't just any pixie dust. It's meant to honor Gaius. There's no reason the Sylph guard would lie. Faylan tradition calls for all clans to bring a tribute to a royal funeral. And no matter the level of conflict, tradition always rules in Faylan.

Gaius is really gone.

"H-how did he..." I cough out the words.

"Gaius was training for the Ethodine when it happened."

My mind shoots to the competition every port has been buzzing about for weeks. An ancient event where the eldest heirs of every clan used to face off in a series of dangerous trials to see who could master all the Ethos, deciding which clan was fit to rule Faylan next.

With clan tensions, rebellion, and threats of war on the rise, the high and mighty Sylph leader, the faerie queen of all Faylan herself, had done the unthinkable. She reluctantly agreed to resurrect the Ethodine. Even more surprisingly, she'd also agreed with the clans' final demand: whichever heir wins, their clan will rule permanently.

When I'd first heard the news, I'd laughed. I hate the Sylphs as much as the next faerie, but every clan has their faults. Being in my line of work, I see them all. None of them are fit to rule, and holding a pointless competition isn't going to change that.

Besides, it's almost a pity that we might soon return to peace. These tumultuous times have been kind to the pirates. With every clan at each other's throats, it's been that much easier for crime to slip by unnoticed. Or at least, there's always another clan to pin the blame on.

But I'm not laughing now.

"Which of them killed him? I swear, whoever it was, I'll..."

Though I'm fuming, Whit remains calm. "Shade, he contracted the Knolls before the competition could even start."

My face falls. *The Knolls Plague?* The rare faerie-killing disease rises and falls as quickly as a knoll on a hillside. With no direct cause or cure discovered yet, once he caught it, Gaius didn't have a chance.

I look to the waters, but I can feel Whit's eyes on me.

"He passed within a week." She places a hand on mine. "The funeral is at dusk."

I lick my lips, searching for words. "I have to go."

Whit throws her hands up. "And this is exactly why I didn't want to tell you." Clasping them together in a Dryad pose of peace, she tries to calm herself, taking a deep breath. "For once in your life, listen to me, okay? Returning is practically suicide."

More like inciting homicide. If I return, who knows what Feyden will do to me.

As I picture the Gwyllion Lord, heat singes my fingertips, and I hiss in pain. Anger rises, the heat threatening to release. A heat I've successfully kept at bay for four years. I see Gaius on the ground again, smoldering in smoke, and my breath hitches.

That disaster was my fault, but this one—this one is Feyden's. The Knolls is something the malnourished or weak contract. Not strong, healthy Gwyllion princes. The only reason Gaius could have gotten it was if Feyden pushed him too hard in training, expected too much, blind to the consequences. Everything I've seen the Gwyllion Lord do before. I run my hands along my scarred arms.

It could have been me. It *should* have been me.

That settles it.

Even though I know it will only aggravate her more, I move to the helm, ignoring Whit's piercing stare.

She sighs, knowing I'll do whatever I want in the end.

I have to go. Not only to say goodbye, but also to make *His Highness* pay. We just have to be smart about it.

As I look toward the Gwyllion province embedded in the distant mountains, the burning in my hands grows. I clench them into fists, nails digging into my skin until I think they might draw blood.

"Let's ready the crew," I tell Whit. "I have a plan."

~

"Strip the Sylphs of their uniforms." My boots pound down the weather-worn deck, and my crew's celebration comes to a halt. Whit trails close behind, but I don't give her time to interject as I dole out orders. "Line up those dust chests and bring up every barrel of rum you can find."

Some of the crew looks at me as if I've gone mad, but I give them a warning glare. They scatter to obey. A group emerges from below with the rum first.

"Here you go, Captain," says Colt.

"Perfect. Take the pixie dust out of the chests and store them in the barrels."

Colt looks at the others, then tilts his head at me. "And what do you want us to do with the rum?"

"Dump it overboard."

"What!" The whole deck explodes into an uproar. I put my head in my hand. Maybe I should have explained the full plan first, but I can barely think straight.

"All right, all right, calm yourselves! If you listen to me, I've got a way we can get five times as much rum after this next job."

"Next job?" Zale says. "I thought this *was* the next job?"

"Are we not headed home?" Luna wrings her trembling hands. The storm must have really shaken her up.

"Not yet." I put a hand on her shoulder, raising my voice so all can hear. "Instead of leaving the Sylphs and their ship to rot, we're going to use them to our advantage. We'll bring home more plunder than Maverick could have hoped for. Trust me."

A few hours later, I'm on the Sylph ship with half my crew, sailing straight toward the mountainside, all of us decked out in royal Sylph garb. The fact that I've got everyone dressed in costume this time, even Whit, is definitely lifting my spirits. Now, if only they can act the part.

I breathe in deeply, the palpable tang of seaweed and impending victory in the air. Shielding my eyes from the sun, I watch the other half of our party back on the Minnow as it sails farther away and disappears around the cliffside. They have the barrels of pixie dust hidden on board along with the real Sylph soldiers locked in the brig—wearing nothing but their undergarments. Picturing that actually makes me smile.

THUMP.

"Ow!" Zale cries as he fumbles one of the chests onto his toes.

"Don't forget to lift those like they're extra heavy when we reach land," I remind the crew, who are preparing the now-empty chests.

"Are you sure about this?" Whit asks from beside me.

I nod as convincingly as I can. "It's a good plan."

"It's *your* plan."

"Exactly." I grin. "Dressed as Sylphs, carrying the chests in as a tribute, you'll have no problem gaining access to the treasury. With the funeral, there will be more guards than usual, but this crew can take them. Fill the chests with as much plunder as you can carry and exit through the same passageway we used when I helped you escape the dungeons."

I swallow hard, trying to forget that I'd also been running from the vision of Gaius' body smoldering on the floor.

"And what will you be doing?" Whit's question brings me back to my plan for redemption. And revenge.

"I'll be at the funeral with a few of the mates. We'll pick-pocket the crowd for extra loot. If anything goes wrong for either of us, we'll use our sparrow call."

Whit considers me for a moment, like she can tell I'm not sharing everything. I avert my eyes. If I tell her what I'm really up to, what I'm truly aiming to steal, she'll just try to stop me. I can't have that.

She wouldn't understand. She'd call it an unnecessary risk. But for me, it's worth more than all our plunder combined. Maverick can have all the loot this time. But the item I desire is priceless.

After a moment, Whit nods passively, knowing she can't change my mind. It'll be fine, just like all our other missions, she'll see. Sure, my impulsiveness sometimes gets us into trouble. But if everything goes according to plan, Maverick will be more than pleased with our plunder, and Feyden will be punished for Gaius' death. If only I could see Feyden's face when he realizes his treasury has been robbed from right under his nose, but we'll be long gone by then.

My confidence quickly diminishes as a familiar beach at the base of the mountains comes into view. The long stretch of sand is not only for merchant ships, but is also where the Gwyllions' royal funerals take place. I exhale, and my breath takes a misty form in the cool mountain air. Memories flood back in a rush, and I grip my dagger tighter to keep my hand from shaking.

I try to picture Gaius' face, but it's been so long. The one thing that never fades from my memory, though, is his kindness.

Always the understanding one. Cool and collected. My twin, but my opposite in every way. At times the puck frustrated me to no end, but even so, he'd been my best friend. My only friend in that soulless place. The only one I regretted leaving; the one I'd betrayed.

I lick my lips, regretting dumping all our rum into the sea. I could really use something to take the edge off. I nod toward the beach, trying to distract myself from all the things that could go wrong.

"Remember the first day we met?" I ask Whit.

She chuckles. "Do you ever let me forget?"

"I still can't believe you got caught stealing from the fishmongers. You're lucky I was there, they would have taken your hands for sure. You'd probably still be rotting in that cell if I hadn't saved you."

Whit scoffs. "As I remember it, I was the one who saved *you*. You were the one begging me to take you with me." She looks to the mountains she pulled me from. "You were more caged than I was."

"Caged," I repeat softly. Always under close surveillance. Suffocated. Stifled. Feeling short of breath even now, I inhale the sea air.

"You're right," I concede.

Whit's brows rise in surprise. I don't like to admit it, but it's true. She saved me. And it didn't stop with that day. Whit has always had my back. Whether I've said something out of turn to Maverick or mucked up a mission, she's always there to get me out of a jam.

I try to muster the words to thank her. For being such a good friend —my only true friend since Gaius—and for keeping my secrets all these years. But expressing my feelings has never been my strong suit. Good old Gwyllion upbringing made sure of that. And before I know it, like a wave on the sea, the moment passes.

Whit shakes her head, lowering her voice to a whisper so no one else can hear. "Someday, Quinn," she says. "Someday, I fear you're going to get yourself in too deep. So deep that even I won't be able to pull you out." Her smirk is laced with a hint of sadness. "I hope you know what you're doing."

Me too, I almost say.

I lean on the railing, staring at the beach where I'll soon face all I've left behind. My next words come out more confident than I feel.

"Don't worry, I do."

I wait for Whit's clever remark. It's pretty much a given when I'm being this cocky. But when there isn't a reason to speak, she doesn't.

We make port, and the crew unloads the chests onto the beach as I get into character. While the rest of the crew are dressed as common Sylph soldiers, their varied wings retracted into their backs, I proudly wear the garb of the Sylph captain. Donning his large feathered hat should be the greatest thrill yet.

Soon, I'll be wearing one of my own.

I will myself to focus on that instead of the fear seeping in. But though the wide brim casts a concealing shadow over my face, I still feel exposed.

I pace back and forth on the dock, perfecting my captain-like stride and voice. "Be careful with that cargo," I say in a deep tone, obnoxiously accentuating each consonant and syllable as any snobbish Sylph would.

Whit gives me a look at my attempted accent, and I jump down to join her.

"That bad, huh?" I ask.

She purses her lips. "I'd keep working on it."

I look for the small team that will remain at the funeral with me. Before we landed, I'd directed Mira, Colt, and Luna to fly over and hide in specific positions at the site. I can't see them, which is the point, but I pull my hat low over my face and let out our crew's sparrow call. I hear three successively in return.

Good. They're ready.

Another sound bellows through the air. The steady rhythm of a Gwyllion drum.

I freeze as the ominous beat bounces off the mountains, resounding in my chest.

The funeral has begun.

CHAPTER 4

As the drum beat sustains, growing louder every moment, fae from all clans answer the call, making their way onto the beach. Time to make sure my team is at their posts.

I look toward the movement in the water first, where I know Mira has been waiting. Though I've witnessed a royal funeral before, a great crowd of fae suddenly arriving out of the sea still sets my teeth on edge. Their fish tails transform into legs, their skin changing from tinted blue to flesh colors as they dry in the sun. *The Nymph clan.*

As planned, Mira melds seamlessly into their ranks, her fin-like wings draped along her back like an elegant cape. Like those in her former clan, a shimmering, wrapped chiton clings to her body, allowing her to morph in and out of her fish-tailed form with ease. She'll be able to pick-pocket much better if she looks like one of her own. As the Nymphs climb the banks, some lift seashell instruments to their lips as Mira joins in with the chorus of enchanting voices, overwhelming the beach with a traditional funeral dirge. It's void of distinguishable words, but my heart still twists at the tragically beautiful melody.

I turn to the woods next, where a large group of Dryads have emerged, and I catch Colt slyly bringing up the rear. It was hard to spot him at first in the sea of green clothing and tattooed bodies blending into the wooded scene. But out on the beach, their unique features are present for all to see. Like Colt's hooved feet, many of them have animalistic features. Horns, antlers, and whiskers alike don't just belong to the tamed beasts that follow at their sides. As the incense they carry fills the air, Colt follows his folk in lowering his translucent wings in solemn respect for the loss of sacred life. But however peaceful and serene they seem, I know they'll be ready to pounce with a vengeance at the first sign of aggression.

As the Dryads pass a nearby cave, I balk at a throng of beady, glowing eyes peering out from the darkness. But it's just the Kobold clan emerging from the cavern. It's one of the many entrances to the surface from their tunnels below. I smile as little Luna sneaks into the throng from a bush beside the opening, spreading her leathery bat-like wings like the others. She blends in nicely with her patchwork clothing of colors, buttons, and straps. She also dons a common Kobold cap and goggles that keep their heads and sensitive eyes protected while underground.

A gong sounds, pulling all gazes upward.

My breath catches as a crowd of Gwyllions parade from the city above, down the steep mountain path right toward us. I freeze, the sight more overwhelming than I anticipated. My feet sink into the sand, and I almost wish the beach would give way and swallow me whole.

The world moves in slow motion as my folk march as one synchronized unit. They follow those at the front carrying an iron casket, meant to protect others from the disease that killed the one inside. Though the body is hidden from view, my heart sinks.

Gaius.

Of course, I knew this day would come eventually. No faerie lives forever. I just thought we'd both get to a good old age. That I would've gotten the chance to say goodbye. To apologize. My hands grow hot and sweaty. Closing my eyes, I focus on the waves lapping against the shore, the sound calming me. I'll reserve that kind of anger for the one who truly deserves it.

Then, at the back of the procession, I spot him. Lord Feyden, cold as steel and as pious as ever. Even at the funeral of his own son, there isn't a turning down of his mouth. Just a straight, narrow, immovable line. Even through his braided beard, I see it. The rest of the clan follow his lead. Even the sprouts at their mother's breasts and the little sprites that stand at attention around their legs keep silent.

Oh, the sacred Etho of the Gwyllions. Strength above all else.

Their self-crafted weapons of iron and steel are their ultimate sign of strength and power. Even to the point that they take their most prized weapons to the grave. As Gaius' casket passes me, I step toward it without thinking. His weapons, his symbols of strength, are mounted to the box. Which means somewhere on there is the one thing I've come to take.

His dagger.

My hand closes around its twin at my side. My brother's legacy doesn't belong in a dark cave to rust until the end of time. No, with his dagger I will make sure he lives on, sheathed to my side, fighting through life with me. As he always should have been.

"Captain." Whit's voice brings me back, irritation scraping through her words, like she's said my name more than a few times. With the helmet of a Sylph guard concealing her Dryad horns, she's ready. "Are we clear to move out?"

The other clans have groups already bringing their own treasures in honor of the dead. Following a battalion of Gwyllion soldiers up to the mountain city where the treasury lies, some of the Dryads carry baskets of healing herbs and spices, as well as fresh meat from the Woodlands. Nymphs bring precious sea glass, jewels, and pearls found only in the deepest depths of the sea. Kobolds push carts of freshly-mined pixie dust.

I cross my arms, sneering at the tradition. As if any amount of loot could make up for the loss of a son. Especially one as loyal and honorable as Gaius. And their presence, their so-called *gifts*, only add insult to injury. I'm sure they're all silently celebrating the fact they have one less clan to compete with for the crown.

They *deserve* to be plundered, all of them.

I nod to Whit, and her team joins the procession with their empty chests, making sure to walk as if they are heavy with dust. While the procession was lengthy, the actual funeral will be quick. Just long enough to show honor without wasting time on emotional weakness. My troop won't have long to finish the deed.

As I disappear into the crowd, I take note of my team of three, and the Gwyllion guards who move through the crowd toward the front. Colt, Luna, and Mira hold still, all eyeing me until I wipe my brow—the signal that it's safe to act. Slowly and slyly, they begin pickpocketing with subtle movements that only I can discern.

My target, however, is at the front.

Brushing up against all kinds of fae has become normal for me. But I can tell it's a rare and uncomfortable sight for most others, especially the toddling sprites and adolescent younglings who rarely see fae other than their own kind. With the variety of sizes, shapes, and skin colors in each clan, it would be harder to tell the clans apart without their clothes and wings. But today they flaunt their wings and clan garb, eyeing each other with caution.

If I'd been a true Sylph, I'd be showing off large feathered wings. Wings like the high-flying birds in the sky city. But I am no Sylph.

I keep my Gwyllion wings hidden under my wing bones as my weapon-wielding clan proudly stretches theirs out, resembling the most powerful and intimidating creature in all of Faylan.

The wings of a dragon.

At the front, the clan leaders approach a nearby ledge jutting off the mountainside. The Nymph, Kobold, and Dryad lords take the stone-carved seats that are set for them, with Feyden following close behind.

Then the Sylph leader steps up to join them. The Queen of Faylan herself.

Soft gasps drift through the crowd as the tall figure takes a seat next to Feyden, her white feathered wings gleaming brightly against the dark mountainside.

I'm as surprised as anyone. The queen is an elusive creature these days. The list of rumors about her are as long as the train of her purple gown. After the deaths of her three late husbands, debates over her possible involvement has only fueled the increasing division between the clans, though no evidence ever surfaced. While some pity her, believing her to be cursed with bad luck, I've heard others go as far as to accuse her of murder by means of ancient dark sorcery.

"I thought her advisors feared for her life too much to let her leave Eldore," whispers a Gwyllion mother, squeezing the hand of her little sprite tighter.

"I guess a royal funeral is enough to bring her out of hiding," scoffs another as she shushes the whimpering sprout in her arms.

"Or it's a decoy." I whisper it mostly to myself, but the Gwyllion mothers glare at me in my Sylph attire just the same. Ignoring them, I step deeper into the crowd. I want to get a better look, but this supposed queen wears a wide-brimmed hat with so many extravagant flowers spilling over the brim that I can barely see her face.

Trying to steal my look, huh?

Another thought seizes me. I'm wearing the garb of one of Her Majesty's captains. I'd better be careful.

I look back at the ship my crew arrived in. Another Sylph ship now floats by its side. True Sylph guards are definitely in the crowd by now. I'm running out of time. Pulling my hat lower over my face, I move to the edge of the crowd nearest to Gaius' casket.

The closer I draw to his lifeless body, the deeper my heart sinks. The words being spoken from the front fade into the last pleasant memory I have of him on this very beach.

"You have a different kind of strength."

His words echo back to me as I recount the promise I made: that I would never leave him. That he would always have that strength of mine. A promise I broke only hours later.

What I wouldn't give to do that whole day over. To convince him to run away with me instead of flying back to the city. He'd be traveling the world with me right now instead of lying dead in a casket. Now, Gaius will never leave this beach again.

I have to get that dagger.

Finally, my moment comes. Feyden rises from his seat and approaches the tomb in the mountain to give the eulogy. With everyone's attention on the Gwyllion Lord, all eyes have pulled away from the casket. Even the pair of guards stationed around it have looked away, though they haven't moved. Not yet.

My eyes comb the iron box. Swords, axes, maces, and all other forms of weaponry decorate its exterior. But I don't spot the dagger. It must be strapped to the other side.

I look back through the crowd until I lock eyes with Mira, Colt, and Luna, who have slowly moved from the outskirts to the center of the crowd. I haven't told them what I'm after. All they know is I will soon signal them to act, and then we'll get out of here as quickly as we can.

But the sight of Feyden approaching the tomb stops me. A single torch stands at the entrance, its flickering flame a symbol of the faerie life they honor. Remembering funerals of the past, I hold my breath for what will happen next.

Extending his iron staff, Feyden extinguishes the flame.

My chest tightens. Gaius is really gone.

Whit once said the Dryads believe a faerie's spirit lives on after this life. That they are at peace, watching over those they left behind.

That's not the Gwyllion way; I've never believed it myself. But for the first time, staring at Gaius' flameless torch, I hope it does.

Another gong signals the end of the funeral.

It's now or never. I tip my hat to my team.

"Watch where you're going, *Wooder*!" Luna's voice rises over the crowd as she pushes Colt.

As planned, he collapses near Mira and a group of Nymphs. They cry out, pulling back their elegant skirts.

All eyes in the crowd turn toward them. I take a small step backward, toward the casket.

A few Kobolds chuckle with Luna.

Dryads eye her viciously. They move to help Colt up, but he jumps to his feet and pushes Luna back with all his strength.

"You first, *Kobie*!" he dares her. "You must be pretty high on dust to pick a fight with me." Colt fumbles around with a mocking giggle, as if high himself.

Luna takes a threatening step toward him.

"Must you really be so uncivil?" Mira scolds. "At a funeral, of all places."

Her folk murmur agreements as a tall Nymph reaches for his long flute and flips it, revealing a sharpened tip.

Taking another step back, I fold my arms, catching the eye of one of the casket guards. "This doesn't look good. Don't you think you should do something?"

He doesn't answer me, but he eyes his partner, who already has a hand hovering over the hilt of his sword.

Luna glares at Mira. "I'd stay out of this if I were you." She pulls out a knife. The Kobolds around her follow her lead, revealing their own hidden weapons, ready for blood. "Wouldn't want to soil your pretty dress."

With that, the fae around them collide. Gwyllion guards, including those at the casket, dart into the fray to break them up.

Confident my team will escape amidst the chaos, I crouch in the sand and make my way around the other side of the casket. I run my fingers over the series of weapons.

But it's not here, either. The dagger isn't anywhere. How is that possible?

My stomach plummets, and my eyes dart to the Sylph ship we arrived in. It's still vacant, the rest of my crew nowhere to be seen.

They should have been back by now.

I listen for Whit's sparrow call, but even if she used it, I wouldn't be able to hear it over the scuffle on the beach.

I look back to the tomb where Feyden still stands. A Gwyllion guard approaches him, and Feyden's posture stiffens as the guard whispers in his ear.

Feyden's eyes scan the crowd… and lock with mine.

My heart leaps into my throat.

If I take to the skies now, I'll be shot down by a million steel arrows in seconds. Instead, I push through the crowd, my dagger drawn.

Not fast enough.

Breaking through to the back, I come face to face with a dozen Gwyllion guards, their swords drawn. Gwyllion guards are not like Sylph guards; Sylphs train out of obligation and duty. But every Gwyllion is trained from spritehood to use a blade with extreme precision and force, never backing down from a fight.

This isn't going to be easy.

As I yank my cutlass from its sheath, the guards come at me from all angles. They attack as one, but I duck and dodge, keeping my smaller frame out of their reach. Listening for every sound and anticipating every move has always been one of my specialties. Jumping, turning, slicing through the air, I maneuver around every hit and block the ones I can't dodge.

The crowd has now taken notice of this new battle, one against ten. They gape as I take three of them down.

"Ha!" I cackle. "You think you can bring down the great Pirate Shade!"

Gasps sound around me. My blood is buzzing. I've never had an audience of this size watching me fight before. For a moment, I let it get to my head.

Wondering what Feyden must be thinking, I just barely dodge a blade and lose my balance, falling backward into the sand.

Pride before the fall.

The guards don't waste a moment. Those that aren't writhing on the ground pounce immediately. One of them punches me in the face for good measure. Stunned, I let them drag me across the sand without a fight.

I can't believe I've gotten caught. After four years, the possibility ceased to even cross my mind.

Maverick is going to kill me.

As Feyden comes into view, my senses return, and I level a glower at him. The guards force me to kneel before him as they yank off my hat, my dark waves of hair falling over my shoulders.

Feyden is the only one who can see my face. I don't know what I expect to see in his. Shock? Confusion?

But he doesn't even flinch. He doesn't look surprised at all.

Instead, he leans in.

"Hello Quinntessa," Feyden whispers, for my ears only. He stares at me with the same disappointment that used to haunt my dreams. "Welcome home."

I bristle at the sound of the birth name I left behind long ago. Grunting against the restraints, I narrow my eyes.

"Hello, *Father*."

CHAPTER 5

After clapping me in irons, the guards throw a cloth bag over my head, though I can still see a good deal through the holes in the woven fabric.

Feyden obviously doesn't want our clan knowing he has a pirate for a daughter—at least, not yet.

As the guards lead me at spearpoint from the funeral up the steep mountain pass, I can already hear the whispers as we trudge through the crowded Gwyllion city.

"The great Pirate Shade has been captured."

Though they can't see my face, they line the streets as I pass, pushing and straining to catch even a glimpse of the faceless pirate who's eluded the limelight for so long. They gawk as if I'm a myth come to life or a ghost back from the dead, unaware just how much of a ghost I really am.

"I never would have guessed Captain Shade was a pixie. Did you see how she held her own against our soldiers?"

"Sure, but no pirate stands a chance against our clan."

"It was about time she came to justice. Good riddance."

If only they knew the same faerie they mock is their princess: *Quinntessa, the Lost Lady of Greymerrow.*

When I ran away, Whit helped me chop off my hair, change my clothes, and pick a new name before bringing me to Maverick. I considered at least keeping the nickname Gaius had given me, the one our father despised: *Quinn*. But even that felt too close to my origins.

"What about Shade?" Whit had motioned to the hood I'd refused to remove for fear of being recognized. I'd only shrugged. I didn't care what I was called, as long as I was free. And it stuck.

Now, back in this once-familiar city, even with a bag over my head, I feel utterly exposed.

I avoid the wide-eyed Gwyllions as they glare and whisper, looking beyond them to study the city. At first, it appears as if nothing has changed at all. Stone shops owned by the best blade crafters in all of Faylan line the main road. My ears twitch at the nostalgic sound of hammering metal and the high-pitched whining of sharpening wheels. Even through the crowds, the heat from their forges presses against my body, quickening the pool of sweat pouring down my back.

As strong as the iron and steel they wield, the Gwyllions' only civil interaction with the other clans is in trading their weapons. Although, they always keep the best and newest weapons for themselves, of course.

Lost in thought, I nearly trip over two Gwyllion sprites who dart into the street amidst their game of swordplay.

"Watch where you're going—" I start to curse, but stop when I catch their eyes.

My folk have always been muscular, strong in body and spirit, especially the young. But these sprites look half the size they should be, their clothes stained with earth and ash, the cloth hanging loose from their bodies. An older puck grabs them from the street, his expression fierce and wrinkled beyond his age.

I look more closely at the rest of the crowd. Like steel, they've been beaten down, losing their luster. Faylan's dwindling resources and clan conflict hasn't been kind to them—and neither have us pirates, who often take advantage of each clan's plight.

Unable to look at them any longer, I focus my attention on the mountain snowcaps, where it's rumored some of our kind once lived. Those in Greymerrow City claim that true strength must be earned through suffering, believing even the use of magic to be a crutch. So much so that most acts of magic are forbidden among our folk. Relying on it is the ultimate sign of weakness.

Our brethren in the snowcaps, however, embraced the use of magic wholeheartedly, calling themselves *The Mystics*.

Legend has it that they developed an ability to produce fire out of thin air, but those in Greymerrow rejected their ways. My folk preferred to work hard, creating fire to craft their weapons the "old-fashioned" way rather than resorting to the Mystic sluggards' seductively dangerous magic.

Magic like mine.

After my experience with it, I can't blame them.

Still, the Mystics claimed that all Gwyllions could wield such magic. That our fire and the similarity of our wings are evidence that we descend from the dragons themselves. But the dragons do not see us as family so much as a source of food.

As we turn a corner, we pass a stretch of buildings scorched from dragon fire. I stop at the sight of a spriteling doll burnt to a crisp on the path. From the distant mountain peaks, the roar of a dragon bellows, and I shudder.

Each year the Gwyllions spend months fighting the beasts off, while others are spent rebuilding from their destruction. The Mystics, on the other hand, haven't been seen in so long that many Gwyllions believe the dragons have wiped them out for good.

A jerk against my arms pulls me back to the present.

The guards tighten their hold as we approach the stone fortress I once called home. Like much of the city, it seems frozen in time, as dark and dreary as when I left it. But it too looks tired and worn. The blood-red flags have faded and, if possible, the air is even more frigid inside, the narrow windows allowing infrequent beams of light. As we walk through the large cast iron doors, ghosts of little Gaius and I running down the long, stone hallway haunt me all the way to the one room I always hated most. *The Hall of Judgment.*

My father passes us on the way in and heads toward his throne high above the crowd of guards, advisors, and courtiers. I stare up at looming stone pillars, scarlet flags, and the heads of open-mouthed dragons mounted on the walls.

Today, I am the one to be judged.

Once seated, Feyden spreads his dragon-like wings wide and locks eyes with me. Anyone might expect a father to be joyous over the return of a lost youngling, especially one who was supposed to be dead. But as he lifts his regal, bearded chin, his nostrils flare. Not only because I've disrupted his son's funeral, but because I'm an embarrassment just for being who I am—his daughter, the *vagrant*. The pirate. The disappointment.

As I'm led farther into the room, I spot my crew being guarded in the far corner. Even Luna, Colt and Mira didn't escape the skirmish on the beach, and are chained to the others who were sent to the treasury.

I scan their faces, searching for Whit, but I can't find her. I hope she got away to warn the others who stayed behind with the Minnow, awaiting our return. Perhaps they've already fled, sailing back to Maverick right now.

I wouldn't judge her for it. Whit and I always agreed, if it came down to one or neither of us surviving, one of us would survive. I'd left my brother by birth in this forsaken place to die. I'm not going to let my sister-in-arms pay the same price.

"This worked out well, mates," I joke.

Some of them laugh.

Gleefully, I notice my father recoil at the sound.

I love that something viewed as a weakness in his eyes sets him on edge, giving my crew a level of power, even while in chains.

"It was like they knew we were coming, Captain," Zale whispers as I pass.

"We were ambushed," another adds.

"Silence!" Feyden commands. The guards force me to kneel as he stares down my crew, motioning to me. "Do you know who this is?"

I struggle against the guards, wanting to lunge at him. *Don't. You. Dare.*

"This here is Captain Shade," Colt says, bold and proud.

"Oh yes, the famous Captain Shade," Feyden says slowly. "She is also Quinntessa, the Lost Lady of Greymerrow... my daughter." He chokes out the last phrase, motioning for the removal of the bag over my head.

A collective gasp settles over the room, but I'm not surprised. It's so like my father to manipulate a moment like this to serve his purposes. Fae forbid that he not control every moment of my life.

My crew's mouths are agape. We all have our secrets, but I can tell that they never would have guessed this was mine.

Feyden twists one of the rings around his finger. "At their birth, the late Lady Lafi and I were surprised that we were having not only a strong, healthy puck, but also a pixie. Twins." A note of pride, however briefly, warms his voice; he always seemed to love telling this part when we were young. Twins are a rarity, usually a sign of good fortune.

But that's where any kind of *love* usually ended. Especially for me.

"It was in their thirteenth year when our dear Quinntessa was taken from us." He looks at me, but I avoid his gaze. "We believed she had been kidnapped, perhaps by pirates. We searched far and wide, but regretfully, we soon believed her to be dead."

I study his stern face. Had he really been concerned? Had he really wanted me back?

"But now it seems she's become a pirate herself, with many crimes to her name, not least of all her attempt on the treasury today." He pauses with a dramatic sigh. "Gwyllion and Faylan law alike leave me no choice but to severely punish her and her crew."

The Gwyllion way. Never mercy, always punishment.

"Of course," I say aloud so everyone can hear. "Your lost daughter is found to be alive and well, and your first thought is to send her to the dungeons."

"Actually," he says, his eyes narrowing, "Since you seem to love pixie dust so much, I thought you and your crew might enjoy working in the dust mines for the rest of your days."

My blood goes cold. *No.*

The underground Kobold tunnels are dreary enough, but being confined to the dust mines is a slow and painful death sentence. Kobolds are already used to breathing high levels of pixie dust. While it still makes them extremely eccentric, that level of exposure won't kill them. Constant inhalation for any other faerie-kind, however, is the worst kind of torture. Most either die from the dust's effects or drive themselves mad enough to end their own miserable lives. Either way, it won't be pretty.

"Typical," I murmur under my breath.

"What did you say?" Feyden demands.

The guards force my chin up to meet his eyes.

"I said, *typical*!" I raise my voice. "First you let Gaius die, and now it's my turn."

Feyden strides toward me, pulling back his hand.

I brace myself for the slap, but I continue anyway. "He wanted to please you so much, he worked himself to death!"

Feyden's hand stops midair, and his face slackens. Is that guilt?

I hold his gaze. For once, I've won.

Feyden breathes in sharply and clenches his fists. "You left him first."

His words hit me like a ton of steel. The truth I'd been trying to stuff down all day comes up like bile in my throat.

I'd left him. Gaius asked me not to leave, and I did it anyway. If I'd been here to protect him, take care of him, maybe he would still be alive. Maybe…

I shake the thoughts away. My father isn't getting out of his own guilt that easily.

"So you'll cause the inevitable death of your only living heir, simply out of spite?"

We stare at each other for a long moment, the throne room silent until he speaks.

"Guards, prepare this lot for the tunnels." He waves a hand toward my crew before turning back to his throne.

My crew yells and thrashes, but it's no use. They look at me with pleading eyes, hoping for one of the masterful plans I've pulled off so many times before.

But my mind is blank. Every action, every word I've spoken today has only quickened their demise.

"No!" It's the only word I can muster as guards drag them out of the room.

They trusted me, and now we're all going to die because of *my* weakness. My need for closure and revenge. If I'd just listened to Whit and taken the Sylph ship back to Maverick in the first place, none of this would be happening. My dream of spending the rest of my days sailing the seas is going up in smoke.

Feyden's muscles relax as he settles back into his chair.

"You bring them back immediately," I demand, as if I am the one on the throne.

Pressing his lips together, he turns to his advisors and courtiers. "Leave us."

They obey, leaving only myself and the guards at my sides.

"I cannot bring your rabble back, but I have an alternative." He wraps his ringed fingers around the arms of the throne, as if bracing himself for what he's about to say. His tense stare makes the hairs on my neck stand on end. "I spoke with the queen before her departure, and she's agreed to let your crew go free without penalty, provided you return her Sylph guards and their ship." He pauses. "And if you agree to take your brother's place in the Ethodine."

My eyes grow wide. "The same competition that killed him?"

"Don't be dramatic, Quinntessa. He fell ill during training. Death was inevitable." His voice is so matter-of-fact, his face unaffected by the depth of his words.

"My name is *Quinn*," I say through gritted teeth. "Your son's body hasn't been in the tomb for an hour, and you're already thinking about your precious power?"

At least I know I'm a criminal. Rulers like Feyden hide their selfishness under a mask of benevolence and goodwill. The whole thing makes me sick. He doesn't deserve to sit on that throne.

"Nothing will bring him back!" Feyden's voice echoes through the hall as he fights for composure. "There's still a kingdom to run—"

"And a world to conquer," I finish his thought.

Though there are few left to judge his words, Feyden leans in and lowers his voice. "If we don't compete, we forfeit Faylan's crown to the Sylphs or one of the other ridiculous clans." He throws up his hands in disgust. "Imagine the Nymphs or the Kobolds trying to rule a world they only ever see half of. Or the Dryads. They'd turn us all into tree-hugging tribes!"

And the Gwyllions would throw the world into a heartless frenzy.

I shake my head. There's no way I want to return to court, never mind rule all of Faylan. I've had enough trouble keeping my crew of thirty from dying at sea or being thrown into the mines. I don't need a whole world at the mercy of my decisions. But what's the alternative?

Feyden watches me struggle. "You may not be the ruler this clan wants," he says slowly. "But you're our only choice."

I let the words sit in the air between us. It's probably the closest thing to a compliment I can ever hope to get from him. He's putting my life and the lives of my crew in my hands, and I don't have long to decide. A life in the mines, slowly losing my mind—or a life chained to my duties, caged by a crown.

My father speaks again, his voice almost… kind. *Almost.* "Gaius would have wanted you to take his place."

Even if he doesn't truly mean it, even if it's just a ploy to get me to agree, I know it's true. Gaius believed in me, even when I didn't believe in myself. Even when I failed time and again.

I measure Feyden up. It's not the Gwyllion way to go back on your word. But I need to make sure. "If I do this, you'll let the entire crew go free?"

He nods.

"You won't pursue them afterwards?"

"They'll have full immunity," he says dryly. "However, the next time they so much as fly over Gwyllion soil, I won't be so lenient."

I take a moment, sensing this is my last chance to bargain. "The pixie dust," I say. "The crew will be allowed to keep the Sylph dust they plundered."

At least this way, Maverick will get his expected shipment. The crew will be welcomed back as victors, and Maverick won't come after me for my head. Though, that fate might be a mercy compared to what my father is offering.

I take a deep breath. "Agree to this, and I'll do it. I'll be your pawn in the Ethodine."

Feyden hesitates, and for the first time a smug smile tugs at his lips. "Oh, your friend has already negotiated that much."

Feyden signals, and out of the shadows come two guards, holding back a scrawny pixie. She's trying to say something through her gag as she jerks side to side, her stubby horns cutting through the air.

"Whit!" I launch myself toward her as the guards yank me back.

But she isn't trying to communicate with me. She's looking at Feyden.

He waves to have her gag removed, and the next words out of her mouth cut me to the heart.

"Feyden, you snake! You promised she'd never find out!" she seethes, nostrils flaring.

I've never seen her so angry. My muscles lock, my mind ricocheting to a million things she could mean, but none of them make sense. None of them can be *true.*

"I'm sorry, my dear, but I had to slightly adjust our deal." Feyden lifts his self-righteous chin. "I had to ensure my daughter would have no reason to abandon her vow and return to you."

No. My daze lifts. "What in Faylan is going on here?"

Whit's face softens, but Feyden speaks first. "You were always clever, Quinntessa, but not very observant when your guard was down. Soon after Gaius passed, your friend visited me. I was intrigued when she claimed she could resurrect my only other heir. For a price, of course."

That's why he wasn't surprised that I was still alive. But how can that be possible? Whit was...

I stare at Whit, but her head hangs low, refusing to meet my gaze.

She'd been so calm when relaying the news of Gaius' funeral. Could it be that she'd already known he was dead before we even attacked the Sylphs? But that would mean...

She hadn't been on some solo mission from Maverick. She'd been here, plotting my demise with my own father. My mind spins.

"In exchange for you, I agreed to release your crew with not only the Sylph's dust, but also some of my own. I was doubtful her plan would work, but she assured me you wouldn't be able to resist returning for the funeral."

I stare at Whit. She betrayed me. Manipulated me, using my brother's death. I'm going to be sick. "Why?... Why would you do this to me? After all this time..."

"Don't you blame this on me." Whit struggles to keep her tone even. "I gave you so many chances. I wanted to believe we could work together as *equals*. But in the end, you always insisted on doing things your way. Nothing I said mattered. Or, if you *did* listen, you took the glory for yourself." She sighs. "I told you that someday you'd dig yourself in too deep. Today, I gave you one last chance to prove me wrong. One last chance to listen to me for once and go back to Maverick while we still could. But you didn't. You chose yourself over us. Again."

She takes a long look around the hall. "You really do belong here, you know. That's what you've proved today. So I'm taking the crew and leaving. I'll take care of them the way you should have."

My shock is wearing off, her biting words stoking a fire in my gut. As much as she might be right, I can't process anything but anger. My hands curl into trembling fists, painful heat singeing the surface of my palms.

Feyden motions to the guards holding Whit, and they start to lead her toward the door.

Before they pass me, she halts. The guards let her linger for just a moment.

Her voice is soft. "We always said if only one of us could survive, one of us would."

I lunge, but the guards at my arms stop me just before I reach her, our faces close enough for me to whisper, "When I'm queen, we'll see which one of us survives."

CHAPTER 6

C rossing the threshold of my old chambers is like being thrust
back in time to my former self. This room should be my
sanctuary. Instead, it's once again my prison.

I'm no stranger to house arrest: guards stationed right outside my
door, flying back and forth outside my window. Growing up, Feyden
always treated Gaius with trust, blessing him with preference and
freedom while treating me with reservation, something almost akin to
fear. I never quite understood it—not until the day my fire manifested.

I guess I should be grateful I'm not spending the night in an actual
cell, but at least there I wouldn't be surrounded by so many memories.
The entire room has been preserved as if I'd never left, probably the
doing of my sentimental brother. But with Gaius gone now, and me
shipping off to the competition, I'm sure it won't be long until my
father turns it into his own personal armory.

I collapse backward on the bed, a gazillion frilly pillows falling over
my face.

How in Faylan did I get here?

In just a day's time, I've gone from almost-pirate-captain to being a
slave to my birthright. It'll be one night of sleep for me, then off to the
competition. The slaughter. All because I let my guard down. Because I
trusted someone. Whit's face flashes before me. I don't know whether I
want to get up and start throwing things or curl up in a ball and never
emerge again.

Instead, I pace around the room. Maybe there's something valuable here I can take with me. I move to my dresser, wondering if anything there could sell for a pretty pouch of copper farthling coins.

As I search, I avoid eye contact with the large mirror over the dresser. I don't need to look at it to know I'm a mess. Even so, the mirror's judgmental stare weighs heavy, discomfort burying its fingers under my skin. I rake my knotted, mangled waves into some semblance of order and pull at the stiff Sylph attire they left me in. I rub at my tired eyes but wince, remembering the punch I'd received at the beach.

That's going to leave a mark. Lovely.

Not finding anything of real value, I glance above the mirror, where two large paintings hang. One is a portrait of myself, commissioned just before I turned thirteen. The other is of my mother.

I'd been a plain-looking sprite growing up. My features matched more of my father's, causing me to appear more puckish. My mother, on the other hand, was a stunning sight, lovely in every way. My only saving grace was that I'd inherited her long, dark curls. Not that I cared much about looking pixie-like when I was younger. But as I've gotten older, I'm glad to see more of my mother poking through.

If only I'd known her.

Though I'd asked endlessly as a sprite, the nature of her death has always remained hidden from Gaius and me. Our father refused to speak of it, and all I could get from the servants was that he'd never been the same since, whatever that meant. I couldn't imagine him any other way.

Supposedly, our mother had been his anchor. They may have even been in love. Perhaps if she hadn't died, my relationship with my father would've been different.

But this is my life. Always losing anyone and anything I love. Trapped in a destiny I don't want.

I slam my hand against the dresser. I can't believe I'm stuck here. Again. Unable to escape my past, while my crew is probably on their way to Maverick to receive their prize. *My* prize. Whit will no doubt be named captain in my absence while I'm crushed under the weight of this life. Just as my brother was.

As each element of the room calls forth another memory, whispering to me, the walls close in. My breath quickens. I have to get out of here before I pass out. Even just for a moment. The guarded door isn't an option, nor are the windows. Finally, I look at my reflection as if she'll have an idea.

Though my mirror-self doesn't speak, a glimmer of light flickering through a crevice in the wall behind me catches my eye. I turn around and draw toward it, lifting the edge of a tapestry to reveal a latch. Relief floods my veins. *It's still here!*

Pulling at the handle, the stone panel lifts, just as it did years ago. Inside is a pulley system that leads to only one other room, where light peeks through below. *Gaius' room.*

Gaius and I had unearthed the sealed up dumbwaiter as sprites. We'd frequently used it to transport notes—and sometimes even ourselves—back and forth without Feyden knowing. Great for getting in extra dueling practice to sharpen our skills.

And now, it could be the key to escaping this whole place.

Approaching the hole in the wall, I hesitate at the tight fit. My once much-smaller body used to fit through our makeshift passageway perfectly. But this might be my only chance. Ensuring no guards have come to check on me, I try not to hyperventilate as I just barely squirm inside and lower myself down.

I breathe with relief as I enter Gaius' room. Though toy soldiers and dragons have been replaced by medals of honor, it still smells like him.

And I smell something else. Sea water.

It's coming from Gaius' window. It's *open.*

I rush to it, breathing in the fresh scent, my heart racing at the sight of the evening sky littered with moons and stars, calling my name. While my room has all eyes on it, Gaius' room is unguarded, and this window faces a side of the fortress that isn't being watched.

I look over Greymerrow City, to the beach below. My wings are still developing; they won't be strong enough to reach the beach in one go. But as long as I take breaks on a roof here and there, I can probably make it out of here without being noticed. If I'm lucky, I might even catch my crew, tell them the truth of Whit's betrayal, and claim my rightful place. Even if I have to challenge her for it, it's better than staying here.

Sure, I'd given my word that I'd enter the competition, but it wasn't like I'd had a real choice in the matter. Like always, I'd been manipulated into making the choice my father wanted. And since when was a pirate good to their word anyway?

Going over the plan again, my fingers clutch the dagger at my side for assurance when another thought hits me.

Wait. I look at my dagger.

If Gaius' dagger wasn't with his casket, then just maybe…

Frantically, I turn around and strip the bed, kneeling to look under it. Nothing. I thrust open the wardrobe drawers, tossing clothes and trinkets to the floor. *It's got to be here.* As our last gift from our mother, Gaius treasured the daggers as much as I did, maybe even more so. If it wasn't on his casket, he must have hidden it before his death.

Above his dresser, a portrait hangs over his mirror, just like mine. I startle at the sight. It's Gaius, though obviously a more recent painting.

His stark white hair is shorter than I remember, wisps and spikes revealing the points of his ears more. A cut my father would have approved of. He may be physically gone, but the painting somehow comforts me. He'd definitely grown up, his posture straighter, his features sharper and more pronounced. The artist had even included the scars that marred his otherwise perfect complexion, probably because it made him look tougher. I shudder, recalling the night he'd gotten them.

The night I gave them to him.

I've imagined returning to Greymerrow many times. In my imagination, Gaius always forgives me, welcoming me with open arms. Now that reunion will always remain a dream. I touch the picture gently with my fingertips, then pull away as bits of stone trickle down the wall under the frame. *What the…*

Clasping the portrait, I shift the frame away from the wall to reveal a hole chiseled in the stone. Inside is a myriad of dusty scrolls and old maps. I shouldn't be surprised; Gaius always hid his inquisitive mind from our father. But in the midst of them, there it is: his dagger.

Pulling out the all-too-familiar blade, I take my own dagger and put it side by side with its twin, both of them engraved with the same maze of ornamented symbols. Placing the daggers together, they fit into the single blade they were made to be once again.

An unfamiliar pressure builds behind my eyes. My hand rushes to my face in search of tears, but as expected, none come.

The truth is, I haven't cried since I left four years ago.

Either my harsh upbringing finally forced out all possible tears, or I've simply forgotten how to produce them. Even now with Gaius gone, though my heart is aching so hard that I fear it will stop any moment, no tears appear. Instead, the room spins, and I lean against the wardrobe, trying to catch my breath.

I've lingered too long. *It's time to go.*

I rush to the window, but before jumping, I look back at Gaius' portrait. I nod in thanks.

Always helping me, brother, even in death.

∼

I'm panting as I reach the beach, searching for the Minnow. My wings ache, so I urge my feet to hurry, cursing the impeding sand. But there's no sign of my crew or the Minnow. Breathlessly, I scan the sea for any sign of a ship's shadow until I spot them. A small speck now on the horizon.

I'm too late.

There's no way I can force my wings to fly that far. What in Faylan am I going to do now? I whip around, ready to scream, not caring who will hear. But the scream catches in my throat.

I'm face to face with my brother's tomb.

I approach, my stomach twisting. Though separated by a stone that covers the entrance, I feel strangely alone with him, so close to the body that used to be full of life and promise. It feels as if he's watching me, shaking his head as I betray my last chance to make up for what I did to him. Exhausted and distraught, my knees hit the sand, my head in my hands as it all comes rushing back.

"There was no way I could've stayed, Gaius. I had no place here. You didn't need me. You were supposed to become the next Gwyllion Lord. You were supposed to be fine." My fingers dig into the sand, squeezing hard. "I'm so sorry. This is all my fault. I should've been here." My voice cracks, but the tears won't come, the pain inside me only growing.

My breath hitches, and I collapse to the ground. Rolling onto my back, I try to breathe as I stare up at the stars, Gaius' words resounding in my head.

"You can't just run away when things get hard... You have a different kind of strength, I know it."

He's right. I can't run this time.

There's literally nowhere to go; Whit made sure of that. All I can do is face what's right before me. My life as a pirate has been stripped from me, my own mission lost to sea. But my brother's mission, his destiny, still lingers here, unfulfilled. My birthright, my place as the Lady of Greymerrow, is his only hope. Maybe this time I can actually fix things instead of screwing them up. Maybe I can still honor him, even in death.

As I stand, my eyes move to the torch beside the tomb. It's still unlit, an eternal reminder of a once-vibrant existence snuffed out by life's cruel winds. I shake my head resolutely.

"I won't let you die in vain."

Approaching the torch, I reach out and close my eyes. Having repressed the curse within me for so long, I'm not sure what will come, but at this point I don't care. Instead of fighting and stuffing it down like I usually do, I channel the memory of Gaius, allowing the pain and anger to flow.

My father's disgust. Whit's betrayal. Every rage and regret I've tried to forget since the day I left home. It's as if a volcano awakens from its sleep, and a rush of heat courses through my veins.

In an explosion of pain and light, my eyes shoot open as the same orange and red flames I'd burned Gaius with burst from my hands.

But this time, they bring Gaius' torch back to life.

I won't let his legacy end this way. I tremble with a mix of anger and adrenaline. An odd sensation of victory and fear. My anger subsides, and the fire recedes from my hands. I stand back, gazing at the torch's flickering flame, ready to make my vow.

"I'm going to finish what you started, Gaius. And this time, I won't let you down."

Having made my promise, I release my wings and make my way back to the fortress. I command myself to leave my fire behind, channeling everything my brother embodied instead.

This is going to be my greatest disguise yet.

CHAPTER 7

I don't sleep much. As the sun rises, I'm led back to the beach. Back to the same Sylph ship my crew captured just the day before. It's ready to set sail again, only this time, I'm its prisoner.

Normally, my father wouldn't trust the other clans with anything. Especially with something as important as transporting his only hope for Faylan's crown. But the faerie queen had one other condition for me joining the competition: that I be delivered in chains. Royal lineage or not, I'm still a criminal. That means no attendants to cater to my needs. Just restraints and wary eyes.

"You can't be serious," I tell my father. "What am I supposed to do if *Her Majesty's* lackeys decide chains aren't humiliating enough?"

"Do not think me a fool, Quinntessa." Feyden calls forth two of his guards.

They carry what appears to be a soldier's breastplate. They fit it around my chest, locking it at the back with a key.

"I assured the queen that you would be chained, but she failed to specify *how*."

My fingers graze the metal, and I lift a brow. "What is this?"

"Our newest form of punishment. It's made from a lighter metal that allows one the freedom of their limbs for labor, but the wing holes are sealed. We call it a *Wing Restraint*."

My eyes widen, and I frantically attempt to release my wings. They don't budge, as if they don't exist at all. They might as well have been severed off. What is a faerie without her wings? The shame is so overwhelming, I nearly beg for normal chains.

"You won't manage flying away while in their custody," my father explains. "But you'll at least be able to defend yourself. You should be good at that, considering your life of crime."

The guards hand me some of my smaller weapons, all of them easily concealable—including my daggers. Warmth spreads through my chest as I look from the gift to my father.

But he avoids my gaze, watching the Sylph ship beyond me.

"When you get there, the queen might tell you to play fair. To be diplomatic in the case of someone else winning and rising to power." He sneers, finally looking down at me. "But you must not trust anyone. Though, I'm sure you've already learned that lesson very well with that pirate pixie."

I glare back at him. *Thanks to you.*

Still, he's right. From now on, I'm on my own.

"Besides," he continues. "Losing the crown is not an option. There's too much at stake. More than you know." His eyes fixate on mine as if they can bore the truth into me.

"More than the crown?" What isn't he telling me?

"There isn't time. Hurry and hide your weapons before they see."

As I stash the blades on my person, I go to prod further, but my father turns to head back to the city without another word. I clamp my mouth shut, pursing my lips.

I don't know what else I expected. Heartfelt goodbyes are not the Gwyllion way. He's done what he can to protect his investment. Now it's up to me.

Leading me onto the Sylph ship, the guards hand my restraint key to the captain. He receives it smugly, reveling in how the tables have turned as I fuss with the fit of the restraint.

The rest of the ship falls silent. All eyes are on me. Some of the Sylph guards glare and sneer, still nursing wounds from my crew's attack. It probably doesn't help that I'm wearing the Sylph garb I stole from them. In an effort to keep my transfer a secret, the captain and my father agreed that having me look like a common Sylph, with the Wing Restraint posing as simple armor, would be best. I'm missing the captain's hat, however. Handing that over was like finally admitting I'd lost my last chance at captaincy.

"I see you've gotten your clothes back," I mock one of the crew before I can stop myself. "Might take a few washings to rinse out the smell of pirate though." I should be trying to channel Gaius' poise, but I can't resist testing the waters, feeding off their hate.

One stocky Sylph looks ready to lunge, his right eye staring me down while the left remains hidden by a bandage covering half his face. I reach for the dagger hidden at my side. One of my crew obviously did a number on him, and he looks hungry to retaliate. His taller friend places a hand on his shoulder, breaking our tension.

Smart friend.

I continue down the deck with my head held high as the Sylphs hoist the sail. It's a relief to be back at sea, but I miss the Minnow and my crew. If I'm being honest, I even miss Whit. What she's done is unforgivable, but maybe she was right. Maybe I was never meant to be a pirate. Captain Shade is dead and gone. With my curls as my only cover, my true face is now exposed to the world.

"Raise anchor!"

The call pulls me from my sulking. As we depart, I gaze one more time at Greymerrow. Even just barely pulling away from its shores, leaving behind its memories, I feel lighter. Before any kind of hope can take its place, a different heaviness settles in: the uncertainty of what lies ahead.

In just a few short days, I'll be in Eldore, standing in my brother's place, face to face with four other younglings bent on my demise.

~

The next day at sea is unbearably hot. Everyone on board is irritable, especially me. I'm uncomfortable, crabby, and bored out of my mind. I try to stay quiet and diplomatic, I really do. It's what Gaius would have done. But every time I open my mouth, whatever I planned to say comes out the exact opposite.

Distributing water to the crew, the guard handing it out pours my portion into his mouth and spits it back out in my face. After that, I decide taking on the persona of a mute will probably be the wisest decision.

Thankfully, the evening brings a reprieve of cool air. It's so quiet, I can hear the creak of the ship as it sways on the waves. The crew is below deck, but I stay topside. I can't sleep knowing what lies ahead.

I lean on the ship's railing and look at the starry sky, my chest aching with longing. My mouth is so dry. If the drought ever decided to end, this would be the perfect time. But the moons shine brightly with no clouds in sight, mocking me. I lick my lips as I look at the water below.

"Wishing you could drink the stuff, eh?" a gruff voice asks. Before I can react, fingers clutch my arms. "Let us give you a hand!"

A scream builds in my throat, but they force me down, covering my mouth with a cloth—the same cloth my crew used to gag the Sylph soldiers. I thrash, telling my arms to grab for my hidden weapons. But the Sylphs hold tight, relieving me of them one by one. There's at least four guards, and none are careful of where they place their hands, either.

"You won't need these where you're going," one of them sneers while the others chuckle.

Every touch, every weapon removed leaves me more helpless and exposed than ever. If there was ever a time I wished my hands would catch fire, it's now. But instead of anger, paralyzing shame and fear overtake me, leaving me cold. One Sylph grabs for my daggers. My heart sinks.

No, anything but those.

With the last connection I have to Gaius snatched from me, it's as if all the fight within me leaves with it.

"We don't care what deal the queen made with you, *pirate*," one whispers venomously in my ear, his spittle hitting my cheek. His breath reeks of rum. "We don't want you on our ship a s-second more." His voice slurs. "Besides, getting rid of you means one less obstacle for her heir in the Ethodine."

He jerks me around, pulling my face close to his.

It's the Sylph with the bandaged face.

My heart pounds, but I narrow my eyes. I can't let him see the fear ripping through me.

"You pirates think you can do whatever you damn well please." He leans in close. Too close. "Well, now it's *your* turn to be thrown to the mercy of the sea."

He rips off his bandage, a crescent-moon scar staring me in the face.

My stomach clenches. *It can't be.*

It's the same Sylph I'd sent to the depths during our raid.

As I try to fathom how he survived, he offers a drunken smile and looks me up and down, clicking his tongue. "Such a shame."

Suddenly, his lips are pressed against the cloth over my mouth, giving me a sloppy, rum-tasting kiss. The others chuckle until *Moon Face* pushes me back with a sneer. Picking my limp body up off the deck, they toss me over the banister, their laughter echoing into the night as I spiral down to the ocean below.

～

Striking the surface of the sea feels more like shattering through a floor of ice. The underwater current whips me in circles, my muscles nearly numb with shock. My pulse pounds in my ears as I flail, lungs burning like they're about to burst. Though saltwater stings my eyes, I desperately try to tell which way is up and kick with all my might. Thankfully, I break the surface, spitting out the salty water and gasping for breath beneath the gag.

I reach for the cloth and relief washes over me as I realize—my arms are free.

Stupid Sylphs. I untie the gag as my legs kick furiously to keep me afloat. *If they weren't so drunk, they would've thought to tie me up properly.* Shivering with cold and fury, I frantically swim toward the ship.

My rage stokes the heat within that I wanted earlier, coursing through my blood, fending off the possibility of hypothermia. But I only make it a few feet before fatigue sets in.

I can't process why, until I remember—the Wing Restraint.

I kick harder, but I only tire faster, the weight of it like an anchor threatening to drag me under and pin me to the ocean floor.

Now is the time to panic.

Spinning around, my breath quickens as I look for something, *anything* that might keep me afloat. Besides the ship speeding away, all I see is open ocean in every direction.

Sluggishness joins the fear and cold seeping back into my body. I beg my limbs to keep moving, but they won't obey. As I sink, the starry sky above blurs, and my eyes adjust to the ocean's darkness. A school of fish swims by while other much larger shadows float in the distance. Creatures yet unseen and probably hungry for a taste of pirate.

Panic slowly turns to acceptance as what I've been pushing deep down bubbles to the surface.

I deserve this.

I believed I couldn't be caught. That I was invincible. But all my decisions have led to this moment. From Whit to my failed heist. Did I really think I could gain redemption by taking my brother's place in some stupid competition? I've failed him again. I don't deserve any more chances.

The sea wraps around me like the arms of an old friend, and I embrace her in return. She and her creatures lurking nearby will finally claim me as their own.

Releasing one last breath, water fills my mouth…

Then two arms wrap around my waist.

CHAPTER 8

C oughing violently, water rips from my throat and I heave in gulps of air. I flop onto a wood floor, my vision out of focus. A puckish figure leans over me. He's saying something, but the sound is garbled. An impossible thought floats through my mind.

Gaius?

I correct my foggy brain. Even in my delirium, I know that can't be true. Besides Gaius being dead, the faerie over me has blue-tinted skin. As he comes into focus, the gills on his neck pulse and relax.

Nymph.

His wrapped garment reveals a mostly bare chest, dripping water highlighting every lean muscle in the moonlight. As his skin dries, it fades to a warm olive tan, and his teal, oval eyes narrow with concern. Curling Nymph symbols are etched in the buzzed sides of his midnight blue hair, while the longer hair on top hangs toward me. It drips salty water droplets into my mouth, and I swipe them away. I never want to taste sea water again.

"She lives!" Like most Nymph voices, his is as smooth as honey. Warm and soothing, but never to be trusted. "You're going to be okay. Just stay still." My head whirls as his words echo and reverberate around me, making me dizzy.

I must still have water in my ears.

"Now, what's a beauty like you taking a midnight swim in the middle of the ocean for?" He chuckles, his hand reaching for my face.

Even in my foggy state, my Gwyllion reflexes are sharp. I grab his wrist, and his eyes grow wide. He tries to pull away, but I hold firm.

Taking another sweet gulp of air, my voice croaks out with as much intensity as I can muster. "No one… touches me."

I let go, and he gingerly rubs his wrist, his face shifting from surprise to intrigue. A dimple forms on his right cheek. "I think the phrase you're looking for is *thank you.*"

Thank you? I try to remember how I've gotten… wherever I am. The Nymph's voice doesn't sound watery anymore, and as my fogginess clears, visions of being grabbed and thrown overboard send me frantically turning every which way.

"Where am I?" I demand. I'm definitely on a ship. But this time I'm surrounded by Nymphs, the iconic trident on their flag waving in the evening breeze.

"Whoa, whoa." The Nymph moves toward me, but then thinks better of it, pulling back. "Our ship spotted you as you were drowning. I saved you." He seems particularly proud of that last fact.

"Spotted me?" I hadn't seen another boat anywhere.

"Well, underneath the water, that is. She can travel underwater, too." He pats the ship's floor as if it's a pet. Slowly, I recall the large shadow looming in the depths before I was saved. Though I'm mortified to be rescued by a Nymph, at least it wasn't a hungry beast.

"We almost passed right by. But lucky for you, the moonlight was shining through at just the right angle, reflecting off your… fancy armor there." He points to my Wing Restraint, unaware of what it truly is. For once, I'm glad I'm wearing it. "And now I welcome you aboard my ship, *The Kalypso.*" He opens his arms toward the vessel and his crew.

I recognize the name. This is not just any Nymph ship. It is the ship of the Nymph heir. I must be looking at one of my competitors. Growing up, I was never taken beyond the borders of Greymerrow, let alone allowed to meet the other heirs, so I take in his features afresh. He doesn't look much older than me. Though I'm encumbered by a rampage of shivers, my wet body cooling in the frigid air, I try to stand to better meet his stature. He offers his hand, but I wave it away.

"Here." My competitor turns as one of his crew surfaces from below deck with a blanket. He takes it and gently holds it out to me. "My name is Sir Aeron, or just Aeron if you prefer." Instead of the usual fearful gaze I'm used to, intrigue and concern color his expression, as if I'm a small, frightened creature he doesn't want to scare away.

Oh, how wrong you are. If he comes close again, I'll teach him that fear is the appropriate response. But when I reach for my daggers, I remember that I've been disarmed.

"I know who you are." I snatch the blanket from him, wrapping myself in the dry fabric.

"You do, do you?" Aeron's chest puffs up, but there's an odd quirk to his brow. "And who might you be?"

I wrap the blanket tighter, hesitating. If I tell him who I am, there's a good chance he'll throw me back overboard, and I'm in no hurry to return to the icy deep. I was cocky and careless on the Sylph ship, but I won't make that mistake again. To the Nymphs, I'm already a hated pirate who acts like she owns their ocean. Now, I'm also one of the few who can keep this particular Nymph from gaining the crown. He's probably on his way to Eldore right now. *What a twist of fate.* The fact that I am alive at the hand of a rival makes me wonder if Gaius has been watching over me from the beyond, after all.

"Well?" Aeron's brows dip, as though curious why I haven't answered.

If I want to keep living, I have to think fast. Whether I like it or not, I have to be cautious and cunning. I have to think like Whit. "D-do you always go out of your way to save faeries you don't k-know?" I ask, teeth chattering, attempting to buy more time so I can think of a good story to spin.

"Only the pretty ones." He smiles.

I nearly laugh in his face. I'm sopping wet and huddled under a large blanket. I'd heard the Nymph heir was a flirt, but I didn't expect him to be desperate. His confidence tells me he's used to other pixies falling for his typical Nymph charm and good looks with ease. But even if I had time in the last few years to have a type, fish-boy wouldn't be it.

"Come now, we have to be able to call you something. Obviously you're Sylph militia." He points to the uniform peeking out from the blanket. "How in Faylan did you end up out in the middle of the ocean all by yourself?"

"Whit. My name is Whit," I stall, blurting out the first name that comes to mind as I try to channel my former friend.

To get out of a jam, Whit has a gift of telling more or less the truth, with enough twists to make her seem the innocent one. It can be tricky, but over the years she's taught me this particular art. Since this Nymph already believes me to be a Sylph with some strange armor, I begin my tale slowly, watching Aeron's reaction, working out the details as I go.

"I was aboard a ship with my comrades, traveling back from the Gwyllion prince's funeral."

"Ah, yes. Gaius." His smile fades. "I was sorry to miss it. I had... a previous obligation."

I cock a brow. Is his regret authentic?

"What a time for the Gwyllions to lose their only heir able to compete in the Ethodine," he adds.

I try to remember I'm playing a Sylph, but the next phrase comes out of my mouth faster than I can catch it. "On the contrary. Seems the Gwyllion princess has been found alive and well. In fact, she's been hiding all these years as the Pirate Shade." I pull the blanket closer to hide my smugness, peeking out at Aeron's reaction.

He cocks his head, then bursts into laughter, his crew following. "You mean to tell me that crazy loon is a bloody princess?"

Though their laughter surprisingly stings, I use the detail to my advantage. "It's true! My crew was commissioned to bring her back to compete, but she tried to escape. When I attempted to restrain her, she knocked me overboard."

Their laughter dies down. I try not to smile as the half-lie comes out better than I hoped. Maybe I don't need Whit after all.

My body warms as I continue my story with gusto. "While she mercilessly tore through my crew, my armor caused me to sink." I tap the metal restraint. "Obviously, this stuff wasn't made for swimming."

"Typical pirate." Aeron snorts, and the others murmur agreements. "Not an honorable bone in their bodies, especially *that* one. Feyden must be desperate or a fool to consider her as his champion, let alone a possible queen of Faylan."

"You could say that again," I agree, trying to dismiss the strange pang of his words. Feyden *is* a fool, and I don't really want the crown. But pirates carry a different kind of honor. And I'd sure as hell make a better leader than any Nymph.

"Well, our clans might not be on the best of terms, but any enemy of the Pirate Shade is a friend of mine." Aeron physically shakes off the thought of the pirate he doesn't realize is standing right in front of him. "As an act of goodwill, I give you my word that I'll personally assure that you make it back to Eldore safely. As it happens, that's exactly where we're headed." He takes a few careful steps forward, extending his hand. "Welcome aboard, Whit."

I shake his hand firmly. *Perfect.* I can't wait to see Aeron's face when he realizes he's helped his own competitor and sworn enemy safely reach the sky city.

Now all I have to do is keep my big mouth in check until then.

~

The rest of the night, I watch Aeron and his crew carefully. I've been offered my own sleeping quarters, but unlike on the Sylph ship, there's no way I'm letting my guard down again.

This is not a ship packed with militia, however. On closer inspection, most of Aeron's crew don't look much older than myself. But, there is, of course, much frivolity among them.

As one puck plays his fiddle, Aeron joins the group dancing to the tune. He's light and free on his feet as he falls in perfect step with a Nymph jig, one I've seen Zale and Mira dance many times before. Laughter turns into hoots and hollers as those on the sidelines gulp down their drinks and clap in time.

In spite of myself, I have to admire them. Unlike the Gwyllions, Nymphs always look for a reason to celebrate, and celebrate *loudly.* With beauty as their Etho, they're the greatest entertainers and party throwers in all of Faylan. They drink up life, deal with the hangover, and go right back in for more.

The crowd's clapping speeds up, challenging the player and dancers to keep up with the tempo. Some falter and are forced to join the growing crowd, but Aeron isn't skipping a beat. Beating out the last Nymph standing, he lands a triumphant pose as the tune comes to a finish. He bows, basking in his crew's applause. He then motions to the fiddle player, bowing to him as well.

Catching his breath, Aeron saunters over to the much shorter Nymph who nearly bested him and claps him on the back. "Hey Fynn, nice footwork out there."

"Not as good as you." Fynn pushes blond ringlets off his sweaty brow and hands him a drink. "Just like Aeron to show us all up. Is there anything you can't do?"

"Or any lady who won't fall for your charms?" adds another with a nudge.

Aeron opens his mouth, but catches me staring through the crowd. He smiles, but I quickly turn away before hearing him say, "The sea herself, lads. The sea herself."

They laugh. Being their prince, I'm surprised to see him treat his crewmates less like the lower class they are and more like brothers. Their camaraderie reminds me of my own crew, and a small part of me wishes I could join in.

But this is not some joyride to Eldore. This is my chance to learn more about my competitor. Perhaps I can find a weakness to use against him in the Ethodine. I've caught Aeron glancing my way more than a few times, but I don't want to appear desperate for information. I'll stay aloof. *Make the sea devil come to me.*

Finding a stray piece of wood, I swipe a switchblade from a Nymph who's taken one too many swigs of ale and settle near a crate on the starboard side. Whittling the wood should help me stay awake as I wait. It could also come in handy if any of the Nymphs decide to try any funny business.

"Why aren't you drinking?" Aeron appears just as I hoped he would, offering me a pint. "You just escaped the jaws of death. You should be celebrating!"

My eyes grow heavy as I stare at the glass. All I want to do is consume the whole thing and sleep through the rest of the voyage. But I can't get Whit's wary voice out of my mind, warning me I can't trust what it could be laced with. Regretfully, I shake my head.

"Suit yourself." Keeping his distance, Aeron shrugs and sits, guzzling down his glass as well as mine.

I curse my caution, wanting to grab what's left in the glass and wash it down myself. Instead, I raise a brow at his gluttony and focus on my blade, taking out my lack of ale on the block in my hands.

He flashes me a winning smile. "What?"

"Just wondering what *you're* celebrating. It's not like you've won the competition yet or anything." I wonder what his strategy to win might be. And how long it will take to get him to reveal it.

"Oh, there's always something to celebrate," he says jubilantly, but then sighs. "I guess I should celebrate that I've just been married off."

I nearly drop the switchblade. "You just got *married*?" I tell myself that my interest is strictly business. Research. But I am definitely intrigued. I can't imagine being married at our age.

"Pretty much." He shrugs.

"Let me get this straight. You got married and then left your bride to risk your life to *possibly* win the crown?" It's more of a judgmental statement than a question.

"More or less." He goes to take another swig of ale but frowns at his empty glass, putting it down in defeat.

"You don't seem very happy. About the marriage, I mean," I prod, hoping for some juicy details. Maybe a personal confession I can use as leverage once the competition starts.

"Oh, she's gorgeous, don't get me wrong," Aeron assures me, as if that's all that matters. To a Nymph, it's usually all that does. He looks to the starry sky, leaning his head against the ship and heaving another sigh. *So dramatic.* "And yet…" He hesitates. I feel like I'm listening to one of Whit's stories, waiting for the cliffhanger to drop and let me off the ledge. "There's something missing, you know? I don't feel the way I should."

I roll my eyes. "Feelings aren't everything." I return to my whittling, growing uninterested with his vagueness. "Feelings can be dangerous."

He turns to me with curiosity. "That's a pretty Gwyllion thing to say."

Blast, I curse myself as I hasten the blade against the wood. That's *exactly* what any Gwyllion would say. After years away from my clan, all it took was one lousy day back there for its poison to sink back in. Still, I have to admit there's some truth to my statement. I see it every time my fiery anger surfaces. Gaius' smoldering body flashes in my mind before I realize I haven't answered Aeron. Why am I talking so casually with him? I should be gaining information and trying to stay alive.

"I've done a lot of study on the Gwyllion way." I try to play off the Sylph Etho of Knowledge, hoping it will dispel his curiosity. "They have some good points."

"Yes, yes." He waves his hand dismissively, and I breathe a sigh of relief. "But emotions bring life!" He leans in, speaking more passionately with every word. "They fuel our dreams. Give us a reason to wake up and pursue what we want most."

I keep my eyes on my carving. "They can also drag you down into a pit of misery and make you never want to get out of bed." What am I saying? It's like word vomit coming up from who knows where, and I haven't even had a drink yet.

Swiping violently, my blade misses the wooden block that's now almost half its original size and nicks my finger. This time I curse out loud as blood breaks through the skin. That's it. It's time to get out of here. Besides, Aeron is starting to sway from the ale, and I'm not going to hang around to see what drunk-Aeron is like. Sober-Aeron is quite enough, thank you.

Throwing the block to the floor, I tuck the switchblade into my boot and put my finger in my mouth. "Excuse me," I mumble, standing to leave.

I'm wasting my time. I'm not getting anything useful out of him tonight, and I know his type. Sure, he might have saved me, and he might be kind to his crew, but he's just like every other proud, pixie-prowling puck I've come across. One that always wants something in return. He's only thinking about himself. I'm sure of it.

"Whit."

His hand clasps my free one, and I turn.

Aeron is so close, his breath tickles my skin. Instead of reeking of spirits, it's sweet. I freeze, captivated by the intensity of his surprisingly sober gaze, his teal eyes boring into mine.

For a moment, I think he's about to kiss me, which would definitely earn him a slap across the face. Instead, he tears off the end of his sleeve with one quick motion and guides my finger out of my mouth. Before I can stop him, he gingerly wraps the wound. Everyone else on board is too consumed with their own frivolity to notice us, but I suddenly feel self-conscious as his fingers graze mine.

"There." He smiles as he gently ties it off. "Now, do you really mean to tell me that you'd rather spend a life denying all that you feel just to avoid the possibility of a little pain?"

His eyes search mine, and for the first time, I notice how many other shades of blue swim in them. Like the rolling ocean waves on a calm day. I rush to think of a quippy answer to his question, but my mind is blank, and I don't have time to think anyway.

I feel something. A *heat*.

Not the same heat as when anger rises. No, this one ebbs and flows through my veins, bringing a flush to my face and a tingling to my fingertips. Aeron must feel it too; his eyes shift from my face to my heated hand in his.

Before I can stop it, a spark ignites.

"Ouch!" we say at the same time, both pulling away.

Blast! I examine my hand, but thankfully the spark disappeared as quickly as it flashed. Like those that sputter off of a sharpening wheel.

"What was—" There's a surprising laugh in Aeron's voice as he shakes his hand, looking at me with one eyebrow cocked.

"No idea." I hold my wrapped finger close and take a shallow breath, encouraging the heat to dissipate. "Thanks for this, but I think it's time I try to get some sleep."

And with that, I leave him on the deck.

CHAPTER 9

O nce I find the room I've been assigned to, I lock the door behind me and pace, still holding my finger.

What in Faylan was that? My heat has never felt like that before. Never conjured as a spark. How did it...

Without warning, the vision of Aeron gingerly wrapping my wound and looking at me with those sincere teal eyes floats into my mind.

"Would you rather deny all that you feel just to avoid the possibility of a little pain?"

Yes, yes I would. That's what I should have said.

I wave the image away. Aeron can't have caused this. His kindness was just a ploy to get whatever he wants from me. And whatever this is, I just want it to go away so I can actually get some shut-eye.

But my hand is still warm. What if it sparks again? Setting my sheets on fire would not be good.

I spend the next hour trying to get the heat to cool down. I even think about returning to the deck to find a bucket of water, but that would mean facing Aeron again. Finally, after much pacing and feeling foolish as I wave my hands in the air to try and cool them, the heat dissipates enough that I'm willing to lie down. But it doesn't feel long after my head hits the pillow that a call stirs me from sleep.

"Land ho!"

Of course. Light peeks through the room's small window, and I sigh, somehow even more exhausted than before. Deeper sleep will have to wait.

Back on deck, nothing but tall, twisting trees line the shore behind Dunestone Harbor. Like past visits with my crew, boats from all over Faylan dock around us as shouts of hovering seagulls mix with the salty air. Trading sailors and impatient fishmongers push crates and barrels up and down gangplanks and through the streets, strictly keeping their distance from opposing clans.

Dunestone Harbor's location makes it the closest port to the center of Faylan, the city of Shree. We'll have to go there first to get to Eldore.

As the crew unloads, I step off the ship and spot Aeron poring over a map with one of his crewmen. Thankfully, he is fully clothed this time, his royal garb representing the true prince instead of a half-dressed sailor. Playing with the cloth still wrapped around my finger, I try to put our previous encounter out of my mind.

"Where to next?" I ask, hoping he was too drunk last night to remember anything. Or, at the very least, how my hand heated in his.

"Morning, Whit," he greets me cheerfully.

I try not to bristle at the name. Every time I hear it, Whit's betrayal stings afresh, but there's no changing it now.

Aeron motions to the Nymph at his side, the same short puck from the dance-off. "Fynn here thinks it'll be a straight shot if we go through the forest."

"That's right." Fynn's blue eyes light up. His golden curls bounce along with him as he traces a direct route to our destination on the map —right through the Woodlands, the home of the Dryads.

I shake my head. "You've obviously never come face to face with a Dryad while strolling through the Woodlands before."

My crew and I used to loot through the forest regularly, but even with Whit's thorough knowledge of the terrain and the skill of our crew, we always just barely escaped. I'm not about to trust this group of carefree Nymphs to protect me, especially one like Fynn. Though his dancing was impressive, his slight frame tells me he's never been in a fight in his life.

Fynn crosses his arms. "I've always heard the Dryads are a peace-loving clan."

"That's right," Aeron defends his friend. "Aren't most of them healing mediks?"

Oh, sheltered prince.

"They'll peaceably slit your throat if you even think about damaging the home they love so dearly." I shrug. The Dryad Etho is indeed centered around Life, cultivating and protecting it. But it's completely up to the Dryads which lives they deem worth protecting.

Fynn rubs his neck, swallowing hard. But Aeron gives him a glare, and Fynn's hand quickly returns to the map.

I lower my voice. "It's the *changeling* Dryads you really have to watch out for. You might have your half-fish form, but some Dryads can shift entirely into an animal or even a tree or bush." I motion to the trees just a few yards away, their twisted limbs creaking in the breeze. "For all we know, these here could be changelings themselves, listening to our every word, preparing to attack…"

Aeron and Fynn hold their breath as if a tree will spring toward us any moment.

"Well, in that case!" Fynn yells, as if alerting any Dryads who might be listening. "With all the cargo we have, it's probably best to take the Kobie Express, anyway!"

Aeron nods, and the two start back to the Kalypso to gather the crew. That is, until Aeron notices my feet haven't budged. "What's wrong now?" he sighs.

I press my lips together. I don't care how clever the Kobolds are, most of them are plumb-crazy. Except for loyal pirates like Luna, I don't trust most Kobolds as far as I can throw them, let alone the dust-powered machinery they create. This particular contraption, fondly called the "Kobie Express," travels on tracks that wind throughout Faylan's lands. It's the most efficient way to get almost anywhere, but I've always refused to take it in the past. Unlike my ship, once inside it, I have no control.

"You trust that thing?" I ask Aeron.

"Do you have any better ideas?"

I try to think. Walking around the perimeter of the forest would take days. And even flying over the Woodlands would be dangerous. We'd still have to land in the forest to rest, more often if carrying the cargo Fynn mentioned. Besides, I can't fly without revealing what my *armor* really is, and that would unravel the entire story I've spun. *Blasted thing.*

I huff and march toward the lesser of two evils. "The Kobie Express it is!"

As Fynn and Aeron direct the crew with the cargo, the blaring whistle of the Express cuts through the air, and I flinch. A crowd of fae are already waiting by the tracks, ready to board.

Someone's voice rises above the gathering, and I spot two Sylph guards near a cargo car. I take a step back toward the ship, not wanting to be seen by them in my uniform. But they're too consumed in yelling at a young Kobold pixie for mishandling their goods. The larger Sylph pushes the Kobold to the ground as his shorter companion laughs and tilts back his head, his crescent-shaped scar coming into view.

Moon Face.

The pixie cowers before him, and it's as if I'm seeing Luna at the mercy of Moon Face's rum-scented breath. The memory of his lips on mine rushes back. But this time, instead of fear, my blood boils. Whatever flame lingers from the night before bursts forth with a vengeance. In a fury, I bolt down the port until I leap forward, tackling Moon Face to the ground.

"You bastard!" I seethe, delivering a few good punches to his face. I yell to the pixie, "Go!"

She scrambles away as I pull out the switchblade in my boot. But the larger Sylph knocks the blade out of my hand, yanking me off his companion. "You better be thankful you took my weapons, because if I had them now…"

"What the—" Moon Face starts. Wiping the blood from his nose, he catches a good look at my face. "You… but you're supposed to be—"

"At the bottom of the ocean?" I sneer, kicking to be released by his buddy. "You're not the only one who can make a masterful escape. Next time you try to kill someone, you better make sure they're good and dead before you sail away."

"What in Faylan is going on here?" It's Aeron's breathless voice. He must have seen me rush off. He turns on Moon Face with a vengeance. "What did you do to her?"

"What did I do to *her*?" Moon Face points to his bloody nose. "She's the loon who jumped *me*!" The Sylph eyes Aeron's garb. "What's a Nymph prince doing defending a fiend like Captain Shade anyway?"

"Shade?" Aeron cocks a brow at him, then at me.

His look sobers me instantly. There goes my cover. My head drops.

I tried, Gaius, but I couldn't even last a few bloody days.

Aeron isn't convinced yet. "What are you talking about? Captain Shade threw her off one of your ships. She's been traveling with us ever since."

"This is definitely her." The Sylph looks me up and down with disdain, pointing at my Wing Restraint. "That's a Gwyllion device that keeps criminals from flying away. I have its key right here."

He dangles it in front of Aeron.

I lunge for it, but the Sylph holding me pulls my arms tighter behind my back. I wince.

Moon Face sneers. "And she didn't throw anybody overboard. We—"

"Jasper," his bigger and obviously wiser companion interrupts. "*We* were unsuccessful in stopping her from throwing *herself* overboard, isn't that right?"

Jasper. So the scum has a name. I still prefer Moon Face.

"Liar! You threw me overboard and left me to sink to my death, you coward!"

"So, it's true." Aeron's words slice through my anger. "You're Shade?" He stares at me as if I've just transformed before him. "Which means you're... the Gwyllion Princess." His voice trails off, his teal eyes flipping through emotions like turning the pages of a book. Confusion, shock, anger... perhaps even hurt?

My muscles relax under his gaze, but only a touch. "That's *Captain Shade* to you. Menace of the Five Provinces. Master of the Silver Sea."

Aeron closes his eyes. My words are barbed, meant to sting, but he shoots me an amused glare. "Funny. I thought you'd be uglier."

Whether an insult or a compliment, I don't know. And frankly, I don't care. I turn back to Moon Face. "I'll take my weapons and my key now."

"Not even for all the pixie dust in Faylan," he scoffs. "Our captain will be very pleased to see you alive and well. He nearly took our wings when we... I mean, when *you* went missing." He walks forward with a slight limp. Their captain might have not gone *that* far, but that doesn't mean there wasn't a flogging. Taking a pair of cuffs connected by a clinking chain out of his belt, he claps them on my wrists. "So, no, *Your Ladyship*. You're coming to Eldore with us."

As the Express whistle sounds its last call, he gives me a sinister smile and moves toward the locomotive while his buddy pulls me along. I don't know which is worse: traveling to Eldore in the hands of these buffoons, or in the company of a betrayed prince. But I look back, my eyes pleading for Aeron to do something. Anything.

His look is hard and unreadable, until he finally puts a hand up. "Wait."

To my surprise, the Sylphs obey, stopping in their tracks and slowly turning around. Aeron strides up to Moon Face and stares directly at him.

"You're not taking her," he says slowly, holding out an open hand. "She's more trouble than she's worth. You're going to hand me the key to her restraints. I'll take her to Eldore myself."

More trouble than she's worth? Then why is he helping me?

Then I hear it. His voice has that watery effect again, like when I first woke on his ship. My head swims in the sound as the taller Sylph's grip loosens, dropping me to the ground. I look up.

Moon Face and his buddy appear to be in some sort of trance, their eyes glazed, and I realize I'm witnessing something I've only heard about: the *silver tongue* of the Nymphs. Though all Nymphs are graced with great beauty and an alluring voice of velvet at birth, only a rare few are rumored to be graced with such a dangerously persuasive gift.

Though I am in no position to request anything of him, I whisper to Aeron. "My weapons. Don't forget my weapons."

Aeron puts up a hand, not breaking his concentration on his targets, warning me not to press my luck.

Finally, he relaxes.

Released from his spell, Moon Face shakes his head. "You know what, this one's more trouble than she's worth," he huffs, tossing the key to Aeron. "She's *your* problem now."

Aeron plays with the key in his hands, a smug quirk to his lips as the Sylphs walk onto the train.

Though my weapons are still unaccounted for, I breathe a sigh of relief. Once in Eldore, I vow to track them down and retrieve my darlings by any means necessary. Then Moon Face will be sorry. For right now, I'm safe. Or so I hope.

Aeron steps toward me, wearing a solemn expression.

"You may think you're clever, Whit… Shade… whatever your name is. Maybe it was wise to keep your true identity a secret. If I knew who

I was saving in those waters, I probably would have let you drown."
He pauses, letting me feel the weight of his words. "Still, I'm a puck of
my word, and I promised to deliver you safely to Eldore."

I hold my breath as he gets close enough to whisper in my ear.

"But once the competition begins, *pirate*... there will be no holding
back."

CHAPTER 10

"A ll aboard!" the conductor calls.

I tentatively approach the train with Aeron close behind.

For a moment, I think of making a break for it. Sure, I'm glad to no longer be in Moon Face's clutches, but now I'm wondering why Aeron would go through the trouble.

My father's warning echoes in my mind: *"You must not trust anyone."*

There's a decent crowd around us. I could catch Aeron by surprise, knock him out, grab the key to this restraint from hell, and get lost in the shuffle. With tons of ships in port, I could easily hide out on one and try to start over once again.

But then what? Right now, I'm weaponless and homeless. Surely Whit has alerted Maverick to who I really am by now. He wouldn't take me back even if I begged.

And most of all, there's Gaius.

Recalling the torch at his tomb, I remember my promise to enter the Ethodine in his name. To make up for all the ways I hurt him. All the times I wasn't there to save him. The Kobie Express is still the fastest way to Eldore. Once there, I'll be able to find Moon Face and get my daggers back—maybe some vengeance too.

I reach the passenger car and take the first step up. As if alarmed by my touch, the locomotive lets out another loud squeal. I jump, losing my footing and falling backward—right into Aeron. He catches me easily, but I squirm out of his grasp as he nudges me into the mechanical beast.

Blasted Kobolds. I shake my head, examining the inside of the contraption they've created. Never satisfied with the same old thing, the Kobolds are always coming up with something bigger and better, faster and stranger. It doesn't help matters that the Sylphs encourage their eccentricity. In exchange for all kinds of treasures, the Sylphs commission them to create and build whatever they desire. Things that benefit Eldore and keep the Sylphs safe and in charge.

Sellouts. All the clans are, really. They claim to hate the Sylphs and their rulership, threatening uprising and war that's led to this crazy competition's resurrection. But they've all enabled the Sylphs to stay in power in their own ways, too.

The Gwyllions protect Faylan's borders and keep the Sylph soldiers stocked with weapons and tools. The Nymphs maintain their luxurious living conditions, supplying entertainment for their royal events. Dryad mediks keep them living long lives, while the Kobolds keep their sky city running with inventions and all the pixie dust they need to use them. The Sylphs monopolize most of the wealth, leaving the rest of us crawling back to them for these kinds of jobs to survive. Sometimes I wonder: if every clan simply stopped giving the Sylphs exactly what they wanted, would they eventually lose everything that keeps their power intact?

But what do I know? I'm just a pirate, after all.

Passing through the train's narrow walkway, I brush past tight booths on both sides. Everyone on board eyes my cuffs with wariness and judgmental stares. Feeling as if the walls are closing in, I choose the first open seat and press against the window, seeking any semblance of open space I can get. But it isn't long before the train moves, jerking me forward into the seat in front of me, earning me a glare from the elderly puck who occupies it.

No, I'm not going to like this one bit.

"Mind if I join you?" Aeron doesn't wait for an answer before dropping into the seat next to me, his voice edged with tension of his own. Obviously, I don't have a choice as his prisoner, but as a prince and all, he seems to be keeping up his gentlemanly appearance.

I'm glad I have no appearances to keep up anymore.

"You don't have to be my keeper." I motion to the enclosed space. "It's not like I can go anywhere."

Aeron leans back, settling into the seat. "Trust me, I don't like this any more than you."

"Then why did you...?"

"I couldn't just leave you with those lowlifes, could I? Who knows what else they would've done to you?" Disgust simmers in his voice.

I lift my brows in surprise. He was worried about me?

Catching my gaze, he coughs and turns away again. "Plus, if you don't make it to Eldore, I don't get to beat you fair and square in front of all of Faylan."

I smirk. I should be thanking him. *Again.* However begrudgingly, this is the second time he's saved my life. But I'm not going to give him the satisfaction.

"Suit yourself." I close my eyes, settling into the seat as well. "If you're going to sit here, then no *talking.*"

I don't need his silver tongue messing with my head. With the train picking up speed on the rickety tracks, the bouncy ride is already messing with my stomach. I wrap my arms around my sides.

Aeron cocks his head. "I didn't know a pirate could get seasick on the shore."

"I think you mean *train*-sick," I correct him. On a normal day at sea, ships rock gently. And if needed, I can direct a ship into more stable waters. Here, I'm at the mercy of the machine. The clicking of tracks grates against my nerves, growing louder every minute. I open my eyes to glare at Aeron. "And no talking, remember?"

"What's wrong?" Aeron grins, inching closer to me. "You afraid I'll make you do something you don't want to do?"

I can tell it's more of a tease than a threat, but my stare must communicate that the concern has crossed my mind.

"Don't worry." He leans back again, crossing his arms and closing his eyes, mimicking my posture. "My gift only works on the weak-minded. Ones that are simple, uncertain, or unstable. The Sylphs at port were bold, but easily influenced. You, on the other hand, have already proven twice that your mind is stronger than I thought."

I raise my brows in surprise, remembering the swimming sensation of his gift. I hadn't succumbed to his tongue when I woke up on his ship, or while he was controlling the Sylphs.

He opens one eye to see me still staring back at him, then closes it. His dimple surfaces. "You're a hard one to crack, Shade. But I guarantee you'll fall under my spell someday."

I roll my eyes in a huff, turning back to the window. His cockiness is infuriating, but I'm glad to hear my mind is strong. That I can't be controlled. I sit a little taller.

Hearing Aeron use my pirate name should make me feel stronger too, more at ease. But somehow, it doesn't sound right. Not now.

I look at my chains around my wrists and sigh. No, not Shade. Though, I definitely don't want to be called *Whit* anymore either. I look out the window, and Gaius' smiling face flashes in my mind.

"Quinn," I say softly, mostly to myself.

"What?" Aeron asks, but I don't turn to him.

"Quinn," I repeat more confidently. "Call me Quinn." Whether out of surrender to my fate, or because the nickname reminds me of my vow to Gaius, *Quinn* seems the most tolerable option.

Letting the confession hang in the air, I brace myself for a snarky retort. But Aeron only shifts in the seat without a word, which doesn't bother me one bit.

Out the window, there isn't much to look at. My beloved sea is long gone, and in its place stand trees upon twisted trees, lining the boundaries of the Woodlands. We're one train ride away from our final destination: Eldore. That's when the real challenge will begin.

I breathe, trying not to think too far ahead.

I'm still on my way, Gaius. I haven't failed my vow to you yet. Wherever you are, I hope you're happy.

The movement of the train evens out, the gentle bobbing of the car changing from sickening to soothing. Before I can stop it, my eyes close, and I fall asleep.

∼

Nudged awake, I jolt, arms flailing as I try to remember where I am.

It seems like Aeron is getting used to that, though. He catches my arm just before it collides with his face. "Wake up, drooling beauty. We're almost there."

"Almost?" How long have I been out? I try not to panic, wiping at my mouth. I scowl when I find no drool.

"Take a look." He points out the window.

The sun has started its descent, cascading colors running across the sky as the blur of trees clears to reveal our destination. The trade city of Shree, the direct center of our world, with the only entrance into Eldore.

As our train crosses one of the few bridges that spans the moat surrounding the town, we leave behind the wide-open land and barrel into a city of smoke, looming structures, and crowded cobblestone streets.

In a more peaceful time, Shree had been a collection of outlying Sylph villages. A central place for all the clans to trade freely. But after the royal family took over trade and stationed a base there for their military, the city took a new shape, with Sylph guards at every intersection.

At Shree's center stands what they are really protecting.

The Sacred Vine.

Exiting the train, I look up at the Vine until my neck hurts. Its green branches are thick as a village hut, twisting together in a gigantic stalk-like tree trunk stretching to the sky. Though its vast roots begin down in the Kobold tunnels, it grows all the way beyond the clouds, where its branches support the foundations of the Sylph city of Eldore.

Though my crew and I have been here many times before, this is the closest I've ever been to the Vine. Security in Shree is extremely tight. Even the strongest faerie wings can't make it all the way up to the clouds without landing on the Vine for a breather, and Sylph guards are stationed all the way around so that no one can enter unauthorized. The only way up is by yet another Kobold mechanism that winds up the Vine's stalk.

Kobold torture machine, more like it.

Drawing deeper into the city, we cut through the crowded markets. Faeries of all kinds push their way in and out of alleyways amidst the carts and shops. They carry everything from Sylph parchment and quills to Kobold gears and rare pixie dust concoctions. And the smells! From Nymph perfumes to Dryad spices, roasts and bubbling sauces, the mingling aromas intoxicate me. I think I even smell the tang of lily tarts in the air. I salivate, my stomach grumbling. Thankfully, no one can hear it above the vendors and patrons tirelessly bartering over mere farthlings.

Any other day, I could've easily swiped a whole meal by now. But Aeron's hand on my shoulder keeps me moving forward as I eye it all longingly.

Distracting myself, I look up to the high buildings, the air clear of flyers. To minimize thefts, Shree is a no-fly zone, so we inch through the press of bodies. With such diversity, it's common to see strange things or skirmishes between clans break out, but I still jump when a Dryad yells at the top of his lungs.

The area hushes as he climbs on top of a barrel and lifts his hands over the crowd. His intense cat-like eyes reflect the freshly lit lanterns, his voice growing louder with every word.

"The time has come! The prophecies are true. The end is near. The Numa are coming!"

"What's he yammering on about?" I ask.

"Just another loon hopped up on pixie dust." Aeron motions to a group of Sylph soldiers making their way toward the Dryad. Though they are twice his size, the Dryad's passion increases.

"You don't understand!" He puts up hands toward them as they advance. "We're all in grave danger! Look at our Sacred Vine. The leaves are turning brown. The stalk is growing moss. As the ancient writings predicted, the land will tremble and the creatures will revolt. Even the prophesied plague has come. It's the beginning of the end!"

My ears twitch. He's referring to the Knolls. The sickness that took Gaius. Though the Sylphs and Kobolds have studied it for years, so much about it is still a mystery. I take a step closer to hear more, but Aeron pulls me back as the guards descend on the Dryad, gagging him.

"It's a shame your brother did not heed the prophecy. At least, not at first," says a voice beside me.

I whip my head around.

Aeron is standing there, but he gives me a curious stare. "What?" he asks.

It wasn't him. The voice was too low and scratchy to be Aeron's. I look around, but there's so many fae passing by, it could have been anyone.

I scan the crowd again. As many hustle back to their routines, on the other end of the square a cloaked figure doesn't move a muscle. Though his hood shades his face, I swear he's staring right at us. At me.

"If you want to learn what really happened to him, you will follow me." It's then I realize this voice isn't external. It's in my head. Coming from this… whoever this is. And somehow, he knows something about Gaius' death. What could he know? My heart quickens in my chest.

As Aeron tugs me forward, the figure moves back into the crowd.

Shrugging off Aeron's arm, I bolt toward the hood.

"Quinn!" Aeron calls, but I'm already gone. And with the no-fly zone, he'll be forced to follow on foot.

Darting through the crowd, I push aggravated folk out of my way and just barely catch sight of the figure's cloak disappearing into an alley. I chase him down it, to another and another.

"Wait!" I call. But when I enter the final one, it's dark and completely vacant.

How is that possible? He was *just here*.

Aeron enters the alley behind me, clamping a hand on my shoulder again. "Did you really think you could run away that easily?"

"I wasn't running away." I turn to him, but my eyes dart around the alley.

"Oh really? Then what were you doing, exactly?"

"I was chasing… someone."

"Someone who?"

"Someone who was talking to me… in my head."

"Quinn, I really want to believe you, but when you make up stories like that—"

"Would it surprise you that I don't really care what you believe?" I snap, though there's a small part of me that *does*. I shake off the feeling. "I'm not making up stories."

"Okay, then who were you chasing?" he asks.

I shake my head. "You wouldn't understand."

"Try me." He takes his hand off my shoulder and folds his arms. Before I can speak, his eyes widen, and he pushes me to the side. "Look out!"

A shadow darts between us, and Aeron tackles him to the ground. The hooded figure.

Without thinking, I launch forward, wrapping the chain that connects my wrists around the attacker's neck and pulling it taut.

Aeron scrambles to his feet, eyes wide. He looks as surprised as I am at what I'm doing. Then his eyes dart behind me.

"Quinn… turn around slowly and let him go."

"What?" I hiss as the figure tries to wriggle out of my grasp. "Why in Faylan would I do that?"

Steps sound behind me, and I whip around, keeping the chain pressed into the hooded figure's throat.

Looks like the goon has friends. All hooded as well. They take a collective step toward us, not saying a word.

"I think now would be the time to do something," I whisper to Aeron, but his brows furrow. "*Tell* them to stand down," I try again, hoping he'll catch my drift.

"There's ten of them," he whispers sharply.

"So what, you have a limit or something?"

"Just let the puck go and let's get out of here."

No. I'm not finished yet. "This one knew about my brother," I say to the hoods. "Tell me what he knows, or I'll snap his neck."

But as I give the hooded figure a warning tug, I feel his bare hand on my arm and freeze.

Fire. Everything I see is on fire. Heat licks at my skin. I'm running but getting nowhere.

"*Quinn!*" *I hear a voice call my name. A familiar voice. Gaius' voice.* "*Quinn!*"

The next thing I know, I'm waking up on the ground in Aeron's arms. "Quinn, are you okay?"

"W-what happened?" Realizing where I am—and how close I am to Aeron, *again*—I squirm away, looking around for the hooded figures. "Where did they go?"

"I don't know. After you passed out they just... disappeared."

CHAPTER 11

Aeron and I keep our guard up as we make our way to the middle of the city. Thankfully, the hoods are nowhere to be seen. That probably wasn't my brightest moment, chasing a random figure into a dark alleyway with no plan. *Good one, Quinn.* Maybe I'd just imagined the voice I'd heard and frightened the poor sap into feeling the need to defend himself. Him and his mysteriously silent friends.

But who were they? And what about what I saw when he touched my arm? Was it even real?

"You sure you're all right?" Aeron cuts into my thoughts. His voice is soft, his brows knit with concern, like I'm about to crumble where I stand. Less like I'm a prisoner and more like I'm a weak little creature in need of protection. A part of me wants to hit him, but another part can't forget when he pushed me out of the hood's path.

"I'm fine," I say as coolly as I can, keeping my attention on our destination, the Sacred Vine.

Passing through the last security checkpoint, we finally approach The Vineway. The Kobold contraption starts at the base of the Vine and will take us all the way up the stalk. The wooden carrying car creaks as we walk across the platform, which doesn't help my nerves.

I'm nearly there, I remind myself. I made a promise to Gaius. And the possibility that there could be more to his death makes it that much more of a promise I intend to keep, even if it kills me. Even if it means being a Nymph's prisoner for a little while longer. I need to find out the truth.

I repeat my vow under my breath. "I won't let you die in vain."

"Kindly keep wings and belongings inside the car at all times," a bubbly Kobold pixie announces. She pulls a lever and the car lurches upward. "Here we go!"

As we move up the stalk, the car spirals around its trunk in a diagonal fashion. I hold tightly to the railing till my knuckles turn white. With my wings still restrained, heights are now my greatest enemy. Feeling dizzy, I shut my eyes.

Aeron chuckles. "Allergic to trains *and* scared of heights?"

"Nope." I force a smile. "Just tired." To prove it, I take a deep breath and look straight ahead. *Just don't look down.*

Though I've seen much of the land's terrain from atop the mountains, surveying all of Faylan from this height is unlike anything I've ever experienced. This high up, the mountains bordering our world seem so very small. The Silver Sea looks like it could fit in my hand, its maze of connecting rivers making their way through the Woodlands and back to the moat around Shree. The only thing not visible are the Kobold tunnels below. Above, all I can see are white puffy clouds.

As we rise above them, I glimpse the place I've never been able to break into before.

Eldore.

Just like the stories I've heard, most Sylph structures sit atop the Vine's massive branches while others float or fly above us, suspended by Sylph magic and the power of pixie dust. There are a few villages on the outskirts, but in the center stand the gates to Eldore.

Sadly, I think of my crew and all the times we've tried and failed to get here. Vine security was always too tight to break through.

They're going to be so mad they missed this.

As we walk through the golden gates, the city of Eldore unfolds. Unlike Shree, these streets are spotless and not nearly as populated. Only a few Sylph families casually walk and fly by us.

As evening sets in, we're so close to the sun that sweat runs down my back. Many Sylphs carry parasols decorated with a variety of intricate patterns. Some take notice of the Nymph prince and his entourage leading what appears to be a Sylph guard in chains. But besides a few strange looks and whispers, their own priorities seem much too important to care about us.

At the end of the road that divides the city in two stands the Sylph palace. As the sun sets behind it, the white towers gleam so brightly in the diminishing rays of sunlight that it nearly blinds me. It's even taller and more glorious than I'd imagined. Looming statues of famous Sylph leaders and philosophers hold up the entryway like columns, and winding vines from the royal gardens peek out from behind its tall walls.

The tension in my shoulders releases, and I breathe. *We made it.*

Once inside the palace, Aeron hands over my restraint key to the guards who receive us, and I'm finally released from my bonds and this blasted Wing Restraint. Heaving off the heavy burden, I take great pleasure in tossing it to the ground with a grunt. I spread my sore wings with exceeding pleasure as both sounds bounce off the entry walls. A chorus of *shhhhh* follows. Sylph scribes carrying scrolls and heavy texts have stopped their routines to scowl my way, but I don't care. It's the first bit of freedom I've felt in days.

Before they lead us to our quarters, however, I spare a glance at Aeron.

He's looking at me too. Having just escaped the band of hoods in Shree together, it's as if there's a level of understanding in our silent exchange, knowing we're about to enter an even more deadly competition for the crown. Whatever just happened with the band of hoods, I can't think about that now. Not with the looming threat in front of me.

I haven't quite decided what to think of Aeron yet, but whether we've been friends or foes during the journey here, we're now most certainly competitors. And soon there will be three more added to our ranks.

I shoot him a smirk to break the stare. "No holding back?"

Aeron returns a smile, remembering his vow to me at the port. "No holding back."

PALACE OF

POTIONS

THE SYLPH TRIAL

CHAPTER 12

As Aeron and I are escorted to our chambers, the hallways of Eldore's palace are so deathly quiet I feel more like I'm in a whitewashed tomb. I stifle a shudder, though I tell myself it's more because the blazing sun is now gone, leaving the sky city as cold at night as it is hot during the day.

I'm used to the roar of waves, chattering crewmates, and the view of vast open seas. But here it's an endless maze of towering hallways filled with bookcases, paintings, and more sculptures of important fae of the past than actual living ones. And it doesn't help that every Sylph we do pass peers at me like I'm the one speck of dirt in their pristine sanctuary.

As I wonder if they were born with their noses stuck up in the air like that, the guards lead us past a series of windows that carry a much more impressive scene. The lights of the Sylph city sparkle against a darkening sky. Flying vessels sail among the clouds as if they ride on white waves, glittering pixie dust trailing from their rudders. I drag my feet, wishing I could fly up to one of the ships right now and get a better look, but the guards push me forward.

"I've definitely got to get me one of those," I say under my breath.

"Strangest ships I've ever seen," Aeron whispers from beside me, the gills on his neck pulsing.

"Strange?" I scoff. "More like miraculous! Do you know how much pixie dust it must take to power one of those things?"

"Tons, I'm sure." His mouth twists. "Seems kind of unnatural."

"You mean like how your precious Kalypso can travel underwater?"

"That's different. At least it's still *in* the water."

"Sure," I humor him but continue to watch the ships. "By Faylan, if I had one of those, it'd be so much easier to pillage wherever…" I stop. Aeron's giving me a look. "Oh, come on, you can take the pixie away from the pirates, but you can't take the pirate out of the pixie."

"I'm sure your father wouldn't approve of that kind of vessel. With it being powered by magic and all."

"My father doesn't approve of anything I do," I mumble.

"That makes two of us."

"Really?" I look up curiously. "And here I thought *fish-boy* could do no wrong."

"You'd be surprised," he says and grows quiet.

Before I can press further, a distinct, familiar sound breaks the silence.

The call of a sparrow.

My head whips up, and I nearly expect my crew to come barreling around the corner to break me out of here. But it's just a wishful thought. Whit would have made sure that wasn't a possibility.

Instead, a parcel of birds swoop in and begin placing the books in their talons back onto shelves. Though I'm impressed by the well-trained fowl, I sigh.

I wonder what my crew's reaction was when Whit told them what happened. What must they think of me as one of the royals we used to jeer at together, entering a competition for the faerie crown? Now I'll be the one they jeer at.

"I'll take her from here."

Panic claws at my stomach as I face a familiar guard who grabs my arm roughly. His smug grin yanks at the scar I gave him. *Moon Face.* Just what this terrible day needs.

I catch Aeron's eyes as they dart to me, then narrow at Moon Face. But he doesn't say a word. We both know he can't do anything now. And he shouldn't. He got me to Eldore, but I'm no longer his concern. I'm his competition.

"Are you sure, Jasper?" The guards who've brought us this far look at each other. "Because we were told—"

"Queen's orders. I'm to help Her Pirateness settle in properly. You two escort the Nymph heir to his room down the hall. Now, get moving." Moon Face gives them a foul sneer.

Immediately, they clamp their mouths shut and hurry away with Aeron in tow. Aeron glances back at me one more time as I hear Moon Face unlock a door nearby.

"Not so tough without your weapons, huh?" Moon Face hisses as he pushes me into my room.

"What have you done with them?" I demand. Did he toss them overboard back at sea? If he was smart, he would have sold them. They are Gwyllion-crafted after all. But then again, he doesn't seem too smart.

"They are being safely stored. Away from you." He crosses his arms. "I've come to tell you two things, pirate. First, you've been instructed by Her Majesty to stay put until you're summoned. So don't get any funny ideas. The windows are bolted shut, and a guard will be posted outside your door for good measure."

He's obviously prepared them for me. No matter. I shoot him a glare that says I'm not through with him yet. I'll find my weapons and get them back, somehow. Especially my daggers.

"And the second is a warning from me." He takes a step forward, lowering his voice to a growl. "Now that you're in my territory, you'd better watch your back."

I step toward him as well, standing as tall as I can. "Oh yeah? Or you'll do what?"

With one quick motion, he grabs my wrist and twists it backward. I curse the whimper that releases before I can bite it back.

"As you well know, I'm not the only soldier who despises your presence here," he snarls. "And no one's going to care if you show up a little damaged to the competition. Not even your father. Everyone's heard the whispers that he only cares about the crown. Not you."

He pushes me back, and I cradle my wrist to my chest, the truth of his words stinging sharper than the pain. "Like I said, I'd watch your back, pirate." He strides to the door and glowers at me one more time. "Especially now that I know where you sleep."

He locks the door behind him, and my stomach plummets.

Trapped again.

His threats could be empty, something to scare me just enough, but it's working.

Quickly, I scan the room for anything I can use as a weapon. Grabbing a candelabra from the bedside, I yank off its three candlesticks and sit on the bed, watching the door.

My pulse is racing, but if he or anyone else returns, I'll be ready.

I'll stay up all night if I have to.

CHAPTER 13

I can't catch my breath.

I'm flying at top speed toward the Minnow, but no matter how hard my wings flap, I'm not getting any closer to the sea.

Birds and all kinds of creatures whip past me to escape the danger lurking behind. Heat licks at my back. I don't have to look to know it's swallowing everything in its path.

Ahead, a raging windstorm rocks the Minnow to and fro. My only chance of escape.

I falter and topple to the ground. I squeeze the sand between my fingers, dragging myself through the coarse dust.

Then I feel it—the ground is shaking. I look back.

Faylan is engulfed in flames. The towering Vine creaks and rocks in the wind like a reed.

Crack!

My heart pounds as the Vine leans. It's falling straight toward me. It's going to crush me, but I can't move. I call for help, but my voice is ragged and hoarse. There's no one in sight.

Throwing my hands over my head, I accept my fate.

Someone pulls me up by the shoulders. They thrust something into my hand.

My daggers.

I face my rescuer only to stare into my brother's eyes.

Paralyzed by the sight, all I can do is watch the Vine's falling shadow cover us in darkness as Gaius opens his mouth.

"Quinn!"

"Gaius!" I sit up straight, soaked in sweat, panting for breath.

I look around the dimly lit room, light peeking through billowing window drapes. There's a half-moon, half-sun symbol etched into the fireplace mantel at the foot of my bed, and I remember where I am.

Eldore.

Though the images that jolted me awake flee my mind before I can grasp them, a shuddering feeling remains. I shake my head. Whatever it was, it was just a dream. Probably the result of Moon Face's threats last night.

I pull the velvet comforter closer, and the candelabra shifts in the sheets. I stayed awake as late as I could last night with the makeshift weapon in hand, but I must have nodded off. Curse this feather bed and all its comforts.

A crackle sounds from the foot of the bed, and I'm wide awake.

Gripping the candelabra again, I leap down, ready to pounce on the intruder.

It's just a fire in the hearth. I relax.

But a fire means... someone was in my room while I was sleeping.

I reassure myself it was probably just a servant, but even as the flickering heat reaches out to warm me, the pit in my stomach grows cold.

Wait. Heat.

The images from my dream return with vengeful clarity.

Flames. Faylan on fire. Flying, but getting nowhere. And then... Gaius.

They're the same scenes I saw when the hooded figure in Shree touched me.

Gaius' face flashes in my mind again. The same kind face I remember, but in the vision, he was older. As old as the painting in his room depicted him. Pain pulses in my chest as I picture Gaius' tomb, remembering my vow.

He was calling my name. Handing me something... *Our daggers.* They're the only form of defense I had against any dangers I might face in this place, including my fellow competitors.

What use will it be entering this stupid competition if I'm killed before I can compete?

The memory of Moon Face's laugh scurries over my skin like fleas. I can't get into the adjoining bathing room fast enough to wash away the thought of him. He must have my weapons somewhere in this place.

That's it. Today, I reclaim my weapons.

I rush into the white room, forsaking my clothes and stepping into the porcelain shower. My wings release, and I expand them to their full length for the first time in days. Though I wince at the soreness, the rushing water brings me back to the sea, calming my entire being, giving new life to my bones.

I feel halfway normal as I dry off, but then I spot my dirty Sylph captain clothes on the ground. Braving a whiff, I nearly retch at the stink. I can't very well put those back on. Spotting the wardrobe on the other side of the room, I cling to my towel and fly over the bed to reach it.

I sift through the collection, disappointed. It's packed with Gwyllion garments my father sent with me on the Sylph ship. Rummaging through plain-colored dresses and fur-lined cloaks, I finally settle on a set of light trousers and a tunic. They're meant for training, but at least I won't melt under Eldore's blazing sun.

After putting them on, I gaze into the full-length mirror. I've dressed up as so many different faerie folk in the past to hide my true identity. These clothes are meant for the Gwyllion heir I was born to be. And yet, I don't recognize myself at all.

Will I ever feel like me again? I ask the mirror.

Once you get your weapons back, you will, the reflection seems to say.

I nod in agreement. All I need to do is give the guard outside the slip. An impish smile forms just thinking about what I will do to Moon Face if he ever enters my chambers again. I can't finish getting dressed fast enough.

Finding the candelabra again, I hold it behind my back as I approach the door, ready to knock out whoever enters.

"Hello?" I call as sweetly as I can. "Can I get some help in here, please?"

No answer.

"Hello?" I say louder, with an edge to my voice. "Seriously, I could be dying in here!" I jiggle the handle to show my imaginary need—but the door is unlocked.

Pulling it inward, I peer through the crack. The hallway is empty.

Strange. I step out tentatively. This could easily be a test from Moon Face. A trap.

With each step, I whip my head in either direction down the hall, but no one appears.

Finally, I shrug. If the guards are going to be lazy and irresponsible, they're the ones who will have to deal with Moon Face later. I'm not going to complain.

This time, I sneak through the hallways unescorted. Careful to evade servants and nobles, I keep a lookout for Moon Face and anywhere he might have my weapons stored.

I also steal more glances out the windows at the floating city and flying ships. Among them, I spot an outdoor stadium below. There seems to be some kind of construction going on as five stone platforms take shape. Though I'm curious, I move on. There'd be no point in storing my weapons there.

Hearing voices, I peer around the corner, where a handful of guards are loading cargo into a room with a large metal door. The sign above the door draws a smile across my face.

Armory.

"Make sure those are tucked far in the back. Jasper doesn't want them to see the light of day until he says so," one of them orders another.

I squint at the blades he carries. The careful detailing and craftsmanship are distinctly Gwyllion.

My heart races, and I'm tempted to launch at them. But there's no way I can take on all of these guards unarmed. Unless there's another way in. Maybe a hidden entrance or even a vent.

I back away slowly—and knock into a pedestal behind me. A vase painted with Faylan's map teeters dangerously on top. I scramble to catch it, but it slips through my fingers, shattering against the stone floor.

"Hey, what's she doing here?"

Blast. I've been spotted.

My wings release, and I fly down the corridors as the guards dart after me. My heart thuds in my chest, but I'm all smiles. How I've missed flying, and the thrill of a chase.

"Watch out!" I knock over a scribe who impedes my escape,

sending his scrolls flying into the air. The scribe yells at the guards to help him.

I smirk. *That should slow them down a bit.*

Turning a corner, I dart into a vacant room. I stifle my heavy breathing as I pull the door in until all I can see is a sliver of the hallway.

"I think she went this way!" a guard calls as they whisk right past me and turn down another bend.

I release a soft chuckle and turn to face the room, only to realize I have no idea where I am.

Great. Well, I can't go back the way I came. Not yet, at least. Forward it is.

The narrow room I've stumbled into is lined with a series of beautiful murals that reach from the floor all the way up to the high ceilings. As I walk toward the other end, they seem to tell a story. The origin myth of our world. Emphasis on the word *myth*, of course.

As I pass each scene, I recall the tale I heard as a sprite.

On the first wall, the mural is black, with one orb of light glowing in the center. This, they call the Seed, the start of our world. I roll my eyes at the idea that all of Faylan could come from something so small.

In the next scene, the sun and moonrain give life to the Seed as it grows into the Sacred Vine. Its sprawling roots form the land, the waters, and spawn Faylan's creatures.

Then, come the fae.

Five different-colored stones gleam at the top of the next mural. Green, blue, red, gold, and purple. Each of them hover over a different faerie race. It's said that the stones came from the moons above, each of them giving life and power to the faerie clan that possessed it. Not that I've ever seen them myself. Every clan leader keeps their moonstone hidden away, passing it down to their heir when they rise to rule.

A heaviness settles in my stomach as I realize I'll be the one to bear the weight and responsibility of the coveted red Gwyllion stone next.

Each successive mural then depicts how the different Provinces were formed. The Sylphs took to the skies while the Kobolds created tunnels in the ground, leaving the rest to divide the territories in between. Gwyllions flew to the mountains, the Nymphs to the waters, and the Dryads to the woods. As if it was ever going to be that easy— that we'd all just claim a place and be happy with our lot.

I trail my fingers across the next scene, where all Faylanians are depicted separately but at peace, sharing resources and happily using their Ethos to serve the greater good of Faylan. I nearly laugh. Such harmony is certainly something I've never seen.

The next mural displays where things went terribly wrong.

Grotesque, wingless, murderous giants salivate for faerie blood. *The Numa.* Though I know the images aren't real, I can't help but inch back. The painting shows them invading our land, enchanting the dragons to attack the cities, and forcing the fae to do their bidding.

My heart twinges, and an unfamiliar sadness tugs at me, but I shove the feelings away. That's not the end of the tale. The faeries fought back.

In the next scene, the Sylph Lord leads the charge against the invaders. In his hand, he holds up a magical weapon. *The Sylphic Scepter.* Supposedly, he used it to banish the Numa to a dark realm called *The Neverworld.* However, the magical staff disappeared long ago, along with any evidence of that dark realm. *How convenient.*

Still, the story says that the rest of the clans felt so indebted to the Sylphs that they made the Sylph Lord and his clan the permanent rulers over all, securing their station ever since.

I sigh, staring at this last image longer than the others. The Sylph victory is where the murals end, depicting them as Faylan's benevolent heroes.

But, as my father always loved to say, the trouble just got worse from there.

"Without the Ethodine competition to provide balance, the greediness of those blasted Sylphs just keeps growing to new heights," is how Feyden tended to finish the story.

While traveling with the pirates, I'd learned just how right he was. The Sylphs abuse their power, favoring certain clans based on what they can provide, pitting them against each other. Of course, the moonrain drought and dwindling supply of pixie dust hasn't helped, only adding to the conflict. Still, each of the other clans somehow believes they'd be able to fix things, if only they could rule.

With the Ethodine resurrected, I guess we'll find out if any of them will get the chance.

CHAPTER 14

R eaching the end of the mural room, I nudge open the door and peer out into another hallway. Empty, for now. I'd better get moving.

As I slink along the walls, I take in other aspects of the palace. Everything here is so polished, so grand, so... *expensive*. Gold elements decorate the walls, begging to be swiped. After making sure no one is watching, I pause by an ornate table and pick up a gilded bowl.

What were they thinking letting someone like me in here, let alone inviting me in? I turn the bowl over in my hand. *Just one of these would feed my crew for a month.*

My crew. My ship. My freedom. For a moment, I wonder what would've happened if I'd gotten back to the Minnow in time. Could I have won them back to my side?

I shake my head. It's not worth dwelling on. I'm bound to the competition, still caged. If only I could cling onto something familiar, even just the smell of the ocean. I close my eyes and breathe in wistfully, imagining my ocean view. I call back the feeling of being at sea. The wind in my curls. Sea salt in the air—but it isn't my seawater home that I smell. Something else tickles my nose. Something syrupy sweet.

I set down the bowl. *I'll be back for you later.*

Right now, I follow my nose to an arched doorway that leads

outside. Stepping into the warm sunlight, I find myself in the royal gardens.

Flowers, fruits, and vegetables of all different colors grow in rows upon rows. As I'm trying to decide where to start exploring, my stomach rumbles, never ashamed to remind me when it's hungry. I pull down a piece of faerie fruit from a nearby tree and bite into its crisp skin, the delicious juices running down my chin. I haven't tasted fruit this fresh in… maybe ever.

My taste buds satisfied, I turn my attention back to the original scent. It grows stronger as I follow it to a clearing encircled by a series of tall rose bushes. I duck down behind them, peering through the thorns.

In the middle of the clearing, I spot the back of a lone puck. He's busy humming a jubilant tune as he paints at an easel in front of him, but it's his long hair that catches my attention. Though he looks my age, it's stark white—a color I've only ever seen on one other youngling.

"Gaius?" I whisper softly. *It can't be.*

I hold my breath as I shift around the bushes to get a better look. But this puck's wings are more bat-like, and his face is much too long and pale to be my brother. There's something strange about his features, though. His ears are unusually long, flopping out to the side, but that's not it. I squint, trying to pinpoint what it is.

"Actually, that would be Hickory," a sharp whisper corrects me out of nowhere.

Startled, I move to throw my fruit at the possible assailant. But all I see is a gardener kneeling beside a nearby bush, tending to the soil. The pixie gives me a tight smile from under the wide brim of her straw hat, her many freckles shifting with the crinkling of her nose.

"Ah," I sigh, relieved it isn't a guard. "What did you say?"

"The puck you're observing." The gardener motions to the white-haired puck with her shovel. "His name is Hickory, heir to the Kobold Lord."

Ah, another competitor. I watch in wonder as I realize he's coaxing the paint colors out of jars with dramatic motions, the paints obeying every wave and flick of his hand. A wide grin draws across the puck's lips as if he's pulling off some great scheme.

"He looks like he's enjoying himself," I say. I've seen artists paint along the docks before, but none as gracefully or joyfully as this puck.

"He always does." The gardener snorts, returning to her work as she mutters, "Especially when his paints are laced with *dust*."

Pixie dust. I knew I recognized the smell. Hickory might actually be a competitor I want to know more about. This gardener seems knowledgeable enough, unsurprising for a Sylph, of course. Perhaps I can draw out a bit more information. If she's anything like Whit, all I need to do is start challenging her, poking holes in her intellect.

"Strange…" I start. "I don't think I've ever seen a Kobold painter before. Are you sure that's him?" Though the Kobold Etho is Creativity, their skills are usually more mechanical. A much more lucrative ability in these times.

"Of course I'm sure," she huffs, a defensive tone rising in her voice. "He's just as crazy as any Kobold, particularly fond of fae history and wild conspiracy theories. But he's such a fantastic painter, pretty much all the murals in the castle are his."

My eyes grow wide, recalling the scale and masterfulness of the murals I just saw.

"It's a pity he's only got one good eye." She peers up at me. "If he's this skilled with one eye, imagine how incredible he'd be with two."

I see it now. That's what bothered me before. One of Hickory's eyes moves frantically as he paints. It's a dark brown. The other, however, is icy-blue and barely moves, shaded as if covered by mist.

"There's a risk he could lose sight in the good one as well," the pixie adds, her voice softening for a moment. "But that only seems to spur him to paint more while it lasts."

I press my lips together in pity. *At least he still has time to do what he loves before it's taken away from him, like it was from me.*

I shift to the other side of the gardener, catching a better view of Hickory's latest work. The painted gardens come to life on the canvas with a glorious waterfall pouring into a stone fountain. In front of it, a figure takes shape, but not enough to make out who it is.

"Unless you want a portrait without a head, you might try holding still," Hickory calls to the subject ahead of him.

"Well, then it wouldn't be much of a challenge for you, would it? Everyone knows how talented you are with still objects. What's life without a little test of skills?"

I know that voice. Following Hickory's gaze, I move a few steps and glimpse where the circle of bushes opens into an alcove. There, I spot none other than Aeron. He's dramatically posing in front of the same fountain in the painting, standing strong and proud, his fin-like wings extended in the air. His expression is hard and focused as he gazes upward, dressed to the nines below the torso but unsurprisingly bare-chested yet again.

The pixie on the ground must see me staring. "Ah, and that masterpiece—" she whispers half-mockingly "—is Sir Aeron himself."

"Heir of the Nymphs," I finish. "Yes, I've had the... pleasure of meeting him already." Though I still don't know how I feel about *that*. For all his kindness, he's still the reason I'm weaponless.

As I pull back the shrubbery a bit more, the branches crack and Aeron's eyes shift, finding me through the leaves. Now, aware he has an audience, he puffs out his chest and gives me a wink.

Oh, put a shirt on.

The gardener notes my disdain and her eyes spark. "Interesting. Most pixies find him irresistible. Until they realize what a pompous, self-absorbed flirt he is."

I raise a brow. The grit in her voice makes me wonder if she knows this from personal experience. Does he flirt with everyone, even the help?

"The pixie he married must not know him too well," I say, biting into my fruit again.

"Oh, didn't you hear?" The gardener's brows shoot up, a smug smile pulling at her freckles. "He fled Nymph territory right before the wedding, leaving his blushing bride at the altar."

"What?" I nearly choke. "Where'd you hear—?"

The garden grows dark, as if the sun has suddenly disappeared. A chill runs through me, and I look up. It's not a cloud or a flying vessel. The deafening roar of a beast booms through the air as a massive green dragon descends upon the gardens.

Its muscular wings send a whirling wind through the bushes, and Hickory lunges for his paints, darting behind a tree. Aeron slips behind the waterfall, practically disappearing into the water as his skin shifts to blue.

I tell my body to run too, but my feet are bolted to the ground. Memories of dragon attacks on Greymerrow flash in my mind. *This is exactly why I need my daggers.* I curse and take a step back, readying myself to flee.

"Wait!" My informer waves to me hurriedly while ducking behind a tree. "You're going to want to see this."

Heart pounding, I hold steady as the dragon lands with a thud. The dust settles, and I spot a figure sitting atop the beast. A pixie. Dressed from head to toe in black, she swoops down on translucent, jade-colored wings and walks casually toward its smoke-breathing head, placing a gloved hand calmly on its nose. I can't believe my eyes.

"Wh-who is that?" I can barely get the words out.

"That beast-taming phenomenon—" the gardener says, nodding to her "—is Alys, heiress to the Dryad throne."

The Dryad lifts her hood to reveal a petite brown face, its perimeter lined with black vine-like tattoos. From her tightly woven ebony braids to her toned figure, everything about her says huntress and warrior—but something in her eyes tells a different story. She rubs her cheek against the dragon's face, and my mouth hinges open. "How in Faylan is she doing that?"

"Pretty incredible, huh? Even Dryads usually stay clear of dragons, but they found that one as an egg. Alys grew up right alongside him, training him herself. She even named the creature. Tomah. Barely knows he's a dragon."

Tomah's long tail wags before Alys sends him on his way.

"There's a lot of mystery surrounding that pixie too," the gardener adds.

"What do you mean?"

"Take her gloves, for instance. She never takes them off. Rumor has it she wears them because, instead of a healing gift, she has a gift of death."

The pixie looks for my reaction as I cock a brow and cross my arms. "A gift of what now?" I've heard of many types of magic, but this one sounds too powerful, too dangerous to be true.

She shrugs. "Believe what you will, but her older sister really should be the one up for the Dryad crown, competing in the Ethodine. She died very young. And shortly after her death, Alys started wearing those gloves. But don't bother asking her if it's true."

"Why's that?" Sizing Alys up, she's obviously a fantastic beast tamer, but from her gentleness with the dragon, I wouldn't have pegged her as a killer.

"She's mute," the gardener says matter-of-factly. "All three of them are pretty impressive competitors, don't you think?" Gathering her tools, she looks up at me. "A competitor like yourself might be intimidated by such a challenge."

I freeze. This pixie servant is sharp. Though it's possible my Gwyllion garb gave me away. I relax.

"Yes, well... I guess I should be thanking you for all your valuable insight." I put out a hand toward her. "How do you know so much about them, anyway?"

Standing to meet me face-to-face, she's taller than I expected. She laughs, this time with a darker tone, as she pulls off her hat and long red locks fall over her shoulders.

"Oh, I always make it a point to know my competition." There's a disdain in her voice that wasn't there before. She pulls off a glove and grips my hand, hard. "I'm Princess Vale. And you must be the pirate my mother invited."

CHAPTER 15

I blink in disbelief.

"You sure don't look like a princess." I bite into my faerie fruit and cross my arms, sizing Vale up in her dirt-stained trousers.

She wipes a bead of sweat from her brow before pulling her scarlet hair into a ponytail. "I could say the same about you."

"Pirate, yes. Princess, not quite," I mutter.

"Well, you're definitely not queen material." She glares, ruffling her white feathered wings.

I narrow my eyes, but before I can shoot something back, a familiar voice cuts through the growing tension.

"Why don't you lovely ladies come out here and mingle with the rest of us unfortunate souls?" Aeron is peering through the brush, still drip-drying from the fountain as his skin returns from blue to warm olive, while Hickory and Alys stand inquisitively behind him.

Wishing to get as far away as possible from Her Spoiled Highness, I emerge, and Vale reluctantly follows. Now out in the clearing, all of us stand in a circle. All five rivals together for the first time, eyeing each other.

"Good to see you're out of your stuffy room," Aeron comments to me. "Any trouble with the guards?"

"Actually, there weren't any…" I halt at his smirk. "Wait, did you get rid of them?"

"I may have strongly *suggested* they take a nice long walk." Aeron shrugs casually.

I grin in thanks, but Vale looks between us with a scowl. "Hickory, Alys. This is Lady Quinntessa of Greymerrow… the vagrant." She grits her teeth, motioning to me in feigned courtesy. She obviously wants to make sure everyone knows who I am. What I am.

Surprisingly, Hickory's good eye lights up. "Ah, yes, Captain Shade." He offers his hand amicably, but it awkwardly lands off to my right. I reach for it and give it a shake, appreciating his use of my pirate title.

"Forgive me." He laughs. "Depth perception is not my strong suit. Must be why I tend to stick to two dimensional planes." He motions back toward his canvas.

Despite my usual distrust of Kobolds, I smile back. His easy demeanor reminds me of Gaius even more. My heart twists.

"Please, call me Quinn." The politeness in my voice surprises even me, but I find myself wanting to keep it up. This is what Gaius would've done. He would've been diplomatic instead of cutthroat. If I'm going to truly honor my brother, I have to play the part.

Alys holds her hand out to me next, though her face is void of any readable emotion. I hesitate. I have no reason to trust Vale, but if Alys' gloves don't do the job, I don't want to find out firsthand if the rumors about her death grip are true.

I glance at Vale, but she shrugs as if to say, *It's your funeral.*

Alys' mouth purses as she starts to retract her gesture, but I shoot my hand forward and grab hers with a firm grip, relieved when I don't drop dead.

"It's Alys, right?" I ask.

She nods, her rigid stance slightly relaxing. But just as quickly, she flinches and yanks her hand back as if I'm the one who's hurt her. I rub my hands together to subtly check. I didn't feel the heat rise, and my palms are cool. *What was that?*

"You look confused," Aeron says with an amused expression.

"I, uh…" I look from Alys to the rest of them. "Honestly, I expected you all to be at each other's throats."

They let out a chorus of snickers, giving each other strange smiles.

"Oh, we all hate each other's guts," Vale assures me, hand on her hip. "But there's too much history between our families to act like animals. At least in public arenas."

"History?" I wrack my brain, trying to recall if I met any of them before I ran away.

"It must have been a year or two after you disappeared," Hickory says. "When we reached mentoring age, we all began formal training as future clan leaders. Our parents even brought us along to the queen's council meetings. That is, until the gatherings became more, let's just say, uncivilized."

"You could say that again. Hence, the council completely disbanding." Aeron crosses his arms. "Our parents get to act like spoiled imps, threatening war and uprising, but we're not allowed to say boo to each other."

Alys grimaces in agreement.

I picture them all as fresh younglings, privy to the ever-growing tensions between the clan leaders. But I know one face is missing from their usual company today.

"You all knew my brother, then?" I ask softly. Their countenances drop.

Hickory nods solemnly, his eyes softening. "What happened to Gaius was a tragedy."

Alys bites her lip, and Aeron nods slowly, avoiding my gaze.

I let their condolences wash over me, grateful.

Until Vale scoffs. "Oh, please…"

"Vale…" Aeron scolds.

"Oh, come on, Aeron," she says. "You can't tell me you weren't relieved with one less competitor to challenge. Not that Gaius was a real threat to begin with."

I know she's trying to get to me, but my fist still tightens around the fruit in my hand, the juices oozing over my fingers. The others look apologetic, but Vale's words make me question their sincerity.

"No disrespect to the dead, Lady Greymerrow." Vale bows mockingly. "But don't let these sad faces fool you. We weren't friends, and you couldn't have cared about him much, either."

I grit my teeth, grasping for composure. Princess or not, who does she think she is? "You don't know anything about me." A warning rises in my voice.

"You're right." She shrugs. "All I know is that you only cared to come back after he was gone and you could take his crown. For all we know, you killed him yourself."

Something inside me snaps. I throw down the fruit and extend my wings, lunging in her direction with a warrior-like yell.

Vale's eyes go wide, bracing herself as I come crashing down on her. Without weapons, we throw punches—mine hitting harder and more accurately, of course—yelling as we pull at each other's hair like little sprites. The others rush to break us up, but we don't yield.

"Enough!" a commanding pixie voice echoes through the garden.

We freeze. A circle of Sylph soldiers surrounds us with swords drawn and ready. We stand, brushing ourselves off in embarrassment. But Vale and I glare at each other, silently vowing that this isn't over.

One of the guards steps forward. "You have been summoned. Please, follow us."

We obey, but his voice is not the one that stopped us before. I look around for who commanded such attention. Before we disappear into the castle, I spot her on a balcony. Or at least her back. Her cape is a blur of purple as she retreats into the shadows.

The queen.

～

The Queen's Hall is the grandest room yet. Footsteps echo off the walls up the tall pillars and high ceilings, as all five of us make our way across the marble tile.

At the far end, three tall windows line the wall, highlighting the grand sky city outside and the gleaming white throne in front of us. Out of its back grow elegant white branches that reach up and outward with a flock of birds perched within them. They ruffle their feathers at our approach.

Below them, sitting poised in all her glory, is Queen Gwendolyn.

From the stories, I imagined her face would be cold and haggard, the visage of a terrifying tyrant. Taking in her presence now, she's indeed powerful, but also stunning. From her golden blonde hair to her light skin, she shines like a star standing out from the darkening sky behind her.

With Vale's fiery red hair and freckled skin, I can barely tell Queen Gwendolyn is her mother, save for the same tilted smile creeping up in the corner of her mouth. Vale obviously takes more after her father, the late Sylph King.

As we approach, we're guided by our escorts into an arc around the throne. The other four take a knee, and a guard touches the tip of his blade to my back, giving me the hint that it isn't optional. I drop down as well, but sneak a glance upward as the queen stands to greet us. She's tall like Vale, almost as tall as the rest of her guards, and she commands complete attention.

"Welcome, all of you," she says warmly, motioning for us to rise. "You've been summoned here for a great honor. To compete for the crown on my head." She touches it lightly before gracefully folding her hands. Though she knows the hatred the other clans have for her, there isn't a touch of resentment in her voice.

But I've learned not to trust first impressions. Everyone is always hiding something.

As she descends the dais steps, a dove flies from her throne and lands on her shoulder. Picking a seed from a pocket in her gown, she feeds the bird and strokes its head as she walks down the line of us, starting with her daughter.

Vale straightens under her stare, her reverence and admiration evident in every muscle.

"In the first era of our kind, the clans decided who would rule through a series of trials. Each of the five trials focused on one Etho: Knowledge, Beauty, Life, Creativity, or Strength. All five formed the collective Ethea. Our ancestors wisely decided that the clan leader who proved to be the Master of the Ethea would be crowned king or queen of the fae. And so, each clan created its own trial for the heirs to pass."

She stops in front of Hickory as she reaches for the amulet hanging around her neck, playing with the crystal gem on the chain. "And why have we not held this competition for over a millennium?" she asks the history expert.

Hickory straightens. "After the Sylph Lord defeated the Numa, they peacefully did away with it."

"Correct," the queen continues. "Sadly, peace is dwindling more every day. Never in Faylan's history have we fae been at such odds with each other. Thus, the clans have decided to resurrect this ancient event in the hopes that we can circumvent war, settling once and for all which clan is worthy to rule."

She pauses, brows knitting together. "But this time, it will be the Ethodine to end all Ethodines. Each clan has agreed: whichever heir wins will secure their rule permanently. No more grumbling or talk of uprising or war. In fact, the losing heirs will show their allegiance by pledging a blood oath and handing over their moonstone to the winner."

My eyes grow wide. I can't believe the clan lords have agreed to such humiliating and intense conditions. Spilling their own blood in honor of another clan? Losing their most sacred stones of power forever? But the queen isn't done.

"I also warn you to be just as concerned with your diplomacy as with your training. Whoever wins the throne will also gain the power to dispose of any difficult clan leaders they so choose and select another, more agreeable faerie from that clan to rule instead."

I swallow hard. No wonder my father is so desperate to win. Without me to compete, he's already lost everything. Potentially even our family's claim to the Gwyllion throne. With me, he and our family line could rule all of Faylan, forever unchallenged.

"Over the course of the next five weeks—" the queen continues "—we will travel to the different provinces for each round of the competition, beginning here in Eldore… and ending in Greymerrow." The queen stops in front of me, looking deep into my eyes. Even the beady eyes of the dove on her shoulder seems to watch me carefully.

I glare back. The fact that she allowed me to take Gaius' place is the reason I've been dragged into this. But the queen only smiles before returning to her throne, the train of her purple gown trailing behind her.

"You will have a few days in each province for final training. But once a trial has commenced, there is no turning back. At the end of each round, you will be ranked by that particular trial's standards, awarding you points based on your ranking. And at the end of the Ethodine, we will have a new ruler of Faylan."

Her eyes grow soft. "I must warn you, however, the Ethodine is not for the faint of heart. It will stretch you in every way. And, unfortunately, I cannot guarantee you will all survive."

Hickory shifts uncomfortably, while Aeron shoots a side glance at Vale. Even Alys' mouth parts in surprise before she clamps it closed again.

They've been trained with a royal education, but also pampered and cared for their whole lives. I, on the other hand, have taken care of myself since I was a sprite. Even with parents, it is the Gwyllion way to make their young strong. At least I have that going for me.

"That being said, there are rules set for your protection. While you will be at odds during each trial, you will not show aggression otherwise."

I expect her to glance my way, but instead, she gives Vale a look of warning. Vale lowers her eyes to the floor.

"You will be escorted to training sessions and meals, and your rooms will be guarded at night, but you will not be constantly monitored. You are old enough to take care of yourselves. If you are found to have attacked or harmed any of your fellow competitors off the battlefield, you will be disqualified and sent home in shame."

Now her gaze lands on me.

"Your first challenge will take place at the end of this week. All I can tell you is that it will require a thorough knowledge of our world and history. I send you off to the royal library to begin your studies. You'll surely need it if you wish to survive."

CHAPTER 16

A s we walk through the gilded doors of the royal library, they open to reveal a vast area filled with rows upon rows of bookcases. Three levels of them line the room on either side of us, connected by grand, winding stairs, though many Sylphs seem to prefer flying from level to level instead. As we walk past scribes scrawling away at wooden desks, the smell of parchment and ink fills the air.

"Ouch!" I yelp as something whacks the back of my head. An owl with a heavy book in its talons flies over me. It lands on one of the scribe's desks next to a raven and a dove.

"Oh yes, do watch out for the *parakeeps*." Vale smirks. "Well-trained keepers of the library, but not always the most considerate flyers."

"Thanks for the heads up," I mutter crossly, rubbing the bump growing on my head. I keep an eye out for more flying vermin as I survey the space and notice this is much more than just a library.

Above us, the sky spans the entire ceiling behind a pattern of glass panes where puffy clouds and flying vessels pass by. Thankfully, the panes are tinted just enough to let the scene in but keep extreme heat out. A series of terraces punctures an outer wall for outdoor viewing.

"Happy studying," Hickory says as he flies off to one of them. A few Sylph apprentices peer up from their telescopes, shooting him irritated looks at the invasion, but Hickory's too busy gazing over the city to notice. He leans on the rail and pulls out a sketchbook and quill from the canvas satchel slung across his body. I guess he'll be leaving his studies for later. Though, as far as I can tell, he may not need it as much as the rest of us.

Obviously, neither does Vale. She'd much rather order us around.

"Go on now." She waves dismissively toward the shelves. "You'll find the books and study areas that way."

I hold my ground in protest, but Alys doesn't seem bothered by Vale's tone in the least. She promptly turns and flies to the second floor, where a flock of parakeeps pause in organizing the shelves to let her pass. Some of them abandon their duties to flutter after her. *Interesting pixie, that one.*

Sighing at the overwhelming number of options, I look for a place to start as Vale steps closer to Aeron.

"Unless anyone would like a *personal* tour?" she asks him, a suggestive smirk pulling at her mouth.

"I'm good, thanks." Aeron shoves his hands into the pockets of his breeches and takes off toward the first level of stacks.

Vale huffs and turns her focus to a wall of shelves ahead, filled with not only books, but also bottles and vials of all shapes and sizes. The area is sectioned off by a half-wall where students hunch over tables of ceramic cups and rounded, long-necked flasks filled with strange bubbling substances. Gray-haired Sylphs in professor's robes loom around them, doling out instructions.

"The potions section is restricted to approved staff and students only." Vale eyes me as if daring me to follow. "You may look, but not enter. No vagrants allowed."

My lips twist into a scowl as I watch her take the pouch of herbs she gathered in the garden from her belt and flutter over the half-wall. As she approaches two of the professors, they bow low and beam at her findings.

I turn to leave, but pause in front of a nearby bookcase when snickers from a table just over the wall find my ears.

"Vale thinks she's so smart," grumbles a pixie, fidgeting with the pink bow around her high collared blouse, matching her pink-tinted feathers. "I can't wait to see her face when I finally surpass her in marks this semester."

"And how do you plan to do that?" one of the pucks whispers, peering through spectacles as he pours a powdered substance into his beaker.

"I've been staying up till sunrise for a week studying, but you'd never know it." Making sure their professors aren't around, the pixie plucks what appears to be a compact perfume bottle from her clutch. "I swiped this from the professors' private stash. One spray of this puts me right into a deep sleep for a single hour, but when I wake, I feel like I've slept all night."

"Brilliant," murmurs the puck as the others nod emphatically.

More like brilliantly boring. I roll my eyes. All that intelligence, and that's what she chooses to use it for?

No longer intrigued, I turn back to the bookcases. I'm not sure where to start, so I randomly grab texts from each stack I pass, ranging on topics from Faylan history and celestial bodies to the art of potions and other Sylph magic.

For a brief moment, I wonder if there's any information on an ability like mine amidst all of these records. I shrug off the idea. If nothing else, at least these will be effective in putting me to sleep.

Finding a table near a window, I crack open the first one on Sylph society and their city's construction. As I predicted, it isn't long until I find myself re-reading the same sections over and over, jumping from book to book for anything that will keep my attention. The words are blurring together and barely anything is sticking in my brain. There aren't even any interesting pictures.

Eventually, I slam the book in my hands shut and push it away. This is impossible. I could study all day and never learn enough. How do I even know if any of this will come up during the trial?

I stand to put back the books where I found them, but I'm too turned around in the maze of stacks. I look up and down the aisle I'm in. With no one in sight, I place the books randomly on a shelf they obviously don't belong on.

Then, an idea hits me.

I might not be able to beat the others in knowledge, but it would definitely be harder for them to study if they can't find the books they're looking for.

Quietly, I walk up and down the stacks, pulling out random texts and purposely reshelving them in the wrong spots.

As I remove one at eye level, Aeron's face appears behind it. "What are you doing?" he asks.

I fumble with the text in my hand and nearly drop it. "Trying not to have a heart attack, no thanks to you."

"You know the parakeeps are just going to reorganize those later," he says. "They scour the shelves each night to make sure everything is where it belongs."

"I knew that," I say, keeping my inner grumbling to myself. *Stupid birds.* "One less reason to care about where they go then, right?"

I force the book back on the shelf, covering his face. I turn to leave the aisle, but he pops out right in front of me, startling me again.

"Will you stop doing that?"

"So skittish all of a sudden." Aeron observes me with a smirk.

"Well, getting jumped in a dark Shree alleyway might have something to do with it." Not to mention Moon Face's threats to watch my back. I cross my arms.

Aeron frowns. "Right. Well, whoever they were, I'm sure they won't be able to get all the way up here." He nods to the bookcases. "I'm guessing the studying isn't going very well?"

"Not even a little bit," I say, wiping dust from one of the spines.

Aeron leans against the bookcase, watching me with curiosity.

"What?"

"Nothing. It's just interesting seeing how different you are." I raise a brow at him, and he clarifies, "From Gaius, I mean. He seemed to like this place. He was always…" His voice tapers off, his eyes dropping from my face. "Sorry, I didn't mean to—"

"That's okay," I say softly, picturing Gaius—my twin, yet opposite in every way—walking the same stacks. "It's actually kind of nice hearing someone talk about him like he's still…"

"Here?" Aeron finishes.

"Yeah," I say, appreciating that he didn't use the word *alive*. "You know, he'd never admit it to our father, but he actually really enjoyed books and learning about the world outside our province."

I can still picture him begging me to let him finish one more page before we started training, making me promise not to tell Feyden.

"You miss him." Aeron nods.

"Well, of course I miss him…" I start, with an edge to my words, but the truth dies on my lips. An ache settles in my chest as I put a hand to the empty holster in my belt. The nightmare of Gaius handing me our twin blades flashes in my mind. "The daggers that were taken from me were the last things I had of his."

"Oh. I see." Aeron's voice is soft, perhaps tainted with guilt. Now he knows why I pleaded for them in Dunestone. He takes a step toward me. "I'm sorry, Quinn. I didn't know."

"It's fine." I draw back, shrugging it off, though the ache in my chest grows. Gaius should be the one that's here, not me. I don't belong here. How in Faylan did I think I could do this in his stead? "I should go."

I brush past Aeron before he can stop me and rush out the library doors into the hallway, never wanting to go back there again. Yet another place for Gaius to haunt me.

Marching down the hallways back to my room, I turn a corner and halt as a chorus of arguing voices flow through a large archway. It's the loudest, most boisterous sound I've heard since entering Eldore.

Finally, something interesting is happening.

Taking a tentative step through, I enter a shallow hall that opens into the same outdoor stadium I saw when I first arrived. Staying in the shadows, I notice the five stone platforms that were under construction are now complete. Above, the lowest rows of stadium seats are filled with shouting Sylph nobles, the tassels of their purple and gold sashes fluttering in the wind.

Ahead of me, the queen stands with one of the nobles at a podium, one word chiseled into the wall above them. *Cognisium.* Surprisingly, I recognize the word from one of the books in the library. If I remember right, this is where events like Sylph court, academic lectures, and intellectual debates are held.

Well, look at that. I guess I did learn something.

"Order! We will have order," the lead noble commands through a long bullhorn.

"We will have order when Her Highness explains how pixie dust is continually disappearing from the royal treasury," one calls out from another horn stationed in the stands. "Or what we're going to do about our wilting vegetation during this moonrain drought."

A contingent shouts their agreements as another speaks up from the other side of the stadium. "Why are we rewarding the other clans' insolence with a chance at the crown?"

"Yes!" another agrees. "And how does she plan to keep the Knolls from returning to Eldore when the other clans enter our borders for the first trial? Our city has been without infection for five years by holding our borders firm, and it only took one Gwyllion prince to bring it back to our doorstep."

I cringe at the mention of my brother and the ever-growing onslaught of questions. I look back to the lead noble and the queen, wondering how they plan to bring such a ruckus to order. If I were in charge, I would have already drawn my blades, challenging anyone to speak one more word.

But the queen has patiently listened to their grievances with the same poise she displayed in the great hall. Now she holds out her hand to the noble with the horn, who gladly relinquishes it to her.

"Unless your desire is for war to be at our doorstep next, the Ethodine is our best option," the queen says calmly. "The Knolls incident was successfully isolated. There's been no spread, and those that are cleared to visit for the trial will be screened before they enter. Finally, I assure you, those who have been stealing from the royal coffers will be found and severely punished. In fact, we have a fresh batch of new recruits ready to triple our ranks and security."

She motions above her as a ship flies in from above, landing in the middle of the stadium. The nobles quietly lean forward as ten rows of Sylph younglings in violet uniforms swoop out on their feathered wings in practiced formation. They land in perfect lines, inspected by more seasoned guards as the nobles murmur and nod approvingly.

Though these young soldiers are not nearly as tough-looking as Gwyllion ones, the sight reminds me of standing in similar lines with Gaius as the Gwyllion Guard tore us a new one over our performance each day.

Two of the senior guards stride toward me, taking a post near the Cognisium entrance, and I draw further back into the shadows.

"Did you hear?" One bumps the other with his elbow. "New recruits will be taking the midnight shift tonight."

"Perfect," sighs the other, stifling a yawn. "I needed some good news today."

I grin as an idea takes hold, my mind shifting from preparing to plotting. *Me too.*

CHAPTER 17

Back in my room, I keep myself busy until the dead of night. Gathering the tasseled ropes that tie my curtains, I place them on the bed and pace back and forth for a few other items I'll need. The last thing I want is to drift off to sleep. I'm not sure what I fear more: the nightmare of Faylan in ruins returning, or spending another night without protection.

I got distracted earlier, but I can't wait any longer. It's time to get my weapons back.

Aeron can't get rid of the guard outside my room this time, but at least whoever it is will be new and won't be expecting me. Fueled by the visions of Gaius and pumping adrenaline, I swing my chamber door open.

"What the...?" The guard on duty goes for his sword, but I'm faster. Flying toward him, I press my finger to a pressure point in his neck that Maverick taught me. I swipe the blade from his scabbard as he collapses to the floor. Best to leave no sign of injury if something goes wrong.

Still, with my opponent down and a real weapon in my hand, I'm alive again. This sword isn't nearly as well-crafted as my own, but it'll do for now.

I drag the guard into my room, hastily tying him to the bedpost and dressing in his garb. I've impersonated a Sylph before. I can do it again.

I pull my curls back into a tight braid and adjust my uniform in the mirror. Grabbing the guard's keys, I lock the door behind me.

With the night shift underway, there's barely anyone in sight except for a few servants. Still, as I make my way down familiar stairs and hallways, I keep my hand on the hilt of the stolen sword and nod courteously to the few I pass.

Finally, I reach the armory door with two new Sylph recruits standing guard. I know it's the middle of the night, but frankly I'm insulted that they don't have more guards on duty knowing there's a pirate under their roof. Oh well. Makes things easier for me.

The shorter of the two eyes me curiously as I approach, but I stride over to him with confidence. "I've been sent to relieve you." I lay on the Sylph accent thick, saluting him as I've seen other Sylphs do.

He lifts a brow and looks at his pal. "We just got here not half an hour ago."

I shrug, racing to remember Moon Face's real name. "Jasper says he wants to see you immediately. It sounded urgent, and he didn't look happy."

Thankfully, the guard's face turns from skepticism to panic, and he flies down the hall.

"He's in the dungeons," I add with urgency, chuckling to myself. *And Sylphs are supposed to be the smartest of us all.*

"What's so funny?" The remaining guard eyes me, still not buying my act. Good.

"You know, I think it's this perfume I bought in town today," I say, pulling out a tiny pink bottle from my pocket. "Ever since the first spray, I can't stop laughing."

The guard takes a step back, but I've already puffed a cloud in his face. He blinks rapidly as it dissipates, and for a moment I fear it won't do anything but make him sneeze. But then his body goes slack and falls forward into my arms.

"See, I just can't stop," I snicker again, lowering him to the floor, silently thanking the pixie I tracked down and stole the potion spray off earlier.

Taking the ring of keys from my victim's belt, I hurriedly try each one on the bolted door. The last one finally snaps into place, and I drag the young guard in with me.

Walking into the armory is like walking into a Gwyllion's dream.

Blades and daggers, bows and axes of every size and material line the walls.

And standing out from all the rest, clearly made by the best Gwyllion welders, are my weapons.

I fly toward them, sifting through the collection of knives and other small weapons Feyden gave me before I left Greymerrow. My hands run over them tenderly. *My oldest and dearest friends. You'd never betray me.*

After my inspection, however, two very important pieces are missing.

Where are the daggers?

"Don't move!" a gruff voice calls from the doorway.

I curse. I was so excited, I forgot to close the door behind me.

"*You*," Moon Face snarls, pointing his sword in my direction. "I should have known it was you. Don't you ever give up?"

"Never."

I grab two of my knives and sling them at him, but his feathered wings shoot him up out of range, and he lunges toward me. I need a weapon to match his blade, so I grab the nearest broadsword off the wall and release my own wings to meet him. The sound of steel twangs through the air, filling the armory.

"Where are my daggers, you imp? What did you do with them?"

"I have no idea what you're talking about." His brows knit with rage as boots sound from the corridor.

I'm about to be overrun. I have to get out of here—fast.

I swipe at an opening in Moon Face's stance. He dodges, and I fly toward the door—only to come face-to-face with the queen herself and a dozen of her guards. *Blast.* I lower my sword in surrender.

"I was about to bring her to you, Your Highness," Moon Face explains breathlessly. "It seems she was after her weapons. I believe she was trying to make a run for it." His dirty mitts are on my things again. My fingertips prick with heat, and I wince.

I glare at him before turning pleading eyes to the queen. Even with her night clothes and crownless head, she looks regal and powerful, a sword of her own in her hand. Her face is firm, but she stares at me as if waiting for my side of the story.

"I wasn't trying to run away, I swear," I say, though I have no credibility to stand on. "And I wasn't stealing. Those weapons are mine, and I want them returned."

"Do you really expect us to let an armed pirate stroll about the palace?" Moon Face scoffs.

The other guards chuckle.

The queen does not.

I plead directly with her again. "Please, your Majesty." I bow, desperate. "You say we're not supposed to attack each other, but if anyone comes after me, I have no defense. All the other competitors grew up learning their magic. But those…" I point to my weapons. "Those are my magic."

Of course, I also have flames that spontaneously burst from my hands, but I have no real control over them or the excruciating pain they cause. I have no desire to do anything but stuff them down and pretend they don't exist.

My weapons are my true power.

I hold my breath. It's the queen's turn. This is her domain. She has the power to jail me, execute me on the spot, or worse—send me back to my father. Finally, the queen nods to Moon Face, who gives her a satisfied smile and returns my weapons to the armory shelves. I sigh, staring longingly after my darlings.

"Quinn." The queen's gentle voice brings me back. I blink at her, thrown off by her use of my nickname. "I've heard that's what you prefer to be called. Take a walk with me?" She motions down the hallway. Assuming the alternative could be the dungeons, I follow.

Returning her sword to the sheath at her side, she leads me down the corridor and outside to the same garden I'd been in only hours ago. Moonlit and completely quiet now, it's as if even the plants are asleep, swaying in the evening breeze, casting shadows. In all my years on the sea, I've never seen the stars so big and bright before. The moons appear close enough to touch.

But the queen isn't looking at the sky. She brushes a hand along the plants and herbs as she walks. "There are many rumors about how I came to power, Captain. But I want you to know the real story."

I'm about to ask why, but for once, I keep my mouth shut. There's something about the queen's presence, how she carries herself, that holds my attention.

"As you've probably heard, I didn't grow up in the Sylph court as most queens do. I grew up in Shree. My father was a Sylph guard while my mother learned the Dryad ways and became a Sylph medik. She always loved studying plants and herbs." She pauses to pluck a dead leaf from a vine.

"When my father died on duty, my mother began bringing me to the palace as her assistant in serving the royal family. A particularly aggressive wave of the Knolls plague had just begun. Even the king couldn't escape it. Tending to him is where I met his three sons: Markas, Lato, and Caleb. Unexpectedly, feelings developed between Markas and me. It was young love between two faeries who didn't have any business being together, but Markas didn't care. Our wedding day was the most wonderful event…"

The moonlight floods her skin, making it appear as if she's reverted to her youngling age along with the memory. But her sparkling eyes soon grow vacant and far-off.

"It was wonderful, of course, until Markas' father collapsed in my arms at the reception."

It's then that I remember this marriage doesn't have a happy ending.

She turns into the shadows to walk along a line of rose bushes.

I hurry to follow, needing to hear what happened next.

"In one day, I became not only a princess, but also queen of all Faylan. A whirlwind of mourning and preparing for my new life all at the same time. Markas, being the hopeless romantic he was, spent more time talking about us running away together than taking care of the kingdom. I loved him, but I also grew to resent him as I took up the responsibilities he let fall by the wayside.

"Lato was always lurking in the shadow of his brother, wanting the crown. And as I was to find out later, also wanting me. So when Markas died of the Plague as well, Lato didn't waste any time proposing, promising to be a better ruler and husband than his brother. I didn't love Lato, but I had nowhere else to go. I accepted his proposal.

"Lato was a hard king, ruling with an iron fist. The more I found out about his true self, the more I spoke up against him. And the less I wanted to give him an heir. This infuriated him, and in a rage, he admitted to exposing Markas to the Plague in order to gain the crown and me, threatening that I could be next. I could only sit back as Faylan stood at his mercy.

"The clans hated him as much as I did, so when an assassin poisoned his goblet, I wasn't surprised. This time, however, I wasn't alone. In my estrangement from Lato, his youngest brother Caleb had grown into a strapping young puck who served in his brother's army. Only a couple years younger than me, Caleb could see where both of his brothers had failed as kings and husbands. When he was home, we'd take long walks through this very garden. When he was away, we wrote letters in code, sharing information but also sharing our hearts.

"After Lato passed, Caleb returned to mourn his brother and propose to me. In marrying the third brother, however, there were no loud celebrations. Many thought I killed off the previous two myself and somehow enchanted Caleb, only to dispose of him too, so I could rule alone."

The queen looks away, but I can see the tears welling in her eyes. "I had nothing to do with Caleb's death. In fact, I begged him not to return to patrolling with his troop. But as much as he loved me, he missed the life of a soldier. And I think, after experiencing so much loss, he was afraid to fully let anyone in…" Queen Gwendolyn trails off. "The day he left, something told me I would never see him again. And a month later, after I got the news he'd been slain in battle… I found out I was pregnant with Vale."

Like many of Whit's stories, I'm caught up in this one until the very end. If she's telling the truth, the tales about her have been blown way out of proportion. Before me isn't the strong queen from the great hall, but a young pixie trying to figure out her place in the world. Not unlike myself.

"Your Majesty," I begin softly, finding new admiration for this royal. "Forgive me, but why tell me this story? Why not just punish me and send me on my way?"

Queen Gwendolyn gives me a small smile. "We are not so different, you and I. We are both powerful, great leaders, and yet we want to be free."

I swallow hard. It's scary how much she's right.

"Tonight you demonstrated impressive cleverness and ambition. I know you don't want the throne any more than anyone wants you on it. So, I have a proposition for you."

"You mean a bribe." I draw back, my guard up again. I should've known this was coming.

"More of a bargain. One where we both get what we truly desire." She smiles. "Vale is the obvious choice for the crown, and I am confident she will excel in this competition. As Vale was meant to be the future ruler of Faylan, I have personally ensured she's been trained in every royal responsibility and Etho since she was a sprite... except one."

She looks to the stars. "I'm sure you can see why I never taught her to fight. I never wanted her to have a reason to go to war like her father. But now, I worry for her success in the final Gwyllion challenge. I want you to train her well enough to defeat the others. Even you."

I take a moment to process. She wants me to train her daughter? To help her beat me at the only thing I excel at? I try to imagine Vale going through the same training exercises I took my crew through, complaining and insulting me all the while. Me struggling to even be in the same room without wanting to knock her out. I scowl.

"And what good will that do *me*?" I cross my arms, ready to turn her down.

"If you accept," she says slowly. "I will have Vale make sure you're ready for all the other phases of the competition. Your survival will be as important to me as hers. If Vale succeeds in surpassing the other competitors in the Gwyllion Trial of Strength, including you, I'll ensure that Vale releases you from your responsibility to the Gwyllion throne and bestows full immunity for your past crimes. If all goes well, you'll have a clean slate, your freedom, and the ability to return to your ship and crew."

I hesitate, mentally combing through every aspect of her deal. If I do this, not only will I gain my freedom, but I'll also still technically fulfill my vow to enter the competition, all without having to become Queen of Faylan or ruler of Greymerrow in the end. But what will I do after everything is over?

My head falls, the sting of Whit's betrayal hitting me again. "I'm not sure I'll be able to return to my ship."

"Quinn, my dear." The queen lifts my chin to meet her eyes. I search her face for agitation, but there's only concern. "I know you grew up with only a father to raise you, so let me give you some motherly advice."

I find myself leaning forward, wanting to hear what she has to say. Is this what it's like to have a mother? Or even just a parent who cares?

"Everyone has their place in the machine. Each clan and faerie has their position in the cog of life. But you don't need anyone else to make it in this world. If your crew has rejected you, you'll find a way to rise above and start afresh."

Warmth spreads through my chest as she speaks, and I'm suddenly unafraid of the future. I want to be the pixie she sees. Perhaps we are more alike than I thought. Perhaps, like me, she's just misunderstood.

I'm about to speak when Gaius' face appears in my mind, and I hesitate.

Gaius wouldn't want me to represent him in the Ethodine this way. But surely he couldn't fault me for getting what I want out of this as well. Maybe *this* is what I'm best at. Being a pirate. Making crooked deals. Surviving.

But before I can start over, I need a bit more from the queen. And right now, she has more to gain than I have to lose.

"I have a stipulation. I want my weapons returned to me now, plus enough riches to purchase a Sylph flying ship and hire a new crew when I've secured Vale's victory." *Maybe that much could afford me some revenge.* I stand a little taller. "These are my terms. Take them, and we have a deal."

"I like your spunk, Captain." The queen smirks as she considers me. "Prove to me you can behave yourself this week—no more knocking out my guards and stealing their clothes—and I will *consider* returning your weapons. As for a new ship and crew, make sure my Vale wins, and you will have your reward."

CHAPTER 18

"This is ridiculous," Vale mutters under her breath. Both her red ponytail and knee-length dress with gold trim furiously swish behind her as I follow through the corridor. Not a speck of garden dirt on her today; she finally looks like the princess I expected.

Once in her chambers, Vale walks to the back of the room, approaching a pair of double doors near her bed. As she throws them open, I expect to see a walk-in closet arrayed with rows of frilly dresses. Instead, we stand in a tall room of floor-to-ceiling bookcases with a white stained desk and two purple-cushioned chairs in the center. Her own private library. I shouldn't be surprised.

Vale has been charged by her mother to help me study in secret so that no one will know she's helping me. Staring at the looming bookcases around us, I try not to feel intimidated. While this is a room Whit would drool over, I know that there's no way I can memorize all this information in just a few days, not even with Vale's help.

I sit at the desk already piled high with books.

Vale glares at me, no longer trying to hide her disdain with any amount of tact.

"You know, I could probably pass this trial without studying at all. Instead, I'm stuck here with *you*." She obviously likes the idea about as much as I do.

"You really think you're that smart, huh?" I cross my arms.

Vale shrugs. "I'm first in my class every year. I've practically memorized every book in this room." She motions to the walls of bookcases with a raised brow.

I whistle, feigning an overly impressed look, though I really am.

"I don't see what the big deal with this trial is," I deflect, flipping through a few pages of a book before tossing it to the side. "If I don't finish first in this one, it's not like answering a few trivial questions wrong is life or death."

"That's what they'd like you to think." Vale smirks. Her white-feathered wings lift her into the air until she reaches the top shelves. "Never forget, underestimating a Sylph is to truly beg for death."

She thumbs through a line of book spines, dusting off the jackets as she goes, and pulls one out before returning to the ground. She plops the book in front of me, and I read the title.

How to Kill Without Getting Caught.

"We literally wrote the book on it." She smiles.

In spite of myself, I grin. This is a book I could definitely be into. But as I reach for it, Vale pulls it back, wagging a finger and clicking her tongue.

"Wouldn't want you getting any new ideas on that subject. It's all the others we need to focus on." She places the book on a shelf behind her, then spins around with intensity. "Let's start with something that should be easier for you, shall we? How many moons do we have, and what are their names?"

"Well…" I picture the sky at night, but Vale doesn't wait for my answer.

"In what year did the first Ethodine occur?"

"Uh…" I hesitate again, my brain spinning.

"How many grams of pixie dust can a Kobold be exposed to before slipping into insanity, as opposed to any other faerie kind?"

Not wanting to miss another question, I throw out a guess. "Four!"

From Vale's expression, I can tell I wasn't even close. She collapses into the chair across from me, flinging her hands up. "Didn't you have any kind of schooling before throwing your life away to piracy?"

"Wasn't really my thing." I huff, frustrated as well as bored out of my mind. "Half our schooling was in the art of sword play, weapon welding, and iron casting. You know, the important stuff."

Vale sighs. "This is going to be a lot harder than I thought. Good thing I came prepared." She pulls a vial out of her pocket and shakes it vigorously before placing it on the desk between us.

"What is it?" I peer curiously at the slimy green substance swishing around in the bottle.

"It's called Notting Potion," Vale says with a glint in her eye. "It helps you retain massive amounts of information at a time. After drinking it, you have about an hour to read or listen to whatever you wish to remember. Normally, someone who takes it can retain what they've learned for only the following day. But this concentrated dose should allow you to keep the information in that sorry head of yours until the end of the week."

"*Should?*" I ask, still eyeing the vial with suspicion. "Why don't all the competitors use it?"

"Because not everyone is as smart as I am. Concocting this stuff isn't easy, you know."

"You *made* this stuff?" I lift it off the desk, observing it from all sides.

"I'm a master at many things," Vale says, lifting her chin with pride. "Like any Sylph, I love the study of the sun, the moons, and the stars. I have quite the knack for ancient languages as well. But potions are my specialty. There's nothing more enjoyable than spending a day in the sun, gathering rare herbs in the garden, and experimenting with them late into the night."

"You've really got to get out more." I uncap the bottle, take a quick whiff, and hold back a gag at the putrid scent. "How do I know this isn't poison?"

Vale's smile widens. "Only one way to find out."

I weigh my odds. There's no question I'm not Vale's favorite person. But she'll also have to deal with her mother's wrath, never mind being banned from the Ethodine, if she kills me. Besides, Vale still needs me to train her for the Trial of Strength. At least, I hope that's how she sees it.

Tired of debating my odds, I gulp the sticky liquid down as fast as I can. Choking on its acidic taste, I wait. "I don't feel any different."

Vale rolls her eyes, tosses a book in front of me titled *A History of Sylph Culture,* and opens it to the first page. "Wait for it."

Immediately, the words start whizzing by my eyes so fast, it makes me dizzy. Even crazier, I'm *retaining* what I'm reading. All of it. I flip the page. Then again. And again. My focus only breaks when Vale rips the book away and stares at me with a smile. "Okay, what is a Sylph youngling's main subject of study?"

"The orbiting sun, moons, and stars, and their effect on our world and weather patterns," I say without a second thought.

"Good. How many types of plants are grown in the royal gardens alone?"

"Including edible vegetation?"

"Yes."

"Ten thousand, seven hundred and forty-five."

"Excellent." Vale beams. "All Sylph wings are most similar to that of birds. Which bird's feathers did the great King Zor's wings resemble most?"

"A phoenix."

Vale snaps the book closed, beaming with a triumphant smirk. "And that's how it's done."

"This stuff is amazing." My brain is still buzzing with all the information, my pulse racing. "You use it too?"

"Please!" Vale laughs, tapping her temple. "This brain is a library of information all on its own. You don't mess with perfection. The real question is, are *you* okay with cheating your way through this one?"

"Um, pirate!" I point to myself.

We both laugh. It might have actually been a pleasant moment if not for the footsteps we hear coming toward the door. Vale and I go still, watching the entrance. It could be the queen coming to check on us, but if we're found by the wrong faerie, we're in deep weeds. The door creaks open, and I hold my breath as Hickory casually walks in.

I freeze, but Vale exhales with a wave of her hand.

"Oh, it's just you. I'm busy at the moment. Go away now."

Hickory lets out a light chuckle. "It's really hysterical how you think you can order me around like one of your servants." Hickory holds out the book in his hands to her. "Just making a return."

"It wasn't an order," Vale protests, snatching the book from him. "Just a *strong* suggestion."

It's Hickory's turn to roll his good eye, which then settles on me curiously. A bead of perspiration rolls down my face. I'm nervous about Vale and I getting caught, but I also feel warmer than usual. At first, I'm afraid my fire ability is going to spontaneously make an appearance, but this feels different. Perhaps perspiration is how the potion works its way out of my system. Either way, it's definitely making me look guilty.

I've only just begun this charade, and I'm already done for. I look to Vale. *Why isn't she freaking out too?*

Instead of asking why I'm here like any normal faerie might do, Hickory sniffs the air, following his nose until he's right in front of me. Completely disregarding my personal space, he leans in.

"Can I help you?" I press up against the back of my chair.

"I had a question," he says, still inspecting me while addressing Vale. "But I can see you're busy. I'll come back later." And with that, he leaves.

The door clicks shut behind him.

"Very odd, that one." Vale confirms my exact thought, still seemingly unconcerned.

I nod at the book Hickory returned to her. "Are you helping all the competitors pass the trial? Don't you think that's a little counterintuitive?"

Vale laughs. "What, Hickory? With his love of history, he might know more than I do, if that's possible. He borrowed this for pleasure reading, but just now he was probably also hoping for a pixie dust fix."

"What, are you his supplier or something?" I joke.

"Up here in the clouds, I'm the only supplier."

I nearly laugh out loud, but her expression is dead serious. Though I'm skeptical, being the queen's daughter, I can see her easily gaining access to all the pixie dust she wants. *Typical Sylph, taking advantage of the plenty they already have.* I'm still worried about Hickory, though. "Do you think he knows you're helping me?"

"Perhaps. He probably smelled the potion. Not having full sight can really heighten all other senses, you know," Vale says casually as she inspects the condition of the book he'd returned. "But he won't say anything."

"How can you be so sure?" Sweat gathers at the nape of my neck.

"He's too dependent on the dust. It dulls the pain in his bad eye." Vale finishes with the book, placing it carefully back on the shelf. "He knows if he spills any of my secrets, I'll cut him off."

"You really do have everyone wrapped around your little finger," I comment, a bit impressed. As she said, I shouldn't underestimate her.

Still, I can't leave her feeling too sure of herself. "Everyone but your mother, that is."

Vale's demeanor goes from tolerating my presence to loathing me all over again in a matter of seconds. She comes at me in a stoic fury, her freckles gathering in a contorted expression.

"Bet you think *you* can do that though, don't you?" She leans over me. "I heard all about your little stunt last night. How my mother showed you mercy, offering you this ridiculous deal. She may feel sorry for you, *pirate*, being motherless and all. But don't think that means you'll get into her good graces. Sure, she'll reward you, but she'll throw you away in the end. She only has room in her heart for one, don't you forget that." She looks at the vial still on the desk and back to me as a smirk emerges through her anger. "Well, at least for this week, I know you won't be able to forget it."

I blink, taken aback by her venomous insults. But as she stomps out of the room, I realize the one who is really hurt is Vale.

~

I spend the rest of the hour feverishly reading as many books as I can before the potion evaporates out of my system.

Vale doesn't return. *Finally, some peace and quiet.* But even with my temporary speed-reading abilities, I don't get through even half the books in her library. With the hour almost up, my heart rate slowly returns to normal. I'll need a nice long bath after all this sweating the potion has caused.

Just one more book, I tell myself, grabbing the next one on the pile.

The edges of the cover are bent, coated in a layer of dust, much older than any of the other books I've come across. I start to wipe away the dust but pause, my fingers brushing over the well-worn leather.

There, in the middle of the cover, sits a singular symbol, engraved in gold: three circles, each smaller than the last, fit inside each other. A decorative flower is overlaid on top of them; its ten delicate petals stretch out to the perimeter of the outermost circle.

An uncanny notion washes over me—I've seen the image somewhere before. I wrack my memory, but I can't place it. Peering closer, I graze my fingers over the gold embellishment.

The moment I touch it, a bright light fills the room. A surge of energy shoots through my fingers, spreading through my body like a lightning bolt.

The book drops with a thud, and I squeeze my eyes shut, shaking my head until the surge of energy dissipates.

What in Faylan was that?

I spot the book on the desk. The blinding light is gone, but no way am I touching that thing again. Either this text is cursed, or the potion is still messing with me. A distant bell chimes the hour. Whatever that was, it's definitely time for a break.

The initial effectiveness of the potion might've worn off, but I still have a few more days to prepare the old-fashioned way. If I really want to survive the Trial of Knowledge, I need to be ready. Picking up as many books as I can carry, I head back to my chambers. I'm more than done with this stuffy room and the strange happenings inside its walls. In my hurry, I knock into something in the hallway, books flying everywhere.

Perfect. I'm about to curse when I notice Hickory sprawled out on the floor, covered in my books and a collection of his paint brushes and sketches. Maybe it's because his misty blind eye is staring at me, or that he still reminds me of my brother, but somehow I find myself apologizing.

"I'm so sorry." I nearly trip over the books while trying to help him up.

"I'm pretty sure *I* bumped into you." Hickory laughs, waving me off kindly while picking up his art supplies and a couple of my books. "A little light reading?"

"Just a bit." I sigh. "Got to get ready for this first trial somehow. Though I hear you're more than prepared."

"Perhaps," he says, struggling to hold back a smile at the compliment. "But you know, it's what's *not* in these books that's the really interesting stuff." He holds out one of them to me.

I tilt my head before taking it. "What do you mean?"

"Well, for instance…" He pauses and looks around at the empty hallway, lowering his voice. "The history books claim the Sylphs banished the Numa from our world entirely. But some faeries believe the Numa still hold some power over our world. That they still cause mischief and disaster, growing stronger in the shadows until they will one day return. Some even believe the Numa cursed our land with the Knolls plague as their parting gift."

Ah, here are the conspiracy theories Vale was talking about. Interesting. "That is, if the Numa even existed at all," I challenge.

Hickory's brows lift. "You don't believe—?"

"Please. The events happened so long ago, the story of the Numa and the Sylph King could have easily been inflated over time." I've seen it happen firsthand with legends created about my own pirate persona. "I wouldn't be surprised if it's just a way for the Sylphs to justify their place in power." Though, recalling Hickory's mural depictions of the terrifying Numa salivating for faerie blood, I can't help but shudder.

"Sounds like you have some conspiracy theories of your own, then?" Hickory eyes me with a smirk.

I shrug. *Hmm. Maybe I do.*

Hickory picks another book off the floor, and his eyes go wide. "Where did this one come from?" He holds it out to me, and I nearly jump back.

It's the book with the strange symbol.

I put out my hands as if it might leap forward and attack me. "Ah… I have no idea. I didn't mean to take that one." Thankfully, it doesn't seem to be doing anything strange while in Hickory's hands. "What is it?"

"Oh, just another ancient tome, but one I have yet to read myself." Hickory holds the book close to his chest, as if it's more precious than possessed. "Mind if I take it off your hands?"

"Please," I say, relieved. "Just make sure Princess Pouty-Pants gets it back."

"Sure thing." Hickory laughs again as I pick up more books. "And don't worry," he says in a softer tone. "Whatever you and Vale were doing earlier stays between you and Vale."

I slowly pick up the last book, glancing around the empty corridor before I meet his eye.

"Just like whatever transpires between Vale and me stays between Vale and me." He pulls out his pipe, and I realize he's referencing their pixie dust dealings.

"You don't want to rat me out?" I ask. "One less competitor to worry about?"

"You could do the same to me, I suppose," Hickory counters, striking a match on his belt and lighting the pipe. "But I'm fairly sure I don't have a chance at winning. Of course, I'd never hear the end of it from my parents if I didn't at least try. Being able to travel and paint all of Faylan as its king does sound pretty amazing. At least I'd never have to go back to the dark abyss of the tunnels." He shivers, clutching the tome tighter.

"Wait, you're a Kobold who's afraid of the dark?" I startle at the thought.

"I know, it's ridiculous. But with only one working eye, I don't see as well as other Kobolds do, especially in the dark." Hickory shakes his head in good-humored embarrassment. But glancing at some of his murals on the walls nearby, his face grows more serious. "There've been times my good eye fails to glow in the dark at all. Each time, I fear I've finally lost my sight completely, never able to see or paint anything ever again."

My heart breaks for him. "I hope you don't mind me asking, but how did you lose your vision in the first place?"

"I was diagnosed with a disease a few years ago," he explains.

"The *Knolls*?" I chance a guess.

"Our mediks thought it might be that at first, but since the disease stayed centralized to my eyes, that theory was dismissed. They were able to slow the effects dramatically, but I eventually lost this eye completely." He points to the hazy one that barely shifts. "My parents wanted our mediks to gouge it out and replace it with a mechanical eye, but it was a risky procedure. I could have lost all sight if things went wrong. So, I refused. Besides, I think this eye actually gives me an edgy, vagrant kind of look." He flicks back his white locks, revealing more of his misty eye with a smirk. I can't help but smile back. This puck has spunk, and I appreciate his candor more than he knows.

"By the way, I wouldn't take what Vale said yesterday too personally. About Gaius, I mean."

My smile fades as I replay her accusations in my mind.

"I think Gaius' passing reminded us all how vulnerable we are. None of us, no matter our station, are immune to death. I think your presence may be a reminder for Vale that's too close for comfort."

I wonder at his wisdom. His reasoning doesn't make Vale's words sting any less, but it does help me see things in a different light.

"Plus, I think she sees you as a real threat. You're the only wildcard she hasn't quite figured out yet." His smile returns. "Vale is afraid of the dark too, in a way. She hates being blind to something she feels like she should understand. I'm afraid she'll probably keep pushing your buttons until she knows what makes you tick."

"Great," I say sarcastically. There's some satisfaction in knowing that Vale might actually see me as a threat, but with my current deal with the queen, it doesn't matter. If Hickory's analysis of how Vale functions is accurate, this is going to be a very long few weeks.

A door down the hall creaks open. Alys emerges from her room, dressed in all black as usual, her gloved hands securing the satchel at her side. She stares at us. Every time she gives me that cold, blank look, I feel as though she can see right into my very soul. It's starting to give me the creeps.

Hickory gives her a short wave. He's obviously the friendliest of all of us. But she breaks her stare and continues in the opposite direction.

"Don't mind Alys." Hickory shrugs. "She tends to prefer the company of creatures over her own kind. Nothing personal, of course."

I stare after her and her gloved hands. "Have you ever seen her, you know… kill someone?"

Hickory snorts. "Alys? I think you've been listening to too many stories. Folk are rarely what they appear to be, Captain. You of all fae should know that."

I agree, but his statement isn't exactly a denial either.

"I'd stop hanging out with Vale, though, if I were you," he adds, turning to leave. "Aeron too, if you know what's good for you."

CHAPTER 19

As much as I'd love to heed Hickory's warnings and never see Vale again, there's no way that's possible. Not when I'm contractually obligated to train her every blasted day.

Once we're in the other provinces, it will be a lot harder to be discreet, and Vale has a lot to learn about swordplay in five short weeks. So, to our dismay, the queen has given us access to a private training room and insists that I give Vale as much instruction as possible while we're still in Eldore.

Lucky me.

There are some upsides, however. At least during these sessions Vale is in *my* wheelhouse of expertise and under *my* instruction. Our weapons might be made of wood to start, but knocking her around with them is still fairly entertaining.

"Ouch!" Vale cries as I strike at her rib. "You did that on purpose."

"After the last few sessions, you'd think you'd have learned not to leave that spot vulnerable anymore." I circle her, poking at her legs. "And your stance is still all wrong. Didn't you practice anything I showed you yesterday?"

Vale glares. "I was too busy reading through all the royal library's books on swordplay. Boring as ever, but I know all the weapons and fighting terms now. I bet I know even more than you."

"A lot of good that's doing."

While I'm giving her a hard time, I'm honestly surprised by some of her natural instincts. Like her gleaming red hair, she probably inherited some genetic skill from her late father. But I'm not going to risk giving her a bigger head than she already has. It's time to take this princess down a peg and show her what true strength really is. And how hard she'll have to work for it.

"You know head knowledge is much different from actually applying it in real life, right?" I say.

Vale rubs her side. "You still don't have to hit so hard."

I sigh. "Look, if you want everyone to believe you can beat me in the final trial, you have to at least make it look convincing. You've got to toughen up, Princess. If I'm not hard on you, you'll never learn."

As my father's exact words come out of my mouth, I wince.

The last time I remember him saying it, I'd gotten cocky during a dragon-raiding drill and led my troop to failure. Feyden made me duel him right then and there. In front of everyone. That was when I got most of my scars. I touch my arms, and my wings shudder behind me at the memory. I couldn't fly for a week.

Still, I can't deny that his methods produce results. Though I've never been quite as harsh, I've seen their effectiveness with my own crew. And, if I ever want to get through this competition and return to my life of piracy, I have no other choice but to use them on Vale as well.

"What's wrong with you?" Vale's voice snaps me back to attention.

I must have spaced out.

"Besides the fact that I'm stuck here with you?" I run a hand through my sweaty curls as I think of the litany of things that are wrong.

There's the nightmare of Gaius that's still haunting me. It's been coming back most nights, keeping me tossing and turning. Frankly, I'm exhausted. But I don't tell Vale that.

There's also the annoying fact that I can feel a faint hum of the Notting Potion's magic constantly buzzing through my body. "I don't think your stupid elixir is agreeing with me," I finally say. "I keep feeling this tingling sensation."

"That just means it's still working, helping you hold onto all the information you learned. When you stop feeling that sensation, that's when you should start worrying,"

It's true; I can still recall every single piece of information I learned that day in Vale's library. Honestly, it's kind of creeping me out. I just hope it will all be worth it.

"Well, I think I've had quite enough of you for today anyway." Vale waves her hand dismissively. "You may go."

"With pleasure," I say under my breath. I don't like obeying her orders, but at this point, I want nothing more than to get out of here.

"And if you know what's good for you—" she calls after me "—you'll grab that pile of books on the way out. You still have to survive the first trial, after all."

I grumble as I pick up the towering stack of books and head to my room. I feel a headache coming on just thinking of another study session. All I've done since arriving in Eldore is stare at pages and pages of text until my brain hurts. Listening to Vale's whining isn't helping either.

I yearn for a distraction. Some fun. Unconsciously, Aeron's smile pops into my head.

Stop that! I shake off the image.

He's caught up with me a few more times while at meals or studying in the main library. But ever since Hickory gave me that warning, I've tried to keep my distance.

I don't know why Hickory said what he said. Maybe he knows about Aeron's silver tongue too? In any case, getting too close to Aeron —or any of them, for that matter—will only lead to trouble. It's better to keep to myself.

But trouble is my middle name, and I know it the moment I turn the next corner and spot Alys walking down the hall. I quiet my steps, watching her carefully until all I can hear bouncing off the walls is the sound of her heavy boots.

And something else.

A faint but distinct sound of metals clinking together. I search for the source, but it leads back to Alys. The sound matches the rhythm of her steps, muffled by the long black cloak she wears.

Could she be hiding weapons? I quicken my pace.

Alys seems like the sort who could sneak weapons onto the premises. We haven't exactly gotten off on the right foot, but maybe I can convince her to share.

"Hey, Alys!" I call, trying not to drop the pile of books. "Wait up!"

But if anything, Alys quickens her pace. She turns the next corner, out of sight.

"Wait a minute!" I walk faster, ready to throw the books to the ground and leave them in my wake. "Come on, I know you're mute, but you're not deaf!"

Turning the same corner, I come face-to-face with a very unhappy Alys. Arms crossed, she stands in front of an arched opening leading out to the gardens. As the sun shines through, it highlights her small but strong frame and her stern brown eyes. She obviously didn't like my last comment, but at least I've gotten her attention.

"Ah, off to take a stroll through the gardens?" I ask, adjusting the books in my arms.

She taps her foot impatiently and lifts a brow.

"Anyone ever tell you that you're a fast walker?" I stall. How can I get her to show me what she's hiding under that cloak?

But Alys isn't in the mood for chitchat. She rolls her eyes and walks outside, disappearing into the foliage.

"Wait!" I huff and follow.

Once through the archway, I freeze. Up ahead, Alys approaches a green dragon flying overhead, the same one she arrived on earlier in the week. *Tomah.*

I slide behind a tree, waiting to see what she'll do.

With a flick of her wrist, the dragon halts in midair, only flapping his wings to stay suspended. He watches her intently for her next command.

Alys raises her hands in a fluid motion and the dragon obeys, flipping through the air.

It's like Alys has a secret language that only she and the dragon know. A dance only the two of them share. It's mesmerizing. When she brings her hands down, he darts toward her and lands with a thud, the ground trembling.

Unlike the menacing dragons in the mountains, one could easily miss Tomah in this setting; his emerald-green scales blend into the plants around him. The hair under his chin and chest billows out like a regal mane, while the rest hangs off his body like drooping vines. He practically disappears into the foliage until he shifts to growl and snap at the birds flying overhead.

Though he sits curled up like a bobcat, playfully wagging his tail at

Alys' approach, I'm still unable to move. Dragon raids on Greymerrow replay in my mind, the smell of smoldering stone returning. Is getting hold of a weapon really this important?

After taking a deep breath, I decide it's now or never. Do or die. I gulp down my nerves, leaving the books on a nearby bench.

"Hey, Alys," I say as casually as I can, my focus more on the dragon as I approach. I stand near his tail. It's safer than going near his smoke-breathing head.

At the sound of my voice though, Tomah whips his head toward me, watching my every move.

"Got a question for you, one warrior to another," I continue to Alys, but she passes right by me, circling around the dragon, her eyes roaming over his body. She's inspecting him. Looking for something.

I decide to take her silence as permission to keep talking. "You see, I'm in need of a weapon or two, and I'm willing to do whatever's necessary to acquire... well, anything, really."

Surprisingly, Alys reaches into her satchel, and my heart leaps with hope. But instead of a weapon, she pulls out a half-eaten lamb leg that I recognize from the afternoon lunch spread. Tomah licks it into his mouth, bones and all. I grimace as she wipes the dragon saliva onto her cloak.

I press on, taking a tentative step forward.

Tomah's attention shifts back to me as he licks his lips, daring me to come closer.

I hold my breath, chancing another step.

This time, he bares his sharp teeth, launching toward me so fast I barely have time to react.

Alys darts in between us. She glares at him, using her hands to sign another order. The dragon snorts out smoke but settles back down, eyeing me.

I breathe out, but I can't stop now. One last try. "I wouldn't need much. Preferably a weapon that is small and easily *concealable*." I lower my voice to a whisper. "Maybe we can make a deal for, say, whatever you're hiding under your cloak?"

Alys' eyes finally snap to mine and narrow, the black tattoos that frame her brown face creasing with the movement. She slowly moves her hand beneath her cloak, and I draw back, realizing she could just as easily use whatever it is against me.

But what emerges from her belt isn't any weapon I've ever seen. More like a ridged blade connected to a pair of large metal shears. Or pliers, or…

Alys huffs and turns toward the dragon. Making sure to give him another piece of lamb from her satchel first, she kneels and uses the device to begin… clipping and sharpening his claws.

My shoulders slump.

"Ah, I see." I pinch the bridge of my nose. *Stupid.* I guess that means no weapons today. Back to hitting the books for me.

But as I move to leave, I notice two figures on the other side of the garden. One has midnight blue hair, his back to me. The other faces him, and I recognize her fiery red waves.

Aeron and Vale.

I'm too far to hear what they're saying, but Vale doesn't look happy.

Her eyes shift from Aeron and find me. At first, her look grows even more agitated, as if I've purposely been spying on them. But soon, a mischievous smirk tugs at her lips.

Aeron moves to follow her gaze but Vale grabs his hand. Batting her lashes, she lures him away into the shadows, shooting me one more poignant grin before disappearing out of sight.

I step forward, wondering what they're up to, but then stop. I push away the thought and snort. I don't care.

The rasp of Alys' filing stops, and I glance her way. She and Tomah stare at me in curiosity.

"What?" I ask, annoyed at the whole situation.

Alys and Tomah look at each other, then back to me. Alys shrugs. As she resumes tending to her dragon, I pick up my books in defeat. But not before taking one last glance at Alys' back. I swear her shoulders are bobbing up and down with silent laughter.

CHAPTER 20

On the morning of the first trial, I'm dragged out of bed before I can even open my eyes.

"What the—?" I wake out of my stupor and throw a punch toward the first blurred face I see.

A hand with rough, calloused skin grips my wrist firmly before I can make contact. This is no Sylph. My eyes focus. I'm surrounded by five Gwyllion servants who are already pulling my night shift dress over my head and yanking brushes through my unruly hair.

"What are you doing?" I try to pull away from them, but Gwyllion servants are not demure or frightened of me like the Sylph servants have been.

"Pleasant morning to you as well, my lady," the large one with my hand still clutched in her fist practically growls. "Lord Feyden sent us to make sure you represent Greymerrow well in the trial today."

Of course. I sigh and eventually concede, letting them drag my exhausted body into the washroom and scrub me down, knotting my curls into a tight braid.

When they're done, I turn to the mirror. With little to no make-up used in Gwyllion culture, my face looks plain. Cold. If that isn't enough, the muted fabrics I wear wash out my already earthy complexion, threatening to kill my soul. My transformation is complete. I glower at the mirror, the Gwyllion part of me evident again.

Exiting my room, I don't bother to hide my misery. But no one seems to notice, let alone care.

The usually peaceful palace is bustling with servants rushing past me, preparing for the day's events. Evading wings and the items they carry, I find solace in a quiet alcove with windows that stretch from floor to ceiling, letting in cascading beams of light.

There, I find Vale gathered with Aeron, Hickory, and Alys as they stare out over the city. I haven't spoken to any of them except Vale since my incident with Alys. I've spent most of my time studying alone in my room while trying to avoid more awkward encounters.

Though I sense their eyes on me, I keep my focus on the window, where we survey the city and the hordes of faeries that fill the usually clear streets. All the different clans are arriving from the Vineway, pouring into the city in droves.

"Quite a sight, huh?" Aeron asks.

"It's a rare sight, for sure." I nod. Memories of the clans gathering at Gaius' funeral rush back as if it was yesterday and a lifetime ago all at the same time. I try to ignore the twinge in my heart. "I can't imagine this many non-Sylphs have ever been welcomed here."

"It's the first time in *decades*, actually." Vale avoids my gaze, but that doesn't stop her insatiable desire to correct my error. It's also meant to grab Aeron's attention away from me, no doubt. "It's only for today, so the rest of Faylan can view the trial. Mother says it's a sign of goodwill that will further promote peace and cooperation between the clans. The others have agreed to do the same for their trials, but I don't know that it's the best idea."

"Why's that?" Hickory squints his good eye at Vale. "Isn't that what this whole competition is supposed to be for? Finding peace?" His voice is laced with sarcasm.

Vale glares at him before returning to the window. "All I'm saying is that we've kept our clans separated and our borders guarded for so long. Letting everyone in all at once, it just makes me… nervous."

Everyone? My eyes dart through the crowd afresh, wondering if any of the pirates made it through. "So, they're just letting anyone in?"

"Don't be silly. There's still a screening process before entry. You're definitely the only *vagrant* permitted, that's for sure."

I smirk. "Good thing I had my own personal invitation then."

Vale looks at me, and for the first time, a hint of a smile appears. "Yeah, well, let's see if you last the day."

～

Flying into the outdoor stadium is a shock to the senses. Today, the Cognisium is packed to the brim as trumpets blare. The crowd's chattering turns to roaring cheers as my competitors and I descend into the deafening noise. Though nearly every seat is filled, the separation of clans is stark. Each clan keeps to their own section, maintaining a healthy distance from the others as they wave clan flags and display their wings proudly.

Still, the Sylphs were sure to select an arena that reminds us whose territory we're in. Sylph statues with large feathered wings loom from the five corners of the structure, peering at us with their stone-cold eyes.

Sweat beads on my forehead, but at least I can blame it on the midday sun beating down on us. Of course they chose a day without a cloud in the sky.

In the rafters, the clan lords and ladies gather in their own separate booth. It doesn't take me long to pick out my father with his large frame and sour expression. He hates being outside the safety of his mountains. And he's probably nervous I'm going to screw this up. Badly.

The crowd seems to agree. As we land, the audience grows quiet, all eyes on me. In any other situation, I would've welcomed the attention. Maybe given the crowd a wave and an obnoxious smile. But today, everyone in the stadium not only sees the elusive face of Captain Shade for the first time, but also the Gwyllion princess who abandoned her clan to become a vagrant.

I can't worry about that now. Striding forward, I focus all my attention on what lays ahead. As instructed, the five of us step onto our designated stone platforms. They are strangely long and narrow, running parallel to each other. The queen stands in front of us as a team of Sylphs haul over a bullhorn twice their size on squeaky wheels. The clans grow quiet as the queen approaches the mouth of the horn.

"Welcome to the first trial of the Ethodine," the queen announces, her voice filling the stadium. "Today marks the end of conflict and the beginning of peace as we take one step closer to crowning the next ruler of Faylan."

The ground shakes. Reflexively, I release my wings and hover above the shuddering platform. *What's happening?* I look at the others, but they just stare wide-eyed at the floor.

The ground around our individual platforms splits open, and walls of multi-colored glass rise from the ground. In seconds, each of us has four glass walls surrounding our platforms, closing us in. My heartbeat pulses in my throat.

But it's the sharp glass spikes covering the two far walls that catch my attention. As they reach maximum height, Sylph servants fly overhead, carrying thick glass sheets. They secure them to the top of each of our enclosures, sealing us in.

I inhale sharply. *Trapped again.*

The queen continues. "For our part, we Sylphs bring forth our Trial of Knowledge. In a moment, the walls of each champions' enclosure will begin closing in toward them as they are asked a series of questions. A wrong or delayed answer will cause the walls to pick up speed, while a correct answer will slow them down."

The Sylph guards wheel out an hourglass as tall as the queen.

"If a champion answers enough questions correctly before the timer is up, the floor beneath them will open and whisk them to safety. The order in which they finish will determine their ranking for this round."

Fresh sweat breaks out on my forehead. There's no mention of those that don't answer the satisfactory number of questions. A fact the crowd has also noticed.

Murmurs grow louder as the clan leaders stand up, shouting their outrage. My father even dares to take a step forward, as if ready to fly down to stop the whole thing. But Sylph guards swiftly block them in, reminding them whose territory they're in and whose game they're playing.

I fly toward the ceiling of my prison, banging my body and fists against the glass. If I only had my daggers, I could probably crack the structure, but the walls are too thick to break by myself.

I look at the others, my shock and fear reflected in their faces.

All but Vale, that is. The queen nods to her, and Vale rolls her shoulders, ready for the first question.

Slowly, the other heirs follow suit, their faces hardening, readying themselves for the trial they've unknowingly been preparing for their whole lives.

I force myself to keep it together, the tingling in my body reminds me that Vale's potion is still at work.

I'm going to be fine. I hope.

The queen lifts her hands. "Let the first trial begin!"

The hourglass is flipped, and the spiked walls begin closing in.

"First question," a voice echoes within my enclosure. I spin around to face my questioner, but no one's there. *What kind of magic is this?*

I don't have time to find out as the spikes inch closer.

"Moonrain glows with a unique element. It nourishes Faylan's grounds, sustaining the land and all its resources. What's the resource we'll run out of first, if the moonrain doesn't return?"

My heart races, but thankfully the potion humming through my system jolts my brain, pulling forth the information.

"Pixie dust!" I yell. I don't want there to be any reason the questioner doesn't hear my answer and speeds up the walls.

They slow, and I breathe in relief. But they're still coming, the sun glinting off their sharp spikes.

I turn to the hourglass. The sand is speeding its way down.

I have a long way to go, and not a lot of time to work with.

The voice moves on. "List five major uses of pixie dust and five major dangers."

My brain jolts again as the words come to me, slower this time. "Medicines... incantations, fuel, euphoria, and... floating!"

The spiked wall picks up speed with each moment I hesitate. I wipe sweat from my brow, racking my brain for the rest.

"Dangers come with overexposure or mixing certain herbs which can cause... susceptibility to sickness, depression, loss of memory, lunacy and... death."

The walls decelerate again.

I pant, glancing at the other competitors' boxes. I can't hear their questions, though their hurried mouths move to answer, and Alys' hands fly around in a series of signs.

Hickory and Vale's walls are moving even slower than mine, their natural knowledge even faster than my potion-enhanced brain. But Aeron and Alys are not as lucky; the spikes are closing in.

Finding myself hoping we all survive, I wrench my attention away from them as the questions seem to go on for eternity. Thankfully, most are either ones I already know or topics I studied while under the Notting Potion's influence.

"How many Sylphs have ruled since the Numa's banishment, including the three brothers who were married to Queen Gwendolyn?"

"Thirteen."

"Younglings reach mature faehood when their wings are fully developed. Which clan reaches this stage faster than others?"

"Gwyllions."

"Dryads are sometimes born with physical characteristics and advantages of animals because of their deep connection with them. What were the characteristics that Dryad ruler, Lady Bayu, was born with?"

"Yellow eyes and whiskers."

"Many think infant faeries were originally called *sprouts* because they sprout from their mothers. But what is the true origin of their name?"

"The first faeries are believed to have literally sprouted from the Sacred Vine."

Considering my terrible education, the potion's effects are nothing less than miraculous. But the questions keep coming. Maybe it's stress or fatigue, but the tingling through my body eases.

Suddenly, the whole section of Kobolds in the audience rises to their feet in applause.

I glance at Hickory's containment box. His spikes haven't moved far, and he's nowhere to be found, assuring me he hasn't been impaled but is safely below us. I sigh with relief.

Unsurprisingly, Vale has already escaped her box of terror as well, leaving me, Aeron, and Alys left in the race.

The next question comes. "How many faeries died in the first wave of the Knolls plague?"

I wait for my brain to jolt the answer. Nothing happens.

"A hundred?" I guess.

Wrong. The walls speed up.

I must not have studied that one, I try to reassure myself.

"Which herbs are mixed together to create the Dryad's most common healing balm?"

Nothing again. Absolutely nothing.

"Um… well…" It's no use. I have no idea. The tingling of the Notting potion is gone. "Next question!"

"Who was the first Kobold to experiment with pixie dust as a fuel source?"

Nothing.

"Nymph skin turns blue when wet. What are the main benefits of this?"

The spikes continue picking up speed. I can barely breathe as sweat coats my back. I look frantically at my father. The queen. Anyone.

Aeron and Alys' containment boxes are now empty too. They're safe.

I'm the only one left.

No one can help me now.

With the spikes only a few feet away, I fly to the ceiling once more and slam into the glass with the full force of my body. It doesn't budge.

My skin burns with panic. I desperately consider letting my fire loose on the glass to melt it. But the enclosure is only growing smaller. Even if I used my ability, I'd only incinerate myself. What else?

I dart to the floor, banging my fist against the metal door, begging those below to let me in.

No, no, no! Vale, if I get out of this, I'm going to kill you!

The questioner speaks again in his monotone, unsympathetic voice.

"The Mystic Gwyllions claimed to be descendants of dragons because of their wings and fire-wielding ability. Where did they claim their fire released from: their eyes, their mouths, or their hands?"

I look at my fists. Though the answer can save me, I hate that I don't need to read about this one in some book. Hoping this is the last question, I speak the truth I know all too well.

"Their hands."

The floor opens up, and I fall into darkness.

CHAPTER 21

S afely under the arena, I've finished in last place, but I'm still alive. That has to count for something.

Gwyllion servants rush to attend to me, but I push past them and fly through the doors, desperate for air. Flying up a stairway and into a hall, I find myself back in the palace. I dart toward my room.

"You didn't do half-bad in there, for a cheating pirate."

I look back. It's Moon Face. Just the faerie I did *not* want to see.

"If you're accusing me of something, sky-boy, you might as well say it." I continue on my way, barreling through the halls. Almost getting impaled on a wall of glass daggers is enough for one day, thank you.

"You think you can do anything you want, don't you?" His voice intensifies as he follows. "That you can just waltz in here and cheat your way to the crown?"

I spin on my heels. "Why don't you just say what's on your mind?"

He advances, pushing my shoulder. "Little birdie told me you stole some herbs that helped you retain all the information you just spouted in there."

So, he's not as stupid as he looks. Still, he dared to shove me.

I reach for a weapon at my side, but of course, they're still in the queen's armory, thanks to the idiot in front of me. "If you value that hand, you will not touch me again."

My comment only encourages him. "You mean like this?" He

pushes me harder this time, cornering me against a wall. "I warned you to watch your back."

"Maybe you should watch your front." I move to knee him. He shifts just enough that I make contact with his gut instead.

Blast. I was aiming somewhere else.

He hisses with pain, but the impact isn't enough. With one quick motion, his hand wraps around my hair and pulls my head backward into the stone.

I stifle a cry. I'm about to go for his eyes next when I hear a blade released from its sheath.

Aeron is behind Moon Face, pointing a sword right at his head.

Moon Face moves for his own sword at his belt, but it isn't there. Aeron took it right out from under his nose.

"Unless you'd like me to dull the point of your ear, sir—" Aeron warns "—I would step away from the lady."

Moon Face releases my hair and backs away, but his stupid smirk remains. "Just fooling around. No harm done."

"You better be glad about that."

Aeron doesn't lower the blade until Moon Face walks around the corner and out of sight. Sliding the sword into his own belt, Aeron looks pretty pleased with himself, but I brush past him.

"Where are you going now?" he calls after me.

"Far away from *here*," I call back, heat in my face, not slowing down. For Faylan's sake, I must have looked like such an idiot.

"You've got to be kidding." Aeron follows close behind. "I just saved your life. Again!"

I shake my head. He still doesn't get it. A Gwyllion who needs saving is weak and inferior, indebted to their savior. It's the greatest shame, and there's no way I'm going to feel indebted to him. Besides, he might've fended off Moon Face for now, but Aeron showing my inability to defend myself puts an even bigger target on my back.

"I don't need you saving me at every turn. Gwyllions don't need help. I had everything under control."

"Are you serious?" His own frustration grows. "You didn't even have a weapon to defend yourself."

Reaching the door to my room, I spin around so fast, Aeron nearly crashes into me.

"And whose fault is that?" I bark. I don't know whether I'm more embarrassed or angry at my failure to protect myself. I curse. If only Aeron had gotten my weapons back when he had the chance in Dunestone Harbor, perhaps I could've snuck them into Eldore with me.

"Well, if you weren't in such a hurry to run away from me, you would've noticed I brought you something." Aeron huffs, reaching under his cloak to reveal not one, but both my daggers.

"Where did you...?" I gape. They were missing from the armory the other night, but here they are right in front of me. He must have stolen them from the armory even before I tried to retrieve them. "How long have you had them?"

"Does it matter?" He lifts a brow, allowing his smile to return.

Unclenching my fists, I go to accept them, but stop. "What's the catch? I mean, thank you, but..." I'm taken aback, happy to see my daggers, and yet so confused. What's his angle? He has to have one. Everyone does. "Why do you keep helping me? I'm your competition, remember?"

"No catch." He sighs, pushing the daggers into my hands. "By all accounts, I shouldn't even give you one of these. But when you told me how important they are to you..." He grows quiet as I remember our chat in the royal library. "And seeing how you handled yourself in the competition today, well, maybe I've judged you too quickly. I thought you deserved to have them back."

Aeron's eyes focus on me, soft with sincerity. It's as if I'm seeing them for the first time, noticing how blue and clear they are, like the ocean. Perhaps if I lean in a bit closer, I can dive right into their cool waters. He might be a privileged Nymph prince, but he keeps surprising me. Much like being at sea, my feet are steady and firm one moment, and then a surprising wave hits, threatening to whisk me off my feet.

I've been staring too long. Aeron speaks up with a slight chuckle in his voice. "Plus, you're right, I can't keep saving you. It's bad for my image. Might make other fae suspicious that something else is going on..." He winks playfully, but his smile is genuine, his stare not straying from my face.

Warmth builds inside me again, the same kind I felt on his ship. It starts deep in my gut and rushes upward as if I'm going to throw up right then and there.

Heat. The warmth changes to panic. I clutch the daggers.

"Thanks." I dart into my room, leaving him in the hallway.

I lean back hard against the door, sliding to the ground.

What's wrong with me? And why did Aeron go through the trouble of returning my daggers? If he thinks using kindness will give him an advantage over me, he's sadly mistaken. I'm not going to let him, or anyone else, find any weak spots to exploit.

I swallow hard. The metal of the daggers' handles glows red from the heat in my hands. I drop them to the floor and curse as the red handprints fade. But it isn't just my hands that are hot.

Slowly, I bring the back of my hand to my face, finding my cheeks are also warm to the touch.

CHAPTER 22

The next morning, it isn't a nightmare or Gwyllion servants that wake me, but a racket outside my room.

I roll out from under the warm covers and stagger to the door to find the palace bustling yet again. Fae servants from every clan fly back and forth, carrying an assortment of garment cases and baskets of food. One Sylph nearly hits me over the head as he whizzes through the air with a large trunk.

Ducking just in time, I snag the nearest servant I can find. "What in the blazes is going on? Can't a pixie get her beauty sleep?"

"Sorry, M-Miss," stammers the Kobold, nearly dropping the stack of books she's carrying. "It's a traveling day." She stares up at me, recognition and panic igniting in her eyes. With my angry face and mane of messy curls, I must be quite the sight.

Reluctantly, I soften my tone. "Traveling day?"

"Y-yes, Miss," she answers, still wide-eyed. "You and the others set off to Isinglass for the next stage of the Ethodine today."

The horrific details of the trial return in a blur. Trapped in the quickly enclosing box. Glistening glass spikes reaching out to impale me. I shudder.

They don't waste any time. Don't we deserve a break?

As I rub the memory and sleep from my eyes, an old, dusty book sitting on top of the stack in her arms catches my eye.

It's the tome with the strange symbol. The one that glowed at my touch.

I step backward. "Is Hickory returning these books to the princess?"

"Actually—" she says, more confused than scared this time "—Sir Hickory has asked that these be stored with his belongings for the trip ahead."

I smirk. Hickory is slyer than I thought. He doesn't intend to return the book to Vale after all. What could be in that old text that's so fascinating? I'm about to ask the servant another question when a familiar laugh echoes down the hall.

Amid the bustle, there's Aeron. My stomach flips. Thankfully he's distracted by his conversation with a Nymph maid, but they're headed toward my end of the hallway.

Without another word, I scurry inside my room, slamming the door shut.

I shake my head. What's happening to me? Even without using his silver tongue, he keeps messing with my head. Whatever Aeron's effect is on me, I need to keep myself in check and stay focused on my mission. But it'll be a lot harder to do so, knowing where we're headed next.

Isinglass, the province of the Nymphs. Though I'm not looking forward to being in Aeron's domain, going there does mean we'll return to the sea.

That thought spurs me to start packing right away.

Pulling out my trunk, I know the first thing I'll put inside. *My daggers.* I stashed the blades between the mattress and box spring last night.

I move to hide them in the trunk before anyone can come knocking, but I pause, my fingers lingering over the weapons.

My old friends. It's been so long since I used them for their intended purposes. I slice them through the air, an extension of my body once again. I fit them together into the single blade they were initially made to be, and a sense of wholeness rushes over me. The connection to my skill, my twin, and even our mother, returns.

Aeron did this for you.

The thought comes before I can swat it away. I sigh. Just for a moment, I allow myself to recall Aeron's soft ocean eyes. His fingers briefly grazing mine as he gave back my daggers.

Then, without warning, the scene in my mind violently shifts.

Aeron's gentle eyes morph into Gaius' terrified gaze from my nightmares.

Instead of Aeron, Gaius hands me the daggers in the chaos, screaming my name. My stomach swarms with confusion and terror.

Trying to soothe myself, I run my thumb over the dagger's handle. My finger traces the pattern of engraved icons and swirls, one after the other—until one of the symbols catches my eye. My racing heart halts as the tome from Vale's library snaps into my memory.

It can't be.

The once-strange symbol that was on the book doesn't seem so foreign anymore. There, embedded in the dagger's intricate designs, is a circle, within a circle, within a circle, and the unique flower with ten petals. The same symbol that decorates the tome's cover. They're identical.

What connection could my mother's daggers have with some ancient book collecting dust in the Sylph princess' library?

Gaius' face from the nightmare flashes across my vision again. The sound of him calling my name rings in my head.

"Quinn!"

A knock sounds. I shove the daggers behind my back just as a tall Gwyllion servant bursts through the door.

"Good, you're up," he says gruffly, the words ruffling his overgrown beard. "You'd best get dressed and finish packing, Lady Quinntessa. You don't have much time."

He shuts the door and I don't waste another second, burying my daggers under a mound of clothes. I just got my weapons back—I'm not going to let them get taken away again.

After closing the case hard and locking it for good measure, I sit on top of it and sigh. I should be thinking about the upcoming trial, worrying about whatever madness the Nymphs are going to throw at us. Thanks to my agreement with the queen to help Vale secure the crown, surviving the remaining trials is my only path to freedom. But that freedom is still weeks away.

Right now, my thoughts are focused on the symbol, the tome, and the daggers. There's got to be a connection. I think back to my nightmares. Has my subconscious been using Gaius to tell me something all along?

I curse. I was too quick to let Hickory take the book before. And it was nearly in my grasp just a few minutes ago in the hallway. No matter how eerie it is, it's my only clue to these horrifying visions.

I need to know what's in it. I need to figure out the connection. If I do, maybe the nightmares will finally stop. I might even find out more about my mother.

If I don't, I have a feeling I'll never be free of Gaius' ghost.

Whether Hickory will be willing to share the book with me or I have to find another way to get my hands on it, I'm not sure. But I am resolved. Throwing the last of my few possessions into the trunk, one thought repeats through my mind.

I must have that book.

SEA OF SECRETS

THE NYMPH CHALLENGE

CHAPTER 23

This is not how I pictured returning to the sea.

On one hand, I can't help but smile as I approach a ship whose flapping sails are pulled taut to catch the wind, prepared and ready for adventure. The comforting calls of gulls pass over the dock, and I breathe in deeply. A breeze blows through my hair and the smell of sea salt in my nose intoxicates me, reviving my bones. It's as if I've been holding my breath the entire time I've been away.

On the other hand, this is not the Minnow or my crew. This vessel is crawling with Nymphs, bound for Isinglass. And after a full morning of travel from Eldore—riding back down the Vineway, pushing through the streets of Shree, and taking one more terrifying ride on the Kobie Express —the jangle of chains around my wrists reminds me how *not* free I am.

"It's only a precaution," the queen assured me before we left the sky city, as her guards clapped metal bracelets on my wrists. The queen is no fool. Me being an outlaw provides the perfect excuse for her to protect her investment. Though I've made no effort to hide my great displeasure, I don't blame her. Our verbal deal doesn't guarantee that I won't try to escape.

At least it's not a Wing Restraint, I try to comfort myself.

Crowds around the harbor gather as we board the ship. The queen steps on first with her attendants. They carry heavy trunks and bird cages with her precious feathered pets squawking inside.

Following her, we proceed up a plank in the order of our rank from the Trial of Knowledge. Vale walks on first, flicking a long red braid over her shoulder, with Hickory close behind, his nose already in his sketchbook. Alys pulls at her gloves as she strides on next, eyeing the crowd warily. Aeron waves to them warmly, even though he trails behind in fourth, flexing his fin-like wings with unhindered anticipation.

And finally, in last place, is me.

The memory of being rejected from the Gwyllion Guard stings like a reopened wound as I follow them. At least my father left Eldore before the ranking ceremony took place, so I didn't have to face his disappointed scowl. Not that I've had a hard time imagining it all on my own.

I shake my head. Vale is still on track to win the crown, and as far as the deal for my freedom with the queen is concerned, that should be all that matters.

As we pass, some fae wave and cheer on their representative, but many stare at us as if we're lambs sent to slaughter. News has spread fast about how dangerous the Ethodine's first trial was. If anyone envied us before, none of them do now.

I step onto the deck's creaking floorboards, working to keep my posture poised, strong, and indifferent. But once aboard, my body grows tense, exhaustion creeping in. How I wish for a mask or a hat to disappear behind.

I'm not the only one under close surveillance. Up until now, we've all been constantly surrounded by our respective clan entourages, which has made plotting a way to get the mysterious tome back from Hickory particularly difficult.

The book that is somehow connected to my daggers. My nightmares. My brother.

Hickory is perched on a barrel, scribbling in his sketchbook at the other end of the deck. As I watch him, the possibility that he'd be willing to simply give me the book or even share it with me, nudges itself into my mind. But asking only creates the equal opportunity for him to say no. Or worse, he might ask *why* I want it. Then if I stole it, he'd know it was me who took it for sure. No, my chances are better if I just keep quiet and wait for the right time to nab it. The only problem is, his things are already packed away and heavily guarded in the belly of the ship.

I sigh. As with everything I want lately, I'll have to be patient.

Though that's very unlikely.

I try to distract myself. I walk the deck, finding my sea legs again as I take in the wide open stretch of ocean, keeping watch for any other ships on the horizon. Maybe a pirate ship.

If we were on the Minnow, my crew would be singing songs as they swabbed the deck, calling out bets on card games. But out here, the ocean is void of any other vessels and, except for the creak of boards underfoot, this ship is quiet.

Suddenly, I feel very alone.

It's better to be alone, I tell myself. *Then no one can betray you. No one can let you down.*

I lift my chin toward the sea. I don't need them or anyone else. In just a few short weeks, I'll take all of Faylan by storm with my new flying ship and crew. I'll be so unstoppable, Maverick will be begging me to come back.

Picturing the Pirate Lord pleading before me tides me over for a while, but as the boring trip drags on, even visions of grandeur can't stop me from complaining.

"I don't see why I'm still locked up." I hold out my chains to a passing guard. "It's not like I'm going to jump overboard."

"I wouldn't put it past her," Aeron speaks up from a few feet away. He leans over the side of the ship, his fin-like wings fluttering as if he himself will jump any second. "She is a pirate, after all."

The guard snorts and continues on.

"I know I told you to stop helping me, but you don't have to do the opposite either," I say glumly as I join him at the railing.

Aeron's dimple appears. "I'm sure the queen will free you once we arrive."

As I gaze out over the open ocean, I wonder if I'll ever be truly free again.

"Where exactly is this grand land of the Nymphs, anyway?" I ask, trying to think of something else. We've been on the sea for hours, and the horizon is still void of any structures.

"You Gwyllions have your weapons to protect Greymerrow," Aeron starts to explain. "Kobolds live safely underground. The Sylphs have a giant vine between them and the rest of the world. When threats of clan war escalated, the Dryads obviously used some kind of magic to hide their central city. Perhaps we chose to do the same."

"It must be some serious magic," I say.

After Isinglass disappeared, Pirate Lord Maverick always had us searching for it, but to no avail. Next to his constant obsession with pixie dust, the priceless treasures the Nymphs collect from the depths of the ocean were always next on his list.

"You'll see soon enough. Look there!" Aeron shouts, like a little sprite whose wings have finally grown strong enough for flight.

I peer over the rail. A series of fish tails kick up along the side of the ship, more appearing every second.

"That's a rather large school of dolphins." A blur of red appears at my side. Vale pushes loose strands of hair out of her face to get a better view.

Hickory and Alys join us on her other side and peer down as well.

"Those are not just dolphins," I laugh. Beside the dolphins, Nymphs in their fish-tail form jump out of the water, some of them spinning in midair.

Vale waves to a particularly attractive Nymph with luminous green hair who's showing off for her.

I yank her hand down. "Don't encourage them," I whisper sharply, making sure Aeron can't hear. "Most Nymphs are like spurious roots: beautiful to look at, but should never be trusted."

Vale turns away from me like a pouting sprite. She might be book smart, but her real life experience obviously doesn't extend far beyond Eldore and her academic studies. In fact, I wonder if she's ever been this far outside of Eldore before.

Ahead, the sound of rushing water breaks beyond the bow of the ship. A bubbling geyser is spouting up from the middle of the ocean, growing larger every second.

"Come on, you're not going to want to miss this!" Aeron calls over his shoulder as he rushes toward the front of the ship.

Little by little, towers made of coral emerge, growing into a single structure four times as tall as our ship. Fountains of water pour off its glistening surface.

The palace of Isinglass in all its glory.

Has it been hidden at the bottom of the sea all this time? The grand towers of coral loom over us while its large, colorfully tinted windows gleam in the sunlight.

Hickory quickly ties his white hair into a low ponytail and yanks his sketchbook out from his satchel. He must want to capture its majestic form before we get too close.

"Now that's what I call a masterpiece, wouldn't you say, Kobie?" Aeron elbows Hickory.

Hickory's quill shifts out of place, earning Aeron a piercing glare.

Though I agree that it's breathtaking, I shake my head. "There's no way in Faylan you're getting me in there."

"Why's that?" Hickory asks, still scribbling.

"That's why." I point below us.

At first glance, the Nymph palace appears to be floating on top of the ocean surface, but its lower levels are still submerged underwater. Though I'm grateful to be back at sea, I have no intention of physically reentering its waters anytime soon. Flashes of nearly drowning at the hands of Moon Face and his rabble twist my insides. I hate how he's tainted my connection with my beloved sea.

I scowl. "Once we're in there, what keeps the castle from sinking back down and drowning us all inside? The Nymphs may be able to breathe underwater, but we can't."

"The palace doesn't take in water," Aeron assures us. "We have magical barriers that take care of that. Besides, if we wanted to kill you, we'd have much more imaginative ways of doing so." He pauses for effect, but then gives me a wink.

I roll my eyes, though a lump forms in my throat. Aeron might be joking around, but as I peer down into the depths, I know I can't yet speak for his clan.

CHAPTER 24

I'm still hesitant as I step off the ship onto the Nymph palace's surrounding platform. Unlike the gentle rocking of a floating vessel, I'm surprised by how solid the ground feels.

A troop of Nymph guards in ice-blue uniforms open the seaweed-covered doors. With harpoons in hand, they stand at attention, waiting for us to enter. Nodding to the guards, Aeron takes the lead.

As we approach the threshold, I notice a glossy, transparent sheen that stretches across the doorway. I hesitate, and so do the others, but Aeron walks on. The sheen bends like a liquid and fluctuates around his body, elastically bouncing back to its original shape once he's through. Like an unbreakable bubble.

Noticing he's alone, Aeron turns and waves us on.

Alys is the first of us to stride forward. She puts out a gloved hand to the sheen's surface, presses on it slightly, and then steps through just as Aeron did. She turns to us and nods. She seems fine.

If Alys can do it, so can I. I take a deep breath and follow. A cool, tingling sensation washes over me as I pass through. I shiver, but at least it's dry on the other side.

Aeron meets me with a smile. "I told you. Magical barrier. Or as we call them, *aquagates*."

Though the entrance hall is thankfully void of water, it's completely submerged in song. Melodious laughter and the most beautiful music I've ever heard fills the air, lifting my spirits. A symphony rings out from an orchestra that lines either side of the hall, comprised of every instrument from lyres and harps to fiddles and flutes.

As we cross the pale pink and orange floor made of polished coral, crowds of Nymphs in elegant chiton tunics turn from their conversations with intrigued smiles.

"Well, well. Look who decided to finally grace us with his presence again," a tall puck calls from ahead of us. I can't tell if his seaweed-colored hair is slicked back with water or grease, but it seems to glow brighter at the sight of us. I realize he's the same Nymph who waved to Vale on the way here.

The group he's with turns, and a gaggle of three pixies practically shriek with delight.

"Aeron!" one shiny-haired blonde squeals. She rushes toward him and wraps her webbed fingers around his arm, completely ignoring the rest of us.

I give the next pixie a wide berth as she latches herself to his other side. "We're so glad you're back," she coos, batting her unnaturally long lashes at him.

"Have you seen Arista yet? She's going to die when she sees you," says the third.

The other two deflate at the name. Maybe she's talking about his betrothed? I purse my lips, wondering how beautiful this Arista must be if these pixies were overlooked as Aeron's potential mate.

Aeron sucks in a breath and produces a strained smile as the green-haired puck and two of his friends approach.

"Don't be rude, Aeron. Why don't you introduce us?" says the green-haired Nymph, intrigue sparkling in his matching emerald eyes. I can already tell I don't like him one bit.

"Everyone—" Aeron says, looking back at us "—this is some of the lot I grew up with. These lovely pixies are the Callan sisters. And these two pucks are Tal and Wayde, who've faithfully followed Nile everywhere since we were sprites." He motions to the pucks flanking the one called Nile, who runs a hand through his slimy green hair with pride.

"Hey!" Wayde gives Aeron's shoulder a good-humored push.

"Harsh, but not untrue." Nile smirks, then turns to Vale. "You must be the lovely Sylph Princess I've heard so much about." Nile steals a glance at Aeron as he takes Vale's hand.

Aeron narrows his eyes, but Nile brushes his lips against Vale's knuckles. Her freckled cheeks blush a pale red and, noticing Aeron's expression, she seems to revel in the attention all the more.

"I'm Nile, son of Duke Seaton of the royal Nymph court." His voice is smoother than honey but slyer than a sea serpent. He nods behind us.

I turn to see an older Nymph with matching green hair and billowing robes. Nile's father is speaking with the queen, along with a few others who must be a part of the Nymph court. I wonder what the queen would think if she saw Nile kissing Vale's hand. I turn to remind Vale of what I cautioned her about on the ship, but I find Nile eyeing me next. I step backward.

"And this must be—"

"This is Lady Quinntessa of Greymerrow," Aeron says formally. I'm surprised that his comment isn't matched with a pirate joke, but a warning tone instead.

"Ah yes, the long-lost Gwyllion princess." Nile goes to take my hand next, but stops at the sight of my metal cuffs. He coughs out a laugh, lifting the chain between my irons with a finger. "Quite the fashion statement you're sporting. Must be all the rage where you come from."

The Callan sisters giggle and I pull my hands back, balling them into fists.

"Touch me again and you'll be *sporting* a black eye." I dare him with narrowed eyes.

Aeron stifles a chuckle, and Tal elbows Wayde. "She's got you there, Nile."

"Feisty one, isn't she?" Wayde adds.

"Ugh, a pirate through and through, indeed," Nile sneers, sticking his nose in the air. "Just as I expected, not a lady at all. Right, Aeron?"

Aeron's dimple disappears as he looks from Nile to me, seemingly at a loss for words.

"Right?" Nile steps closer to him with a provoking tone.

"Aeron, all your things have been brought to your room." A short Nymph with familiar golden curls bounds up next to him.

"Thanks, Fynn." Aeron nods, looking grateful for the interruption.

Ah yes, Fynn. He was part of Aeron's crew that I'd met after Aeron rescued me from drowning. If I remember right, he's the naive map reader who suggested we travel straight through the Woodlands during our travels to Eldore.

"Hey, guppy." Nile puts a heavy hand on Fynn's shoulder, making him slouch shorter than he already is.

Wayde and Tal chuckle.

"You know, I was hurt when I wasn't invited to your runaway party boat," Nile says to Aeron. "But if you brought this guy along, it couldn't have been that much fun."

"Cut it out, Nile," Aeron warns protectively, but stands idly by as Nile ruffles Fynn's hair.

"What?" Nile laughs. "I'm only having a bit of fun. Right, guppy?"

"Sure." Fynn doesn't look pleased, but he takes it. He bows to Aeron and then leaves.

I narrow my eyes at Aeron. What's up with him? Fynn is supposed to be his friend. He could have done more. What in Faylan does Nile have on him?

But there's no time to find out as the orchestra's melody changes to a more triumphant blast.

On the grand staircase ahead of us descends the Lord and Lady of the Nymphs. I remember seeing them at the first trial, though they looked far too young to be Aeron's parents. I guess that's to be expected. Obsessed with appearances, the Nymphs are known for making use of every material and charm imaginable to keep up their youthful complexions.

"Welcome, all of you, to Isinglass!" Lord Kaito calls out. His voice is just as jubilant and melodic as the music that fills the room. His wife, Lady Delphine, follows close behind as Kaito stretches his arms wide like a performing ringmaster, motioning to the beauty around him with his jeweled trident.

As he makes his way down the stairs, his fin-like wings fan out behind him, and he points the trident toward the fountains on either side of the staircase. The cascading water spurts upward at the trident's movement, shooting ten times higher and circling in the air, taking on a variety of shapes.

A few of the lavishly dressed Nymphs at either side of the stairway follow his lead, adding to his water display with the movement of their hands. *Water Manipulators.*

The Nymphs around us cheer and applaud as I marvel at the use of such magical abilities being displayed so openly. At the way it's admired and encouraged rather than hated. I rub my own hands together as I watch, wondering what it must be like not to fear your own magic.

As the Nymph Lord draws closer, he smiles broadly, reveling in the attention. Aeron clearly gets his sea-colored eyes from his father. They also share the same midnight-blue hair, but I can only tell that from Kaito's shortly-trimmed blue beard. It's etched with the same swirling Nymph symbols that adorn the sides of Aeron's hair. The rest of Kaito's head is waxed clean, highlighted by a small golden hoop hanging from one ear and a line of sea diamonds climbing up the lobe of the other.

Reaching the bottom of the stairs, Kaito's eyes focus hard on Aeron. "My son," Lord Kaito says, his tone low. He wraps his long fingers around Aeron's shoulders, clasping tightly. Too tightly. "I'm so glad you're home." Kaito smiles broadly, but the gills on his neck pulse. His eyes narrow as if to say, *I'll deal with you later.*

Aeron swallows hard, but he forces a smile as well. I wonder if this is their first encounter since he left home. Or rather, *ran away.* Bristling at the thought of my own father's punishments, I wonder what Aeron's will be for ditching his own wedding.

"We will have time to visit with Aeron later, my love," Lady Delphine cautions softly, her voice ringing like bells. She lays a gentle hand on Kaito's shoulder.

Unlike Aeron or her husband, she's more slender in frame and smaller in stature, jet-black hair cascading down her back. But as she tucks delicate strands behind her fin-shaped ears, I can see Aeron's thin, oval eyes and gentleness in her gaze. Her beauty and grace are unmatched by anyone else in the room.

She gives the rest of us a surprisingly warm smile, her eyes sparkling as brightly as the shimmering blue gown that clings to her body. "You all must be tired from your journey," she says. "Please, follow us and we'll show you where you'll be staying."

Releasing his grip on Aeron, Lord Kaito ushers us forward, past the orchestra, toward the stairs that lead below. As we descend, the view out the colorfully tinted windows progressively changes from the gleaming sun over the mountains to the expanse of the underwater world.

Instinctively, I suck in a breath.

Below sea level, the city of coral structures appears, lit up by jellyfish lanterns and other glowing sea creatures. A group of Nymphs swim by on the backs of their sea stags, curiously eyeing us.

But I'm more focused on the glass in the window itself. More importantly, what would happen if it were to break. I lightly tap on its surface, bracing myself.

"No need to fear," comes the Nymph Lord's silky voice as he joins me by the window. As he surveys his realm, I try to ignore the hairs standing up on the back of my neck. I might've been the queen of the sea on the Minnow, but down here, I'm in his territory with no crew and nowhere to hide.

I expect him to glare down at me for my many sins against his clan over the years, but instead, he addresses the group. "These windows are made of sea glass, thicker and stronger than even most Gwyllion metals. In fact, it looked like the enclosures you were all in during the first trial were made of the same glass."

His eyes focus hard on the queen, but she stares straight back at him, as if daring him to challenge her further. Though sea glass is a common Nymph trading commodity, Kaito obviously doesn't approve of the Sylphs using their prized material to nearly kill his only son and heir.

"Still, the show must go on!" His practiced smile returns. "We Nymphs have our own test we've prepared; one where you will have to use your beauty in more imaginative ways than ever before. I'm sure it will prove to be even more *entertaining* than the Sylph trial. At least for us." The Nymph Lord's wild eyes narrow in on me with a strange smile. "And for the viciously unforgiving judge you'll face."

CHAPTER 25

V*icious judge?*

What could he mean by that? As I mull over Lord Kaito's words, wondering who this mysterious judge could be, Lady Delphine and a handful of Nymph guards lead us the rest of the way to our rooms.

"Right this way." Aeron's mother ushers us into a hall with a line of giant white orbs, so polished they look like pearls. Each has sea glass windows and an aquagate on one side. "We will take one of our transports to travel to the guest pods."

What? The blood drains from my face at the thought of being stuck in some kind of underwater bunker.

Lady Delphine must notice, because she adds, "Don't worry. You can return to the palace at any time using our tube bridges." She points to a system of transparent glass tubes that span from the palace to other structures beyond. "But I thought you might want to get a closer look at the city on the way."

Two by two, we're led into the transports with a water manipulator to guide us. Aeron follows me into mine, and I suck in a breath at the tight fit. Our shoulders brush against each other, which doesn't help my quickening pulse.

Suddenly, the orbs lurch forward, exiting through an aquagate in the wall one by one, the ocean pressing in all around us as our guides steer us toward the Nymph city below.

Among normal citizens, the city is alive with performing fish trainers, musical entertainers, and water manipulators on every corner. While some of them keep their distance from us, swimming out of the way with looks of suspicion, others get way too close.

A few Nymph beauticians swim around our transport, fighting for my attention, pressing their beauty charms and colorful garments decorated with rare sea gems against my window. Another waves for us to enter her shop, which appears to be enclosed with aquagates as well. She offers me lower and lower prices as we pass.

"Don't mind them," Aeron says. "The shopkeepers have gotten even more pushy since clan tensions increased. Few of them feel safe enough to sell on the surface. You're probably the newest clientele they've had in a while. Fresh meat for hungry sharks."

"Great," I say sarcastically, though I tuck the information away. Might be useful later.

As we continue, I try to picture Mira and Zale swimming through these streets together before becoming pirates. I wonder if they ever miss it. Before I can stop myself, I'm picturing them on the Minnow, too busy with whatever mission they're on now to think about the home they left behind. Could they be missing me at all?

Once we reach the other end of the city, we approach what appears to be a giant glass dome.

Passing through one of its aquagates, our transports enter the dome and land on a wooden dock attached to a small island. Thankfully, water doesn't fill the dome completely. Instead, it only fills the lower half with the island floating on top.

I don't wait to be told to exit the transport, sucking in a deep breath in the open space as I step out onto the dock. Water flows *below* my feet again—right where it belongs.

This is far from the underwater bunker I feared. I turn in a circle, marveling at everything around us: our view of the palace, the city, and streams of colorful fish, whales, and other creatures swimming around the dome's perimeter.

Even more awaits us on the island. With the others, I follow the dock that surrounds the land as we pass clusters of palm trees, cascading fountains and bubbling hot springs. Finally, the dock leads to our accommodations: a series of rounded pod-huts made of coral that arc in a horseshoe shape around the edge of a small bay.

"How lavish," Hickory speaks my thoughts out loud, his good eye bouncing around to all the sights. I can tell that sketchbook of his won't be empty for very long.

"We aim to impress," says Lady Delphine. "Please, make use of any of the amenities on the grounds during your stay."

Drawing nearer to the pods, we pass a few Nymphs repairing one of the many fountains. Though I still don't love the thought of the dome being underwater, the gentle sound of rushing water soothes my anxious fears.

One by one, we drop off the queen and then each heir to their pods. At the end, only Aeron and I remain, as my pod is last. Lady Delphine unlocks my door, and I go to reach for the handle, but the clink of my chains stops me.

Blasted things. How long am I meant to stay like this?

"Oh, I nearly forgot." Aeron's mother pulls a key from her pocket. "I believe this is for you." I'm still surprised by the warmth in her voice, and the gentleness of her fingers as she unlocks my cuffs. "Now, that's much better, isn't it?"

"Yes, thank you." I rub my wrists gratefully.

"The queen handed me the key for you earlier, but I nearly left with it. I'm getting so forgetful in my old age."

I hold back a laugh. With not a wrinkle to spare, she looks more like she could be Aeron's older sister rather than his mother.

Lady Delphine clasps her hands together, but then looks curiously at Aeron. "Speaking of, your father mentioned I should meet him somewhere, but now I cannot for the life of me remember where."

"I believe it was the throne room. He's summoned me there as well." Aeron gently touches her shoulder. "Are you sure you're all right, Mother? Maybe you should go lie down."

She pats his hand. "You've been home less than an hour and look at you, already fussing over me." She turns back to me. "I'll leave you to your room now. I'm sure you'll want to rest and refresh yourself before our party tomorrow."

"Party?" I perk up.

"Oh, yes." Her eyes brighten. "We've planned a splendid celebration to properly welcome you all to our province."

"Mother throws the best parties in all of Isinglass," Aeron says to me.

Delphine's smile widens at the compliment. "Oh, how I've missed you, my son." She gives Aeron's hand a squeeze. "Now, don't be long. You know how much your father doesn't like you *skipping out* on things." She says it lightly, but I can hear a hint of seriousness too, probably referencing the wedding again. Without another word, she turns to leave the way we came.

"Your mother seems nice," I say, though I get the sense there's something off about her.

"She is." Aeron smiles, but then it fades. "My father, not so much."

"Can't argue with you there."

"Hey, look at us actually agreeing on something." He grins. "Here, let me get you settled in." He reaches for my door and opens it for me.

I hesitate. "Aren't you supposed to meet your father?"

"He can wait a few minutes. Come on. I think you got the pod with the best view." He's already inside, walking straight toward the curtains. I enter, but tentatively, making sure to leave the door open behind me. I don't want him, or anyone else who might see us, to get the wrong idea.

As he pulls at the drapes, light filters through the floor-to-ceiling sea glass window, brightening up the room. My trunks from Eldore have already been brought in, some of them sitting beside a luxurious circular canopy bed adorned with sheer drapes and a seashell headboard. The pile of plush pillows are already calling my name, but I scan the room for the case that I know holds my daggers. Thankfully, I spot it sitting atop a vanity decorated entirely with shells and starfish.

As I turn back to the window, the view nearly steals my breath away. It might not be the wide-open ocean view I'm used to, but it's the next best thing. The sparkling saltwater that surrounds the island spreads out before me, small currents rippling up toward my window. Since my pod is at the end of the arched arrangement, the other pods can't obstruct my perfect view. I'll take it.

"I told you, you have the best view," Aeron says proudly, as if he had something to do with it. The glint in his eye tells me maybe he did.

I try not to dwell on the possibility too long, glancing around the perimeter of the window until I find a latch to the right. I pull at it, and the window slides open like a door. I breathe in the salty air with a sigh.

"Sorry about earlier, by the way," Aeron says softly. "With Nile, I mean."

I turn to him, brows raised. "You don't owe me anything." I shrug, though I find I don't mind the apology. "What's with that puck anyway? And why in Faylan do you, prince of the Nymphs, tolerate the likes of *him*?

Aeron shakes his head. "If I don't, he'll report me to my father, and I already have him mad enough at me about the wedding."

"What would he tell your father, exactly? That you weren't bowing down to some jerk?"

"Oh, Nile would spin some story to get me in trouble, I'm sure."

Interesting. "I thought you were supposed to be pals," I say.

"I thought we were, at one time. When we were growing up, he used to seek my favor endlessly, reserving his venom for others like Fynn. I think he's always been a bit jealous of me, perhaps hoping that being close to me and my family would gain him power someday. But ever since the Ethodine's dangerous nature was made known, he's gotten bolder, turning his venom on me as well. I guess he doesn't have much confidence that I'll survive. Now it seems Vale's favor is what he seeks."

I crinkle my nose, remembering Nile's lips on Vale's hand. "It did seem that way. What do you think he wants with her?"

Aeron shrugs. "She's in the lead for the crown after placing first in the Sylph trial. If she wins, perhaps he figures she'll hold the power to dethrone me and choose another to rule the Nymphs. If he gets in her good graces, why not him?"

"Well, if it's possible, I like him even less now." I cross my arms. I'm going to have to keep my eye on that one.

"I don't blame you." Aeron sighs. "But while I'm here, until I secure my place as Nymph Lord, I must do what I can to make allies instead of enemies."

"Not like my opinion matters, but I don't think you should have to change who you are for anyone. Especially for someone like Nile. You should stand up for what you believe in. Be yourself."

"Easy for you to say. You don't care what anybody thinks of you." At first his words sound like a jab, but when he turns to me, his eyes are soft. "I kind of admire that."

Heat rises in my face, but I force it down.

Aeron looks as if he wants to say more, but must think better of it. "Anyway, I shouldn't keep my father waiting."

As I follow him out, I spot Hickory exiting the next pod over. He's got his dust pipe in his mouth and his satchel of art supplies slung over his shoulder. Probably off to paint everything in sight.

I steal a glance at his door. He must have the ancient book in there, but there are too many witnesses to try and break in now. I'll just have to track his comings and goings to figure out the best time to sneak in and find the tome.

～

"I can't believe they're having us engage in a bloody beauty contest," I groan.

By the queen's request, I had snuck past the Nymph guards late at night and into Vale's room so she could help me prepare for the next part of the Ethodine: the Trial of Beauty.

Vale sits at her vanity, which is covered in tiny pearls. It's piled with books, of course, but also brushes, powders, and the Nymph oils she's currently using on her fair, freckled skin. As she applies a dab of one, it makes a few of her many freckles disappear.

I collapse on the plush couch behind her. This is going to be a long night.

"Always so dramatic." Vale peers at my reflection before continuing to admire herself. "It's not really a *beauty* contest, lucky for you. Think of it more like a trial of talent."

I huff. I don't want to be here. What I would rather do is figure out where Hickory is keeping the ancient tome. Maybe I can sneak into his room and search for it when he's out for a meal or something. Until then, I have to try to focus on this trial. "I don't see how beauty or talent is necessary to rule a land."

"In Nymph society, it is," Vale assures me. "They believe each faerie has been born with a particular gift that gives them power, bringing beauty and light to the world."

Beauty and light? Between my sword fighting and flaming hands, my only skills seem to bring destruction.

"And what's your gift, exactly?" I ask. "Talking everyone to death?"

"Very funny." Vale shoots me an unamused stare through the

mirror. "Actually, I sing."

"Really?" I ask with an arched brow. Singing and music are usually more of a Nymph specialty.

"I might not have been trained in swordplay day after day like you, but my mother made sure I had a tutor in every other subject imaginable. She even paid the great Marcelline to travel to Eldore and give me lessons when I reached youngling age."

I sit up. Marcelline is one of the prima donnas of operatic Nymphs. I once saw her masterfully captivate an audience while my crew pickpocketed the crowd. I had nearly dropped my spoils at the breathtaking sound of her voice.

"This I've got to hear." I lean in.

My intrigue must tempt her to show off. She puts down her brush, closes her eyes, and takes a deep, low breath.

The sound that comes out doesn't match her at all. While her natural speaking voice has a high, whiny pitch, her singing timbre is round and full. I don't recognize the words—the language must be one of the ancient ones she loves studying so much—but the vowels are soft and lovely to the ear. She only sings a few phrases, but when she finishes, my mouth hangs open. Thankfully, I close it before she opens her eyes.

"Not bad." I put my hands behind my head and lean back. "You're not afraid Aeron will choose to sing as well and show you up?" Not that I've heard him sing, but being a Nymph and all, he's bound to be very good.

Vale tilts her head down, but I don't miss the small smile crossing her face. "I have it on good authority that he will *not* be singing."

The memory of Vale pulling Aeron into the shadows of Eldore's gardens returns to my mind. My stomach twists.

"Is that *his* authority?" I ask nonchalantly as I play with the seashell tassels of a pillow, telling myself that my interest is more about gathering intel than jealousy.

A slight blush joins the freckles on her cheeks. "Perhaps." Vale's eyes narrow in on my reflection as she pulls a coral comb through her hair.

I furrow my brow. With Nile's interest in her, it could very well be him who told her instead. *Two can play at this game.*

"Because if it wasn't, I could find out for you, you know. Aeron likes to talk to me for some reason. Can't seem to leave me alone, actually."

Vale's blush vanishes. "No, no." She grits a smile, pulling her brush through her hair with more force. "I'm supposed to be helping *you* and your talentless soul."

"Helping?" I laugh. "You mean like your Notting Potion? You almost got me killed!"

"Hey!" She spins in her chair, no hint of a smile now. "You're still alive, aren't you? My efforts got you further through that Trial than you would've ever gotten on your own."

I look away. She's right. I hate when she's right.

"Seriously, now. Every creature has *some* measure of beauty, no matter how *small* it might be." Vale looks me over as if it's impossible to find a single speck of beauty anywhere on my person.

I throw up my hands. "I assure you, I have no such gift."

"Well, you'd best make one up fast, or you'll be disqualified. And you know we can't have that." She gives me a weighted glare, reminding me of my deal with her mother.

"No, we certainly cannot," comes the queen's voice.

Both Vale and I straighten as she enters the room and closes the door softly behind her. "You two are quite impossible," she scolds. "If you argue much louder, you'll alert every sleeping fae in this dome of your little meeting."

"Sorry, Mother." Vale stands, her tone and demeanor instantly changing. "What're you doing here?"

"Vale, my dear," the queen places a hand on her daughter's cheek. "You know I have every confidence in you. However, since watching Quinn nearly get skewered during the last trial…" She turns to me, and I lower my eyes to the ground. "I had a feeling she might be needing *my* help for this round."

At that, I perk up.

"Really, Mother, that's not necessary. We don't want to bother you." She shoots a glare at me. "Knowing Quinn, we might be up all night trying to think of something."

"Don't be silly, Vale." The queen cuts her off with a wave of her hand, still smiling at me. "I'm sure I'll be able to think of a talent our pirate friend would be perfect for." She looks me up and down as she rolls up her draped sleeves. "I do my best work with impossible odds."

CHAPTER 26

I f the Trial of Beauty wasn't enough to worry about, the next day we're invited by Lord Kaito to a celebration, just as Lady Delphine promised. Kaito called it an *Underwater Masquerade*, which is to be held in our honor. But as I step down into the large circular banquet hall, I'm sure that's not his only motive.

Honestly, it feels more like I'm inside a massive aquarium. Below the ocean surface, the walls are entirely made of sea glass. It gives view to the endless ocean world outside, creating the illusion that all the attendees are underwater.

As I fight the fear of drowning clawing at my stomach, I focus on the faerie folk trailing along the dance floor instead. The rippling water plays off the glass walls. Sea diamond chandeliers cast colorful hues across the room as fae meld into the ocean scene. Water manipulators make a show of arcing cocktail drinks through the air into goblets. Dancers and showmen put on an evocative display, enacting the band's sultry song.

To complete the scene, each faerie present wears an elegant mask that represents a different creature of the sea, their attire complementing their choice.

The Callan sisters are already taking turns dancing with Wayde and Tal. The girls resemble sea stags in their matching azure dresses, masks, and coral antlers. Wayde wears turtle shells on the shoulders of his tile-patterned suit, while Tal appears to be a clown fish with orange and white stripes.

Whatever their part in the night's festivities, every Nymph displays their talent and beauty with elegance and grace. My hands tighten their hold on my skirt. How in Faylan am I supposed to compete with any of this?

When asked by the Nymph servants what creature I would like to emulate, I'd first asked to become a swordfish. But when my request for an actual sword was rejected, I decided to go with something a bit flashier.

Eight long trails of gathered lace weave around the skirt of my blood-red gown as I make my way through the sea of fae—the tentacles of my octopus persona. With a matching red-and-white-spotted mask to cover most of my face, at least I'm back in my element. I'm a shadow in the night, blending in with the masses, walking around unnoticed through the room with my head held high. I love that my face is hidden again. My pirating habits kick in, and I keep my eye out for anyone not paying attention to their farthling coin purses.

If only my dress had true tentacles to aid me.

In the maze of masks and music, it isn't long before I spot my fellow competitors. As if her distinct fire-red hair isn't enough of a giveaway, Vale wears a brightly colored mask and strategically low-cut orange dress. The bottom fans out to reveal five pointed ends as she dances through the interchanging steps, passing from one available puck to another. Of course, the Sylph princess would want to be the star of all fish.

As she twirls into her next partner's arms, I realize it's Nile. Even though he's sharply dressed in a bright red suit and mask that reminds me of a lobster, it's hard to miss his bright green hair.

Vale breaks into a smile, but this time I catch Queen Gwendolyn's tall figure on the outskirts of the dance floor, watching Vale with an eye of caution. Though she still wears her crown and royal purple robe, her semi-transparent top ends in a skirt made from hundreds of fluorescent strings. Her luminous dress makes her an elegant yet powerful crystal jellyfish, gliding across the floor as she nods to each guest, still keeping an eye on Vale.

It isn't until I reach the tables of delectable seafood hors d'oeuvres that I spot Alys. The only pixie in the room not taking the opportunity to dress provocatively, she's covered from head to toe in a black seaweed fabric, emulating what I assume to be an eel by the way it shines. Her black braids are in a tight updo, and she's cross-armed, scrutinizing those on the dance floor as if she might electrify anyone who even thinks about asking her to dance. I get the impression that the Masquerade doesn't amuse her.

What she hasn't seemed to notice is that through the glass wall behind her, actual fish of all shapes and sizes have gathered, hovering around her frame.

Such a mystery, this one. Besides the question of her gloved hands still sitting unanswered in my mind, I admire her no-nonsense, quiet rebellion of the event and find myself drawn to her. If only I could find a way to communicate. If I stick to simple yes or no questions, I might be able to get somewhere.

I approach with caution, trying to appear busy choosing between a platter of crab cakes and a bowl of clams on the table nearby. It isn't hard to do. After a night of failed attempts at identifying a talent I can use for the upcoming trial, and a morning of servants dressing me for the Masquerade, I'm starving.

"Doesn't this whole party seem silly? You know, in light of everything?" I toss a crab cake into my mouth and hold out the platter to her as a peace offering.

Alys wrinkles her nose and looks away.

"Not much of a seafood fan?" I ask.

"Alys isn't much of a *meat* fan, in general." Hickory appears on my other side. "She's a vegetarian."

"Really?" My brows shoot up, not only at Hickory's words, but at what he's wearing. He's decked out in a shimmering silver suit and pointed hat with an eye patch over his blind eye. "And what sea beast are you supposed to be?"

Even Alys peers over at him, her head tilting slightly.

Hickory opens his mouth to answer, but a voice interjects from the dance floor.

"Sorry to disappoint you, mate," Nile says, approaching with Vale on his arm. "But I don't think a pirate is technically a creature of the sea."

"Though we can't speak for Quinn, of course." Vale eyes me.

I shoot her a look.

"I'm a deep-sea squid, thank you very much." Hickory gives Nile a cold stare I've only ever seen him give Aeron. He points to his good eye. "One eye at the front." He turns around. "A smaller eye on the back." A decorative symbol that emulates an eye is stitched into the back of his jacket while ten tails trail off the hem of his coat. "Two eyes for two different purposes. But as a faerie of the sea, I'm sure you knew all that."

Vale puts a hand over her mouth to cover a smile, and I catch Alys stifling a smirk as well.

Nile's lips twist. "Ah, of course," he says tightly. It seems Hickory is one of the few that can get under Nile's skin. Good for him.

Hickory stands a little taller. "Besides, this getup gives me a reason to carry this around." He reaches into his pocket and pulls out a vial of black liquid that sparkles; probably tainted with pixie dust. "Ink, anyone?"

"Ha!" Vale laughs and claps her hands. "Very clever!"

Nile gives her a look, but Hickory smiles victoriously. "Thank you." He beams at her and places the vial back in his pocket.

"Look out, thirsty pucks coming through." Wayde and Tal push past us to get to the sea breeze cocktail bowl on the other side.

Alys glares at their backs, and I'm more than happy to follow her lead.

But Nile must think I'm eyeing the cocktail. "You and your dust-smoking friend better not get any ideas about spiking that bowl."

"Yeah," Tal agrees with a mouth full of shrimp. "The last time we did that, the Nymph Lord *beached* us for nearly a month."

Nile looks like he's about to pummel Tal.

I raise my brows. "Beached?"

Vale sighs, ready to instruct me as always. "It's when a Nymph is exiled to the land for any amount of time. It's quite embarrassing, and—"

Nile rolls his eyes and puts a hand on hers to still her chatter. "I think she gets it."

A conch shell sounds, pulling our attention to the staircase entrance. The band halts, and the whole room of dancers stills. Aeron and a pixie I assume is his bride-to-be appear at the top of the staircase.

"Presenting Sir Aeron and Lady Arista," the announcer calls.

The quaint way their names go together makes me want to gag. Still, I step forward, peering over the crowd for a better look.

Despite Aeron running out on their wedding, his betrothed's smile stretches from ear to ear as they descend into the hall. He lied about the status of their relationship, but he hadn't lied about her beauty.

Arista's long magenta hair trails down her curved figure. The pleats of her pale form-fitting dress mimic the oyster shell she's meant to portray as a string of pearls drapes down her sweetheart neckline.

It's hard to behold her true beauty, however, with the seashell mask she holds in front of her face. I hope against hope it hides an underwhelming visage. A long, crooked nose perhaps. A unibrow. Anything, really.

But as they descend, she lifts the mask to reveal a perfectly shaped nose, full red lips, long batting eyelashes, and a whole list of other desirable traits, none of which are underwhelming. A self-conscious twinge trickles up my neck. All eyes watch her as if mesmerized.

All except Aeron.

He's dressed in a blue-gray suit with fabric that stretches from his arms to his sides like wings and a long tail at the back of his coat. He appears to be a sharply dressed stingray. But Aeron isn't matching Arista's smile. Peering through his mask, his eyes are glazed over, locked in a forward, uninterested gaze. Until they shift, finding me.

His lips part as his eyes lower to my dress and back to my face. His dimple appears, and I struggle to fight the blush rising in my cheeks. But as they reach the bottom of the stairs, Arista leads him onto the dance floor as the band strikes up a new tune in their honor.

As if broken out of a trance, the party resumes. Alys walks off, the fish outside still following her movements. Vale huffs in Aeron and Arista's direction, yanking Nile back onto the dance floor.

Staring at Aeron dancing with his betrothed, I'm left alone with my thoughts. I straighten my skirt with a fierce tug. No one is going to get me down tonight, not even Aeron and his fiancée. I'm escort-free and chainless. With my lavish Nymph-dress and a mask to shield me, nothing can ruin my mood.

"Didn't I tell you that guy is bad news?" Hickory says, stepping up to my side. I startle. He was so quiet, I'd forgotten he was there.

"You say that, but you've never told me why," I challenge.

He avoids my gaze. "Well, for one, look at the company he keeps."

He nods to Nile dancing with Vale. She giggles at something he's said, and I catch a mischievous glint in Nile's eye. Though Hickory definitely has a point, I know there has to be more.

"I don't know, Hickory. You're starting to make me think you're jealous for my attention or something," I say, half-jokingly.

Hickory lets out a guttural laugh and snatches up a goblet from the table. "No offense, Captain, but you're not really my type." He takes a sip, turning toward the dance floor.

"Oh really?" I press with an intrigued smile, watching him survey the dancers. No, wait. His eye is following something. "But there is someone, isn't there? Maybe they're in this very room?" I look around playfully before returning to Hickory.

His complexion turns even paler than usual. "You don't know her, I assure you," he says, though the words come out a bit rattled. His good eye now darts around the room as if trying to avoid giving away who the mystery pixie is.

"Wow, relax, Kobie. I was just kidding," I say, and Hickory's color slowly returns. "But truthfully, I'm not sure sticking around you is much better than Aeron."

"And why's that?" Hickory goes to take another gulp from his goblet.

"Well, you do keep a lot of secrets. You won't tell me the whole truth about Aeron or who this mystery pixie is…" I trail off, getting an idea. "Or why you steal books away from the libraries of Sylph princesses."

"What?" Hickory nearly chokes on his drink, but composes himself. "I'm not sure I know what you mean."

Ah, so he does intend to keep the tome a secret. Even from me. What could he want it for? Whatever it is, it can't be as important as me decoding the nightmares about my brother.

"There you are," comes a low, agitated voice. I shudder and peer behind me where none other than my father stands. He wears a gray suit and mask with a string of sharp teeth looped around his neck.

A lurking shark. How appropriate.

I look back at Hickory. I'm not done with him yet.

But I'm too late. Whether he saw the opportunity to avoid more talk about the book or my father's presence was enough to spook him, he's gone. I'll have to catch up with him later.

Slapping on an obviously fake smile, I spin back around to my father.

"Ah, Your Grace." I give him an overly dramatic curtsy. "I didn't realize that you'd already arrived in Isinglass. Just when I was starting to have some fun."

As expected, my father's face shows no sign of amusement. "Fun," he scoffs, crossing his arms. "Maybe if you were focusing less on having *fun* and more on putting your energy into the last trial, you wouldn't be at the bottom."

My smile disappears. He doesn't care that I was almost stabbed to death by sea glass, or that I survived it. Only the crown matters to him. The crown I'm not even trying to win anymore. But I can't let him know that.

"I'm doing my best." I lower my voice as others pass by, eyeing us.

"Well, obviously *your best* won't make you queen." His tone remains rough as he observes me. "You are distracted. Why?"

"I..." I hesitate.

I can't let him know about my deal with the queen, and I definitely can't tell him about my dreams. Especially *who* is haunting them. Perhaps my father has some knowledge of the symbol on our mother's daggers, but as I stare into his impatient glare, I shake my head. Even I think I sound crazy. I don't need Feyden to confirm it.

"Excuse me," Aeron's voice interrupts. I'm surprised to see him without Arista. Even more so that his hand is held out to me. "I seem to have lost my dance partner. Mind filling in?"

I weigh my options between bad and worse as I look from my father's scowl to Aeron's hand.

"I don't think that's such a good idea—" my father begins.

"I'd love to," I answer emphatically before he can finish.

With that, Aeron flings me onto the dance floor with a twirl. Though I haven't formally danced in years, Aeron guides me through the steps with a strong leading hand. After some stumbling on my part, we fall into a rhythm, and I look back at my fuming father.

"Saving me again?" I ask with a touch of sarcasm, but also with gratitude this time.

"Oh, were you in some sort of trouble? I hadn't noticed." Aeron grins, his dimple making an appearance again. "If anything, *you* saved me. I can't very well be found dancing out here by myself." He looks at our feet, then back into my eyes. "Thankfully you seem to be getting the hang of it."

I smile smugly, but then catch sight of Aeron's bride-to-be. Arista is searching the crowd, the same plastered smile from earlier still draped across her face.

"Better than your fiancée, I assume?" I nod toward the partner he could be dancing with. "I think she's looking for you."

"Ah, there she is." Aeron laughs nervously as he moves us deeper into the crowd of dancers. He leans in close to whisper. "Honestly, I'd rather not be around her right now."

I try not to laugh at the fact that Aeron is hiding from a pixie. "You know, if you wanted to get away from her, you could've asked Vale to dance." I watch for his reaction.

Aeron's brow furrows. "Why would I do that?"

"Well, for starters, you're kind to her. Though I can't imagine why. Plus, I've seen you two sneaking off together doing… whatever it is you two do." I command my cheeks not to burn, nearly stepping on his foot as we spin.

Aeron's confusion morphs back into his smirk. "You're very observant." He pulls me closer, the band moving into the final part of their song. "I'm flattered you've paid so much attention to my dealings with other pixies."

I roll my eyes. How does he always manage to do that? Catching me off guard, twisting my words. *Not this time.*

"I couldn't care less about what you do or with whom you do it. I only started taking note after Vale told me you agreed not to sing for the Trial of Beauty," I half-lie, looking for confirmation.

"She told you I said that?" Aeron stumbles through the next step, but then narrows his brow. "Since when did you two become friends?"

"I wouldn't say *friends* exactly. And don't change the subject." I have to be more careful. He can't know that she and I are helping each other. I lower my voice to a whisper. "As I see it, it only makes sense for you not to sing anyway. We both know a certain other *gift* of yours would give you quite the advantage with the judge. Some may even call it *cheating*."

Not like I haven't been doing my own fair share of the same thus far, but I need Vale to stay ahead in the competition if she is to be queen and I'm to receive my reward. "Are you brave enough to not sing?"

Aeron peers around us to make sure no one's listening in. "What I want no longer matters. I haven't yet told Vale, but I'll be singing after all. My father insists."

I'm about to ask if his father knows about his *silver tongue*, but right now I'm more intent on making sure he doesn't use it during the trial.

"Still, you at least entertained Vale's request." To have done that, he must have some kind of loyalty to her. "If I didn't know any better, I'd think there was something *more* going on between you two."

Aeron's grip around my waist tightens, and he lowers his voice. "Vale and I have… a complicated past." He chooses his words carefully as others dance around us. "She may like to think there's something… *more* between us. But there isn't."

"But there *was*, wasn't there?" I whisper. He looks away. *I knew it.* I smile victoriously at the discovery, trying to ignore the twinge in my chest at the thought of them together.

"Maybe there *was*," he concedes. "But it's in the past, all right? It doesn't matter… not anymore."

I blink up at him. His eyes are searching my face. There's an intensity behind them, as if he's trying to tell me something with just a stare.

"Because you're a Nymph, and she's a Sylph?" I ask.

Without meaning to, I think of Whit and all the ridicule she received growing up for being a half-breed. Private affairs are one thing. Royals taking secret mistresses from different clans are scandals rumored to have happened from time to time. Most of them are kept quiet enough that they're never brought to light. But outright marriages between royal families of different clans are unheard of. Forbidden.

"Well, yes," Aeron starts. "But that's not what I meant—"

"And even if she was a Nymph, you're about to be married to someone else, so…"

He blinks at me, lips parted. "Right…" His voice trails off, a sadness coming over him, and I realize that somewhere along the way, the conversation shifted.

We've stopped talking about him and Vale and moved on to something else entirely.

He's still looking at me, but I drop my gaze to my feet. "Right," I breathe in agreement.

And just like that, the song ends, and we part.

"How poetic. The pirate and the merman." Nile appears at our side, Vale no longer with him. "Your father wants to see you," he says to Aeron before turning to me with an unsettling glint in his eye. "I can take this one off your hands."

"We weren't quite finished—" Aeron begins, but Lord Kaito's voice cuts in next.

"Nile, thank you for finding my son." He says the last part in a low growl, his fingers tightly wound around his trident. Lady Delphine stands behind him, looking apologetic. "Your mother and I must speak to you. *Alone.*" Kaito looks down on me meaningfully, then at Nile.

Nile bows and moves as if to guide me away, but I give him such a glare, he turns on his heels without another word. *Coward.*

Lord Kaito guides Aeron and his wife to the outer wall, and I back away to an hors d'oeuvres table, staying just close enough to overhear their whispers.

"What were you thinking, abandoning your fiancée to dance with that pirate, parading her in front of all our guests to see?"

"Believe me, Father, it's nothing compared to what you did to Arista," Aeron whispers back.

"Ah, you're punishing me. Is that what this is?" Kaito shakes his head. "Honestly, Aeron. After the disappearing act you pulled, what else did you expect me to do? I told your wedding guests that the queen commanded your immediate return to Eldore to start the competition, but Arista already knew the truth. After that pitiful note you left her, with all your 'I don't love you' talk, she needed a bit more *convincing.*"

My brows knit together. Arista looked so happy earlier. Maybe too happy.

Kaito leans in closer to Aeron, whispering sharply. "Now, I want you to act the part while you're home. The alliance with her family's beauty and gem trade will be a strong match. And when you return from the competition, you will marry her, or so help me—"

Aeron turns to Lady Delphine. "Mother, please don't make me do this."

"Kaito," she says. "Do we really have to talk about this here?"

"Enough." Kaito grips his trident tighter and leans toward his wife's ear. "My dear, tell your son he must listen to his father."

I hold back a gasp as I hear the watery effect of Kaito's voice.

Lady Delphine's gaze grows blank and far off. When she speaks again, it's as if all the warmth I sensed from her the other day is sucked from her being.

"Aeron, you must listen to your father," she says flatly.

That's where Aeron got his silver tongue. From his father. Of course.

"Mother." Aeron grabs her arms. "Don't let him do this to you. You're not yourself. Snap out of it. You don't have to listen to him."

A muscle in my jaw ticks. I can't just stand by and watch this happen. But what can I do?

Suddenly, I hear giggles coming from a few tables away. The Callan sisters are laughing and drinking around a cocktail bowl with Wayde and Nile. An idea hits, and my feet are moving before I can stop them.

Commanding my legs to weaken, I stumble toward Lord Kaito and purposely bump into him.

"Oh my! Very s-sorry, Your Grace. I didn't s-see you there," I say, making sure to slur my words.

"What's wrong with you?" Kaito pulls back from me as if I have the Plague and straightens his robes.

I lean on Aeron, putting all my weight on his shoulder.

He eyes my unsteady legs. "Are you drunk?"

"Perhaps," I smile lazily, then look over to Nile and his gang. "Now that you mention it, that cocktail tasted a bit strange. Kind of like pixie dust." I wag a finger in the air. "I think I might have seen Nile pour something into the bowl."

Kaito's eyes set ablaze on Nile, and he adjusts his grip on his trident. "Aeron, get your mother to her room. I will be there shortly."

I shift off Aeron as he takes his mother's arm. Her eyes are still glazed and barely blinking.

My lazy smile shifts into a satisfied grin as Aeron and I watch Kaito march through the crowd straight toward Nile. As he catches the Nymph Lord barreling toward him, even his green hair seems to pale with fear.

Though I'd love to watch Nile's humiliation, I don't want to linger too long, so I take the opportunity to quietly back away. If Aeron catches on to what I've done, I don't want to deal with the whole "thank you" bit that might be coming.

But I only get a few paces before I'm blocked, forced to peer up at the queen's tall frame.

"Your Majesty—" I begin, startled, but she puts up a hand.

"Well, aren't you quick on your feet, Captain. And quite convincing." She nods back to Aeron, who's searching the crowd for where I've gone. "Though I guess I shouldn't be surprised with your many years as a pirate, hiding your true identity for so long."

I turn back to her, waiting for a threat to rat me out for what I've done. But instead, she considers me, a new light in her eyes.

"I've been thinking more on what talent you could display for the Trial of Beauty. And now, I believe you've given me the perfect idea."

CHAPTER 27

I 'm not sure I approve of the queen's idea for my talent. When she first explained it to me, I tried not to laugh. But at this point, it's not like I have many other options. Late that same night we begin my trial preparations, along with a sparring session for Vale. It's still my responsibility to continue building her strength and keep the skills she learned in Eldore sharp.

"Are you sure I can't display my knife-throwing or something?" I offer one more alternative to the queen's plan after directing Vale to start on fifty push-ups.

"One, two, three..." Vale starts her count from the floor. She's doing them too quickly. I place my foot on her back to add more weight.

"Hey!" she shouts.

I ignore her, turning back to the queen. "My aim with a knife got pretty good while I was a Gwyllion Guard recruit. Had the best aim in the entire pirate fleet, too." I can still see Maverick's look of pride when my daggers hit the bullseye every time. Eventually, I could even do it blindfolded.

"Eight, nine, ten..." Vale groans.

The queen doesn't look up from Vale's vanity, where she's recording something on a piece of parchment. The finch perched on her shoulder does though, tilting its head at me. Sometimes her birds give me the creeps.

"This is not Greymerrow, my dear," the queen says, her feather quill flitting about as she writes. "And I don't think the Nymphs would feel particularly fond of Captain Shade being permitted weapons in their crowded arena. Now, come."

I sigh and obey, lifting my foot from Vale's back. Vale takes a moment to breathe, but I give her a warning look. "Have I mentioned how much I dislike you?" she huffs. "Sixteen, seventeen, eighteen…"

The queen folds the parchment and hands it to me along with a small pouch of farthlings. "Here are some instructions on what I want you to practice and a list of supplies to get at the market tomorrow. Go over everything on your own, and we'll review it together tomorrow night."

I take a peek at the list written in Her Majesty's perfect swirling calligraphy. I glance back up at her, still not convinced.

"Trust me." She gives my shoulder a gentle squeeze.

I nod reluctantly. *Do I really have a choice?*

Returning to my pod just before everyone rises for the day, I spend the next morning trying to catch up on sleep. But my nightmares won't leave me alone.

Faylan on fire. The Sacred Vine falling. Gaius thrusting our daggers into my hands.

Even with his panicked gaze, when I see him alive and well in my dreams, it's almost a relief. But then I wake again in a cold sweat to the bitter reality that he's gone.

At this rate, I'll never get any sleep. And if I'm too tired, I'll never be alert enough to stay alive during these ridiculous trials.

I reach for one of the daggers I've stashed beneath the mattress. The symbol on the hilt stares back at me. I know it must mean something important, but I'll never figure it out without that tome.

I've taken note of when Hickory leaves his room unattended, but some of the others are usually still milling about. I could sneak in when everyone gathers in the central palace for meals, but if he notices me missing right before the book is taken, he'll surely know it's me.

Although, maybe I don't have to steal it, exactly. Maybe just flipping through some of its pages will tell me something.

That just might work.

I've already missed lunch, so for now I take a transport orb to the market to purchase the items on the queen's list.

"How much for this?" I ask, motioning to a black top hat in a display of caps and other head coverings.

The Nymph swings a webbed hand onto her hip, pearl bracelets clanging together on her wrist. "It's not your color, darling. What about this one?" She grabs a gem-covered sash that's obviously much pricier and lifts it to my body. "Very pretty," she encourages.

I browse the other sashes, remembering they're also on the list, and point to a much simpler teal one, trying to ignore the fact it reminds me of Aeron's eyes. "I'll take this and the hat. How much?"

"For you…" She eyes the pouch at my side. "Thirty farthlings."

Rookie mistake, not hiding my pouch. She must have a trained eye; thirty is all I have. But this isn't my first time haggling. "Ten," I say.

"Fifteen," she shoots back.

I sigh. I don't have time for this. "Eleven, and that's my final offer. I can just as easily take my business somewhere else. The shop across the way looks much more accommodating." I start walking back toward the shop's aquagate where my transport awaits.

"Fine, fine." She hurries after me. "Eleven it is."

∾

I return right before dinner, passing Vale and Alys as they head out. Hickory is the last to leave. As he locks his door, I nod to the satchel slung around his shoulder.

"Going to paint after dinner?" I ask.

"You know it." He picks up the blank canvas leaning up against his pod and pats his bag full of supplies.

"Enjoy," I say as he continues on. *And take a good long while.*

"Aren't you coming?" he asks.

"I'll be right behind you. Just have to drop these off first." I hold up the sack in my hands.

Once he's out of sight, I toss my things in my room and double back to Hickory's pod. Making sure the coast is clear one last time, I take a knee, pulling a pin from my hair and picking the lock. It gives easily before I slide through, making sure to lock the door again.

For the most part, Hickory's room is laid out the same as mine, save for the canvases, paint supplies, and stack of books sprawled out on his bed. I rush to the books, picking up and shifting them one at a time, placing each one right back where I found them so Hickory doesn't suspect a thing.

Come on, I know you're here.

A few stray pieces of parchment sticking out of a sketchbook catch my eye. Gently, I pull them free. They're covered in ink, but not with Hickory's normal sketches.

Hurriedly scribbled symbols are scrawled over the surface in various sizes, some crossed out with arrows and circles connecting others. My stomach twists. These look like the scribblings of a crazed fae. What's Hickory gotten himself into now?

I rotate the parchment in my hand, but I can't make wings or tails of what it means. I wouldn't be surprised if it's his own code to ward off snoops like me. But then I notice something I do recognize.

In one of the page's corners, circled five times, is the symbol from the tome's cover.

I knew that symbol meant something! I've just started looking through the books again when I hear a key slide into the door's lock.

Hickory can't be back already. He must've forgotten something. Just my luck. Why does this keep happening to me? Ever since the botched funeral heist, none of my blasted plans seem to be working. I'm a crew of one with no lookout and no backup strategies.

The doorknob jiggles. I've got to get out of here, fast.

I look to my only other exit, the curtain-covered window. Swiftly, I stuff the pages back into the sketchbook and dash behind the drapery. Stifling my heavy breathing, I nudge open his window and sneak out onto the dock, cool air coming off the bay behind me. Hickory's door opens just as I pull the pane closed, pressing my back against the pod wall just out of sight.

Holding my breath, I hear him rustling around in the room. Soon the door creaks open and closes again, and I catch his figure walking back toward the transport orbs.

I sigh in relief. He should definitely be gone now. Maybe I can sneak back in and try looking one more time—

"Quinn?" a voice says behind me, and I jump.

CHAPTER 28

A swimming figure approaches in the water, and the jellyfish lanterns illuminate Aeron's face. I relax a bit.

"What are you doing?" he asks. His Nymph tail swishes behind him as he leans his wet blue arms on the landing, looking up at me with interest.

How much did he see?

"Nothing," I say quickly. "Just out for a stroll. Needed some fresh air."

"So you decided to hang around Hickory's window?" He raises a brow.

"I figured I'd check everyone's window locks as I go." I take hold of the window latch again and feign a jiggle of it. "Good, nice and tight. Can't be too careful."

"How... thoughtful of you." He arches a brow.

"That's just the kind of pixie I am." I smile broadly, though I know it's not very convincing. If I try to leave too quickly, he'll know I was up to something. "Honestly, after all the excitement at the Masquerade last night, I didn't feel like being around everyone at dinner. Thought I'd hang back here for a bit of peace and quiet." I sit down at the edge of the dock and lift my skirt up just enough to dip my legs in the water. I bristle at the cold temperature. "I'm guessing you had the same idea?"

"Sort of," he says. "After a long time away from the sea, I've been trying to reconnect as much as possible. It's one of the only places I truly feel like myself, you know?"

I gaze over the water and into the sea pressing up against the dome around us. "More than you know."

"Well then, you should come in!" Aeron exclaims playfully, making me regret my transparency. "It's one thing to look at the ocean, it's another to be in it!"

"I think I've done enough swimming for a lifetime." I shake my head. "Last time you had to pull me from its depths, remember?"

"And I'll be here to save you again, which I know you love so much." He playfully flicks some water onto my dress.

"Hey!" I exclaim, trying not to laugh. "I think I'll pass."

"Oh, come on, you've got to lighten up. Have a little fun." He boldly grabs my hands, ready to pull me in with him. "You know you want to."

I pull back, my teeth clenched together in a warning smile. "Don't—you—dare."

My legs are already submerged. It would be so easy for him to pull me in. But surprisingly, he lets go of my hands and drifts backward.

"Fine. But here's a parting gift so you know what you're missing."

In a flash, Aeron dives back into the bay. His tail smacks down on the water's surface, and I yelp as a frigid wave rushes over me, soaking me through.

Aeron resurfaces with a wide smile.

I sit there in shock, arms held away from my body as water drips off my hair, down my face and dress. My lip begins to quiver.

"Oh no, I'm so sorry." Aeron swims back. "Don't cry, I was just playing around…"

But as he draws close enough, a smile breaks across my face. "Ha! The only one that's going to be crying is you, you imp!" I laugh and jump into the water after him.

Aeron's look shifts from confusion to joy in a snap as he tries to swim away from me. But I grab his arm and drag him back.

"You're in so much trouble!" I allow my signature cackle to ring through the air as I dunk him under the water.

Aeron surfaces and lets out a ferocious laugh. He shakes his midnight blue hair, playfully whipping water droplets toward me.

Grabbing me around the waist, he pulls me close. "Trouble, huh? I think I can take it."

I rest my hands on Aeron's shoulders as his tail swishes back and forth, keeping us afloat. Our laughter subsides, and I realize how close we are. His warm breath brushes against my skin. His teal eyes are so clear, little specks of green reflecting back at me.

Slowly, his face inches closer to mine.

I panic and turn my gaze back toward the pods. *What am I doing? What if someone else comes back and sees us?* Though dinner shouldn't be over yet, I'm still relieved to see no pod lamps flickering to life. All the windows are dark, the curtains closed tight. The only sounds are the periodic flutters of the caged birds in the queen's pod. I double-check Vale's window. If she sees us like this, she might literally kill me.

"I think maybe it's time we go," I say.

"You can go, if you'd like," he says, though his hold on me doesn't loosen. "I'm not quite ready."

I don't dare say it out loud, but neither am I.

"Aeron?" I ask. "Why are you really out here all by yourself? You could go swimming any time. I'm sure Arista is expecting you in the dining hall."

His eyes shift away. "Honestly, I needed to let off some steam."

"Why?" I prod. "It looked like things were all patched up between you and your betrothed at the Masquerade."

"I'm sure it did." He shakes his head, then pauses.

I hold my breath, waiting for him to go on. Will he actually tell me the truth?

"The thing is, when I skipped out on our wedding, Arista was furious. No one knows this, but she called off the marriage entirely. Which, frankly, is what I'd hoped she'd do."

"So… then she forgave you." I try to give him a way out. This is his business. If he doesn't want to confide in me, I'm not going to pull it out of him.

"Not likely," Aeron scoffs. "She doesn't even remember having a previous wedding date. Just the new one both our parents arranged for us after the Ethodine is over." He leans in closer. "My father *persuaded* her otherwise."

"Because he has a silver tongue too," I say matter-of-factly.

Aeron's eyes search my face. "You don't look as surprised as I thought you'd be."

I purse my lips. "I may have overheard him using his gift on your mother at the Masquerade."

"You *heard* it?" he asks, lifting a brow.

"Well, it's hard to miss the strange watery sound on your voice whenever you use it. It was the same with your father. Not hard to figure out."

"I've never met anyone else who can hear it besides me." He looks at me in awe. "You haven't said anything to anyone? If someone at court found out, the clan would lose trust in our family's rule. I might even lose my position in the Ethodine." His grip on me tightens as if he fears I'm setting him up to do exactly that.

"I haven't said anything. And I don't plan to." I reassure him. "I know I can be cutthroat, but I'm not a monster."

Aeron relaxes. "I know—I mean, thank you. Really, that means a lot."

"Of course," I say. "I'm… I'm just so sorry about your mother. She doesn't deserve that." I can't get the image of the light leaving her warm eyes out of my head.

"No. No, she doesn't." Aeron grows quiet. He looks beyond me, his focus hard and sharp.

"Has he always been this way? Your father, I mean."

"Not when I was younger. Of course, I was more naive and compliant at the time." He purses his lips. "I think deep down I always knew there was something wrong with our gift, but I so desperately craved his love and approval that I allowed him to train me in it. For a long time, I used my gift on whoever he directed me to. But as I got older, the things he asked me to do became more questionable, and I started to refuse."

My skin crawls, imagining what Kaito could have demanded. Then another fear creeps into my mind. "Did he ever use his silver tongue on you?"

"Oh, he's tried. Several times. But it seems this type of magic doesn't work well on others with the same gift. When he couldn't control me, he settled on controlling my mother instead." His eyes soften. "He knows I won't fight back if she's in danger."

"And now he's resorted to manipulating Arista too." I shake my head, putting the pieces together. The whole situation makes me sick.

"Exactly," he breathes. Aeron may not love Arista, but his tone is laced with pity at the mention of the Nymph pixie. Even I'm starting to pity her.

"Is there no way to undo your father's manipulation? Couldn't you just persuade her *not* to marry you?" If Aeron has the gift too, surely two can play at this game.

Aeron's brows furrow, and his mouth opens as if ready to respond sharply. But he stops. His jaw shifts, reconsidering his words.

"I know I've joked around about what I can do." He looks deeply into my eyes. "But I really do hate using it. I try not to unless I feel like it's absolutely necessary. Convincing Arista not to marry me still doesn't give her free will back, and messing with her mind even more can be dangerous." His gaze drops to the water. "I'm fairly sure my father's manipulation of my mother is having long-term effects on her memory. He refuses to see it, but I swear she's growing more forgetful."

"How awful…" I say, remembering her lapses in memory the day of our arrival.

"I fear I'm losing a little more of her all the time." Aeron sniffs and blinks as if holding back tears. My heart twinges. "Besides, even if I tried to counteract my father's effect on Arista, he's had many more years to perfect his gift. Breaking his spell would take skill and time I don't have. And if I succeed in ruining his arrangement again, there's no telling what he might do."

For the first time, Aeron's cocky demeanor is fading, revealing someone I never would've expected. How can someone stand to feel this passionately and still be able to function as he does? Though I try to keep my walls up, Aeron's sincerity is bringing them all crashing down one by one.

"So, you're going to go through with it. You're going to marry her." The words catch in my throat.

"Believe me, I've been trying to find a way out. He expects me to keep controlling Arista when we're wed, but that's not the kind of marriage I want. My father may prefer to force others to love and respect him, but I refuse to live that way anymore. If I'm to marry, whoever she is, I don't want to have to *make* her love me." He looks into my eyes. "I want someone to choose to love me back. Someone who accepts me for who I am. Someone like…"

He trails off, staring at me. My pulse quickens. *Don't say it.*

Aeron sighs and gives me a halfhearted smile. "Maybe that's not my destiny. I suppose none of us are really in control of our own fate." His eyes search mine. Perhaps simply for confirmation, but it feels like something more.

"Aeron," I begin softly, this time unable to look away.

"Mmhmm?" His eyes don't stray from mine.

"Why did you lie to me about your wedding that first night we met? Why not just tell me you ran away instead of making it sound like you were already married?"

Aeron looks down as his hand runs over the small of my back, sending shivers down my spine. He leans forward until we're sharing the same breath.

"Though I didn't know who you really were at the time, I sensed there was something different about you. In a good way, I mean."

I swallow hard, thankful for the cool water as my body heats.

"I guess I made it sound like I was married, so I had a reason not to do this…"

Aeron moves toward me again.

For a moment, I let go of all urges to turn away.

A shrill gasp sounds over the water. "Aeron?"

Aeron halts right before his lips touch mine, and we jump apart. Two figures stand on the dock a few pods away. One of them is Arista. She has her hands over her mouth. No spell can make her unsee what she's just seen.

Next to her, Nile has a comforting hand on her shoulder and a smug look on his face.

Blast. I float even farther away from Aeron, back toward the landing. If only I'd left earlier.

"I tried to warn you, Arista," Nile says.

"Arista, don't listen to him." Aeron is already swimming toward her. "It's not what it looks like."

But tears spill over her cheeks, and she turns to flee down the island and out of the dome.

"Arista!" Aeron lifts himself out of the water to sit on the dock and hurriedly pulls his chiton over his head as his tail turns back into legs.

"Good luck smooth-talking your way out of this one." Nile snickers.

Aeron turns on him and, with all his strength, punches Nile square in the face.

I cough out a surprised laugh as Nile stumbles from the force and trips right into the pool.

As I pull myself up onto the landing, I catch Nile's fish-tail form swimming away from us. I knew he was a coward.

Aeron looks at me from the dock. His mouth opens as if he wants to say something. But then he lets his wings loose and darts after Arista.

Left alone in my soaked dress, I stare after him, wondering what he'll do now.

I curse, realizing that I care.

Suddenly, a lamplight flickers on in a window nearby. Before I can see whose window it is, I turn and slink through the shadows back to my own pod.

I can only hope there weren't any other witnesses to our spectacle.

CHAPTER 29

Here goes nothing.

It's the day of the Trial of Beauty, and I'm back above water in the main palace, standing on the stage of a grand auditorium with the other heirs. It's a venue where only the best entertainers in Faylan perform—all of them Nymph, of course. As with any normal theater, I expect to see a large curtain lining the back of the stage. But instead it's entirely open, like a gigantic archway opening to a masterful view of the sea and the mountains in the distance.

I feel like I'm back on the Minnow. The breeze coming off the water tickles my nose and I smile, trying to relax. The last few days have gone my way, though. I've been too preoccupied with trial preparations to try breaking into Hickory's room again, and this is the first time I'm seeing Aeron since that night.

Beside me, Aeron smiles out at the crowd like everything is fine. I want to ask him where he's been, what happened with Arista, but he's busy waving to the excited crowd, which is not only twice as big as the one in Eldore but also twice as loud, the sound bouncing off the inner walls.

I sigh. *Focus, Quinn.* While this talent show of sorts will be extremely humiliating, at least it won't be lethal.

Like the trial before, the clan lords and ladies sit in a private balcony jutting out of the wall above. Alys' parents hold hands while Hickory's look around as if admiring the construction of the stadium. The queen, however, is seated next to my father. Both of them sit upright with stoic faces, waiting for what's to come.

From a side entrance, Lord Kaito and Lady Delphine enter with Arista and two Nymphs who I assume are her parents trailing behind them. Arista's radiant smile is plastered back on her face as she waves to Aeron excitedly and blows him a kiss. He nods to her with a pursed smile.

Though I shouldn't be surprised the spell has been readministered, an ache knots in my chest.

I suppose none of us are really in control of our own fate, Aeron had said.

Based on my luck in life so far, I can't exactly argue with that.

"Welcome, welcome one and all!" Lord Kaito appears on the stage next to us, and the auditorium grows quiet. "Today we have quite a show prepared for all fae, great and small." He flashes his pearly white teeth, which gleam under the stage lights.

Excitement buzzes through the room. The Nymph Lord seems to feed off the attention and his ability to command such a crowd. *A born entertainer.* I almost smile with admiration until I remember how easy it is for him to manipulate folk whenever it suits him.

"For your enjoyment, each contestant will show off their Beauty through their greatest talent on this very stage. Beauty is more than a delight to the eyes and grace to the soul, but a power any ruler must learn to wield. Today, each one must display all of this and more to prove themself the victor of this second trial."

Lord Kaito pauses dramatically, a glint in his eye as he pans the crowd. "I can see you all begging the question—who is unbiased enough to rank our champions for this part of the competition? Well, let me introduce you to our judge."

With this, the Nymph Lord approaches the sea at the back of the stage. The five of us look at each other in curiosity as he lets out a whistling tune.

My blood runs cold at the sound I've heard only a few times before while at sea.

Aeron steps backward toward the crowd, knowing what it is too.

The call of the Leviathan.

"Back up!" I call to the others without thinking, following Aeron's lead. They look to us for more information, but I just shoot them a wide-eyed gaze. "Move!"

An enormous creature breaks the water's surface.

With a crash, it lands on the stage, its red scales gleaming in the sunlight and sharp teeth bared.

With the head of a dragon and the body of a serpent, the Leviathan coils its tail under itself and lets out a threatening hiss as its red eyes scour the crowd.

The other clans gasp and shriek but the Nymphs applaud, cheering on their titanic beast.

I might have once been named the Menace of the Five Provinces, but Pirate Lord Maverick always called this creature the *Demon of the Silver Sea*. No ship has been known to escape its fury.

But the Nymph Lord is not afraid. He walks to the Leviathan with his trident and an equally menacing smile.

The creature dutifully lowers its head toward him.

I hold my breath as Lord Kaito draws dangerously close, close enough to whisper into the sea serpent's ear.

The sea serpent growls but doesn't attack.

My eyes grow wide. This thing might be a terror, but it's trained. Kaito's silver tongue must work on the Leviathan too. It's like watching Alys with Tomah. Only this dragon, however obedient, doesn't seem too happy to see the Nymph Lord or to obey his orders.

I peer over at Alys. She doesn't look impressed in the least. In fact, her expression mirrors the Leviathan's, disgust smeared across her face. To her, it doesn't seem to matter how horrifying a creature might be.

"The Leviathan is a magnificent and terrible beast," Lord Kaito speaks to the crowd again. "But what most don't know is that it is also extremely intelligent. Much like fae folk, it can be entranced and subdued by incredible beauty, evidenced when its scales change color. It may not be beautiful itself but, as you will see, it's a great and vicious critic."

As he speaks, three Nymphs surround the creature, softly chanting as they place the tips of their staffs on the ground, encircling the monster. Black squid ink drags along the stage, creating the outline of a ring around the Leviathan. It must be mixed with pixie dust, as the ink glows with whatever Nymph spell they're casting.

"Each champion will enter the magic ring being drawn," Lord Kaito continues. "The ring will keep the Leviathan within its borders until the spell is broken, though fairies can enter and leave as they wish. We will know it's completely subdued when all the Leviathan's scales change from blood red to crystal blue. The competitors will be timed based on how fast they can accomplish this, stepping outside the ring to officially complete the challenge. If they leave the ring before this point, however, they will forfeit this trial."

He turns to the five of us. "Make it laugh or cry with joy. Make it lust after your gift or slumber at your tune. But be warned, this creature grows hungry when bored, so I wouldn't waste any time. The first to enter will be Vale of the Sylphs!"

Vale's clan breaks out into cheers as the rest of us nervously take our seats in the front row. Vale is visibly shaking. Even with all her practicing, I'm sure she never thought this would be the judge she'd have to impress. She takes a tentative step toward the beast, but the Leviathan responds with a ferocious roar, and her red locks fling backward with the force of his breath.

Now it's the Nymphs' turn to cheer, rooting on the Leviathan. I catch Kaito shooting a glare at the queen. He's obviously anxious to pay Her Majesty back for nearly impaling his son.

The Leviathan calms and watches Vale carefully as a beast might quietly stalk its prey, waiting to pounce. But Vale squares her shoulders, firms her features, and begins to sing as she steps into the ring.

The notes come out much quieter than in practice. On the fifth line, her voice catches in her throat.

The sea serpent swivels closer to her, circling with hungry eyes.

Its tail snakes around her legs.

Vale falters again.

Stop looking it in the eyes. Just focus on the words.

As if she's somehow heard my thoughts, Vale closes her eyes, centering herself. Though the Leviathan has her wrapped around the waist, she takes a deeper breath this time and sings the words with more support. More confidence. Her voice rings clear and true.

Just as Kaito described, one by one its scales are turning from red to blue, its eyes more entranced than ravenous. But there's still many more scales that need to turn, and she's already nearing the end of the song.

Vale circles back to the first verse, her voice growing in urgency as if the song is a spell working its magic, her vibrato filling the hall. By the end of her second time through the song, the scales are almost all blue. Vale belts out a phrase, and the last note cracks.

The Leviathan winces at the sound. It snaps its jaws and the crowd gasps.

But Vale recovers with a final sweet phrase, soothing the Leviathan back into a lull.

Its remaining scales turn to blue.

She did it!

The Sylphs cheer.

Fully subdued and satisfied, the Leviathan uncoils its body from around her and allows her to exit the ring unscathed.

I exhale and give her a small nod as she returns to her seat. Though Vale isn't my favorite faerie, she fought hard for that one. Plus, in order to secure my eventual freedom, I kind of need her to stay alive.

"Well done." Kaito rises, his smile tight. I'm sure it's to mask the disappointment of Vale's survival. "But the show has just begun. The next to face the beast is our very own Sir Aeron!"

The Nymphs explode with cheers, but none are as loud as the Callan sisters and their gaggle of Nymph pixies who are fawning over Aeron near the front. In addition to Arista, it seems he has an entire doting fan club.

I roll my eyes as he humors them with a wave.

He approaches the ring coolly, but my fingers squeeze the arms of my chair.

The creature's eyes are trained on him already, licking its lips.

"For his talent," Lord Kaito adds, "Aeron has also chosen to sing to the beast!"

Vale shoots me a panicked glance, but I avert my gaze. I guess he's going to go through with it after all. Considering the excitement sparkling in Kaito's eyes, Aeron'll no doubt be able to control the beast with his silver tongue just as his father did. If so, he definitely has the greatest advantage of us all.

Relaxing my grip on my chair, I find myself caught between relief that Aeron will survive and worry over how Vale will ever be able to compete with him now.

But before Aeron enters the ring, he waves over a Nymph attendant from the stage wings.

It's Fynn. He hands Aeron a violin and a bow, giving him a nod of encouragement.

Aeron faces the crowd, his eyes focused on his very unhappy father in the front row.

"Sorry to disappoint, but my father was ill-informed," Aeron announces.

The Nymphs moan, but Vale lets out a relieved breath.

"Today I will be *playing* for the beast instead." Aeron lifts up the instrument, and the Nymphs cheer just as emphatically as before.

Then his eyes lock with mine. He nods.

He's really doing it. My heart races. *He's standing up to his father in front of the entire clan. He's not going to use his gift. I actually got through to him.*

Warmth rushes through me at the thought.

The Leviathan roars in impatience, and my skirt wrinkles in my fists as another thought hits me. *Wait. He's not going to use his gift, even against this beast.*

And it's all my fault.

I look to Aeron's parents. Lady Delphine clasps her hands tightly in her lap, her eyes wide with concern, while Kaito's face turns an angry shade of red behind his beard. Arista's spell must be a heavy one, because her smile hasn't even faltered, as if caught in a daze.

I try to catch Aeron's gaze again, hoping I'm not too late.

Whatever I said, forget it! It's too risky. If you've ever had a reason to use your gift, this would be the time!

But he's already stepped into the ring.

Aeron doesn't waste a second as he touches the bow to the strings and begins pulling it side to side across them with a fury. The tune is faster and more lighthearted than I expected and somehow familiar.

The Leviathan arches its spine, seemingly startled by the loud, upbeat tune. It circles Aeron, giving him a wide berth at first, but some of its scales are already turning blue.

Aeron speeds up the tune, bouncing from one foot to the other as he plays.

Some Nymphs around us begin to clap along, and I realize where I've heard the tune before. It's the same dancing jig from the first night on Aeron's boat. Watching him perform now, it's the first time he's looked as happy and carefree as he did that night.

The Leviathan's scales turn faster, and I listen closely to the violin's sound. It isn't accompanied by a watery effect like Aeron's silver tongue. No, he's simply playing, showing off his raw skill. His pure talent and beauty. And it's working.

Then a string snaps.

The clapping stops and Aeron freezes, staring at his instrument and then to the Leviathan. The beast has grown blue from his feet to his neck, but scales are starting to change back to red with every passing second of quiet. The Leviathan slithers forward and growls as if Aeron stopped on purpose, warning him to begin again.

A soft chuckle sounds behind me. I glance back to see Nile with Wayde and Tal, smiling smugly. He couldn't have something to do with this, could he? Would he have stooped so low as to sabotage the instrument?

Aeron's eyes shift to the three strings remaining and takes his player stance again, only this time the tune is completely different.

With slow movements of the bow, the violin sings as sweetly as any Nymph voice I've ever heard. The notes lull and swell into a sorrowful tune that pulls at my heart. The enchanting melody entrances the room into stillness.

I nearly forget that the Leviathan is still on the stage. Since Aeron began the new melody, the creature hasn't moved. It still doesn't look as if it's under any kind of spell. It looks at peace, its chest lifting and falling in even measure. As blue scales climb up its neck, the beast's eyes are soft and glassy. Could that be a tear trickling down its face?

Snap. Snap.

The breaking of two more strings resonates through the quiet auditorium, and the Leviathan's head jerks, snarling at a second interruption. It licks its lips again. Perhaps it's wondering if Aeron tastes as delicious as he sounds.

I swallow hard.

Aeron breathes heavily, staring wide-eyed at the violin as the Leviathan slowly slithers toward him. He only has one string left.

What's happening? My clenched fingers leave sweaty spots on my skirts.

I look back at Nile again. He's leaning forward in his seat, no longer looking smug. Instead, his mouth hangs open. He looks as shocked as I feel, seemingly afraid for his childhood friend.

I turn back. Aeron is staring at me as if I know what to do. I can only think of one thing. I nod hurriedly and mouth one word.

Sing.

Aeron looks to his parents, whose intense gazes seem to agree.

Instead, Aeron takes a deep breath and touches the bow to the only remaining string. Slowly, he moves his fingers up and down the neck in a simple lullaby.

His eyes are closed, totally focused on the music. His fingers know exactly where to land.

Much like me and my weapons, he and his violin are one.

Within seconds, not only are all of the Leviathan's scales crystal blue, but so are its eyes, drooping ever so slowly until its head lowers to the floor and it falls asleep.

Opening an eye toward the creature, Aeron gradually brings the melody to a satisfying end.

No one makes a sound as he steps out of the ring, faces the audience, and takes a bow.

The room explodes in applause. Even fae from the other clans can't help themselves, including me.

At the sudden sound, the Leviathan springs awake, its scales instantly changing back to red as it lifts its ugly head in a monstrous roar, quieting our cheers.

Lord Kaito stands up to address the crowd. Although he appears somewhat relieved, he makes no comment on Aeron's performance or his disobedience. He only announces the next competitor.

"Alys of the Dryads!" Lord Kaito's voice bellows.

Part of me breathes a sigh of relief, my hands landing on my knees, though my legs are bouncing. Not that I'm anxious to be in the ring with the sea beast, but this waiting, seeing one heir after another barely survive, I'd almost rather get it over with. I wouldn't be surprised if Kaito picked this order just to torture me.

Alys rises from her seat. Before mounting the stage, however, she removes her cloak to reveal—a dress. A long, simple garment.

Of course, it's still black as usual, complete with her gloves. The sleeves are long enough to cover the rest of her arms, the skirt long enough to cover her legs. Still, I've never seen her wear a dress before. In contrast to her usual tough appearance, she looks dainty and elegant.

As she climbs onto the stage, her bare feet peek out from the bottom of her skirt, and I wait in wonder to see what talent she's chosen.

On the perimeter of the glowing ring, Alys stares long and hard at the creature. The Leviathan bares its teeth, daring her to enter.

Slowly, Alys lifts her hands above her head and, with a pointed foot extended toward the ring, she steps in.

There's no music to accompany her, no rhythm to follow, but her patterned movements through the space are smooth and graceful. Hypnotizing. The Leviathan seems to agree as it watches her, moving its head along with her movements.

"She's dancing, right?" I whisper as quietly as I can to Hickory, who sits next to me.

"It's the moonrain dance," he whispers back, though his gaze doesn't leave Alys' form. "Dryads believe certain physical motions have magical effects. This one is a traditional Dryad dance. They believe it calls forth the moonrain when the land needs it most."

Considering the length of the current drought, the dance obviously isn't helping. But no one can deny that it's captivating and is at least helping Alys subdue the beast.

Alys' movements change and shift, bigger and more robust, bringing her closer and closer to the creature.

So close that her hand gently lands on its nose.

The Leviathan freezes, and Alys locks eyes with it once again, as if having some kind of silent exchange.

Then, with one fluid, graceful motion, Alys flips herself onto the Leviathan's back.

The creature darts toward the edge of the magic ring closest to the sea.

The ring's no longer glowing.

In their retreat, I glimpse a smudge of black ink on the underside of Alys' bare foot.

Alys and the Leviathan are trying to escape.

CHAPTER 30

"Stop them!" Lord Kaito shouts.

Nymph guards from all directions race after them as the crowd goes into a frightened frenzy. I can't move, not believing my eyes.

Alys doesn't care about winning the trial. She wants to set the creature free. Her dance might not have caused it to rain, but whatever magical movements she did weakened the circular prison's magic enough for her to break it. I've never admired anyone's fearlessness and determination so much.

Alys and the Leviathan barely make it to the water's edge before the Nymph guards throw ropes over the sea serpent's long body, holding it down. As the creature shrieks under the restraints, Alys jumps off the Leviathan's back to try to fend off the guards on her own. But it's no use.

I nearly jump on the stage myself to help her, but more guards fly in to manage the crowd while others rush the stage. They grab Alys, holding her back while they wrangle the creature toward the ring, enchanting the border yet again.

"Restrain her!" Lord Kaito demands as he works on calming the beast.

The guards start to carry her out of the auditorium. Alys is kicking the whole way, a silent scream evident from her open mouth and enraged expression.

"No, wait." Kaito holds up his hand for them to halt. "She will watch until the end. Any ruler needs to learn that there are consequences to their actions."

Alys shoots Kaito one of her piercing glares.

The room calms, but as I watch Alys get tied to a chair, my heart pounds.

An unfamiliar sense of guilt rushes over me, wishing I'd done something. Anything. But what could I have done?

"Alys of the Dryad clan has broken the rules of the Trial of Beauty, and therefore has been disqualified from this round," Lord Kaito announces as the crowd settles back into their seats. "Our next competitor to display their skill..." Kaito looks at me, "is Lady Quinntessa of the Gwyllions."

My stomach plummets as I look at the beast. Smoke billows from its nostrils, still seething from the incident.

My feet are heavy as steel as I step up to the stage. I don't feel any better as an attendant sets the chest of items I prepared just inside the ring. Before entering it, I look at the queen. Though, I hope it appears to everyone else as if I'm looking at my father instead.

When we discussed her talent idea for me, we assumed there would be a faerie judge. Now, standing in front of a giant sea dragon, especially one freshly enraged, I wish I'd fought for my knife-throwing idea all the more.

There's no way this is going to work.

But just as the queen did with Vale during the Trial of Knowledge, she nods to me to proceed. Somehow, her vote of confidence pushes me forward into the ring.

I rush to the chest, revealing a series of props I've collected. Nymph hats and wigs, masks and capes, everything I will need for a one-faerie show.

As I pick up my first prop, the Leviathan is fully red again, an impatient growl emerging.

"Ladies and gentlefae," I call. "I give you, the Tale of the Numa!"

In theory, it's simple. Take my skill of disguise and impersonation, then combine it with story to put on a show. It's something I hadn't even considered a talent until the queen suggested it. Those in the crowd lean in. Even Lord Kaito looks intrigued. But will it be enough for the monster?

Directing my attention to the red demon, I step into the ring and begin.

"Of all of Faylan's faerie clans, Sylph knowledge none shall meet," I say with dramatic flair, placing a crown of seaweed on my head. "The beauty of the Nymphs unmatched, the craft of Kobolds never sleeps."

For each part of the tale, I grab new items from the chest as I recite the poem the queen assigned to me. I switch up my voice and appearance to emulate the different characters I play. A glittering sash for the Nymphs. A top hat for the Kobold miners.

"Dryads nurture all of life. Gwyllion strength no one can beat."

I lift coral branches to my temple as antlers for Dryad changelings, then release my Gwyllion wings, slowly lifting into the air, casting a shadow over the stage.

"But darkness comes with no remorse. All shall crumble at her feet."

Flipping in the air, my props clatter to the ground as I fly back to the chest. I grab pillows next and stuff them under my tunic, throwing a cape around my shoulders before slamming the coffer closed. I stand on top, lifting my hands into the air.

"In her shadow, giants form. Our world the Numa will obtain."

Impersonating the giants, my voice reaches for the deepest tones I can muster, slowing my speech to an idiotic pace.

"They bellow loud, 'We take your land, we bring you plague, we steal your rain.'"

The crowd roars with laughter.

But the monster doesn't know what to make of me. It circles as it did with Vale. He sniffs and hisses whenever I take on a new persona. Some of its scales turn blue, but it's still trying to make up its mind.

Pressing forward with the story, I tell of the Numa's minions next. "The dragons at their mercy rise. With shrieks and wings, they take the skies. With fire, they all terrorize the clans the Numa spurn."

I don't need a prop for this part.

Leaping off the chest, I dart through the air with my own dragon wings, and fly around the Leviathan, making sure I don't leave the perimeter of the circle. The fae in the crowd cheer wildly, but to my dismay, the Leviathan doesn't like it one bit.

As if I'm a fly buzzing around its head, the Leviathan chomps its teeth.

I launch backward only to be swatted by the serpent's tail.

It flings me to the ground.

Retracting my wings just in time, pain shoots through my arm as it breaks my fall and collides with the chest. I cry out, and the crowd gasps.

Holding my arm, I look up to the queen, my father, even Aeron, but there's no way they can intervene. They can only watch as the creature slowly slithers closer to finish me off.

I won't leave the ring, but I'm not going to be eaten today.

I pull out everything from the chest with my good arm. I need something to distract the Leviathan, even for just a moment. No longer afraid, my body burns with the urgency not to die.

Burning. Oh no.

Before I can stop it, my hand sparks a tiny flame, igniting a piece of cloth in the chest.

No, no, no!

Smoke billows, and the crowd murmurs.

Frantically looking around, my eye lands on a long coral stick I'd planned to use as the Sylphic Scepter for the grand finale. Grabbing the burning cloth, I wrap it around the top of the stick just as the Leviathan's scaly tail wraps around my torso and lifts me into the air.

I raise my makeshift scepter and thrust it into the Leviathan's face. At the sight of the fiery weapon, it pulls me away and nearly drops me.

"But one Sylph King, he lifts his eyes. And with his Sylphic scepter, cries!" I yell at the creature, the Leviathan now a part of my act as I play the Sylph King. "The Neverworld is where you'll die. Begone, never return."

Breathless, I wait along with the crowd as I hold the burning scepter. The Leviathan looks at the flame, then into my eyes.

A flicker of revelation seems to pass over the creature's face as it blinks at me—as if it somehow knows the truth, that this fire has come from part of me. The monster's shell has peeled away. I can see its soul. And it can see mine. As if it too is not what it appears to be on the outside. Though I don't understand it, a connection is made.

Is this how Alys feels with her creatures?

As the Leviathan lowers me to the ground, I don't even hear the applause or notice that all the beast's scales have turned to blue. It follows me with its eyes as I step out of the ring, all the way back to my seat, its scales slowly returning to red.

"That was masterful," Hickory whispers next to me. "Where did you get the fire?"

"I had a match in the chest," I lie quickly. "We Gwyllions love our fire, you know. All part of the act."

"Uh huh." Hickory raises a brow skeptically. "How… resourceful of you."

"Thanks." I try to smile back. He can wonder whatever he wants to for now. I'm just thankful it's over. I survived. I can finally relax.

Beyond Hickory, Alys is staring at me from the chair she's restrained in. Her usually blank face also twists with curiosity. Can she tell what I felt with the creature?

"Hickory of the Kobolds will close our show," Kaito announces, the enthusiasm in his voice waning. He turns to Hickory. "Let's try to finish today without another reckless stunt, shall we?"

Hickory nods, taking that as his cue to approach the stage.

The crowd is still settling down as a few Kobolds come out from the stage's wings with Hickory's easel and paints.

Hickory doesn't look nervous. Why should he? He's the greatest painter in all of Faylan. As long as the creature isn't more blind than him, he'll enchant the Leviathan, no problem.

I settle into my seat, trying to put aside my feelings about what just occurred, ready to sit back and finally watch Hickory finish a masterpiece from beginning to end.

Entering the magic ring, Hickory coaxes the paints out of their containers with a wave of his hands. A playful smile draws across his face as the colors glide along the canvas with grace.

The creature's slithering body draws closer to Hickory, and I join the crowd in a collective gasp. But the monster only watches the canvas, its scales already turning blue.

Hickory doesn't seem to notice. He doesn't flinch. He stays fully focused on his work, and it soon becomes obvious that he is painting the landscape of Faylan from a bird's eye view. From the mountains to the Sacred Vine, the sea to the woods, the vibrant colors come alive, as though one could jump right into the painting and fall toward the land below.

I stare at Hickory's back as he remains immersed in his process. It's eerie how focused he is, actually. Even as the Leviathan's scales fully turn to blue and his clan explodes with cheers, he doesn't stop painting.

I lean forward in my seat. *What is he doing?*

Hickory's movements grow faster and more hurried as he suddenly starts to paint over the bright colors. Shades of black and brown splash across the canvas, shadowing the once stunning scene in darkness.

A murmur hums through the crowd at the change.

The Leviathan, while still entranced, tilts its head. It inches away, startled, as Hickory's arms loosely flail over the canvas rather than purposely directing the paints.

Then Hickory's body starts to tremble.

The crowd that was once mesmerized by the beauty of the painting grows loud with concern.

"What's he painting?" a bold puck calls out, and I slowly stand to try to make it out myself. A Nymph attendant draws near him, then returns to the Nymph Lord.

"I can only see the whites of his eyes, Your Grace," she informs him. "I don't think he's in control of what he's painting."

"What exactly *is* he painting?" Kaito asks, his voice more irritated than concerned.

"Death."

"Come again?"

"Death," she repeats. "It's all of Faylan. In ruins."

Before I know what I'm doing, I jump onto the stage, not sure if I mean to make sure Hickory is okay or to get a closer look at the canvas.

A guard grabs me before I can reach him. But as they pull me away, I see it.

In the painting, the Sacred Vine has crashed to the ground, and all of Faylan is covered in ash as if it has been on fire.

Just like in my dream.

CHAPTER 31

Though Hickory technically subdued the Leviathan, the Nymph guards have to help him finish the trial by carrying him out of the ring, rushing him and his painting off the stage. They say it's to attend to his condition, but I have a feeling it's more to ensure no one gets a good look at the disturbing image he painted.

I still can't believe Hickory painted my nightmare. How is that possible?

That's it. I can't wait anymore. I need to talk to Hickory now more than ever.

After overhearing he was brought to the infirmary, I rush straight there. It's located in a pod near the palace, so I have to dart through a glass-tubed bridge to get there. I ignore my heart pounding in the tight underwater space, focusing on the infirmary door ahead. Before I can open the door, I collide with someone who's obviously as desperate to get out of there as I am to get in.

"Alys?" I say.

She stops her retreat, holding a bandage to her arm. Scrapes on her face gather into a scowl, marring the delicate vine-like tattoos that frame her features. The Nymph guards obviously weren't afraid to be rough with her.

It's hard to tell what she's more angry about: me bumping into her already-bruised body, being disqualified from the day's challenge, or failing to set the Leviathan free. Probably all of the above. Still, seeing her bravery during the trial, the way she connected with the Leviathan, I find myself stepping toward her.

"Um…" I try to think of what to say. "Did you—did you see Hickory in there?" I ask.

Alys nods swiftly and turns to go.

"I was quite impressed by your way with the sea creature," I call after her sincerely.

She halts, and her eyes shift to me. Though she still wears a stoic glare, she doesn't turn away.

I swallow hard and proceed. "The escape attempt was spectacular. I'm just sorry it didn't work."

Alys closes her eyes. I brace myself for a sour reaction, but she gives an appreciative nod. Our eyes meet. Her look reminds me of the Leviathan's, intensely holding me captive before releasing me from its clutches.

"Do you know what happened to it?" I press a bit further. "After the trial?"

Alys shakes her head with a defeated shrug. She aimlessly looks into the sea beyond the glass walls that surround us, perhaps hoping to catch a glimpse of the beast swimming by.

"I hope they set it free," I say quietly. "No one deserves to be trapped, made to perform on command."

Alys lets out a breath. Her hands motion to the two of us and then the space around us. Her eyes survey the fishbowl-like tunnel before returning to me with brows raised.

"Right." I smile, understanding. "Including us."

Alys nods triumphantly, then folds her arms.

I'm pressing my luck with the beast-tamer, but she isn't pushing me away yet. Making sure no one is coming, I quiet my voice, chancing another question.

"If you don't mind me asking, I've noticed you have some kind of connection with different creatures. Even one as fierce as the Leviathan. How do you do it? I mean…" I fumble to think of a way I can ask in the form of a yes or no question.

It seems Alys catches my drift. She cocks her head, and the slightest hint of a smile creeps up the corners of her mouth as if to say, *Wouldn't you like to know?*

Then she turns and marches down the bridge away from me.

~

"Please, if I can only speak to him for a minute," I beg the Nymph medik. She won't let me pass as she stands between me and Hickory's open door.

"Many apologies, Lady Quinntessa, but you'll have to come back another time. Sir Hickory is finally sleeping, and he needs his rest."

"Let her in," Hickory's groggy voice calls from inside the room.

I eye the medik. *Asleep, huh?*

She sniffs in annoyance and begrudgingly shifts to the side.

I step in and close the door behind me.

"Quinn?" Though he's the one who called me in, Hickory still sounds as surprised to see me as I am by his condition. Considering his recent episode, he looks fairly normal. He's sitting in an infirmary bed, with no sign that he was convulsing or mindlessly painting the end of the world just an hour ago. "What're you doing here?"

"I..." I stumble, realizing I haven't thought through exactly what I want to say. Tentatively, I step up to his bedside. "I came to see if you were all right." His brows lift, and I add, "What in Faylan happened to you?"

Hickory pauses. "I don't know. One minute, I'm painting, and the next, I'm waking up here. I thought I blacked out, but when I saw the painting, it all came back. Everything on that canvas, I first saw in my mind. It felt like a dream, as if I was living inside it. I think... it might have been a vision."

"A vision?" I ask.

"Shh!" Hickory looks to the door, but the medik doesn't enter.

I lower my voice. "Have you had those before?"

"Not really. Nightmares, sure. But visions that I end up painting without even knowing it? Not that I remember. Either way, it can't be a good sign. The only thing I can think of is..." Hickory pulls his satchel from the nearby chair and tugs out a book from inside. "It might have something to do with this."

It's the ancient tome with the strange symbol.

My eyes go wide. "What, you carry that thing around with you everywhere you go?" That's why I couldn't find it in his room. I try not to show how anxious I am to have it back.

"I've been analyzing it day and night. A bit obsessively, really. You see, this here…" He points to the symbol on the cover, the one that once glowed at my touch. "This symbol is the ancient sign of the Numa."

The Numa?

The gruesome depictions in Hickory's murals in Eldore come rushing back, and I shudder. The symbol on my mother's daggers is the sign of some mythical murderous giants? It doesn't make any sense.

"There are rumors—" Hickory continues, tracing gentle fingers over the symbol "—that the Mystics studied the Numa religiously. That they kept a record about them and their power. It was said to be lost long ago but, Quinn, I think this is it."

I draw back. The Mystics studied the Numa? Great. One more reason to hate them and my similarity to their fire.

"Okay… so what does all that even mean?"

"I don't know, at least not yet." Hickory's mouth purses. "But I have theories."

"Of course you do." I smirk. "Like what?"

"Well…" He hesitates. "I mean, the vision could've just been from a bad batch of pixie dust. Or maybe I'm just sleep-deprived from studying the book." Hickory leans his head into his pillow, looking blankly at the ceiling as if whatever theory he's concocted is beyond even what he considers rational.

In this moment, I know. I alone hold the power to confirm Hickory's insanity by dismissing his vision, or to further his paranoia with the story of my own mirroring nightmare.

I don't know what conclusions he's come to, but he's already studied the book endlessly and knows plenty more about the Numa and the Mystics than I do. Even if I succeed in somehow stealing the tome from him later, it would take me forever to figure it out myself. I need to know, and right now Hickory is the next clue. Perhaps if I solve the mystery of my nightmares, Gaius will finally stop haunting me.

I sigh. "If you're thinking you're crazy, you're not."

Hickory's gaze snaps up.

I raise my hands. "I mean, you're as crazy as they come, don't get me wrong. But with this…" I bite my lip, feeling like I'll regret this later. "I've been having nightmares almost every night for a while now, clear as day ever since my first night in Eldore. Your painting and my dreams—they're practically one and the same."

Hickory nearly drops the book, his good eye focusing hard on me. "You're kidding!"

It's my turn to shush him as a Nymph medik stops outside the room and peers through the window in the door. I force a reassuring smile until she turns away.

"I wish I was," I say. "Something strange happened when I touched that book. I don't know how to explain it. What do you think it all means?"

"Isn't it obvious?" Hickory insists, his eyes wild as revelations wash over him. "My vision, your dreams, the Numa... the Mystic prophecies must be coming to pass!"

Prophecies? I think back to the crazed Dryad in Shree, and the chaos and destruction he foretold. Hadn't the same Dryad mentioned a prophecy too, just before I chased the hooded figure who spoke into my mind?

"What exactly do these prophecies say?" I ask, still lost.

Hickory looks directly into my eyes. I fight the urge to back away as he recites the words with great intensity. "The Vine will wither; the sky will fall. The Numa's tale, take heed you must. A plague will mark the end of all. It comes on wings of ash and dust."

I blink.

The Vine's destruction I can identify from my dream. And we all know of the Plague. But what of the rest?

"Is that it? What does it mean? Has the book given you any more clues?"

"That's been the problem." He opens up the book.

I peer at the foreign markings that litter the pages, which are the same symbols I saw strewn over the parchment in his room.

Hickory looks up at me. "I can't read it."

CHAPTER 32

As Lord Kaito pounds his trident on the coral floor, the clanging bounces off the gleaming walls of the throne room, rattling my already-troubled mind. Around me, the wave of murmuring quiets. Morning light spills through sea glass windows, illuminating the anxious faces of clan leaders and those in the Nymph court who press in from the outer walls.

"Yesterday's Trial of Beauty was quite the spectacle," Lord Kaito begins. "Before we send the heirs off to their next destination, we must award our competitors with their rankings."

I stand at attention with my fellow heirs before the throne, back straight, eyes steady. Inside, my thoughts are a million miles away.

I peer over at Hickory. He seems fully recovered after a good night's sleep in the infirmary. I'd hoped talking with him about his visions, about the tome, would've brought some clarity about my nightmares. My daggers. Anything. But it's only weighed down my weary mind with even more questions.

"The entire tome is written in some ancient language or code," Hickory had told me. "I've been working on deciphering it, but it's going to take some time."

I sigh. I didn't like the answer then, and I don't like it now. I clench my hands into fists, resisting the urge to tap my foot on the coral floor.

Kaito's voice cuts through my thoughts. "In first place for the Trial of Beauty, having finished the challenge in the shortest amount of time —not that we had any doubt—is Sir Aeron of the Nymphs!"

Aeron's mouth breaks into a genuine grin and his clan celebrates with cheers and instruments blasting. As he approaches the dais to receive a first place medallion, my mouth twitches into a smile before I can stop myself. Even with his damaged instrument, he earned the win fair and square.

My smile steals away, however, as Arista breaks through the crowd. She jumps into Aeron's arms with a squeal, nearly knocking him over.

I try to hide it, but I bet I look as happy as the queen who is quietly stewing on the sidelines. Her face may be void of emotion, but her knuckles are white, clasping at the amulet around her neck so tightly I fear one tug will break its chain in half.

That can't be good. I take a breath and look away before she can catch me staring. It's okay. As long as Vale places second, she's still in the lead for the crown. Everything is still going according to plan. Freeing my mind of such worries, my thoughts drift back to the tome as Kaito lifts another medallion in the air.

"And in a shockingly close second... is Lady Quinntessa of the Gwyllions."

My head jerks up. *What?*

Vale's red hair whips around as she turns her shocked glare on me.

A lump forms in my throat. I think back to the trial. I hadn't exactly been tracking how long I'd been up against the Leviathan. I was a little busy trying to keep myself from becoming its dinner.

The crowd doesn't seem to know how to react either. There's no music or cheers, only whispers. As I approach the dais to receive my medallion, I spot my father lurking in a far corner, half-shadowed by a tall Nymph statue. Feyden is as still as the stone figure next to him, but he gives a single, stiff nod.

Approval? Acceptance?

Whatever the case, his thoughts are not what I should be worried about right now.

After Kaito lowers the medallion over my head, I dare another glance at the queen. She's not hiding her feelings now. Her glare bores into me, chilling me to the bone. No chance of my fire making another appearance under that look.

I swallow hard, trying to communicate with my eyes. *I didn't mean to, I swear.*

It doesn't seem to help. After Vale ranks third and Hickory in fourth, I'm swallowed up in the dispersing crowd. A passing Sylph servant bumps into me, and something slips into my hand.

It's a piece of parchment barely the size of my palm. Discreetly, I flip it over and read four words in the queen's spiraling calligraphy. This time there's a hard slant to each word.

My pod. One hour.

FOREST OF BLOOD

BLOOD

THE DRYAD HUNT

CHAPTER 33

M y sweaty fingers clench at my sides as I drag my feet down a long tube bridge, the dark ocean pressing in at every angle.

I should be stuffing my face with delicious seafood along with everyone else in the Nymph palace, our last breakfast before we shove off for the Dryad province next. Instead, I'm back in the depths of the ocean, where the only seafood I see is what's swimming around me. They almost seem to snicker at me as I answer the queen's summons to her pod.

Her twisted face when I ranked ahead of Vale in the Nymph trial plays over and over again in my mind. The queen can't fault me for simply trying to survive, can she?

Whatever the case, I can talk my way out of this.

I start to prepare my defense as I enter the dome, but halt as I near the queen's pod. A stocky feather-winged fae swoops in from an aquagate on the other end.

Moon Face?

Slipping around the pod wall, I wait for him to pass by on his way to the palace. Instead, he stops short, barging into the queen's quarters.

I thought I'd be free of him after we departed from Eldore. What is he doing here?

"Your Majesty, forgive the intrusion, I must speak with you." Moon Face's muffled voice sounds from inside.

"Not now, Jasper."

"But Your Grace, it's about the missing... *item*."

There's a pause, and the queen lowers her voice. I can barely make out the words. "Speak quickly. I have Quinn on her way right now, and no one must see you here."

Intrigued, I press my ear against the pod wall, listening harder.

"As you've instructed, we've been in Eldore searching everywhere for the ancient text, but it hasn't turned up."

The queen's voice takes a biting turn. "Vale said it must be somewhere in her chambers, though I've sensed she's hiding something from me. Return to Eldore and search again. Vale's room, the main library—turn the whole palace upside down if you have to." She pauses. "If it isn't found, I want the other competitors' things searched as well. Thankfully, they wouldn't be able to read it, but you know how detrimental it would be if someone found it who could."

My mind goes to the Mystic tome with its unreadable code. I nearly gasp out loud. It can't be the same, can it? If it is, why is it so important to her? Does the queen know how to decipher it?

"Well, what are you waiting for?" The queen's voice rises. "Get going!"

"Of course, Your Majesty," Moon Face says before shooting out the door and back toward the aquagate he entered from. I've never seen him fly so fast.

I don't want it to seem like I was right outside the whole time, so I wait, pressing my back against the outer wall of the pod. If I'm right— that the Mystic text and the book they're talking about are one and the same—I should warn Hickory. But there will be time for that. Right now, I have to appear before the queen or she might get suspicious.

I knock on the door.

"Come in." The queen's voice is calm and collected again.

"You summoned me, Your Grace?" I enter tentatively and bow, remembering why she called me here to begin with.

The queen's pod is the most lavish of all, filled with ornate bird cages as well as a slew of potted plants that cover the vanity and violet carpet. She must've brought them with her from the royal gardens.

The queen doesn't turn, busy watering a tall hydrangea.

I brace myself for whatever scolding is coming.

"Ah, Quinn. I trust you are well-rested after yesterday's events?" she asks, still consumed by tending to her plants.

"Yes, Your Majesty." I bow my head. That's a lie. After talking to Hickory about his visions and how they'd lined up with my dreams, my nightmares had been especially vivid. I blink, trying to look more awake. "And may I just say how sorry I am to have surpassed Vale in rank. It was not my intention—"

"Well, I should hope not." The queen finally puts down her watering vase and raises a brow. "I assume that from here on out, we will continue to put our best foot forward, while keeping our eye on the *true* prize." She eyes me carefully.

"Of course, Your Majesty." I nod, getting the hint. It's subtle, as I'm learning is the queen's way. If I want to be free of this life, I can't forget that I need to play her game. And make sure I don't outmatch Vale again.

"Now, I have some royal business to attend to before I depart Isinglass, so I'm asking one of my captains to lead the traveling party through the Woodlands in my stead. I'll need you to keep a close eye on Vale and keep her safe."

"Of course, Your Majesty," I say again, wondering if her royal business has anything to do with the mysterious book.

"I'll follow shortly," she assures me. "But before you enter Dryad territory, I want to give you some guidance."

I wait, expecting her to share some advantage for the next trial, but that isn't it at all.

"Do not get distracted by the puck."

"What?" I freeze, my mind racing. With her talk of the tome and Hickory fresh in my mind, I wonder if she's talking about him. Was she in the infirmary when I spoke with him last night? Or did someone tell her?

"I know your tendency is to be impulsive," she continues. "But I need you completely focused on the task at hand. Believe me, I know what it's like to be swept away by young love. It isn't worth it. Not when more important things are at stake."

Young love? I recall her story of falling in love with Prince Markus and how poorly that went for her. "Your Majesty, I'm not quite sure what you mean—"

The queen waves a graceful hand to quiet me. "Focus on the competition now, and you can always try to charm him in the future.

Believe me, I don't have much faith in his marriage arrangement lasting much longer."

Aeron. She means Aeron.

My shoulders relax, but my heartbeat quickens. Everyone saw us dancing together at the Masquerade. Could she have seen us swimming together the other evening as well? A pod lamp had flickered on just as I was leaving the pool that night. *Blast. Could it have been hers?*

"Your Grace, you have absolutely nothing to worry about—"

"Good," she cuts me off, staring at me. "I trust you to take care of this then, yes? Because I'd much rather not have to intervene again."

Again?

I blink.

What does she mean, *again*?

The queen turns back to her plants and begins to hum a tune I vaguely recognize. Then it hits me. It's the lullaby Aeron played during the trial.

The memory of Aeron's violin flashes in my mind. The snapping of its strings jabs at my side, and my breath catches.

I'd first thought Nile tampered with the instrument. Could it have been the queen? Would she really go so far to ensure my focus stays on helping Vale win the crown, even risking Aeron's death? I swallow hard. Before anything even happened between Aeron and me, the queen knew he would have had a natural advantage for his clan's trial. Slowing him down, or possibly taking him out completely, would have been an added bonus for her. She's already gotten me out of the running with our deal. I shouldn't put anything past her.

I stare at the queen with a new level of unease. She glances my way with arched eyebrows, still waiting for me to respond. "Do we understand each other?" she presses.

I try to force words out, anything at all. All I can do is nod.

If the queen is saying what I think she is, I have more to worry about than I thought. I'll just have to stay away from Aeron. I have to convince her nothing is going on between us, or who knows what she might do next.

～

The Nymphs send us off with a display of spiraling water arcs and a grand choir of singers. As we sail away, the towering palace of Isinglass descends back into the ocean depths until only bubbles linger on the surface.

Frankly, I'm glad to be finished with this vain clan and have another part of the competition under my belt. But I also lament, knowing I'm leaving my precious Silver Sea yet again for the most dangerous place yet.

The Woodlands. *Dryad territory.*

As we make port, we leave not only the ocean behind, but also most of the day's light. Twisted trees reach for the sky, blocking out most of the sun, leaving us to trudge through eerie shadows. The forest is too dense to fly through, so we travel on foot through thick greenery.

A screeching owl startles me, then a rustling sound in the bushes. I draw closer to our traveling party as I imagine beady eyes lurking in the shadows. From past pirate raids, I know creatures and even the trees themselves could be rogue Dryad changelings preparing to ambush us at any moment. I feel for my daggers hidden under my cloak. Whether the Dryad Lord has claimed to receive us in peace or not, there's no way I'm walking through the Woodlands unarmed.

As time drags on, the scenery changes. Rotting logs encumber our path and dead leaves crunch underfoot as I swat away humming insects. Branches groan in the stale breeze, many barely holding onto their last leaves.

"What's that smell?" Vale scrunches her nose.

I sniff the air. In place of fresh pine, the mustiness of moss and decay fills my nose. Every time I enter the Woodlands, another part of the forest seems to be dying a little more. I lean my hand against a tree trunk and the bark falls away, dry and brittle. Fiery visions from my nightmare flash through my mind, and I pull my hand back.

"You all right?" Aeron asks, suddenly beside me.

"I'm fine," I say, averting my eyes. The queen's warning from earlier rings in my mind.

Do not get distracted by the puck… I'd much rather not have to intervene again.

I press forward, hoping he'll get the hint. No such luck.

"I've been meaning to talk to you." He matches my pace, his voice a low whisper. I don't answer. "Are you mad at me or something?"

"No. What would I have to be mad about?" I shrug, keeping my gaze ahead.

I can do this. Even if the queen hadn't threatened him, this is for the best. Whatever almost happened between us in Isinglass, he's still promised to Arista. It's pointless to keep letting him in.

"We're competitors, Aeron," I say simply, when he continues to follow. "It's probably time we start acting like it."

"Right... Okay." His voice lightly cracks with a sadness that makes me want to take it all back.

Before I can give into the temptation, I pick up my pace and stride ahead. With every crunching step, I hate myself and this place even more.

Alys' countenance, however, seems to grow lighter the deeper we go into the forest. Her black braids bounce as she and her attendants take the lead. It's her turn to go home, though nothing feels homey to me about this place.

I may not quite understand her, but I find myself happy for her. And without former crewmates like Colt, who knew the Woodlands and always carried handy explosives for protection, I feel a lot safer with her in our company.

After what feels like hours, we finally stop at an open field near a brook for rest and a midday meal. Alys' attendants leave to go on a short hunt for food while the five of us are left behind with the queen's captain and a group of Sylph guards.

We've brought along some dried squid from Isinglass and are allowed to drink from the flowing brook, but we aren't supposed to go too far from the tents and fire pits that the attendants have set up for us.

"Have you ever been to Vyndoria?" Hickory asks me quietly, perched on a log near the flames.

"No." I cup my hands into the brook's cool water and drink deeply. "My crew often pillaged villages throughout the forest, but we never found the Dryad's capital. You?"

"I've been once, to paint a portrait for the Dryad Lord and Lady. But I was blindfolded on the way there and back so I wouldn't be able to return or lead anyone else there. I'm just glad the clans have opened up their borders for the competition so that I don't need to be blindfolded this time." He shivers. Being forced into complete blindness must have been an utter nightmare for him.

He glances behind us. Though a dozen Sylph guards are spread out around our campsite, they're either too busy looking for external dangers or consumed in conversation to notice us.

Taking the opportunity, Hickory pulls his dust pipe from his jacket and sticks a twig in the fire, using it to light the pixie dust. He inhales deeply, his body lifting off the log, floating in midair. He breathes out a puff of smoke into a glittering raven, which majestically glides away from us.

I gawk. Even his pipe smoke is artistic.

Settling down onto the log, Hickory relaxes, leaning against a rock. "By the way." He lowers his voice and peers through his good eye at me. "When are we going to talk about the you-know-what again?"

I purse my lips. I haven't told him about the queen's conversation with Moon Face, and if they were even talking about the same book. There have been too many people around us to get a moment alone. I peer around to make sure no one is able to hear us now.

I'm not sure where Alys is, but I soon spot Aeron farther down the river. Unsurprisingly, Vale is with him. I tell myself not to care. She pulls him by the hand, playfully guiding him deeper into the woods before the guards can notice. My chest tightens and, before I know it, I've shot to my feet.

If Aeron doesn't like her the way she likes him, why does he humor her? And what in the world are they always sneaking off for?

"Quinn?" Hickory says.

"We'll talk later, I promise." I trail after them, careful to not attract attention from the guards. "Let's just survive this place first."

"Okay," Hickory's shoulders slump as he follows me into the brush. "Where are we going?"

"Hush," I whisper sharply. "You don't have to come."

"Quinn, wait—"

I whip around. "What did I just say?"

His usually floppy ears perk straight up. "Did you hear that?" he asks, his good eye alert.

"Hear what?" I'm getting more annoyed as I strain to listen. "I don't hear anything."

"Something's not right." He closes his eyes and I wait, remembering his heightened senses. "I thought I heard—"

A piercing scream cuts through the forest. It's coming from the same direction Vale took Aeron. With one look at each other, Hickory and I dart through the brush, clawing our way toward the sound.

Breaking through to a small clearing, we find two figures standing at the mouth of a cave. Aeron is shielding Vale with a long branch in his hand as they inch back from a gigantic cat-like beast. *A lynxicorn.*

Its spotted fur stands on end as it hisses, baring dagger-like teeth and curling tusks, ready to slash through its enemies. Not to mention the spikes on the end of its swooshing tail and the long, pointed horn on top of its head. It could easily impale either of them in a second.

"Nice kitty, we're not here to harm you," Aeron says calmly. "Let us go, and we'll be on our way." His words warble through the air.

I hold my breath. He's trying to use his silver tongue on the beast. Good. Kaito used it on the Leviathan. Why wouldn't it work now?

But the lynxicorn narrows its cat-like eyes as it takes a threatening step forward. Its shadow swallows Aeron and Vale in darkness. Even on all fours, it's nearly twice their height. They don't stand a chance.

"You've got to be kidding me." I curse under my breath.

The lynxicorn's long, pointed ears twitch my way. *Blast.*

Turning back to Aeron, it gives him a low, menacing growl, seeming to blame him for our sudden appearance.

Aeron nudges Vale back and tightens his grip around the stick in his hand. He's going to try and battle it.

Before he can swing, the lynxicorn lifts a clawed paw and slashes through Aeron's forearm. His stick falls to the ground, snapping in half.

"No!" Vale shrieks, and my heart leaps into my throat as Aeron is knocked to the ground. Vale collapses next to him, trembling.

"Get out of here," he tells her through gritted teeth, clutching his bleeding arm. He then looks behind her where Hickory and I stand at the edge of the clearing and locks his eyes on my face. "All of you!"

The lynxicorn is not one to wait. It claws at the dirt, lowering its horned head, preparing to charge.

My jaw clenches. *Oh, no you don't.*

The queen will kill me if anything happens to Vale, and if I let Aeron die trying to save her, I'll never forgive myself. I whip out my daggers and launch forward to help fend off the beast.

Another figure beats me there, darting in between Aeron and the lynxicorn with nothing but her gloved hands.

Alys. Just like with her dragon and the Leviathan, Alys puts out a hand and stares into the beast's eyes.

The creature pauses, and Alys holds her ground as if expecting something to change.

I hold my breath, hoping it does.

Instead, the lynxicorn whips its spiked tail down right where Alys stands.

She dodges the blow just in time as the spikes drive into the earth, causing shards of rock to go flying. Rolling back her shoulders, Alys leaps onto the beast's back. She yanks at its long ears to reign it in. That only makes it angrier. It rears and bucks with a deafening roar, trying to throw her off.

Alys grips tighter, keeping her hold on the creature, but as it lands on all fours, her face drops.

Five more growling lynxicorns emerge from the brush. They're closing in on all sides, pressing us together.

We're surrounded.

I look at my daggers. They won't be enough.

"I told you I heard something," says Hickory, stepping back.

"Right now is probably not the best time for I-told-you-so's," I say, readying my blades just the same. I'm not going down without a fight.

But as a lynxicorn creeps toward us, I notice something different about its eyes.

They're red.

I look around. All of them have blood-red eyes.

Suddenly, the guards from our campsite burst into the clearing and unsheathe their swords.

"We've sent the attendants for help," the Sylph captain yells. "Get behind us."

As the guards charge the beasts, my stomach turns.

To my right, one lynxicorn slashes its claws through a guard's feathered wings. To my left, another bites through a Sylph's leg, blood spraying the ground.

Screams fill the air, but I can still distinguish the captain's voice shouting one word to the five of us through the noise. "Fly!"

I look at the others, my heart hammering in my chest.

The guards can't hold them back much longer. The lynxicorns don't have wings. Up is our only way out.

Bending my knees, I release my dragon wings and push off the ground with all my strength, hearing the rush of the others' wings catch the air and swoop up after me.

As we fly to the tops of the twisting trees, branches and thorns catch on my clothes, scraping skin. I don't stop until I break through to the open blue sky with the others. Just as I think we're safe, I halt in the air.

Heading straight toward us is a hoard of flying figures. With the sun blazing, I can only see their silhouettes. At first, they look like fae, bodies and wings similar to ours. For a moment, I think it's the rest of our traveling party coming to rescue us.

But as they draw closer, I see that their skin is ribbed and charred. It looks as if they've been burned, flecks of skin flaking off their bodies as they move. They snarl at us with disfigured faces, while flexing irregularly long arms riddled with boils.

One opens its mouth, baring his sharp fangs at us with a hungry expression.

I jerk backward. "What the...?"

"This way!" Hickory darts to the side, but we're met by even more of them.

There are dozens.

We're trapped. Again.

One of them eyes Aeron, who's favoring his wounded arm. It launches toward him with claws raised. Sunlight reflects off its sharp talons and something else between its long fingers, with a pointed end as thin as a needle.

With no time to think, there's only one escape. I grab Aeron's tunic and drag him back down into the forest below, calling to the others. "Come on!"

As we fly down through the brush, the burned creatures shriek, crashing through branches after us. Landing back in the clearing, the five of us huddle together. The dark creatures descend onto the lynxicorns, some of them mounting their backs as the beasts stand eerily still.

"Are they controlling them?" Hickory asks.

"Whatever's going on, I don't want to stick around to find out," says Aeron. "We need to get out of here."

"And how do you propose we do that?" Vale asks.

"Looks like we're going to have to fight our way out." I reveal my daggers again and head straight toward one of the lynxicorns.

Alys intercepts me. Her hands are raised, eyes full of concern.

"Alys, you may be a vegetarian, but these lynxicorns aren't." Hickory points at the remains of our guards sprawled in bloodied heaps on the other side of the clearing. A lynxicorn near the captain's lifeless body turns to us, licking its teeth. Its pack follows, boxing us in again.

Instead of heeding Hickory's warning, Alys puts her fingers to her mouth and lets out a loud whistle.

"What was that for?" Vale asks frantically. "Are we going to whistle them to death?"

"No." Hickory points to the sky. "That whistle was for *him*."

A blast of fire shoots down from above and incinerates two of the burned creatures on the spot. The others' hungry faces turn to horror as a lumbering green dragon breaks into the clearing, smoke billowing from his nostrils.

Tomah.

Fire bursts from his mouth again as he whips his tail around, sending some of the dark figures flying through the air. The others go after Tomah with a vengeance. They claw at his neck and back while lynxicorns sink sharp teeth into his legs.

I wince at the sight, but with Tomah distracting them, the beasts have all but forgotten us. This is our chance to get out of here.

"This way!" Aeron waves us on with his good arm and takes off with Vale and Hickory in tow. I move to follow but Alys is frozen in place.

"Alys, come on!" I shout.

She doesn't move, watching Tomah struggle to fend off the beasts. She steps toward him, but the dragon shoots a wall of fire in front of her, as if warning her not to get involved. She extends her wings to fly over it. He blows another blast in her direction.

"Alys!" I grab her arm.

Fury rages in her eyes as tears stream down her face.

"I know you don't want to leave him, but he wants you to go."

Through her tears, she nods, and we run through the trees, leaving Tomah behind.

CHAPTER 34

"I think we lost them." Aeron breathes hard as we finally stop running. No longer able to hear Tomah's cries, the Woodlands have become eerily quiet.

I look at Aeron's arm. He's still clutching it. The bleeding has slowed, but without treatment, I'm sure it'll get infected. At least we got out of there when we did. He could have been killed. We all could have. I can't get the image of the dark flying creatures out of my mind. And the one moving to stab Aeron with—whatever that was.

"What were those things?" Vale collapses onto a nearby boulder, looking up at Hickory.

"I have no idea," Hickory says, leaning against a tree. "Alys?"

Alys looks back with a vacant stare. She shakes her head. If even *she* doesn't know what they are, we're in more trouble than I thought.

"Do you know where we are now?" I ask her tentatively.

With our guards torn to shreds, and the rest of our party nowhere to be found, we're completely alone. Still, Alys has to know these woods like the back of her hand. "Can you lead us the rest of the way?" I ask.

Alys looks around, trying to get her bearings.

"Can't we rest first?" Vale complains.

"Not unless you're sure those things won't catch up to us," I say. "We should keep moving."

"We're far enough for now," Vale presses. She hauls herself to her feet and points to the brush behind us. "Alys, you and Quinn go look for some berries or something," she directs in a royal tone. "Hickory, figure out some way to start a fire. Aeron and I will look for berries over here."

"What, so you can stumble into another beast's lair and almost get us killed again? I don't think so." I glare, not liking her ordering us around one bit. That, and the fact that her and Aeron would be alone again.

"Ladies, ladies. Pointing fingers isn't going to help anything," Aeron starts, but we ignore him.

Vale strides toward me. "We'll need some kind of sustenance if we hope to make it the rest of the way. We haven't eaten for hours."

"And whose fault is that?" I step forward to meet her. "The hunting party would've brought food back if you hadn't run off." Though we haven't been on our own for long, I'm growing more agitated with *Her Highness* by the minute. "And what gives you the right to play leader? You're not the queen yet, princess."

Vale crosses her arms. "Okay. Do *you* have any better ideas?"

My jaw clenches. On the Minnow, Whit had always been more of the planner, and I was the action girl. I'm always the one who gives the orders. But Vale's right. If we keep pushing ourselves with empty stomachs, we'll only be slower and weaker if attacked again.

"Fine." I snort in defeat. "Let's be quick about it."

I motion for Alys to follow, but she shakes her head. Moving to a tree, she pulls down its leaves to reveal bright blue berries.

"See," I say. "Alys already found food. Now we can keep moving."

But instead of putting them in her mouth, she crushes them with her hand and walks over to Aeron, peering at his wounds.

Aeron tentatively offers her his arm, and she slathers on the sticky blue juice. He hisses at her touch, but then his shoulders relax. Snatching a nearby leaf, Alys dabs at the wound, the scratches now dried into dark red slashes.

"Thanks." Aeron breathes, obviously feeling relief from the pain.

Alys isn't finished. Next, she looks around and points to a glossy mushroom with purple spots.

"Another healing plant?" I ask, feeling like I've figured out the game.

Alys shakes her head violently.

"Not healing. Poisonous," Vale says.

Alys purses her lips and nods.

Vale draws toward it for a closer look. "It's a highshroom. Strong hallucinogen, too. Don't worry," Vale assures her. "I'm an expert in plants, so between you and me, we'll be safe."

Though I'm no less frustrated, this seems satisfactory for Alys, and we depart on our assignments.

∾

Walking with Alys is, well, quiet. Mostly me pointing at plants and her shaking her head yes or no. I don't mind. I go to ask her about yet another plant when rustling comes from a bush nearby.

I grab my dagger, preparing for another dark figure, but Alys puts out a hand to steady my advance. Carefully, she inches toward the bush and pushes back its branches to reveal a jackalope caught in a hunting trap. Though it thrusts its tiny antlers at us, pink nose flaring, blood pools out from where its leg is nearly severed, staining its white fur coat.

"Well, this works out perfectly," I say. "I much prefer rabbit to berries anyway."

After making sure the trap's owner isn't lurking close by, I turn to find Alys glaring.

"What?" I ask defensively. "This poor, suffering creature is going to die anyway. Unless there's a healing plant around here that can reattach a limb."

Alys looks back to the jackalope struggling for breath and rolls up her sleeves. Her arms, usually hidden under her clothing, are covered in marvelous, swirling black tattoos. The same kind that frame her face.

Then she reaches for her gloves, and I hold my breath. I've always imagined her hands were withered or covered in boils, something that would have further incited the death rumor. But as she slips the gloves off, her hands are not evil-looking at all. They are beautifully young and smooth. Only the tattoos reaching all the way to her fingertips mar them.

I relax.

Until Alys reaches out to the creature.

"What are you doing?" I crouch next to her. Am I about to see Alys' death grip in action?

She ignores me and places her hands on the dying animal. The struggling jackalope twitches, then relaxes, closing its eyes.

Well, that was quick. But Alys is only getting started.

With the creature completely still, she gently works the jackalope out of the trap and cradles it in her arms. Alys presses her eyes shut like she's concentrating. Her face contorts, sweat beading on her forehead.

I'm so preoccupied with her expression that I nearly miss what's happening with her tattoos. They're no longer black, but beginning to glow a bright white. And wait—are they moving? I shake my head and blink furiously. It's not a trick of the eye. Her tattoos swirl over her skin as if they're overlaid vines and not a part of her at all. They glow brighter as I watch, creeping further down the sides of her arms.

Captivated by the spectacle, goosebumps climb up the back of my neck. *What in Faylan is going on?*

I look at Alys' face, her eyes squeezed tight, her teeth clenched as if she's the one in pain. The more her face contorts with agony, the more the tattoos glow.

The jackalope kicks.

Though its eyes are still closed, its chest moves up and down. It's still breathing!

Soon, the leg completely heals, leaving only dried blood surrounding the wounded area. I've seen Dryads heal with herbs and incantations before, but Alys isn't using any of that.

Her tattoos return to black, and Alys relaxes, though tears prick at her eyes. She breathes in deeply and releases the animal.

The jackalope's eyes flutter open, and it stands up on its hind legs. Looking at Alys as if to offer her its thanks, it bounds away like it was never hurt at all.

Did Alys *really* heal the creature just by using her hands? It looked as if she even took on the jackalope's pain as her own.

As Alys replaces her gloves, all I can do is stare, mouth agape. She isn't an agent of death or even a common medik. She's one of the ancient Dryad healers I've only heard stories about.

I have so many questions. I've never wanted to communicate with someone so much.

Seeming to understand, Alys rubs a spot on her arm with her

fingers as if it's sore and then points to it. I tentatively step closer as her tattoos return to a stationary state, except for the area she touches.

Like a branch growing out of a vine, a new part of the tattoo grows and swirls around until it settles into a shape. A rough outline of a jackalope.

I reach out to touch it, then stop.

"These aren't tattoos," I say, more of a statement than a question. "They're scars."

Alys nods.

"This is amazing, Alys," I exclaim. "Why in all of Faylan would you keep this a secret?" She could have used her ability to heal Aeron earlier, but she didn't. "And why choose to show *me*?"

Alys sighs heavily, her shoulders lifting and releasing with frustration.

We have to figure out a way to communicate. I look at her tattooed arms as if they can answer for her. My eyes settle on an area I didn't notice earlier.

A familiar symbol calls to me. Three insular circles, overlaid by a flower.

It's the sign of the Numa.

"Alys." I point to it. "How did you get this one? Do you know what it means?"

Before Alys can respond, another scream rings through the forest.

My head snaps toward the sound, and the word comes out of my mouth before I can even register it.

"Vale!"

CHAPTER 35

I t's definitely Vale's piercing scream. Alys and I spring into action. Reaching our campsite, we find Hickory frantically looking around, not sure what to do.

"Did you hear that?" His eyes are wide with panic. "I think it was Vale."

"I know," I say breathlessly. "Which direction did they go?"

Hickory points, and the three of us charge ahead as another scream sounds.

"Help! Somebody, help!"

It's definitely Vale.

"This way!" I call as we follow the voice through the trees.

Reaching a large willow tree, I look up. Aeron and Vale hang amidst its branches, stuck in a Dryad trap. The roped netting has them wrapped in a tight ball. Vale almost elbows Aeron in the face as she points at us.

"See?" Vale shoots Aeron a smug look of triumph. "I told you if I screamed loud enough, they'd find us."

"Did you have to scream right in my ear though?" Aeron says, still holding his hands over them.

I breathe a sigh of both relief and anger. "Blast it, Vale, we thought you were dying!"

"Well, you heard me, didn't you?" She's still smug.

"So did the entire forest! Did you already forget about the flock of dark creatures that almost had us for lunch?"

Vale's freckled cheeks pale.

I shake my head, taking out my dagger to cut them down. "We have to get out of here, and fast, before anyone or any*thing* finds us."

It's too late. The crack of a branch sounds, and we whip around to face our fate.

A large company of Dryad warriors emerge from the brush with bows drawn. Some of them are changelings, shapeshifting from trees and animals into fae right before our eyes.

Alys steps forward, her hands giving signals I don't understand.

From the troop, a large brown and white wolf steps forward, morphing into a youthful and towering Dryad. "Hold your fire!" he calls. His deep brown, muscular chest and arms are covered in Dryad markings. His sharp eyes peer out from white paint, the same coloring the wolf had around its eyes just moments ago. With that piercing glare and facial structure so similar to Alys, they have to be related somehow.

"Alys," he says.

She bounds to him, and he pulls her into a relieved embrace. For the first time, her mouth breaks open all the way into a joyous smile, giving me reassurance that everything is going to be okay.

"Put down your weapons." The Dryad says and his warriors obey. "We've been looking for you ever since your traveling party showed up without you. Tomah returned barely alive. Everyone's been worried sick."

At the mention of her dragon, Alys' hands fly up in a slew of signs. The Dryad gently lowers her arms.

"Tomah will be fine, Alys. Our best mediks are attending to him. After seeing his condition, we all thought… I'm just so glad you're okay." He hugs her again. "What in Faylan happened out there?"

"We were ambushed." The words fly out of my mouth. "We barely made it out alive."

The Dryad's eyes narrow at me. "These must be your competitors." His voice is laced with judgement. "What are you talking about? Who ambushed you?"

"Well…" Hickory starts. "First it was a pack of lynxicorns, but then..." He looks at the rest of us.

"Other creatures came." Aeron presses his face up against the netting. "They had the look of fae, wings and all, but their appearance was twisted—gruesome-looking. Like they were living victims of a fire. Burnt to a crisp."

"It seemed like they had some kind of control over the lynxicorns too," Vale adds.

"Even Alys couldn't reason with them," I say.

Alys' eyes are glassy again. She's probably thinking about Tomah, wishing she could have done more.

The other Dryads exchange knowing looks. Their leader takes a breath, his eyes pressed shut. "Goblins."

"Goblins?" Vale asks, scrunching her nose in confusion.

My stomach plummets. If Vale hasn't heard of them in any of her studies, what exactly are we dealing with?

"That's what we've taken to calling them, anyhow," the Dryad continues. "We have no idea what they truly are, what they want, or where they come from. They appeared a few weeks ago, terrorizing some of our smaller villages and hunting parties, stealing our supplies." He looks to Alys, whose eyes are wide. "We thought we chased them back into the mountains. Haven't seen any of them for at least a week's time." He turns to the four of us. "Not until you all showed up."

"Are you trying to accuse us of something?" I say.

He steps toward me, but Alys crosses in front of him, placing a firm hand on his chest. She gives me a look of warning as well, then signals to him again.

"Alys says that you're competitors… but not *enemies*." He emphasizes the last word with a heavy tone of suspicion. Accepting a bow from one of his comrades, he puffs out his chest as he motions to his warriors. "You'll be safe with us as we travel the rest of the way. I'm Leman, the first of Alys' younger siblings, leader of the Dryad warriors." His eyes narrow at me as he growls through his words. "Welcome to the Woodlands."

～

Once the Dryads cut Vale and Aeron down, Leman and his troops lead us the rest of the way to Vyndoria. The eerie sounds of the woods increase around us as evening falls. More than once, Vale complains as we trudge through mud and brush. I give her a warning pinch every time.

Tired of being her keeper, I look at Aeron to pinch her in my stead.

He grins as if to say, *With pleasure.*

I smirk back, savoring the bit of easiness between us again. I quicken my pace to match my speed with Alys ahead.

"*Younger* brother, huh?" I ask her quietly.

In front of us, Leman towers over pretty much everyone. He shoots a quick look over his shoulder, but doesn't say anything.

Alys smiles and shrugs. She's definitely in lighter spirits now that she's back with her folk and knowing that Tomah will be okay. I want to ask her more about her tattoos and symbols, though. I just need to figure out how.

"You were signing with Leman before," I whisper.

She nods.

"Do you think he could teach me?"

"*Leman* does not cooperate with *pirates*," Leman answers for her.

"Oh, so you know who I am." I smirk.

"Unfortunately. Wasn't hard to pick out the Gwyllion pirate with your dragon wings." He stares straight ahead as he walks. "If I had things *my* way, there wouldn't be pirates or any competitions promising false peace." He scoffs, his words turning to mumbles. "Sacrificing the best of our own. Battling it out for a crown while evil creatures run rampant and there's less pixie dust to go around every day. Ridiculous."

Alys folds her arms in a huff, and Leman eyes her.

"So, you would prefer war," I say.

Leman stops, and like a pack of wolves following its alpha, so does his troop. "That's not for *me* to decide. We've arrived."

In front of us is a wall of gray, speckled rock.

"What do you mean, *we've arrived*?" I ask.

Leman ignores me and reaches into a drawn pouch around his neck, pulling out a lump of green powder. From where I stand, it gives off a fresh, earthy scent.

Dipping two fingers in the powder, Leman approaches the wall and draws a series of Dryad symbols on the surface while whispering unintelligible words. As if the words give the powder a life of its own, the edges of the symbols grow out like vines, forming shapes like Alys' tattoos.

Finally, they settle into the image of a vine-covered door. I lean forward to get a better look, waiting for Leman to push it open or pull at a handle. Instead, he walks straight through it.

I startle backward.

"Did he just—walk through a wall?" Hickory asks behind me, his voice climbing with excitement.

Before I can resist, Alys grabs my arm and pulls me through after him. I brace myself for impact, but I only feel a rush of air before opening my eyes.

Leman stands in front of us as the others step through, motioning to the glorious scene before us. "Welcome to Vyndoria."

$\sim$

No wonder it was impossible for any of Maverick's pirate crews to find Vyndoria in the past.

In addition to the magical door in the stone, their homes are built right into a series of monstrous trees. Their rounded roofs jut out of the trunks, emulating giant mushrooms that surely help to keep them hidden from anyone flying overhead as well.

As evening sets, the light in each of the cabins glows brightly, attracting fireflies that flutter around. It's a magical sight.

The most striking aspect is that Vyndoria is not like the dying, twisted trees that cover much of the Woodlands. Everything is a lush green color, vibrant with life.

As we approach the largest tree, a small group is gathered, too wrapped up in their murmuring to notice us until—

"Alys!" a shrill little voice calls, and the group turns, rushing our way all at once. A whole slew of Dryad sprites and younglings reach us first, practically knocking Alys over.

In the commotion, Leman stops two Dryads on their way over, talking to them in hushed tones. I recognize them as the Dryad Lord and Lady from the previous trials, the lord with his swirling ram horns and his wife with her green tattoos, marking her as a plant changeling.

"Sister, sister!" one of the littlest sprites cries out to Alys as she picks her up.

"We missed you so much!" another exclaims as he hugs her legs.

Quickly moving out of their way before I'm trampled, I mentally count the number of bouncing heads. There are ten of them, plus Leman and Alys, making a total of twelve. I nearly fall over in shock. I've never seen such a large family before.

"The Dryads aren't joking when they say *go forth and multiply,* huh?" Aeron whispers to me, and I choke back a laugh.

"Vale!" The queen rushes toward us from one of the nearby trees. Even with our delay, I'm surprised she beat us here from whatever mysterious *royal business* she had. She breaks into tears as she reaches us, hugging Vale tightly. "Thank Faylan you're safe."

As hard as the queen is on her, it's clear she truly cares about her daughter. Though Vale looks like she might die of embarrassment, I would have taken it any day. If my father were here, he'd probably give me a scolding for not taking out all the goblins myself, then send me back out there to finish the job.

"Thank Faylan, they're *all* safe." Dryad Lord Torlon and Lady Navi stand with Alys and Leman between them. "At least, until the trial," he adds, still smiling.

Some of us laugh nervously. Though our travels have been treacherous, the real challenge hasn't even begun yet.

Standing next to Leman, Lord Torlon is a slighter, aged version of his son, his black and gray beard reaching down to his chest. As if compensating for a battle wound, he leans on his staff of twisted wood that encircles a clouded orb at the top. His deep brown eyes hold a measure of kindness as he looks at each of us.

"Leman has informed us of the dangers that you faced today. Considering the ordeal, I'm instituting a day of rest tomorrow while our warriors scour the perimeter for these goblins. I will also personally give our champions a proper tour of not only the deadly dangers of the forest, but also the vibrant life of our sanctuary here in Vyndoria." He motions to the beauty that surrounds us. "For now, it would do us all good to get some rest."

At the mention of rest, the heaviness in my limbs increases, and I long for a bed. Thankfully, we're led to our chambers nestled in an enormous tree nearby. Entering through an opening at the bottom, we climb up the staircase that winds inside the hollowed-out trunk until I'm dropped off in front of a round wooden door.

Inside is a small, cozy space lit by a firefly-filled lantern. The smell of fresh flowers on the little table soothes me as I notice my trunks have already been brought up and unpacked. I collapse on the soft bean-filled bed nestled in the corner. It's hard to feel completely settled and safe, even as I pull a pillow close to my chest.

My mind is spinning with the events of the last couple of days, so many of them still unsolved. Hickory's vision, the queen's secret conversation, the strange goblin creatures, Alys' powers, and the Numa symbol on her arm.

Besides the trial coming up, I have an unsettling feeling that there are even darker dangers ahead. Fearing the nightmares of Gaius that await me in sleep, my hand reaches down between the mattress and box spring. I've stashed my daggers there once again. I touch them for comfort. Eventually, I succumb to my heavy eyelids and drift off, wondering what the days ahead will hold.

CHAPTER 36

The next morning, I'm groggy, but glad not to have woken up from my usual nightmares for once. After I dress, I'm led outside for breakfast on a sunlit terrace surrounded by climbing greenery and the morning songs of birds.

A series of high-top tables with legs of twisted wood are scattered throughout the space, with platters of varying faerie fruit featured at each. My mouth waters as I walk from spread to spread, ignoring the stares of Dryads mingling around each table as I take one of every juicy fruit I can find.

"Lily tarts!" I exclaim, not even ashamed of my sprite-like excitement. I nearly drop my plate to hurry toward my favorite dessert. I pop a few into my mouth, the fresh, tangy flavors sending my tastebuds spinning.

Lily tarts back home were usually imported, or made with ingredients no longer fresh by the time they reached the mountains. These warm, gooey tarts in my mouth must have just been made. A soft moan of joy escapes my lips.

"Sounds like you're eating something simply awful." Aeron approaches my table, eyes traveling from the platter to my face, which is surely smeared with tart juice.

"Oh, they are," I say with my mouth still full, putting out an arm between him and the delicious treats. "Truly terrible. In fact, I'd best eat all of them so none of you have to suffer."

"How self-sacrificing of you." Aeron folds his arms with a grin.

The wounds on his right arm catch my eye, and I reach toward him without thinking, my fingers grazing the slashes that are now scarred over. No sign of infection.

"These look better," I say, glancing up at him.

"Better now," he says, staring at my fingers and then back at me.

Blood rushes to my face and I pull away, returning to the lily tarts. "Good," I say. Internally, I curse myself. *Quinn, what are you doing?*

"I've never understood fae who like those things." Vale appears on the other side of the table, her eyes flicking between Aeron, me, and the tarts. Her mouth twists as she uses a delicate hand to toss a piece of fruit into her mouth, holding her plate away from the tarts as if they might infect her breakfast. "They're much too sour. How can you stand them?"

I roll my eyes and jam another in my mouth, munching loudly. *Can't a pixie enjoy her favorite food in peace?* I make a face back at her, mimicking her expression. Even with my mouth full, I'm about to respond with something equally snarky when another voice cuts in.

"They are definitely an *acquired* taste, my dear."

The three of us turn to find the queen approaching, and I gulp down the rest of the tart in one forced swallow. Subtly, I shift as far away from Aeron as I can. Hopefully she knows I wasn't the one instigating our interaction.

"I trust you are all well-rested and ready for the day?" she asks, adjusting the amulet around her neck.

We nod.

"Good. We must all put our best foot forward, keeping our eyes on the *prize*." Her stare lingers on me as if to say, *I'm watching you.* My insides twist.

"If I could have your attention," Lord Torlon's voice carries over the terrace as he emerges between two flowering hedges with Alys, tapping the bottom of his staff on a nearby rock. "Once you've filled your bellies, we'll begin the Woodland tour as promised. Leman and his warriors have scouted the area to make sure it's safe, and a few of them will accompany us as we go. You'll also get a glimpse of the nursery where we keep the many young herbs and plants we care for. As you know, the Dryad fae are protectors and cultivators of all life, and defenders of the Sacred Vine. We only kill to eat—and some of us don't even do that." He smiles at Alys.

"No, she only kills other fae with her death hands," Vale whispers to me.

I nod back, not wanting her to know Alys' secret.

"We hope you enjoy our tour today," Lord Torlon says before his expression grows serious. "If I were you, I'd pay close attention to what you learn, as it may help you with the Trial of Life later this week."

∼

As we walk through the forest, Lord Torlon points out a variety of plants and their uses.

Hickory can't stop feverishly sketching in his notebook, taking in all the sights and colors as well as the many small critters that progressively join our trek through the forest.

Like the fish in Isinglass, they seem to gravitate toward Alys. Birds, foxes, and even snakes creep and slither out from the foliage in her wake. At one point, a chipmunk lands on her shoulder, nuzzling her cheek.

I try my best to stay engaged and remember what Lord Torlon is saying. Though it's all unmistakably beautiful, frankly, I'm bored. Trees and bushes, flowers and vines. After a while, everything starts to look the same, making it easy to get turned around. At least out on the sea I have the sun and stars to guide me.

Vale, on the other hand, is having the time of her life, especially as we enter the enclosed nursery with rows and rows of different vegetables, fruits, and other vegetation. She can't help herself, naming as many different plant species and facts as she can rattle off before Lord Torlon even gets the chance to say them himself.

He's patient with her, and I marvel at him. I surely wouldn't be.

"This one is…" the Dryad Lord begins again.

"Oh, that's a marshing fern!" Vale exclaims, rushing to crouch near it. "I've been looking for this exact coloring for ages! May I?" She pulls out a pair of small shears from her dress pocket and gives the lord a sweet smile.

Torlon shakes his head. "Unfortunately, this plant, along with many others in our care, has become so rare that we don't extract it unless it gives itself to us of its own free will."

"I see." Vale slowly puts her shears away, trying not to look disappointed.

"Why have some plants become so rare?" Aeron asks.

Lord Torlon smiles. "An excellent question. Any thoughts?" He peers around at us like an instructor with his students.

Hickory looks up from his sketchbook. "Perhaps because the rest of the Woodlands are much drearier? It's so lush and green here."

"Yes, though the Woodlands weren't always such a dreary place," Torlon says sadly.

"What happened?" I ask, recalling the rotting parts of the forest we passed during our travels.

"To explain that, I must first tell you more about one plant that we will not visit today, though it is our top priority: the Sacred Vine." Lord Torlon motions upward beyond the trees, where we can just make out the Vine's stalk climbing into the sky in the distance. "Does anyone know why the Sacred Vine is so important?"

Vale hesitates. "Because without it, all of Sylph territory wouldn't exist?"

I roll my eyes. *What a tragedy that would be.*

"This is true," Lord Torlon confirms. "But just as all living things in Eldore grow from the Vine's branches, it is our belief that it is the same here on the land. That the Sacred Vine connects us all. As our creation story explains, it's where all life in Faylan began. All plants come from and are connected to the Vine. It communicates to the entire world through its roots that stretch through our land."

A dark cloud seems to fall over Torlon's glimmering eyes. "Ever since the moonrain drought began, the Sacred Vine has suffered and is slowly dying. This is why our clan holds fast to the moonrain dance, hoping it will one day return. Because when the Sacred Vine suffers, we all suffer."

Scenes from my dreams and Hickory's painting spin through my mind. The world on fire. The Vine crashing down. Out of the corner of his good eye, Hickory steals a glance at me, probably having the same thoughts.

"That's why medical and food supplies are dwindling so quickly?" Vale asks, looking back at the marshing fern.

"Precisely." Torlon nods solemnly. "That's partly why we created the protective barrier around Vyndoria, to act as a sanctuary where we've been able to better care for the plants and creatures. We must save what we can. Though, of course, we cannot save everyone."

Lord Torlon motions us forward to a field covered in young, budding trees. They're surrounded by wildflowers and piled stones at their bases. The trees look strategically planted in rows upon rows. A sinking thought seizes me.

"Are those... graves?" I ask.

Lord Torlon nods. "Yes, we plant a new tree for each life we have lost, and we have lost many to famine and plague over the years. Including Alys' older sister."

He points to one of the more mature trees where Alys is already kneeling, her hand on the base of the trunk, her head hung low. An ache grows in my chest, remembering the utter despair that overwhelmed me at Gaius' tomb. By the tree's growth, I can tell it's been many years since Alys lost her sister. Yet, tears trail down her cheeks as if the pain of losing her hasn't softened with time like I would have hoped it would.

"Let us continue. Alys will follow," Lord Torlon says gently.

The others meander after him, but I linger for a moment behind a tree. Alys' hands slowly fall to the ground, her shoulders slumped. Then her muscles tighten as she tears out a handful of wildflowers in frustration and casts them aside. I think about going to her, not knowing what I would do or say, just that I know her pain. I hesitate as Alys wipes away her tears.

Quickly glancing around, she doesn't seem to notice me and replants the wild flowers with care, removing a glove to press them into the dirt. As her tattoos take on a soft glow, the torn, bent flowers reconnect to the soil and bloom even wilder than before.

Sighing, I step back, leaving before I'm noticed. All I can think of is what it must be like for Alys to have such an ability, but not be able to save her own sister.

∾

"Do you believe what the Dryad Lord said about the Sacred Vine?" Vale asks as we spar. The queen has found a hidden cove for us to train in the forest, but all Vale wants to do is talk.

"Would it surprise you that I really couldn't care less?" I bring my blade down, and Vale barely blocks it in time. "What I *do* care about is not having to try so hard to make you look capable of beating me in the final trial."

"That's not fair." Vale pouts. "I've gotten better."

I snicker. "Not good enough. Not yet."

Vale's shoulders slump as she draws in the dirt with her blade.

I shake my head. I'm not going to get anything effective out of her while she's so distracted.

"What's wrong?" I sigh, trying to channel some of Lord Torlon's patience.

Vale shrugs. "I don't know. I guess I figured if my father was such a natural fighter, I would be too."

"Well, you'll never become a great fighter with that attitude. Come, tell me why you want to be queen."

"What?" Vale seems thrown off by the question. She lifts her chin. "What do you mean? It's my destiny as the Sylph princess to follow in my parents' footsteps. Isn't that enough?"

"Battle isn't just about physical strength. It's about strength of mind too." I point a finger to my temple. "And I don't mean memorizing a million facts. You've got to know the goal behind your actions. You've got to have drive behind the swing of your blade to win." I swing my sword toward the branch of a tree, and it slices in two. "The blade is only as strong as the one who wields it."

"I—I..." Vale stammers.

"What would be your first decree as queen?" I try to help her along. She just looks at me blankly. Has she really never thought about this before? "Okay, well, what would you want to do if you *didn't* become queen?"

Vale's fair freckled skin pales even more at the thought. "I... I guess I like learning things. I'm good at it, at least. Ancient languages. Potions. But, honestly? I have no idea. My mother's never really been particularly interested to know what I find enjoyable. Maybe if my father were still here, he would..."

For the first time since I've known her, Vale grows still and quiet. Almost sad.

Remembering the mother I barely knew, I wrap my dark curly hair around my finger, wondering if it's the only thing I inherited from her. I still don't know what connections she and her daggers might have to the Mystics or the Numa. There's still so much I don't know. Things I wish I could ask her.

"Although…" Vale studies her blade and swings it through the air. "It's strange. I might not be as good as my father was, but I do feel closer to him in times like this. Doing something he loved." She looks at me as if she forgot I was here and shakes her head. "Must have been nice to have your father teach you all this stuff growing up."

"*Nice* isn't exactly the word I'd use." All I can remember from training sessions with my father are times filled with yelling and disappointed looks. And Gaius attending to my cuts and bruises when Feyden wasn't looking.

"You didn't really know your mother, right?" Vale asks without reservation, as if she's asking me about the weather.

I sheathe my blade with a snap. "I'd rather not talk about it," I say coolly.

"Oh, so you can pry into my personal matters, but I can't ask you one simple question?"

"I'm the teacher, you're the student." One of my father's favored excuses. I clench heated fists. Obviously Vale is done training for the day, and I'm not about to start a story-swapping session with her. "We'll pick this up again tomorrow."

"Quinn, wait…" Vale starts.

But I've already walked away.

CHAPTER 37

I walk back to the main village in a huff, whacking leaves and branches out of my way as I go.

Who does Vale think she is, asking such questions? It's not because she cares about me or my mother, not really. We can help each other get what we want, but I'm not going to bond with her. It's just not going to happen.

As I enter the village, my mood instantly lightens. Unlike the quiet evenings, the space is alive with activity today.

Lady Navi is gathered with a cluster of mothers, sorting baskets of fruits and healing herbs. Another group flies among the high branches, hanging clean linens as they chatter. One of them yelps as a flock of sprites fly straight through the linens. She scolds them as they swoop around the trees with the local birds in a game of tag.

On my right, a group of mediks brush past, carrying in wilted plants and injured animals from the forest.

"This way." Lord Torlon guides them with his staff toward a new tent set up for overflow.

Past them, Leman and his warriors stand in a fenced-off area. Some practice their shifts to changeling forms while others spar, probably readying themselves for another scouting trip.

Amidst the lively scene, there's something calming about the Dryad folk and their way of life. They move about their day at a much slower pace than the busy Sylphs or performing Nymphs. The air is fresh. The village is at peace. No wonder they've hidden their little sanctuary away from the rest of the world.

Lost in it all, I don't notice Alys until I hear dragon footsteps stomping through. Alys straddles Tomah's back, smiling from ear to ear as she pats his back.

"Well, look who's up and about," I say warmly to the dragon. It's the first time I've seen Tomah since he saved us. He's still pretty beat up, moving much slower than I remember. Surprisingly, he sniffs my hand and gently rubs his nose against it. Not so afraid of the fire breathing beast anymore, I pat his scales gently.

"He's doing a lot better," says a high-pitched voice from atop the beast.

For a moment, I think I'm hearing Alys miraculously speak, until one of her little sisters pokes out from behind her. "His medik said it's time we take him for a walk." She releases her wings and flutters down to the ground, Alys following close behind.

"Well, I'm very glad to hear that." I look down at the little sprite with colorful flowers woven into her long braids. Her bright white smile practically glows against her dark skin, which is lined with green tattoos. "And who might you be?"

"I'm Ivy, Alys' sister. Well, one of them anyway. But the best one, right, Alys?" Ivy smiles up at her before turning back to me, talking a mile a minute. "You're Captain Shade, aren't you? I've heard so many stories! Like the one where you fought off fifty Sylph guards by yourself in the middle of Shree and made off with their trove of pixie dust and weapons."

I smile, seeing my own childhood curiosity and love for adventure in her demeanor. Some of the details of her story are vastly exaggerated, like the number of guards and the fact that I definitely hadn't done that job alone. I wonder whether I should correct her, but she doesn't give me the chance.

"I bet you have so many more stories too! Could you tell me one?" Ivy asks, her big brown eyes wide and eager.

Alys puts a hand on her sister's shoulder, shaking her head, and signs something to her.

Ivy hurriedly signs back.

"What did she say?" I ask Ivy, fascinated by the exchange.

Ivy huffs. "She said your real name is Quinn, and that I should be more polite. Sorry, I get in trouble a lot for asking too many questions."

"That's okay. Thanks for the translation." I laugh as Alys smiles at her sister. "Actually Ivy, I'll make you a deal, if your sister is okay with it." I crouch down until our eyes are level. "Alys and I have been trying to communicate, but I don't know how to read her signs. How about I trade you some stories in exchange for some signing lessons?"

Ivy's eyes light up. She looks at Alys expectantly.

Alys chews her lip. I can tell part of her wants to approve. As many questions as I have for her, I sense there are things she wants to communicate to me as well.

"Ivy." Leman strides up, placing a strong hand on her shoulder.

I purse my lips as I slowly rise to meet his intense gaze.

"I think Mother is looking for you," he says to Ivy, though his glower is still intently focused on me.

Ivy peers up at him. "Aw, but I was just—"

"Now, Ivy," he says firmly. "Alys, why don't you go with her. Make sure she doesn't get into any more trouble."

Alys' brows furrow. Leman narrows his eyes right back until she gives up.

Though Alys is older, Leman obviously sees himself as the one in charge. It reminds me of Gaius, and my chest tightens. I almost miss our bickering. I would give anything to have him here still, even if it was just to have him reprimand me one more time.

Alys doesn't seem to feel the same. She grips Ivy's hand tightly and they fly back to the top of the dragon. With a tap from Alys, Tomah lumbers away. Ivy looks longingly back at me, not happy about the situation in the least.

"What do you think you're doing?" Leman grabs my arm hard and pulls me under the shadow of a nearby tree. "Ivy doesn't need someone like *you* filling her head with any more crazy thoughts."

"Someone like *me*?" I yank my arm away. "I was just—"

"And I don't know what you want with Alys, but I'm warning you —stay away from her too. Eat our food, enjoy our hospitality, and compete in your useless trial. Live or die, I don't care. Just stay away from my family, *pirate*. Or else."

My blood boils. I want to yell back. And yet, how can I hold his threats against him? I *am* a pirate. A pirate who repeatedly looted their clan in the past without mercy. He was probably a part of some of those very hunting parties that my crew used to steal from. There's no reason he should trust me.

"Fine," I say, though I don't really mean it. I don't need him watching my every move, but I don't want him to think I'm weak either. "You better watch yourself too, *Wooder*," I warn, daring to use the term for a lowly Dryad. I lift my chin. "For all you know, I might be your future queen."

"Ha!" Leman spits out a laugh. "Can you really be that naïve? If the Sylphs lose, what makes you think they'll give up their power so easily? Just because of a simple agreement? And if they win, do you think the other clans will accept it quietly? Mark my words, this competition isn't going to resolve anything. So, when that all goes down…" He pats the bow on his back. "I'll be ready." Pointing his finger at me, he backs away. "In the meantime, keep your distance, pirate. I'm warning you—stay away."

As Leman disappears into the crowd, I lean back against the trunk of the tree. I can't even be mad at him. He's right. The queen is already doing everything in her power to make sure that Vale wins. Even going so far as to bribe me. Though I respect Leman's protectiveness of his family, I need the queen's deal to work.

"Well, that went well," a voice says from above. Hickory is lounging on an upper branch of the tree with his sketchbook in hand and a pixie dust pipe in his mouth.

"Leman seems to like me more and more every day," I joke back, shaking off the encounter. "How long have you been up there?"

"Long enough." Hickory shifts over on the branch. "It's a great view from up here. Come and see."

Hickory's right. As I make my way up, more and more of Vyndoria comes into view. Their treehouse homes climb all the way up the trunks into the high branches as vine-wrapped bridges and branch-bended stairs create a maze of connections between them. Dryads poke out of tree holes, calling to each other as the sound of twittering birds fills the air. A group of sparrows fly through cascading beams of light, one landing in a branch above us.

I settle down on Hickory's seeing side so he doesn't have to keep shifting his head, leaning over to view his latest sketch of the village. He's captured each detail perfectly.

"Wow." I whisper, wishing I could create something so beautiful. "What else do you have in there?"

"Mostly sketches of the plants Lord Torlon mentioned, so I can study them. Used some of my watercolors to differentiate them, too. Here's the red kinto berries. Great supply of energy. Not sure how important all of these will be for the trial, but I want to be ready."

As Hickory flips through a few more, I realize I've already forgotten more than half of them. I try to commit them to memory as Hickory continues.

"I think you'll be much more interested in this, though." Hickory's voice heightens with excitement as he flips to the back. "I'm making some progress translating the tome's symbols, though it's slow going."

"At least it's something," I encourage, trying to make sense of the scattered notes he's made on each sheet. It looks like a jumbled mess to me.

"The best part so far—," he continues "—is that I came across the Mystic prophecy I told you about. There seems to be even more to it than I realized. I can't read the extra sections yet, but I'm hoping to make sense of them soon."

"Excellent. What did you write here?" I ask, grabbing the book.

"Wait, give it back." Hickory reaches for it in a panic, but I'm too quick. So quick that some loose pages peek out.

"What's this?" I ask playfully, realizing it's something he doesn't want me to see.

"Nothing." Hickory tries to snatch it back from me again without success.

Holding it far enough away, I tug out the collection of pages, growing silent as I stare.

They're all masterful sketches of us, the competitors, at different points in our journey. Vale tending to the plants in the royal gardens. Alys trying to free the Leviathan in Isinglass. Me threatening a group of goblins with my daggers. Aeron stuck up a tree in a Dryad trap. I let out a chuckle at that last one.

"Hickory, these are amazing." They're not his usual portraits or still-life. "You've drawn all of these from memory?"

"I figure I'll eventually be commissioned to chronicle the competition—as long as I don't die in the trials," he says, running a nervous hand down the back of his neck. "Might as well get a head start while the memories are fresh."

I flip through a few more. There's one of Vale singing. Another of Aeron and I dancing at the masquerade. I try not to blush at that one. Then Vale in her starfish dress. Alys being followed by all the forest animals. Vale in the plant nursery. Vale smiling at Hickory in his squid costume as he holds up the vial of ink…

There sure are a lot of sketches of Vale.

"Wait a minute…" I stop, looking at Hickory with wide eyes. He's the one blushing now. "Do you have feelings for—?"

"Vale!" The sound of the queen's voice chills me.

Below, the queen leads Vale under the tree we're sitting on, and both Hickory and I hold our breath.

"I thought you were supposed to be working with your *trainer* for the afternoon, my dear," the queen says coolly. "Not lollygagging about the village."

"I was, Mother," Vale insists. "But Qu… *my trainer* abandoned me. You should be reprimanding *her*. If Father were here, he would…"

It's hard to see the queen's face, but when Vale halts in her response, I know it can't be a happy expression.

"Well, he's not here, Vale. I am," the queen counters.

"I'm sorry," Vale rushes to apologize. "Don't worry, I'll find her. She has to be around here somewhere."

If they only knew how close I really am.

The queen sighs. "Vale, it's my job to worry. You know I have so many other things on my plate without you being behind in the competition. You cannot fall in the ranks any further. Do I make myself clear?"

Vale's head drops.

"Oh, my dear." The queen sighs, tucking a strand of Vale's red hair back into place. "I'm only hard on you because I know your potential." Her hand drifts to Vale's chin, and she lifts it to meet her eyes a bit forcefully. "*Everything* I do is for your own good. Do you understand?"

"Yes, Mother." Vale nods, her chin still in her mother's grip.

"Good." The queen nods back. "Now come along. Let's go find that *trainer* of yours."

As they leave, Hickory and I sigh with relief. But as much as I fear for myself and what the queen will do when she finds me, regret over leaving Vale in the woods creeps in.

I know the pain of a demanding, disappointed parent all too well.

∾

Thankfully, I'm able to avoid Vale and the queen the rest of the day. The next morning, I make sure to show up to our training session early, ready to get to work. But it isn't Vale who's waiting for me in our usual spot in the woods.

"Hello, Captain," the queen says. An empty bird cage sits on the ground next to her as she inspects the rose bushes nearby.

"Your Majesty." I bow my head. "Where's Vale?"

"Oh, she'll be along in a minute," the queen assures me, taking out a pair of shears to cut a flower for herself. "I wanted to have a word with you first. I don't think I made myself as clear as I intended to the other day—"

"Your Highness, before you say anything—" I begin "—I want to apologize for my behavior with Vale. It won't happen again."

"Oh, I'm sure it won't." She snips the flower. "Because if you don't train my daughter as you promised, I will not allow Vale to prepare you for this trial or any other to come."

She straightens and holds the flower to her nose, taking in the aroma.

"In fact, I will be overseeing your training sessions from now on. Until I am thoroughly satisfied with Vale's progress, she will not help you study for the Trial of Life at all."

There's no tone of anger or frustration in her voice. She simply states the cold hard facts, completely composed. She peers up at me from the flower, a glint in her eye. "Do I make myself clear?"

I swallow hard. "Perfectly, Your Majesty."

"Good."

She bends to pick up the bird cage and opens the tiny barred door, letting out a soft whistle. A sparrow flutters in from the trees and lands in the cage. The queen feeds it a seed and snaps the door shut.

"Oh, and one more thing." She walks toward me and stops at my side, her voice lowered to a whisper. "I would choose your *friends* wisely, Quinntessa. The wrong company can easily lead you astray, distracting you with things that are not your business, nor your concern. Inviting only trouble. Neither of us want that, do we?"

Friends. Distractions. Trouble.

I search her unblinking eyes, panic rising in my chest. *Is she talking about Aeron again or Hickory? How does she know so much?*

Whatever the case, the response she wants from me is clear.

"No, we don't."

CHAPTER 38

Needless to say, I don't skip out on any more training sessions with Vale. And just like the queen promised, she's always there to watch us. I work Vale harder than ever, though I also try not to be as snarky while doing it. She's definitely making progress. But without her help concerning the Dryad plants, I'm panicking for myself.

Though the queen warned me to stay away from the others, she also didn't leave me much choice.

I convince Hickory to let me borrow his sketches to study—in exchange for me not telling Vale about his feelings for her. I still don't understand it. Most of the time, she treats him like dirt. He insists there's more to her. Either way, like anything I might feel toward Aeron, it's a lost cause.

I also catch Ivy alone any time Leman is off hunting or patrolling for goblins. Learning how to sign is harmless enough, right? If I can communicate with Alys about the symbol on her arm, maybe it'll help Hickory and me learn more about the ancient book. With Ivy's constant demands for more stories before she teaches me anything, I don't learn half as much as I'd hoped, but it's a start.

I don't get much opportunity to practice, either. As the next trial arrives, all thoughts about the Numanic symbol and the tome are pushed from my mind.

The sun dips behind the trees and gray clouds form above, as the air grows cold and damp. As usual, no rain comes. The five of us are met by a Dryad servant holding a platter of fruit.

"Is this dinner?" Aeron asks. There are only five round pieces of faerie fruit that the servant holds out to us. "Don't we need our energy?"

"A proper celebration feast will follow the trial," she explains. "This fruit is freshly picked from Lord Torlon's own garden, providing optimal energy for your trial tonight."

I sigh and snatch up the one closest to me. Biting through the skin, I focus on the rich flavors, trying to calm my nerves.

Approaching the edges of Vyndoria, Lord Torlon meets us near a large archway that's been drawn on the sanctuary's stone barrier. It must be where the other clans have entered to witness the trial.

As Dryads look out of windows in the trees, the clan leaders and other visiting fae gather on the ground with us in wonder at the wooded scene. The full moons peek out from the clouds, lighting the small clearing with the help of a series of lit torches and clusters of fireflies dancing overhead.

Alys stands next to me, staring at her mother and the rest of her siblings. Ivy discreetly moves her hands in a motion that I now know the meaning of: *Good luck.* She smiles.

I give her a small nod. I've enjoyed our encounters more than I expected. On the Minnow I had younger crew members, like Luna. But by the time I found them, most were old enough to have lost the innocent spark that still lights Ivy's eyes. If I'd had a younger sister like Ivy, I think I would have enjoyed it.

Looking back at her siblings, though, one is missing.

"Alys," I whisper. "Where's Leman?" Though I can actually sign this to her now, I'm not about to show off my newfound skill in front of all of Faylan.

Alys purses her lips and shakes her head.

He isn't coming? I know he despises the competition, but he can't even come to support his sister?

I chomp into my fruit again as the Dryad Lord calls for attention.

"Today the Dryad Clan brings forth the Trial of Life." He raises his walking staff to address the crowd. "A true ruler protects their folk and their world, valuing the precious gift of life. Having the wisdom to know when to take it and when to preserve it, even at their own expense."

Lord Torlon then looks to the five of us. "To be found worthy of this trial, you must enter the dark forest and gather specific healing plants. You see, each of you has been infected with the same illness which, if not treated fast enough, could be lethal."

My chewing slows, and I gape at the Dryad Lord. He seemed so kind, so fair. But infecting us without us even knowing it? This has to be the cruelest trial yet.

Vale hurriedly inspects her skin for signs of disease. "How did we get infected?"

"You ingested your poison through the fruit you ate just moments ago."

I spit out the fruit, coughing into the dirt. It's too late. I've already eaten most of it.

My fellow competitors look equally shocked. Even Alys. I wonder to what extent her healing abilities stretch. She healed the jackalope, but can she heal herself?

Dryad attendants carry out five potted plants, each of them bearing the exact kinds of fruit we ate, only the plants are glowing.

"Each of you have eaten from one of these plants, enchanted with pixie dust, tying your life source to its own survival," Lord Torlon explains. "While you're in the forest, we'll be able to monitor you based on the condition of your plant. Attached to each, we have recorded the illness and its symptoms. Your job is to identify the three plants that will cure each symptom."

A chain is slung over my head, and I jerk back as a spherical pendant lands on my chest. I turn over the transparent orb with my fingers, and the liquid inside starts to glow.

"These pendants will help light your way," Lord Torlon continues. "The juice inside has been taken from the fruit of your plant. As you traverse the woods, it will glow brighter as you near the remedy plants."

I grasp the pendant tight between my fingers. At least I won't be going into the dark forest completely blind.

"When you have cured yourself, you may return. Those who return first will be ranked higher than the rest, but points will be docked for unnecessarily destroying life in the forest, even if you are provoked."

Lord Torlon motions to the potted plants. "When you are ready, you may learn of your curse and enter the forest."

All five of us dart toward our plants. The leaves on mine are already wilting. I snatch the parchment tied to it with a shaking hand:

Disease: Fascal Delirium

Symptoms: fatigue, rash, hallucinations. If not treated, death.

Great. I take hold of the pendant around my neck and sprint through the archway into the forest. I only remember one of the healing plants out of the three.

I'll be dead by dinner.

~

As I leave the safety of Vyndoria, the dense Woodlands is a maze of endless trees. The light of the moons casts blue hues over the normally green forest, creating flickering shadows that play with my mind as the ominous call of an owl screeches from somewhere overhead.

How in Faylan am I supposed to find anything here?

At least I have the soft glow of the pendant around my neck, but when I hold it out in front of me, it only illuminates a few feet ahead.

As I trudge on, my feet slow with each crunching step. My shoulders slump, as if someone has heaved a burden over them.

No, this heaviness feels deeper than that. As if it's seeped into my body and buried itself in my chest. My eyes droop in the dim light. I force them open. I haven't gone that far; how can I already be tired?

I lean my hand against the cracked bark of the nearest tree, realizing I'm struggling to catch my breath.

Then it hits me. The first symptom is setting in.

Fatigue.

All I want to do is lie down in the moss and sleep it off. Another part of my brain screams that it won't do any good. This will only get worse if I don't find an antidote. And there are worse symptoms yet to come.

Gathering my quickly dwindling energy, I allow my eyes to close so I can focus, wracking my brain for a plant that will help. Lord Torlon's teachings are a droning mumble in my memory. Thankfully Hickory's drawings of the different plants are clearer. I mentally turn the pages until a bushel of bright red berries appear in my mind.

Kinto berries. A plentiful source of energy.

I look down at my pendant again. What did Torlon say? It'll glow brighter when we are near the right plants.

I take a few steps forward and the glow dims slightly. A step to the right. About the same. A few steps to the left and then backward. The glow intensifies.

A headache takes root at my temple, but I force my feet to move in the glow's direction. As I round a large tree trunk, the pendant is blazing so bright it lights everything in sight.

Including a bush of shiny, red berries.

There's already a puck there in front of it with stark white hair. *Hickory.* He has his back to me, pulling off the berries in large handfuls, tossing some into his mouth and more into a pouch at his side. Soon they'll all be gone.

"Hey!" I call, and the puck turns.

It isn't Hickory.

It's *Gaius.*

My breath hitches, lodging in my throat. I was short of breath before. Now I feel as if all the air has been kicked out of me.

It can't be.

But there he is, standing right in front of me. Alive. His hair is longer, but the scars from his burns run from his jawline all the way down his neck. I'm afraid to breathe or blink, for fear that he might disappear.

I take a careful step forward. "Gaius."

His eyes go wide. He bolts.

"No! Wait!" I lunge after him. The underbrush of pine needles and burrs scratch my arms. Branches pull at my tunic, threatening to slow me down. I urge my burning legs to follow after the wisps of white hair dashing through the trees. My clothes grow slick with sweat, my pulse roaring in my ears.

He's alive. Something deep inside always told me somehow, some way, he couldn't be dead. But why is he running?

"Gaius, stop! It's me!" I cry out.

Finally gaining on him, I reach out and pull him backward. I flip him around and pin him against the nearest tree. He tries to wriggle out of my grasp. I hold his arms against the bark as firmly as I can.

"Gaius, calm down." I try to speak softly while using the energy I have left to keep him still.

His frantic eyes dart from me to the darkness around us.

"It's me, Quinn. It's all right. Nothing is going to hurt you."

His eyes narrow. "Nothing, huh? What about *you*?" he practically spits. He looks down at my hands around his arms, and I feel him tremble beneath my touch.

"What?" His words shoot like lightning through my body, and I nearly let go of him from the shock.

He's afraid I'll burn him again. His look is crazed. He doesn't know what he's saying. Something else truly terrible must have happened to him out here. I tighten my grip. I need to make him understand.

"No, Gaius. That was an accident. A mistake. I'm your sister. You know I would never—"

"Never leave me?" His face twists angrily. "You mean like when you promised you wouldn't, and then left anyway. You left me with our *father*, of all folk!"

Another stab to the gut. My head pounds as he squirms to break free.

I can't lose him. Not again. I won't survive it.

"Gaius, I'm so sorry. But you have to listen to me," I plead. "I don't know where you've been. They told me you were dead. We buried you. And ever since that day, I've been trying to make up for what I did."

"You mean by joining the Ethodine?" he scoffs. "Did you really believe that taking my place in this competition would make up for anything? Would *change* anything?" He laughs darkly. "Like always, the only faerie you're thinking of is yourself. Father was right after all. You're a screw-up. And you're dangerous. All you do is hurt others. You're doing it right *now*—"

His last words turn into a scream of pain, and I look down at my hands. They don't feel hot, but they're bright red, burning into his flesh.

"No!" I yell and let go.

He pushes past me, holding his arms as he breaks through the brush.

"Gaius!"

I run after him again. I need to apologize. He needs a medik, and fast. But as I dart after him, I feel myself slowing, the fatigue growing worse. Still, I push off the trees to propel myself forward, desperate not to lose him again.

I trip over something. Something big.

My knees and elbows skid against the ground as I fall hard, dirt and pebbles stinging my skin. I hiss with pain. When I lift my hand, it's covered in something sticky. Mud? Sap?

I flip my hand over, the pendant around my neck illuminating my bright red palm.

It's blood.

It's smeared across my hands and my tunic. I turn to see what I stumbled over, and my heart shreds into pieces.

It's Gaius' body.

His frantic eyes stare up at the sky as his body shakes, blood dripping from his arms and chest.

"No!" I shriek. The sound tears at my throat as I rush to his side.

My hands hover over his body, afraid to touch him. I look for something I can do. Anything. He's already lost so much blood, and his skin is deathly pale. Grief and rage ricochet through my body. I'm shaking. My heart is pounding.

How—how is this possible? I just saw him alive and now—now he's dying. Again.

His eyes roll back into his head, and I grit my teeth.

"No... no, no, no."

I can't stop myself anymore. I clutch his shoulders and pull his limp body against my chest. Squeezing him close, I breathe hard into his shoulder.

"No, Gaius, please don't leave me again. Don't go."

Pressure builds behind my eyes and grows in my chest. It's so overpowering, I think it might crush my heart. I hope it will. But it doesn't. There's no release. No relief from the pain.

"I'm so sorry, brother. This is all my fault. You should have been the one who lived." I squeeze him harder, my voice breaking. "Please, don't go. I can't do this without you. Take me with you. Please, take me with you..."

"Quinn." The word blows into my hair.

I pull back from the body in my hands.

It's not Gaius.

CHAPTER 39

"Hickory?" I ask, shaking my head.

Hickory blinks up at me, mirroring my shock. He opens his mouth to speak, but I cut in first.

"How did you..." I squeeze his shoulders, peering around frantically for Gaius, and then back down at Hickory. His shirt is stained with red. I jump back. "Hickory, you're bleeding!"

"I am?" He looks down and feels for a wound. Instead, his hand finds a pouch looped on a leather band across his chest. He breathes. "It's okay. It's not blood." He opens the flap to reveal half-squished kinto berries.

I turn my red palm over again and slump backward on the ground, so utterly exhausted and confused. I sniff. Instead of the tang of blood, the scent is fresh and sweet. My eyes dart to the forest around us, my chest still rising and falling uneasily. "What—what happened?"

And where is Gaius? Was he ever really here?

"I don't know..." Hickory starts, looking back toward the trees. "After I found the kinto berries, I thought I heard something. When I turned, there was a black figure surrounded by swirling clouds of smoke."

"A goblin?" I ask.

"I don't know, maybe? Whatever it was, it chased me, and I ran. I looked back a few times. Its darkness was growing, swallowing up the forest as it went. It took hold of me once and I got away, but it tracked me here and pinned me to the ground. Everything went pitch black. I couldn't see or hear anything. I could barely breathe, as if the life was being crushed out of me. I thought I was going to die." He looks up at me. "Then I heard your voice."

"My voice?" My heartbeat slows as I put the pieces together.

"I didn't know what you were saying, but I knew it was you. Slowly the darkness dissipated and I found you… hugging me."

I look at the ground. "I—I thought I was holding Gaius," I whisper, realizing what must have happened.

"Gaius?" Hickory asks. Then the answer dawns on him too. "It must have been another one of the symptoms. The hallucinations are kicking in."

I nod. Hickory's eyes soften. I don't have to explain my hallucination for him to know what I saw.

I still can't believe it. It all felt so real, but Gaius was never really here. I was chasing Hickory, and he was running from me. It was all in our heads. Our greatest fears come to life. I didn't think anything could be worse than my actual nightmares. This was much worse.

A rush of cold flows through me, and my eyes grow heavy and droop. I'm either about to throw up or pass out.

"Quinn!" Hickory catches me before I hit the ground. He grabs some of the remaining berries from his pouch. "Eat this. Quickly now."

He pushes them into my mouth, and I force myself to chew and swallow. My headache slowly eases its grip on my skull, and energy returns to my tired muscles. I look up at Hickory, his eyebrows knitted together with worry, and give him a reassuring nod. Though a part of me wishes he really had been Gaius, I'm glad to have someone else looking out for me.

"Thanks," I say, sitting up.

Hickory helps pull me to my feet. "Here, why don't you hold onto these until you're sure you feel one hundred percent." He hands me the pouch of berries. "I ate plenty before."

I nod and tie it to my belt, silently thankful to not be alone in the forest any longer.

"Quinn?" Hickory taps my shoulder. "We can't have the same hallucinations, right?"

"I don't think so… Why?"

"Because I think I see Alys."

Afraid of what I may see next, I turn slowly.

A few yards away, Alys is on her knees, hands over her mouth, tears streaming down her face. As we draw closer, I see she's looking into an open clearing, lit up by moonlight.

Bodies of dead lynxicorns cover the field.

"What in Faylan?" I step toward the clearing to get a better look, but Hickory grabs my arm.

"Look there." He lowers his voice to a whisper, pointing to a group of dark winged figures descending on the corpses.

Goblins.

It seems that they've killed the lynxicorns who were once under their control. Now some of them are bent over the beasts, making horrible chomping sounds.

"Quinn, real or illusion?" Hickory whispers. "Are those goblins doing what I think they're doing?"

I nod, holding back the bile climbing up my throat. The goblins are feeding on the lynxicorns' raw flesh.

"I'm so sorry, Alys," I say softly. This must be killing her, but she doesn't move.

Unsure of what to do next, the glow of my pendant increasingly catches my attention. I hold it out toward the moonlit clearing. To my dismay, it glows all the brighter.

The pendant wants us to go out *there*?

Beyond the goblins feasting, a large stone structure stands on the other side of the clearing, covered in climbing vines.

"Um, guys…" I swallow. "I think the next plant we need might be near that building."

"You mean the one on the other side of the field of death?" Hickory asks, already shaking his head.

"I think if we follow the circle of trees, we can make it there without catching the goblins' attention," I say. "It might even be a good place to hide out until they move on."

Alys isn't listening. Her breathing deepens, turning to seething gasps. Grabbing a fallen tree branch, she lets her wings loose and flies straight toward the goblins.

"Alys, no!" I reach out for her, but she's already out in the clearing, swinging at the goblins. They leave their carcass meals, flocking to her with bloodied teeth and sharp talons.

With the charred creatures distracted, a clear path to the stone structure is laid out for us. I look back at Alys.

She takes down a goblin with one swing to the jaw, another by jamming the branch through its gut. The rest descend on her, yanking her down, raking their talons across her arms and back.

I look at Hickory. His eyes say he can't leave her either.

"Hey! Hey, uglies! Over here!" I step out of the brush, waving my hands in the air.

Hickory follows my cue. "Why have only one faerie snack when you can have three!"

Dozens of goblin heads turn to us, abandoning Alys to begin another chase.

Unfurling my wings, I whip across the field. "Follow me!"

As we fly, I glance over my shoulder. A hoard of them are gaining on us, and Alys is still struggling to take down the few that surround her.

An idea takes hold. I make a wide turn in the air.

"What are you doing?" Hickory follows. "Isn't leading them back to Alys a little counterintuitive?"

"Get ready to grab an arm," I tell him.

Hickory nods.

Reaching Alys, we yank her out of the goblins' clutches. At first, she kicks and swats at us, obviously not satisfied with the extent of pain she was able to inflict on the creatures. Then her body slowly goes slack, growing heavier in our arms. Her bloodied wounds glisten in the moonlight.

"Come on!" I guide Hickory through a wide turn in the air again. The remaining goblins join the hunt after us, shrieking as they chase.

"Where are we headed now?" He struggles to hold onto Alys' arm. His bat-like wings aren't as strong as mine.

"There!" I pull him along, flying as fast as my wings can carry me. If we head back into the trees, the goblins can easily catch up. If we want to survive, the stone fortress is our best bet.

We land and stumble toward the structure's stone door, putting Alys down to push the door open with all our might.

"It's not budging!" Hickory says through gritted teeth.

Goblins land on the steps below, displaying fanged sneers. One of them launches itself at Alys with a growl, but Alys doesn't even bother to shield herself.

Heat rising in my gut, I let go of the door and jump in front of her.

I lift my bare hands to take the brunt of the goblin's blow. "Don't you touch her!"

Before I know it, the searing heat in my gut shoots from my chest, burns through my veins, and fire erupts from my hands.

The ash-colored goblin bursts into flames and stumbles backward as it shrieks and grabs at its burning flesh. It struggles to fly and eventually tumbles to the ground, rolling around to put out the fire engulfing its body.

The other goblins watch in horror, momentarily distracted by their fallen comrade.

Alys' eyes are now wide and alert.

Hickory holds the same expression.

Both of them are staring at my hands.

They've seen my secret. I'll have to deal with that later. We aren't safe yet.

"Hickory, the door!" I point.

Somehow, it's cracking open.

CHAPTER 40

As Hickory pushes against the door, I grab Alys and fly inside. Hickory follows just as the goblins turn from their smoldering friend and spring into the air after us.

Thankfully, we aren't the only ones on the other side of the door. Vale and Aeron must have been pulling on the large handle, because they're now hurrying to push it closed again.

Moving to help, I catch sight of mossy green spots speckling their skin. *The rash.*

"Hey, a little help here!" Vale yells, and I pull my eyes away from her skin, throwing my body against the door.

The goblins whiz toward us. With all of our combined strength, the door closes shut with a loud thud just in time. Goblins shriek as claws scrape against the stone, but we're safe. For now.

Panting, I face the others inside the dark structure.

Alys and Hickory stare at me again.

"Okay, so… real or illusion?" Hickory urges me to answer in a fearful yet excited tone. His eyes dart back and forth from my hands to my face.

Alys looks at me with wide eyes, as if asking the same question, while holding her bleeding arm.

I shrug at Alys. *Guess you're not the only one with secrets.*

"Are you serious?" Vale asks.

I freeze. *Did she see my fire too?*

She's not looking at me though, she's struggling to scratch her back where I'm sure the rash has traveled. "Of course those goblins are real. What were you doing out there, anyway? You could have gotten yourselves killed."

A sigh rushes out of me. At least Vale didn't see my hands ablaze. I give Hickory a warning glance not to say another word.

"I think what Vale means is, are you all okay?" Aeron scratches his chest violently, though his gaze is focused on me.

"I think so." I peer into the dark room.

Thankfully, there don't seem to be any windows that could let in the goblins. Our glowing pendants are the only source of light, illuminating only the small space around us.

"Where are we?" I hold up my pendant like a lantern toward Vale and Aeron. "And why are you two here together?"

"My pendant led me here," Vale says defensively. "I entered through a back entrance covered by some vines, but I haven't found a remedy anywhere. And this rash just keeps spreading!" She runs her nails down her trousers.

"Same here. Just look at it!" Aeron reveals his arms, where his perfect tan skin is tainted by green splotches. "I was afraid I was becoming a plant myself until I came across Vale here a few minutes ago. We were about to leave when we heard your voices outside."

"Well, thanks for that," Hickory says to Aeron begrudgingly, leaning against the nearest wall as sweat beads down his face. "But we don't have much time. Especially Alys."

Alys is still on the ground, holding her arm. Blood streams out, soaking her sleeve.

"If you could show us this back entrance, I think we'd all like to get out of here." Hickory shudders at the darkness. "Then we can each go our separate ways."

"I've got Alys." I throw one of her arms over my shoulder as the others lead the way.

"What's happening to you?" I whisper to her.

The slashes on Alys' arm and back are long and deep, cutting through her beautiful tattoos as a green film oozes out. Is the mossy rash crossing with her goblin wounds? Or are the goblin's talons poisonous themselves?

Alys gives a defeated shrug.

"Blast! What good is your gift if you can't heal yourself?"

Digging my hand into the pouch Hickory gave me, I pull out some of the kinto berries and push them into her mouth. "Here. Maybe this will help."

That's all I can do. Though I hate it, once we leave the safety of this place, I know I should focus on making sure Vale gets back to Vyndoria first. I can't have the queen angrier than she already is. But can I really leave Alys on her own like this?

"Come on, you two," Aeron calls to us through the darkness. "Let's get out of here."

As Alys and I stand, torches along the walls ignite. Blazing light fills the large stone hall, and I freeze with Alys still against my side. The space is nearly three times larger than I originally thought.

"What just happened?" Vale asks.

Hickory looks at me as if I've done something.

This isn't me. At least, I don't think so.

Looking around, the room is fairly empty. There's just a hallway back near the front door. Something moves in the hallway's shadowed entrance, and I jump back as a figure emerges. He's dressed just like the strange cloaked faeries I saw in Shree, his worn hood covering his face. He just stands there, waiting for something. Hold on, is he the one who lit the torches?

The figure bows his head before backing up, disappearing into the dark hallway.

The memory of the voice in Shree speaking into my mind comes back to me. *"If you want to learn what really happened to your brother, you will follow me."*

If this is the same hooded figure, maybe he still has the answers I need.

Against my chest, my pendant's glowing pulses.

"Hey!" I call after him. "Wait!"

I quickly but carefully sling Alys onto my back as her arms droop over my shoulders, and sprint into the hallway.

"Quinn!" Aeron's voice echoes off the walls.

"I saw something. I'll be right back!" I yell.

"It could be another hallucination!" Hickory calls as their pounding footsteps follow me down the hall.

"You've got to be kidding me," Vale complains.

With Alys' arms dangling over my shoulders, I dart down the hallway as fast as I can, chasing the figure's shadow through a doorway into a darkened room. Slowing, I thrust the glow of my pendant forward into the dim space.

There's no trace of the cloaked figure. It's just a dark room with an archway on the other end. It's what's on the other side of the archway that catches my attention. It appears to be a moonlit courtyard full of lush green plants. As I step deeper into the room, drawing closer toward the opening, the glow of my pendant pulses brighter than ever.

"Quinn, where are you?" I hear Hickory shout from down the hall.

"This way," I call back, lowering Alys to the ground. "I think I've found one of the remedies." Was the hooded figure actually trying to help us find it?

The others enter the room after me. The glow of their pendants casts more light into the space as I take a step toward the courtyard.

"Quinn, wait!" Aeron's voice rings with warning.

A tile beneath my foot shifts down before I can pull away. A heavy stone slab slams over the archway to the courtyard. I whip around just in time to see the same happen to the doorway we just came through

"No!" Vale lunges toward it. She's too late. She bangs her fist on the slab and then turns to me. "Look what you've done!"

My stomach lurches. The hood hasn't helped us. He's trapped us in here. I curse. *What was I thinking?*

Vale strides toward me, fingers outstretched as if ready to pull my hair out.

Aeron steps in front of her. "Vale, relax. Quinn didn't know—"

"Of course she didn't. She never does. She never thinks about anyone but herself!" Vale shouts, scratching more vigorously at her neck where the green rash has spread. "Yet you're always defending her."

"Aeron's right," Hickory adds, surprising all of us, especially Aeron. "Turning on each other isn't going to do any good with the little time we have left. Our best chance is to spread out and find a way out of here as quickly as we can. If we do, we might be able to get access to that courtyard again."

Though I can't argue with Vale—I did get us into this mess—I give a nod of gratitude to Aeron and Hickory.

"Fine," Vale huffs, backing up.

As the others split up to inspect the space, I turn and gasp.

My pendant illuminates a towering sculpture of a faerie. Its stone face glares down at me. Glancing around, there are five of them that line the room in a circular formation around us. They're faeries from each clan, their wings spread out above them, holding a small object with an outstretched hand. Replicas of the five clan moonstones.

It's what's behind them that surprises me the most. Archaic images are carved into the stone walls. Flora and fauna, flying fairies, even the wingless Numa with their dull ears.

On the door now barring us from the courtyard, Numanic symbols trail down the newly formed barrier. I recognize many of them from the passage Hickory has been studying in the tome.

"Hickory…" I point to the symbols. "Real or illusion?"

"Oh, this is real, all right.…" Hickory holds up his pendant as he examines them.

"I don't see anything except weird symbols." Aeron looks exhausted as he crouches next to Alys, checking her wounds. "What is this place?"

"I think we're in an ancient Mystic temple." Hickory gently traces his fingers over the etchings. "I thought these were all destroyed."

"A temple?" I ask.

"They once used them to protect rare plants that they believed to be sacred and to worship the…" He looks back at me. He was probably about to say the word *Numa*. He casts a wary glance at Vale. "Anyway, they often set traps for trespassers, like the one Quinn triggered, leaving the only key to escape in secret codes like these."

"It's Numanic," Vale says in a soft, wonder-filled voice that doesn't seem to belong to her. She follows the markings with her fingers, mumbling to herself in a tongue I don't recognize.

"Wait, you can read this?" Hickory's mouth hangs open, looking equal parts dumbfounded and impressed.

Vale pulls her hand away from the wall. "I, um… Yes. Well, sort of."

"You can read the *Numanic* language?" I press.

"I told you, I have a knack for ancient languages," she says. "The real question is, how do *you* know that this is Numanic?"

I hesitate, then get an idea. "Hickory may have taken a book about it from your library."

"Quinn!" Hickory steps forward to stop me, but I put an arm out toward him.

"My library?" Vale asks.

"Yeah," I say. "Old. Dusty. Leather-bound. Strange flower symbol on the cover. Ring any bells?"

If so, maybe I'll find out if it's the same book the queen is after.

Vale's eyes grow wide with recognition as she lunges toward Hickory. "Thief! I've been looking everywhere for that text, and you've had it all this time?"

Grabbing Vale's wrist, I spin her around to face me. "We'll catch you up when we're not all dying and trapped in some creepy temple, okay? Right now, we need to know what these markings say so we can figure out how to get out of here. And, if you help us, we might even consider giving the book back to you."

"What?" Hickory exclaims.

I shoot him a look. *I said might.*

"Fine," Vale sighs as she scratches her shoulder. "I'm not sure I'll get all of it right, but I'll try."

She begins to read:

> *Beasts revolt at darkest death*
> *A tremble in the land will quake*
> *War and famine on your breath*
> *Order, peace, and unions break*
> *The Vine will wither, the sky will fall*
> *The Numa's tale, take heed you must*
> *A plague will mark the end of all*
> *It comes on wings of ash and dust*
> *Stone and dust they must combine*
> *With every royal clan bloodline*
> *Together when the moons align*
> *The key to power is the sign*

Hickory mutters the words back to himself as if trying to memorize it.

"Is it making sense now?" I ask.

"What does it mean?" Aeron adds from the floor. He's got Alys propped up against him, examining her wounds.

"I-I don't know," Hickory stammers. "It's just more riddles."

He scratches his neck, where green splotches have formed. The rash is setting in. I look down at myself, noticing a few spots on my arms. *Great.*

"Guys, I think Alys has the rash too and her wounds are getting worse," Aeron says with more intensity, trying to keep her sitting upright. He puts a hand to her forehead. "She's burning up. We need to get out of here, fast."

"Riddles… riddles," I look around the room, starting to scratch at my own skin. "What did it say at the end?"

Vale translates again. "Stone and dust they must combine, with every royal clan bloodline. Together when the moons align, the key to power is the sign."

"The key to power…" I say.

If the riddle is a clue on how to get out of here, the key to power could be what we need.

"The key is the sign." I look at the images on the walls. "Maybe we need to find the Numanic sign somewhere."

Hickory, Vale, and I each search a different wall. We find vague depictions of the faerie clans serving the wingless Numa, bowing or bringing offerings, but no sign of the symbol.

"Guys?" Aeron is staring upward as Alys weakly points to the ceiling. "I don't know what the sign you're searching for looks like, but I think Alys found the moons."

We lift our glowing pendants to reveal a dome-shaped ceiling depicting the night sky. Indents in the shape of stars speckle the surface with a series of full moons running right down the middle.

"Together when the moons align…" Hickory whispers. "It's the Moon Harvest."

"The Moon Harvest?" Aeron asks.

"It's a celestial event that only happens once every ten years," Vale says. "All the full moons align like an eclipse, so it appears as if there's only one moon in our sky."

"Okay," Aeron says. "So is that the sign we need?"

"No," I whisper, thinking back to the riddle. "Stone and dust they must combine, with every royal clan bloodline…"

I look at the faerie sculptures around us. They're all looking at the only surface of the room we haven't checked. "Everyone, stand back for a second. I need to see something."

All but Alys move to the edges of the room. I point my pendant to the ground. There are grooves in the floor partially covered by dirt and dust. I start brushing it away with my feet and other grooves appear. Frantically, I drop to my knees and swipe at the ground to uncover more.

Hickory follows my lead, and soon we're all brushing away grime until a symbol takes shape. It's so large, it takes up the entire floor. There are the three rings and the ten-petaled flower of the Numa.

Alys is seated in the middle of it all. She's on the center ring carved into a singular stone tile that's slightly pressed into the ground.

"Aeron, help me move Alys," I say. "I think this is the tile that triggered the trap."

Together we shift her off of it, and I point to two grooves on either side. Maybe handles of some kind?

Aeron jams his fingers into the grooves and pulls, the gills on his neck tensing. The stone doesn't budge. "It's too heavy. Even with all of us lifting, I don't think it will come up."

"Wait. Stone and dust they must combine," Hickory mutters. "Remember how Lord Torlon said the liquid that fills our pendants was enchanted with pixie dust? What if we can use the dust's floating properties to elevate the stone?"

He shakes his pendant, and some of the dust sprinkles over the circular stone.

It trembles, lifting a little, then settles down again.

Anxious to see if it will work, we each take positions around the tile and shake our pendants over the stone. Gradually, the tile rises and clicks back into place, flush with the floor. As it does, the stone slabs blocking the doorways rise, the one covering the hallway entrance, as well as the courtyard archway.

"Finally!" Vale exclaims. She rushes into the courtyard as we grab Alys and follow her out into the moonlight.

There's a glass ceiling and four walls. We must be in the center of the temple. Inspecting the overgrown vegetation, Vale follows her pendant until it leads her to a plant with five thick leaves, each the length of my forearm.

"It's a marshing fern!" she exclaims. "If we cut open the leaves, there's a liquid inside that's a perfect remedy for severe rashes!"

Pulling one off and peeling it open, Vale sucks on the inner liquid as well as layering it over her sores. She breathes out in relief, and Aeron follows her lead with the second leaf. Pulling off the other three, Vale hands them to me.

"You and Hickory should drink this before your rashes get bad. First, give one to Alys. It's skin-healing properties may also help with her wounds from the goblins."

As I help Alys drink and apply the salve, Vale looks to the left of us. "Hickory, hurry up and grab your leaf."

"In a minute," he says. He's busy examining one of the courtyard walls. "I found some markings over here that I've never seen before."

Vale sighs and shakes her head as I drink some of the liquid from my leaf. At least the green ooze and blood from Alys' gashes are beginning to dry up. Color returns to her skin and light to her eyes. Alys touches my arm with her gloved hand in gratitude. I smile.

"Leaving so soon?" I hear Aeron ask.

Vale is already heading back inside. We all stare at her. Even Hickory looks up from studying the wall.

"Thanks for the help." There's a hint of guilt in her expression, then she straightens her spine. "This is still a competition, though. One I can't lose."

The queen's face flashes in my mind. *Keep your eye on the prize.*

Our silence speaks for itself. Though there's a measure of hurt in Hickory's eyes, he understands too. Our common purpose is done. At the end of the day, we all have our own agendas, and we can't let each other stand in the way. Still, Vale isn't as cutthroat as she lets on. She could have grabbed all the fern leaves and ran out. She could have let Alys die. But she didn't.

Before I can say anything, she's gone.

I know I should do the same. I should go make sure that Vale safely crosses the finish line first, and that I don't come in last myself. But Alys still isn't in great shape. She won't make it far without me.

As I help her stand, Aeron takes hold of her other side.

I stop. If I let him help, it could slow him down and allow Vale to get a bigger head start back to Vyndoria. But I can't let the queen find me with him again either.

"I've got her," I tell him. "You should go."

"Are you sure?" The ocean of color in his eyes swim with conflict.

"I'm sure. No holding back, remember?"

He smiles sadly at our saying. "No holding back."

Slowly, he releases Alys' arm and steps back toward the door, watching me all the way until he disappears inside.

Making sure Alys is steady on her feet, I turn to hand the final fern leaf to Hickory before leaving too. I find him standing in front of the markings that he's found on the courtyard wall, mumbling to himself.

"Hickory, stop obsessing and take your medicine. We've got to get out of here."

He doesn't move.

"Hickory." I walk toward him. Still nothing. "Hickory!" I pull at his shoulder. When he faces me, his good eye has gone completely white, just like in Isinglass.

I draw back. *Real or illusion?*

"Hickory?"

He grabs my arms, his nails digging into my skin.

Real! Very real!

He chants phrases from the prophecy in an urgent yet monotone voice. "Beasts revolt… war and famine… the Numa tale… take heed, take heed!"

"Hickory, stop. You're scaring me." I try to pull out of his grasp. His hands are unusually strong, his fingers pressing even harder. "Hickory, snap out of it!"

"Stone and dust… moons align… the end of all… it's coming… It's coming!" He chants louder and louder.

"Hickory!" I yell, preparing to headbutt him if I have to.

Alys hits him over the head with a rock first.

Hickory goes limp and drops to the ground.

I look at Alys, who leans against the wall for support.

"Thanks." I let out a shaky breath. I'm still in shock, trying to understand what just happened.

She shrugs with a weak smile, looking exhausted from just walking the few feet over to us.

Hickory moans from the floor.

Alys and I inch back, preparing ourselves for whatever he's about to do next.

"Wow, that hurts." Hickory sounds like himself as he reaches for his head. "How did I end up on the ground?"

I relax. "I think you went into a trance or something. You're going to be fine now."

"Wait." Hickory freezes, still looking down.

"What's wrong?"

He slowly turns his head and blinks up at us, his eyebrows furrowing. His good eye is no longer white. Still, there's something different about it.

His breathing quickens.

I bend down and put a hand on his shoulder, searching his face for answers.

Just like his misted blue eye, his brown eye that usually moves freely is stationary.

"I can't see." Hickory feels for my arm and grabs it like a lifeboat at sea. "Quinn, I can't see anything!"

CHAPTER 41

H ickory closes his eyes and touches his eyelids with trembling fingers. He opens them, blinking frantically, and then does it all again as if trying to make sure his eyes are open. With every passing second, his chest heaves, his breathing more sporadic.

"Don't panic, okay?" I tell him, even though I have no idea what to do.

"*Don't panic*?" he shouts, feeling for my arm again and squeezing it so hard I fear it'll bruise. I've never seen him this undone before. "I've lost my sight. It's finally happened. What am I going to do?"

"We'll help you get out of here. It's going to be all right. First, we have to take care of your rashes." I look at Alys, and she nods in agreement as she dabs the fern's liquid on his blotchy skin.

Hickory shakes his head. "You don't get it. My sight, my art, it's the only thing I can call my own. It's all I have. All that I am. And now it's gone." He pauses. "You said I went into a trance? What did I do?"

When I tell him about his prophetic ramblings, his eyebrows raise. "That's it. I'm cursed!" he cries out.

"You're not cursed. You thought you lost your sight before in the woods, remember? For all we know, this is another hallucination. We just have to find the last plant."

Alys claps her hands to get my attention, and I look at her. She points to herself, and then the remnants of the fern. I don't get what she's trying to say. I look at Hickory, but without his sight, I can't count on him to know either.

I could try something else. I lift my hands.

I don't understand, I sign to Alys. I know the phrase well, since every time I said it out loud during my lessons with Ivy, she made me sign it instead. *Use signs,* I try again, grasping for more words I can remember.

Alys' mouth drops open, her eyes blinking wide. Tentatively, she signs one word. *How?* Then she points to me.

Ivy. I sign back. *Ivy help… little.* I shrug, hoping she'll get what I mean.

The corner of Alys' mouth lifts.

"Quinn, why is it so quiet? What's going on? Don't tell me I've lost my hearing too." Panic rattles Hickory's voice again.

Alys signs to me quickly, and I pick up the words: *I know, healing, plant,* and the number three.

"It's okay, Hickory. Alys is offering to lead us to the third healing plant," I tell him slowly, looking at Alys for confirmation that I've understood her correctly.

She nods emphatically.

I smile.

A small voice inside tells me I should be doing this on my own, but without Alys I wouldn't even know where to start. In her weakened condition, she won't get far without help either. At this point, no matter our rank, we all just want this to be over.

Thankfully, there aren't any signs of the goblins when we get outside. Alys leads us across the field to a pond not far from where we were standing when we first spotted her. She must have been heading here before we came across her in the woods.

Alys picks some orange wildflowers growing at the rim of the pond and crushes the pollen in her hand.

Though Hickory is skeptical that it will help him, he eats the pollen powder with us, and soon his good eye begins to shift and peer around.

Hickory blinks back tears as he turns to Alys and takes her hands in his. "Thank you," he chokes out.

More than ready to be finished with this trial, Hickory and I sling Alys' arms over our shoulders and follow her hand signals back to Vyndoria, keeping our eyes peeled for any other dangers. We're just able to see the magical archway through the trees when the two of them stop short.

"What're you two doing? We're almost there," I say.

Hickory looks at Alys, and she nods. "You go first, Quinn," he says.

"What? Why?" I ask.

"We wouldn't have gotten this far without you."

I stare at them. Honestly, a huge part of me almost takes them up on the offer. The part that fears the queen and wants that beautiful flying ship she's promised. But something inside me can't do it.

What in Faylan is wrong with me?

Shaking my head, I sling Alys' arm back over my shoulder.

Today, these two are my crew, and the trial is the storm we just barely survived.

"No," I tell them. "We finish together."

I wouldn't have known about the kinto berries without Hickory's help, and I could still be stumbling around in the forest looking for the last plant without Alys. I'm in their debt. But that ends here.

As we enter the village arm in arm, gasps flutter through the crowd. I try to avoid the fuming stares of both the queen and my father, and the equally surprised looks on Vale's and Aeron's faces.

It's all easier to handle when Lord Torlon and Lady Navi rush to Alys. She collapses in their arms.

"What happened?" Lady Navi exclaims, trembling at the sight of Alys' terrible-looking gashes.

"The goblins attacked her," I explain.

"And you chose to save her." Lord Torlon looks at Hickory and me with a mix of confusion and gratitude. "Thank you... I cannot change your ranking, but in my mind, you have proven yourselves the true winners of the Trial of Life."

Though I appreciate his sentiment, looking back at the queen, I'm honestly relieved he can't.

∼

Thankfully, the Dryads fully deliver on the feast they promised. As I approach the terrace, a long banquet table is piled up with a vast array of savory and sweet dishes. The smells invade my senses as I look for an open seat.

Her Majesty eyes me and then the seat next to her with intention. Feeling like I don't have much choice, I walk over and settle between her and Hickory.

Vale sits across from her while Aeron and Alys are seated farther down the table with their parents. Thankfully, Alys is looking much better.

Even Leman has made an appearance, sitting next to Vale. He doesn't look happy about it. Next to him is my father. He glances my way briefly as I take my seat, then returns to staring at his plate. What a pair those two make with their matching scowls.

The queen hasn't said a word to me or looked in my direction. Frustration emanates off her like heat. Though Vale successfully emerged from the forest first, I'm sure the queen didn't like the fact that I helped Alys and Hickory, when I could have been helping to keep Vale safe.

Spotting a bowl of lily tarts in front of me, my focus shifts.

Vale shoots me a look of disgust as I reach for them. I don't care what she thinks. To me, the stuff is as addicting as pixie dust, and besides, I could use some comfort food. I pop a few into my mouth. The flavor of this one is even more intense than I remember.

"Before we eat..." Lord Torlon looks my way. I swallow hard, placing my hands back in my lap. "I just wanted to say that you should all be proud of how you handled yourselves today."

"Considering they all almost died," Leman mutters under his breath.

"What did you say, my son?" the Dryad Lord asks.

At first, it looks as if Leman is going to say it was nothing. Then something shifts in his gaze.

"I was just saying—" he speaks loud enough for the whole table to hear, "—that all the clan heirs could have died today, including Alys. And I know you wouldn't want me to be the next ruler."

Many around the table look down at their plates, pretending to be distracted.

Feeling a tickle in my throat, I take advantage of the awkward exchange to let out a short cough. It cuts through the growing tension like one of my blades.

"I've never said that," Lord Torlon assures him.

"Not outright." Leman stabs a piece of meat in front of him and points the fork at his father. "But we all know you'd never agree to how I would lead."

Lord Tylon sighs, caught between the accusations of his son and the judgement of his guests. "Leman, you're a great warrior. A valiant defender of our clan and the Woodlands. But not everything can be solved with brute strength and war." He eyes my father, who grumbles something under his beard. "Unlike *some* clans, we are called to be peacekeepers. That is our place."

Alys tries to catch Leman's attention, warning him with a stare. He avoids her gaze.

The tickle rises in my throat, and I try to clear it again.

"How does risking the lives of your heirs in some stupid game keep the peace?" Leman demands.

The tickle is turning into an itch. I cough louder. *What's wrong with me?*

Leman pounds the table, glaring at me. "Can you please stop?"

I cough again. And again. Harder each time.

My throat is closing. I grab the side of the table tightly in panic.

"Quinn, are you all right?" Hickory asks.

"Can't... breathe..." I wheeze, trying to suck in as much air as possible.

Spots dot my vision. I'm blacking out.

I search for Aeron farther down the table, locking eyes with him.

"Quinn!" He stands, his chair scraping against the floor as I fall.

Hickory catches me, and I look up at a blur of faces. My body goes numb as I gasp for air. My eyes threaten to close. I fight to keep them open. Alys' face comes into focus, her eyes frantic.

"Stay with me," whispers a voice I don't recognize.

"Move her to the infirmary, now!" Aeron calls out.

That voice I know. But all I see in front of me is Alys.

"Stay calm." The voice reverberates in my mind again as if it could be my own thoughts. "This is going to hurt me more than it hurts you."

Then there's only darkness.

∾

Utter darkness and quiet.

Did it finally happen? Am I dead?

"Quinn!" Gaius' all-too-familiar voice screams my name.

Another dream.

I open my eyes, expecting to be back at the port where my nightmares with him always take place. This time, I'm sitting on a metal chair in a cold room. The only sound is a slow, insistent dripping.

"Quinn!"

I jolt in my seat, anxious to rise and follow his voice. I can't move. My arms and legs are bound to the chair. I yank at the restraints. I'm strapped down tight.

"Gaius!" My head whips around to find where he could be.

Torches light, and a gathering of fae make their way toward me. Their faces are blurred, as if my eyes aren't working properly.

"Hello?" I ask tentatively. "I need help, please!"

Their pace doesn't change. Gradually, their torches illuminate different parts of the room. Large pools of water cover the ground. Something is floating inside each of them.

Bodies.

"No." I start to shake, my forehead breaking out in a sweat. "Please, what do you want with me?"

Whipping my head around, I search for any kind of weapon. On a small table beside me is the Mystic tome, the distinct Numanic symbol on the cover staring me in the face. As much as I want to know why it's here, the book isn't going to help me.

My eyes dart to what's next to it. A silver tray of syringes, some filled with murky liquid, others with dark red blood. Next to them, a collection of sharp metal instruments. Torture tools? Maybe I can grab one and turn it on my captors.

As if answering my silent wish, one arm comes free. No, all of my limbs!

I lunge for the sharp objects. Before I can reach them, hands grab my arms, and pull me to one of the pools of water.

I kick and scratch. It's no use. These fae are too strong. One pushes my face toward the pool's surface. It's filled with water, but no body. Not yet. All I can see is my reflection.

No. It isn't *my* reflection. I'm looking at Gaius.

I reach out to the image, then stare at the strange look of my fingers. *Wait. These aren't my hands.*

I'm not me.

"Gaius?" I croak, trembling as I stare back at myself—at Gaius—in confusion.

A second figure appears in the reflective water. A tall, dark shadow stands behind me, their hand lifting high. The faerie is holding something thin and sharp, ready to strike.

"Quinn!" Gaius' reflection screams.

∿

I startle awake in a dim room. I'm in my Dryad quarters. My shirt is soaked with sweat, though my body's chilled.

A fever.

Someone is sitting at my bedside. His form blocks most of the light so all I can see is the silhouette of his large, muscular body.

I tense, fearing I might still be in the dream.

His head is low, his forehead on his folded hands. His breathing is slow and tranquil as if he's fallen asleep.

I lift my head slightly, blinking to clear my vision and identify my keeper. It doesn't help. It only makes the room spin. I lie back down, feeling like I might be sick.

The figure's head rises. My movements must have stirred him.

Still unaware if he is friend or foe, I shut my eyes, pretending to sleep.

The figure takes a deep breath, and a gentle squeeze pulses against my fingers.

He's holding my hand.

My thoughts flit to Aeron, the only faerie I think it might be. As the figure lets go and gets up to leave, I open my eyes again and nearly call out to him.

I stop. This figure doesn't walk like Aeron. He's much too tall, much too burly. With the help of a candle that flickers on the nearby table, my sight improves as he stops and glances back at me one more time.

Dizziness returns with a vengeance as I catch sight of my father's dark braided beard.

Then he's gone, and darkness overtakes me again.

CHAPTER 42

I awake with a start, eyes frantic. I was dreaming of Gaius again.

My breathing hitches. I'm still in my bed, and Aeron is sitting by my side. This time, it's really him.

It was only a dream… wasn't it?

"Oh, thank Faylan." Aeron's voice shakes as he moves toward me, then he hesitates, clearing his throat. In a calmer tone, he peers behind him and adds, "I mean, um… how are you feeling?"

"Uh, all right, I think." My eyes strain to see what he's looking at, hoping I'm truly awake now. "What happened?" I gingerly touch my throbbing head.

"You passed out at dinner. Stopped breathing entirely at one point. You gave me—I mean *us*—quite a scare."

Aeron shifts to reveal Alys at the table behind him. She's examining a series of vials with red-colored liquid.

"She's been attending to you all night, doing some tests with your blood to see what might have happened."

Alys glances at me out of the corner of her eye. The shirt she wears reveals more of her neck than normal. Down the right side is a delicate new scar-tattoo that definitely wasn't there before. The swirls join at the base of the new mark and then splay upwards, almost like… a flame.

My mouth drops open.

"Are you sure you're all right?" Aeron asks, concern creeping into his voice. "Can I get you anything?"

I'm still looking at Alys' neck. "Yeah, um… I'll take some rum," I mutter.

Aeron's signature dimple makes an appearance. "I'm glad you're feeling well enough to make jokes. I think I saw the servants bring in some fresh goat's milk. I'll go get you some."

As he leaves, I almost call after him that I wasn't kidding about the rum, but I need him to leave so I can talk to Alys.

The door closes and Alys approaches, attentive, as if she knows a question is coming.

"Did you… Why did you save me?" I ask.

Alys just smiles.

Blast, I wish you could just talk to me.

Alys places a finger on her new fire tattoo, where a part of me will forever be imprinted.

"You didn't have to do that," I choke out.

Alys puts her hand on my arm. This time it's not gloved; her power runs through me like a calming yet tingling flow of energy.

Then I hear a voice. The one that spoke to me before I blacked out.

Well, I couldn't just let you die, it says.

The voice has a faint raspiness to it and a hint of spunk. Alys' mouth remains closed, but she lifts her brows till it finally hits me.

I'm hearing Alys speak—in my head!

I sit up too quickly. The room spins and Alys guides me back down.

Whoa, you're not ready for that quite yet, she warns without moving her mouth again.

"How are you doing that?" I ask aloud. "Can you hear what I'm thinking, too? Is that how your ability works?"

Alys grins. *Sometimes. At least with animals, my touch connects us somehow. I can speak to them… and they can speak to me.*

I stare. "You can hear creatures speak to you? Like actual words?"

Kind of. It's more like I can feel their emotions so powerfully that I have a pretty good idea what they're thinking. When I'm healing them, sometimes I even see flashbacks from their past, especially events that have caused them pain. Then I just think of how I'd want to respond to them, and it seems like they understand me. Most of the time, at least.

I pause, taking it all in. "You need to be touching them to do so?"

For the most part, skin to skin contact seems to do the trick. But as the bond is strengthened, some creatures and I are able to communicate fairly well without touch or even words.

"Like with Tomah?" I ask.

Alys nods. *Exactly. Even creatures that I haven't touched seem to trust me, as if I have a particular scent. As if I've been marked from all the times I've bonded with different creatures.*

I think back to our time in Isinglass, and the fish constantly swarming around her. Then during the Trial of Beauty… "That's how you communicated with the Leviathan," I say. "And why you were so surprised when the lynxicorns wouldn't listen to you."

She nods again, then her eyes flutter. She sways as if she's about to faint.

"Alys!" I force myself up to help her. "What's wrong?"

I'm fine. She straightens with a tired smile, motioning for me to lie back down. *It takes a lot out of me to heal, especially when it's a larger creature. It seems I take on their pain myself.*

"Like the jackalope in the forest." I recall her contorted face. "You can do all that for others, but your gift doesn't heal your own body?" She looked so terrible during the last trial.

My body does heal itself faster than most fae, it's just not instantaneous. In fact, the more I'm injured, the slower I heal. Like while battling a poison and being attacked by goblins at the same time, for instance.

She pulls up her sleeve to reveal that her goblin wounds are already closed. New pink skin has formed, knitting her slashed tattoos back together.

Relief washes over me, but I know she must still be dealing with my pain too. "I'm feeling much better now," I say, shifting away from her touch. "I don't want you to drain yourself."

Alys pats my arm. *It's okay. It took a while to heal you, but I'm done now. You had a lot of poison in your system.*

"Poison. From the trial?" I ask. "Didn't the plants we found wipe that out already?"

Alys presses her lips together. *I know what that poison feels like, but this one was very different. This one was powerful and poised to kill if I didn't act quickly.*

"What? How in Faylan did I get…" I think back through the evening, to the moments before my throat started to tickle. The only thing I'd eaten was… *the lily tart.* I knew it tasted different.

The image of the tall, dark figure from my dream poised to stab me flashes into my mind.

Was the dream trying to warn me of my attacker? I'm not anyone's favorite faerie. If someone wanted to poison me, any number of fae could be suspect. But there are only a few who knew I'd go right for the lily tarts. And I'm fairly sure I know which one would want me dead.

"This might sound insane," I say. "But I think it might have been the queen."

Alys' eyes widen. *Are you sure?*

"I don't have time to explain right now, but she definitely has reason to be upset with me. And honestly, I think she's up to something."

I go over the details in my head again. Vale basically confirmed in the temple that the missing book the queen is looking for is the Numanic text. If the queen found out what Hickory and I have been up to, maybe she decided it was time to take me out, especially after seeing us finish the trial together.

But would she really want to kill me? She needs me to keep training Vale, after all. Or does she? Vale's fighting skills have improved drastically lately and she's gotten a lot stronger. The only other competitor who could beat Vale in the Test of Strength now is... me. She already threatened to take Aeron's life. Why should I be any different?

Alys studies me as I think. *What do you think she's planning?* she asks.

"I don't know. Not yet anyway. But I might be getting a bit too close to it for her comfort. Actually…" I look at Alys' sleeve. "I think it may have something to do with that symbol on your arm that I pointed out the other day."

Alys lifts up her sleeve to reveal it.

"This is the same symbol we found in the temple, the sign of the Numa. Do you know how you got it?"

She shakes her head. *All I know is it's where my gift began. I was born with this mark and then, like the seed of a plant, every other tattoo has grown out of it each time I heal.*

"You must have healed a lot of creatures then," I say, knowing how extensive her tattoos are in the places I've seen.

Against my parents' advisement, yes. She averts her eyes. *They've forbidden me to use my gift, especially on or in front of other faeries.*

"Why would they do that? It's a lot better than the rumors about you being an agent of death."

Alys lowers her head. *Oh, you've heard about that, huh?*

"It's true?" I ask, now completely confused.

Not exactly, Alys begins. *I wasn't always the eldest of my siblings. I had an older sister, Lorrelle. She was as beautiful as she was fierce, born to be a great leader even from a young age. Then she grew very sick.*

"The Knolls?" I ask tentatively.

She nods. *It took hold of her so fast. My gift had just begun to surface, but my parents forbade me to try it on Lorrelle. I had only healed birds and other small animals. They didn't know what might happen to me. Still, I couldn't just sit back and watch her die. When one of her attendants fell asleep, I snuck in and tried to save her.*

Alys closes her eyes tight. *The pain was excruciating, like nothing I've experienced since. I screamed so loudly, all the realm must have heard. My parents came rushing in to find my hands on my sister, my few tattoos at the time glowing and lighting up the whole room. They pulled me off of her and while they took care of me, a few attendants checked on Lorrelle. But she'd already passed... I couldn't save her.* A tear rolls down Alys' cheek.

My heart aches, remembering how hard it was to lose Gaius. Knowing I couldn't save him. How hard it still is.

Alys continues. *My parents were devastated, and I'd slipped into a coma as well. They thought they'd lost two daughters; their only hope was that my tattoos continued to grow as I slept. Days later they stopped spreading, and I woke up. My body had finally healed and repaired itself. Everything except...* She stops and points to her throat.

"You lost your voice." All the pieces come together. "Is that when the rumors started?"

Alys rolls her eyes, turning toward the window. *Believe it or not, my parents actually spread that rumor themselves, though they deny it's true to anyone who asks. They say it's better for the world to fear me than to know the truth and the extent of my abilities. They're afraid others would try to use me to heal everyone, especially with the Knolls becoming more widespread. Or perhaps the Kobolds would experiment on me to figure out how to make a serum for the plague. My parents think my body wouldn't be able to hold up under the pressure, and I'd fall into a coma again. Maybe this time, I wouldn't wake up at all.* She looks at her gloved hand. *So, I put these on and keep people at a distance so they can't learn the truth.*

"But you don't agree that's what you should do."

Alys gazes out the window; her new fire-like tattoo stares me in the face.

Both of us have a secret gift that we can't reveal to the world. At least Alys can use hers for good. A rush of warmth and admiration flows through me. Perhaps a bit of jealousy too.

Alys turns back to me. *I just feel like if I could be used to save thousands, even at the expense of my own life, it would at least start to make up for the fact that I couldn't heal Lorrelle. But since I'm in line for the throne, they won't let me submit myself for study. They almost didn't let me help you in the infirmary, but I'd already begun before they arrived.*

"Alys." I put my hand on hers. "I appreciate what you want to do and what you did for me—but I'm not worth saving. The queen knows I'm on to her, whatever she's up to. I wouldn't be surprised if she comes after me again. If she does, I don't want you to rescue me. I think you're meant for something bigger, and you need to preserve your strength for whatever that is, okay?"

That's just the thing. Alys smiles. *Ever since we started this competition, this Numanic symbol on my arm has started burning. As I've studied our interactions, it really flares up whenever you're close by. I'm thinking it has something to do with your fire ability.*

Panic rises in my chest. I could still deny the gift. I could chalk it up to another hallucination during the trial. But both she and Hickory saw it. It was as plain as the flame tattoo on her neck.

Alys purses her lips. *I saw some of your most painful memories while healing you, Quinn. I know your first encounter with your magic hurt Gaius.*

I flinch. I never wanted anyone else to know about that, let alone feel the pain of it.

I turn away, but Alys squeezes my hand. *Quinn, gift or curse, your ability doesn't define you. What you do with it, that's what defines you.*

Like her healing power still running through my veins, Alys' words rush over me in a wave of emotions I can't place or handle. I swallow hard, speechless.

And I do believe that I'm meant for something more, she continues. *I saved you because I think it has something to do with you. I have a feeling we're not so different, you and me.*

I blink, processing, still wanting to argue. Wanting to ask so many more questions.

Aeron enters the room with a pitcher of goat's milk and a tray full of biscuits. Noticing our clasped hands and intense stares, he stops.

"Am I interrupting something?" He smiles suggestively.

"You wish." I laugh, trying to look excited about the snacks and not agitated that our conversation was cut short. There's still so much I want to understand.

Alys leaves her hand on mine for just a few seconds more to say one last thing.

Whatever you're planning, Quinn, I want in.

CHAPTER 43

I lie awake in bed, a million thoughts running through my mind. Alys wants *in*. In on what, even I'm not sure yet. All I know for certain is that I was poisoned, there's definitely something going on with the Mystic prophecy, and the queen might have something to do with both.

That, and the fact that I can't keep doing this alone.

The door to my room creaks open and Alys enters, carrying a flickering candle. A few minutes later, Hickory follows, then Aeron, and lastly Vale, who softly closes the door behind her.

Though every instinct in my body urged me to resist, I asked Alys to secretly gather them in my chambers.

If I want to survive another day, I have no other choice. I need help.

Setting her candle down on the table, Alys pulls up a wooden chair near my bedside. She places her hand on my arm, but this time instead of just leather gloves, I also feel her fingertips through small slits.

I hope you know what you're doing, Alys says in my mind.

I nearly flinch. They're the same words Whit used to caution me before the funeral heist. The one that went terribly wrong. Am I about to make another big mistake?

Alys eyes Aeron as he pulls up another chair, and Vale sits on the other end of my bed. Hickory looks at me over the top of his open sketchbook, which I requested he bring. He paces back and forth as his good eye glows faintly in the dim room.

"Okay, we're all here," Vale breaks the silence with a yawn, pulling her robe tighter around her. "What was so important that you needed us to meet in the middle of the night?"

Aeron leans in, examining my face. "Are you feeling worse?"

"Well, I'm not dead," I say with a weak smile. "That's sort of what I wanted to talk to all of you about."

Hickory stops pacing as the four of them stare at me.

"I've called you all here tonight because it's obvious that someone wants me dead. And I think it might have something to do with the Mystic prophecy. Hickory, can you read it again?"

Tentatively, Hickory flips through his sketchbook to where he's written down Vale's translation. After he reads it to us, I proceed to tell them everything. Well, at least what they need to know.

I share about the recurring dream I've been having of Faylan in ruins and how it lines up with Hickory's painted vision. I leave out the part about Gaius, though. That part is personal, and I'm already sounding crazy enough. I also tell them about how the tome reacted to my touch and how Hickory has been working on translating it for us.

"So, *you* stole the book from my library?" Vale accuses.

"No, I didn't… You're missing the point." I shake my head, trying to keep my cool. "Think about all the strange things that have happened. The lynxicorns turning on Alys. The goblins trying to destroy us. The moonrain drought. The Plague. The threat of war. Lord Torlon even said himself that the Sacred Vine is suffering." I take a deep breath, second-guessing my plan and my sanity one more time. "Hickory thinks it may be the Mystic prophecy coming true. *Stone and dust they must combine with every royal clan bloodline.*" I look at each of them. "If the Numa are returning, it sounds like it may have something to do with us."

Aeron blinks before cracking a smile. He turns to Hickory. "You've really got to lay off the pixie dust, mate. Or at least, don't go sharing it with Quinn."

Hickory steps forward as if he's about to tackle Aeron.

"Aeron!" My brow furrows, confused. I know how I must sound, but I didn't expect this kind of reaction from him. "I haven't taken a whiff, I swear. You saw the prophecy yourself. You can't deny it. It helped us escape the temple. It's also in the Mystic tome word for word. There's got to be more to it."

Aeron sighs and softens his tone, leaning forward on his elbows. "I'm sorry, but you just went through a very traumatic ordeal. Can you blame me for being a bit concerned? I mean, you had a dream, Hickory had a vision, some ancient words in some book showed up in a random temple... and now the end of the world is coming? Did I get all that right?"

"I knew he'd make it into some kind of joke." Hickory looks at me. "Quinn, why are you doing this? We were doing fine without—"

"Now, wait a minute." Aeron puts up a hand. "What about you, Alys? Are you in on this too?"

Without hesitating, Alys pulls up her sleeve to reveal the Numanic symbol on her arm.

Hickory's eyes grow wide and he rushes to her side. "Wow... May I?" he asks before examining it further.

Alys nods.

"Well, I'm outnumbered," Aeron huffs. "Vale?"

We all look to Vale, who's been suspiciously quiet.

"I don't have time for this." Vale stands up to leave. "There are still two trials to come, and I don't want to just survive them. I want that crown."

I glare at her. "Vale, it won't matter who wins if there's no world left to rule."

Vale hesitates. "Fine. Not that I'm saying I believe you... but if you want my help, I'm going to need that book back." She puts out her hand.

Aeron's mouth drops open. "You're not seriously encouraging this."

I shake my head at Vale. "No way."

"You obviously need me to keep translating for you," she persists. "How can I do that if I don't have it?"

"You can meet with Hickory and look over it with him," I say. Hickory's ears perk up at the mention of more time with Vale. "But I can't let you take it back."

"Why not?" Vale demands. "It's mine anyway."

I huff. "Because I know your mother is desperate for it, and I know you'd give it right back to her."

Vale gawks at me, then crosses her arms. "So? It's her book."

"You said it was *yours*." I narrow my eyes. "What's really going on,

Vale? What does she want with it?" I try to sound commanding, though my voice is still ragged.

"I don't know." Vale fidgets. "What does it matter anyway?"

I really don't think she knows, Alys speaks into my mind as she looks at Vale. *Her mother is probably keeping secrets from her too.*

"It matters—" I tell Vale, trying to stay calm "—because she's the one who poisoned me."

"What?" Hickory and Aeron exclaim at the same time.

My stare remains focused on Vale. "She's the only one with a motive."

Vale's face slowly turns as red as her hair. "How dare you. There's no way my mother had anything to do with this. I know all of her potions and how to test for them. I'll prove it!"

She crosses to the table and swipes a vial of my blood before storming toward the door, her eyes brimming with tears.

"Vale, wait," I say. She stops right before the door. Either Alys is right and Vale's mother is keeping her in the dark, or I'm dead wrong. "Maybe it wasn't her."

Vale turns, her hand still gripping the vial tightly.

I choose my next words carefully. "But, if it wasn't her, that means we still have a killer on the loose… and we have no idea what they want. Which means none of us are safe."

Vale's gaze drops to the floor before she walks back to my bed, plopping down on the end, wiping at her eyes.

Everyone else seems lost in thought as well, wondering what it all means.

"Together when the moons align…" Vale breaks the silence, sniffing back the last of her tears. "So we have a competition to finish, a killer to find, and a prophecy to figure out all before the next Moon Harvest, huh? Well, I'll start by examining this." She holds up the vial.

Vale is in.

"When is the Moon Harvest again?" Aeron sighs, then gives me a tentative smile. Despite his skepticism, he's in too.

Hickory does a quick tally in the air. "Just a few weeks—after the end of the Ethodine."

Alys gives my arm a light squeeze. *That's not a lot of time.*

"No, it's not," I say aloud, forgetting the others can't hear Alys.

They look at me. "I mean, it's not a lot of time. We'd better get to work."

CHAPTER 44

The sun will be up in just a few hours, so we put together a quick plan.

Hickory and Vale will work on translating more of the book together in secret. Vale will analyze the poison. And the rest of us will take their translation and keep trying to puzzle out what the prophecy actually means.

After we're done, they depart my room one by one.

Aeron is the last to leave.

"Hey," he says, pausing at the door. "I'm sorry about giving you a hard time earlier."

"It's fine. Even *I* think it sounds crazy."

"You only sound a little crazy," he teases, then grows serious. "Just promise me you'll be careful, okay? If something really is going on, I don't want to see you get in any more trouble."

I'm about to scold him for worrying about me again, but he continues, his gaze fixed on the floor. "I... I don't know if I could sit by your bedside again, not knowing if you'll wake up, you know?"

At his words, all the fight leaves my body, remembering him darting after me when I collapsed at dinner, and his great relief when I awoke. Warmth pools in my chest. "I know," I say softly.

"Good." He smiles. "You know what? You look like you could use some fresh air."

"It's the middle of the night." I laugh. "What's going on in that head of yours?"

"Well, before you called this little meeting, I had something I wanted to show you... You're right, though. It's late, and you're still recovering. You should rest." He puts a hand on the doorknob.

"Wait, what was it?" I try to push myself off the mattress, too intrigued now to sleep. My legs give out. Even my wings are too tired to release as I fall.

Aeron darts over and catches me just in time. I dangle there in his arms, his breath on my skin. Heat rises to my cheeks, and while part of me wants to push away, to stand on my own, the other part wants to lean in a bit closer.

Looking down at my useless legs, I try to laugh it off. "Actually, it looks like I'm not going anywhere fast. I'd just get us caught." It's probably for the best. What if the queen finds out? Somehow, she seems to have eyes everywhere. If she wasn't afraid to poison me, she definitely wouldn't bat an eye at getting rid of Aeron.

But he isn't ready to give up. A mischievous smile tugs at the corner of his lips. "There's always the window. This place isn't too far. I could carry you, unless that's too chivalrous for the likes of Captain Shade. I could always go by myself."

Now I have to know what this surprise is. And, if I'm honest with myself, I'm not ready to be left alone in the darkness of my room.

Or for Aeron to leave.

"I guess ... you could carry me," I give in, half-begrudgingly. "Just this once."

"Just this once." His dimple appears.

After making sure the coast is clear, Aeron scoops me up, and we soar out the window into the cool night air, both of my arms tight around his neck. I try to loosen my hold, but remembering the weakness of my wings, I pull closer. Aeron's smile tells me he doesn't mind in the least.

Flying through the branches of the Dryad homes, their lamps doused long ago, the moonlight guides Aeron to his target, right outside the village.

"What's all the way out here?" I ask as we land.

"You'll see."

He carries me through the brush, and the foliage opens up to reveal a scene that makes my heart swell. A lake surrounded by tall trees sparkles in the moonlight. Fireflies dance over the surface as a small glittering waterfall pours into the lake. A hidden oasis.

Resting near the water's edge is a simple rowboat, with a glowing lantern hanging off a hook on the back.

My grip on Aeron's neck relaxes, and my mouth parts. When we reach the boat, Aeron gently lowers me inside, grabbing a blanket to put around my shoulders.

I look up at him. "What did you… How did you…?"

"I came across this place a few days ago and somehow, it made me think of you." As he looks around, I feel a flush beneath my skin. "When we were stuck in the Mystic temple, I vowed myself that if we made it out alive, I'd bring you here. I know it isn't your Minnow or the Silver Sea, but I thought you might enjoy a little time on the water. And I mean *on* it. No swimming this time, I promise."

Warmth spreads through my chest. "It's actually… kind of perfect."

No one has ever done something this…thoughtful for me.

"Good," he says with a contented sigh. It's hard to tell in the dim light, but I swear he's blushing. "Well, shall we shove off then?"

Before I can respond, Aeron rushes behind me, pushing the boat fully into the lake as I struggle not to laugh like a giddy sprite. As the boat settles in the water, Aeron flies over the top and lands on the bench seat across from me. Retracting his fin-like wings, he grabs the oars on either side.

"All right, what first, Captain?" he asks, playing the part of my eager crew.

I laugh again, swelling with joy at the sound of that title coming from his lips. More than ready to play along, I begin giving commands. "Batten down the hatches! Raise anchor! Set the sails!"

"Aye, aye, Captain!" Aeron attempts his best pirate-voice as he mimes the seafaring directions, joining in my laughter as he moves us out to the middle of the lake.

Though the scene around us is lovely, I can't help closing my eyes. The rushing water from the falls is so soothing. It's almost as if I can feel it healing me from the inside out.

I try imagining a clear night back on the Silver Sea. I can't picture what ship I'd be on. In reality, it wouldn't be the Minnow. And if the queen tried to kill me, who knows if she still intends to give me a vessel.

My smile fades as the vision shatters. Without warning, scenes from my nightmares rush to replace it. Gaius yelling. The Vine falling. The tall, dark figure raising a weapon toward me.

No, he's raising it toward me in *Gaius'* body.

I open my eyes to meet Aeron's concerned gaze.

"Is something wrong?" he asks, bringing his rowing to a stop.

"What?" I blink. "Oh, no. It's not you. Or this."

"Are you thinking about your dreams again?" he guesses tentatively.

How did he get so good at reading me?

"Sort of." I swallow, pulling the blanket tighter as if it can protect me from the visions. "One thing's still bothering me about them."

"*One* thing?" Aeron chuckles lightly. "Every part of them sounds pretty awful."

I relax my hands in my lap. "True. But… there's something I haven't mentioned to anyone else yet."

How am I going to explain this? I shake my head. *I shouldn't be sharing this at all.*

"Quinn." Aeron puts a hand on mine. "You can tell me."

Can I? For a lucid moment, I fear his gaze, his sudden yet comforting touch, not trusting his words.

My father's warnings back in Greymerrow echo in my mind. *You must not trust anyone.*

I listen for the tone of Aeron's voice, for the watery effect it takes when he uses his gift. But his voice remains normal, filled with sincerity. The only sound of water comes from the falls.

"Gaius is in the dreams too," I say.

Aeron's comforting grin fades. He pulls back his hand, taking in my revelation. Then he shakes his head, his lightness returning. "That makes sense. You're going through a lot right now. You miss him."

"That's what I thought too," I agree. "But if these visions are real, they have to be coming from somewhere. What if the Dryads' beliefs about spirits are true? What if Gaius' ghost or whatever has been trying to tell me something?"

Aeron just stares. "...About the Numa?"

"Yes, but maybe more than that, too." I pause. "I had a different dream before waking up from the poison. One where I was attacked, nearly tortured. Someone was about to stab me with something."

I think of the syringes of murky liquid. Were they attempting to inject me with poison?

"And when I looked at my reflection, it wasn't me looking back. It was Gaius."

As I speak, Aeron's skin ironically turns a ghostly shade of white. Or perhaps it's just the reflection of the moons.

When he doesn't respond, I continue. "At first I thought maybe he was trying to warn me about my attacker, about the poisoning. But why would he warn me of something that already happened? I know it sounds crazy... but what if Gaius is trying to tell me something about *his* death? What if Gaius was poisoned, just like me?"

"Quinn," Aeron says, finally finding his voice. "Gaius died from the Knolls. The Plague isn't something you can bottle up and distribute."

"Not that we know of," I press. "The Dryads bottled up the delirium infection they gave us during the Trial of Life. Who's to say someone couldn't do it with the Plague, too?"

Aeron stares blankly.

I'm probably not making any sense. I'm so tired. Worn out. I lower my face into my hands and groan. "Blast... I'm losing my mind, aren't I?" My voice cracks.

"No. I mean... I'm sorry, Quinn." Aeron's voice falters as he shifts closer, placing a hand on my knee. "Don't cry, okay?"

I nearly laugh into my hands. "You don't have to worry about that. I don't cry."

"You don't cry?" His voice lightens in humored surprise. "Are you serious?"

"Very," my voice is muffled by my hands.

"Like, *never*?"

"Not for a long time."

He sighs. "That's so..."

"Strange?" I finish for him, fearing the answer.

"Sad." Sympathy laces his words.

"Sad?" That isn't the reaction I thought I'd get. I look up to challenge him, then stop.

Aeron has moved closer to me, his face much closer than I expected. He's looking at me with those mesmerizing sea-blue eyes.

"Shouldn't that be a good thing?" I swallow. "I mean, who wants to cry, anyway? What's the point?"

With one smooth movement, Aeron brings my hands down into my lap and tucks a lock of curly hair behind my ear. His touch silences me. "My mother says tears can actually be healing. They help process and release pain, carrying it from the body and out to sea." He looks into my eyes as if searching my soul. "You must be carrying so much pain..."

You have no idea. I can't bring myself to say it out loud.

"I wish I could take it away for you," he says.

I try to give him an encouraging smile. "Thanks... but you can't. No one can."

I think of Alys and how she can take away sickness or even near-death with only a touch. Even she can't uproot the inner turmoil of someone's heart.

Aeron's hand moves to my cheek, only taking his eyes off mine to glance at my lips. "I can try." He shifts closer.

"But..." I say breathlessly, trying to think of an excuse to stop him. There's so many I could give. Deep down, I don't want to.

I've fallen willingly under his spell after all.

"No more holding back," he whispers.

And gently pulling my face toward his, he kisses me.

Alarms go off in my mind, bells that ring with the queen's warnings. They're quickly drowned out by the roar of my heart and the press of his lips. My body ignites—not into actual flames, thankfully, but a warmth courses somewhere deep inside as I lean into him. It's as if we're the only two faeries in the world.

And even if it's just for this fleeting moment, the dull pain I carry everywhere drifts away with the gentle waves.

CAVERN OF TERRORS

THE KOBOLD RACE

CHAPTER 45

I dreamily drop garments into my trunk as morning light filters through the window; visions of my night with Aeron won't leave me alone. I walk a few paces, get lost in thought, and completely forget what I was about to do. After I drift off for the fifth time, I curse.

This is why I told myself not to let Aeron become a distraction. At every turn, I see the lake, the boat, Aeron kissing me.

Blast! Why were his lips so soft? So comforting? He tasted like the sea. Like a home I've never truly known but have always yearned for. It thrilled and frightened me all at once.

It wasn't even a long kiss. Aeron was a perfect gentleman, though part of me wished there'd been more. We didn't exchange many words afterwards. Aeron rowed us to shore, flew me back to my window, and asked if I needed anything before he departed. That was it.

I woke up wondering if it'd been another dream. But I'm not one to have pleasant dreams. At least for a few moments, Aeron had chased the nightmares away.

It can't happen again. I shouldn't have let it happen even once. The queen's warnings and her subtle threats echo in my mind. If I don't distance myself from him, then he could be in danger again.

Besides, we still have two more trials ahead of us, an unknown assailant, and a prophecy to unravel. Aeron did what he set out to do—he felt sorry for me and took away the pain, even if it was for a short time.

It didn't mean anything more, not really. He's still a betrothed Nymph prince, and I'm still, well… me.

It was a nice dream, while it lasted.

A knock at my door yanks me back to the present. As I go to answer it, I halfway expect it to be Aeron coming to tell me that he regrets the kiss. That I should just forget it happened. Or perhaps it's Hickory coming to berate me for spilling all of our secrets last night. Or worse, the queen—or whoever poisoned me—coming to finish what they started.

Anyone but who it actually is.

"Leman?" As I stare up at Alys' brother, I hold onto the edge of the door, keeping it only partially open. If he's here to yell at me again, I'm prepared to slam the door right in his face.

Uncertain eyes peer down at me from his wolf face-paint, replacing his usual glare. "Good morning. Yes, uh…" He straightens, muscles tensing. His hands fidget at his sides as if he doesn't know what to do with them. "You look… well."

Is he trying to make small talk?

"Thank you…?" I drawl. *What does he want?*

"I, um… Ouch!" Leman jerks his leg as Ivy peeks out from behind him with an impish smile.

"Hi, Quinn!" She beams at me, then reprimands her brother. "No dawdling. We don't have much time. Now, go on."

"Fine. What I've come to say is…" Leman starts begrudgingly. "I'm glad you're feeling better."

"And…" Ivy motions him along.

"And…" A muscle twitches in his jaw as he puts down his foot tenderly. "I just wanted to… say thank you for helping Alys during the Trial of Life." His gaze strays to the wall. "I'd heard Alys barely made it out alive, but I didn't know you had helped her until after you collapsed at the feast. I don't know why you did it, and frankly, I don't care. Just… thank you." His eyes are glassy. Is this tall, burly puck about to cry?

"You're welcome." I'm still holding onto the door, not sure what I should do next.

"And…" Ivy prods Leman once again.

Leman rolls his eyes. "May we come in?"

If it was just Leman, I would have said no. All Ivy has to do is blink her big brown eyes at me, and I give in.

"Oh, I can't stand it anymore!" Ivy says excitedly as I shut the door after them. "Leman's come to teach you some more signing before you leave us. As a thank you!"

"*More* signing?" Leman eyes her and then me.

"I only taught her a few phrases," Ivy lies as she tugs at both our arms to sit down. "My father says that you leave for the Kobold tunnels at sunset. Not very long to learn. Still, I'm sure anything would help. I'm not a very good teacher, but my brother's the best, aren't you, Leman?"

He still looks unsure, and I'm tempted to tell him that he can just forget it. That Alys can already speak to me just by touch. That would probably make him even more upset. Besides, knowing how to sign to Alys when she isn't near me could prove useful.

"If you're willing, I'd like to learn," I say as politely as I can. "I'm a fast learner."

A smile tugs at his mouth. "Let's see how fast."

With the sun low in the sky, all the competitors are called down to meet outside the Dryad village, where a line of fishing vessels float in a nearby river. The ships will take us to the nearest tunnel, one of the many entrances to the underground city of the Kobolds.

As our attendants climb into the other boats, the five of us are piled into a smaller one, just big enough to carry all of us. And the queen, of course.

"Ah, Quinn," Queen Gwendolyn says as I step onto the boat deck. I nearly jump back out. "So good to see you up and about. We thought we'd lost you."

You would have liked that, wouldn't you?

She sounds sincere enough, but I can't trust anything she says. Not until Vale confirms her innocence.

"Thank you, Your Majesty." I bow my head and brush past her.

As the Dryads bid us farewell from the land, the other four heirs are lined up along the boat's railing. On my way to join them, I bump shoulders with a nearly forgotten, still very unwelcome, foe.

"We meet again. And on a ship, no less." Moon Face sneers.

"Where have *you* been?" I ask. The last time I saw him was in Isinglass. Has he been in Eldore looking for the Mystic tome all this time?

"Wouldn't you like to know?" His crescent-shaped scar creases as he narrows his eyes, his hatred for me as apparent as ever. He looks tired, too. Although it's a perfectly cool day, sweat beads on his forehead. "Make sure not to get too close to the edge there, *pirate*." He lets out a dark laugh as I pass him.

Reaching the others, I try to block out the vision of him throwing me overboard and grip the railing between Vale and Aeron.

"Any progress with the *you-know-what*?" I ask Vale, plastering on a smile for the Dryads below.

"There are so many poisons it could be. I barely slept last night trying to figure it out." A lock of red hair falls over Vale's weary eyes. "So far it doesn't match anything of my mother's, so cool it."

I sigh, telling myself to be patient.

"Speaking of last night…" Aeron whispers from the other side of me, running a hand over the gills on his neck. Vale's ears twitch toward us.

Really? He hasn't sought me out all day and yet he wants to bring this up *now*?

Aeron leans in to whisper again. "I'm sorry if I overstepped. I was… It was—"

"What are you two talking about?" Hickory says from the other side of Vale, his good eye squinting at us. "Did I miss something?" He probably thinks we're referring to the prophecy.

"Yes, what *are* you two talking about?" Vale chimes in, pressing up against my arm.

"Nothing," I blurt out. "It was nothing."

Whatever it was at the time, the kiss can't mean anything going forward. It was a nice dream, but like all dreams, I have to wake up to reality.

"Right… It was nothing." Aeron confirms softly.

In an effort not to take it back, I look over at Alys, who's barely noticed our exchange. She's too busy staring back at her clan. Her family. A wind picks up, tossing her black braids, and tears fill her eyes.

Every faerie in her clan puts their hands over their hearts and then raises them up to the sky. Alys returns the Dryad gesture, and our boat starts down the river.

"Many blessings on your journey, young warriors," Lord Torlon calls.

Ivy waves frantically at Torlon's side while Leman stares directly at me, signing as subtly as he can.

Take care of my sister, pirate. He cracks a smile.

I will, I sign back.

Alys catches our exchange. She looks from Leman to me in confusion—before breaking into a smile as well.

"Wait, when did you learn how to sign?" Vale's eyes are wide as Aeron and Hickory give me curious looks.

"Jealous that I finally know something you don't?" I smirk at her.

"Ha! Jealous of you?" Vale laughs, crossing her arms. "In your dreams."

As our boat rounds the bend, the Dryads disappear behind the trees, and I realize how much has changed in just one short week. When we first entered the Woodlands, most of us were still fairly fierce competitors. Now we leave as… maybe not friends, exactly, but definitely with a certain level of understanding and respect for each other. Something I don't think anyone expected, especially not us.

We keep all this to ourselves, of course. During our voyage, we continue the usual bickering, throwing around a few insults for good measure. In fact, it soon becomes a game to see who can come up with the best jabs. Alys actually comes up with some of the best ones, but with her signing, only I can understand them.

At one point, I catch Hickory at the stern of the ship, staring out at the passing Woodlands as daylight quickly dissipates.

"No sketchbook?" I join him at the railing, far enough away that the queen or anyone else would think nothing of it.

"Not this time." Hickory sighs. "After thinking I'd lost my sight for good during the last trial, I figured I'd spend more time actually looking at the real thing than trying to capture it on a page. Especially since… you know."

I nod. He means before we enter the dark abyss of the tunnels.

"So," he says, lowering his voice more. "Are we ever going to talk about this fire of yours?"

I let out a soft groan, pretending to look at the passing trees. "Do we have to?"

His lips quirk up. "I thought something funny was going on when you pulled fire out of nowhere during the Trial of Beauty. I can't believe that you've kept it a secret this whole time. I know your clan is not exactly *magic friendly*, especially toward Mystic magic—"

"I'm *not* a Mystic," I say adamantly, looking around to make sure no one is listening.

"Of course you're not." Hickory plays along. "*But*, if you were…"

I roll my eyes.

"That would be sort of amazing. I'd be lying if I didn't admit I was jealous," he says. "And you know, finding out more about your possible heritage and Mystic-like gift could help us figure out their prophecy." He looks at me out of the corner of his good eye.

"It's just… I can't control it. The fire, I mean." I lean on the railing, flexing my fingers. "The fact that it aided us against the goblins was a fluke. It doesn't always obey. In fact, it usually causes more harm than good." I grow quiet, thinking about Gaius.

"Well, I'm no Mystic," Hickory says. "But once we get into the tunnels, I may have something that could help you learn more."

I look up with hopeful eyes. Maybe Alys was right. Could I really learn to master this ability, instead of it mastering me?

"We're nearly there," the queen announces from the bow of the ship where Alys, Aeron and Vale stand with her.

As Hickory and I join them, I see that the river is guiding us to one of the many caves throughout Faylan. One that will lead into the tunnels of Tartarus. Kobold guards gripping pickaxes watch us carefully, eyeing the queen before letting our boats pass.

As we slip into the shadows of the cave, water rushes around us. I look at Hickory, whose good eye has started to glow.

"I'd hold onto something." He nods to me, taking hold of the railing himself.

The rest of us follow his lead just in time for the river to bend and shoot our line of boats down a winding canal. Descending further into the dark underground world, I hold my breath until our boat finally evens out and slows at the bottom.

"That was exciting," Aeron says with a relieved laugh.

"Sure, exciting." I shake my head. Usually I live for adventure, but I was not prepared for that.

As we float along, the tunnel feels more like a damp dungeon or the belly of a beast who's swallowed us whole. Lanterns dispersed along the walls are the only light to our path. Soft plinks of dripping water and the twitter of bats leaves an unsettled feeling in my stomach as the arched ceilings narrow, inching closer to us the farther we go.

I loosen the collar of my tunic, suddenly aware of how loud my breathing is. I've always been curious about the tunnels, but I was right to never volunteer for Maverick's raids down here. Give me a sea storm over this any day. I close my eyes, calling forth images of my wide-open ocean. It's not helping.

My eyes search for Hickory in the lantern light. He's behind us, holding fast to the ship's mast as a cold, stale wind sends ghostly whirls through the cavern. The glow of his good eye flickers in and out, and his grip tightens until his knuckles turn white. No wonder he dreams of escaping this place for good.

"Do you hear that?" Vale asks, stepping curiously toward the railing.

My ears twitch as the rest of us shuffle forward to join her. The sharp ping of metal and the echo of distant voices grow louder and more distinct. "It sounds like—"

"It's singing!" Aeron says, surprise and excitement dancing in his torch-lit eyes.

"It's the pixie dust miners." Hickory nods ahead.

Soon, lanterns cast their golden glow over a stretch of Kobolds who drive pickaxes into the walls on either side of the cave. They chisel away at crumbling debris, and sparkling pixie crystals of varying colors emerge from roots in the dirt as they sing in deep, sorrowful tones. Listening to the melody, I vaguely remember little Luna humming it from time to time while mending the Minnow's nets. I half smile at the memory. This tune is sadder than I remember.

The music in Isinglass was beautiful, but this simple song is just as enchanting. A lament of the miner's plight. Even Aeron's eyes glisten with emotion.

As the sound envelops us, the song turns into a round, and my heart tightens. A pressure builds behind my eyes and stings at the

ON WINGS OF ASH AND DUST

corners. Like Aeron spoke of on the lake, I want so badly to experience the release of tears, but none come.

Just accept it. You'll never cry again.

We sail through many different parts of the tunnels, even one that brings us under the sea itself. Above us, a transparent material takes the place of the rock ceiling. Lit up by bioluminescent plankton, a cluster of sharks looms over us as crabs scuttle across the surface.

"What's this?" Aeron shoots Hickory a hard stare. "Has your clan been trying to spy on my folk?"

"Don't flatter yourself." Hickory chuckles. "We have countless tunnels that lead to all different parts of Faylan. Since the deep sea is the only part we can't physically enter, the Kobolds built tunnels like this to escape the darkness for a time and study the sea creatures that pass by."

"Ah." Aeron nods curtly, though his gills remain tensed.

As we go deeper, more of the distinct, sweet scent of pixie dust mixes with the pungent smell of smoke. It nearly overwhelms me as our boat enters a large cavernous opening, leading us right into the heart of Tartarus. Following the underground river through the busy center of the city, we sail around smoke-billowing structures and under arched bridges.

"Well…" The rest of Hickory's words are swallowed by the deafening cacophony of bustling voices and churning machinery.

"What did you say?" I yell, resisting the urge to cover my ears.

"I said, this is home!" Hickory yells back. "And the crazy lot who live here."

As nearby Kobolds notice us, they lift their caps and cave helmets to reveal bright, glowing eyes. While many blink with curiosity, others straighten their vests and patchwork clothing, lifting their proud soot-stained faces.

Alys draws closer to my side. This is a stark contrast from the lush, tranquil forest we just left, and it seems she's struggling to adjust too. Everywhere we turn is earth and rock, gears and tubes, pulleys and smog. Smoke clouds rise from the city, up toward vents in the cavern ceiling. The only signs of plant life are the massive roots of the Sacred Vine that weave in from the tunnel's ceiling, along the walls and throughout the city.

As we leave the city's center, I've just begun to think we're clear of most of the noise when a churning rumble comes from the cavern walls. Rock debris explodes like ship cannons, and an odd machine with a sharp twisting head plows through. Alys' eyes widen, and I rush to shield our heads with my wings as flecks of rubble sprinkle onto the ship's deck.

Thanks, she signs gratefully.

I nod. "What was that thing?"

"That's a Tunneler," Hickory explains, then points to his head. "Another reason why Kobolds are fond of their hats."

Around the newly formed opening, Kobold homes are carved into the sides of the enormous cavern, kind of like the mountainside city I grew up in. Stories of them are stacked high, one on top of the other, with long rock-formed bridges that span across the city.

Through one of the lower passages, the Kobie Express whistle blows as it makes its final stop in the cave, full of Kobolds who have jobs or other places to be on the surface.

"Wow, the tracks really do reach all the way down here," I say, stifling a shudder. I'm glad we took the boats instead.

As we reach the other end of the city, lanterns illuminate a looming stone castle featuring a huge metal disk embedded in its central tower. Strange spinning arrows rotate over the mechanism of gears that fill the center.

"Hickory, what is that?" Vale draws closer to him, pointing to it.

"My father calls it a timepiece, or a clock, if you prefer," he says. A slight blush rises in his cheeks at her nearness as he seems to revel in teaching something to the girl who knows everything. "Since we don't have the benefit of measuring time by daylight, my father commissioned it so we could measure the hours."

I study the large arrows as they tick by, not sure if I like this contraption. Reminds me too much of how quickly time passes. Lately, I feel like I have less and less of it every day.

Vale seems thoroughly fascinated. "How curious." She smiles, intrigue dancing in her eyes. "How does it work?"

I can tell Hickory is loving the attention, not wanting it to end, but Vale's eyes are pulled upward. A flock of flying figures swoops down from one of the castle towers, casting their shadows over us before landing on the dock.

"Welcome to Tartarus." The Kobold Lord steps through his gathered court, swinging his gold cane with one hand and leading his wife with the other. I remember their ghostly pale faces from the previous trials.

"Lord Zephen. Lady Irina." The queen steps off the boat first and nods to them curtly.

Lord Zephen removes his tall top hat and holds it to his tailored vest as he bows his head ever so slightly. "Your Majesty."

He then peers down at the rest of us. His disturbingly large eyes blink rapidly through jewel-studded goggles. I draw back until he raises the goggles to the top of his head. A slanted smile slides up his alabaster face.

"We're so very pleased to see that you've all arrived safely," he says, with more flamboyance than I expect. "Aren't we, Irina?"

"Oh yes." Lady Irina claps her gloved hands and steps forward with surprising grace, considering her ridiculously tight corset. "There are many dangers in these tunnels." She gazes over her high ruffled collar as we step off the creaking boat, her eyes searching. Once she spots Hickory, she ushers him over to join them, seeming to examine him for injuries.

"Nothing a little creativity can't solve. Am I right, my boy?" Lord Zephen nudges Hickory with his elbow. He then pulls back his cape to reveal a mechanical leg from the knee down. He taps it with his cane and does a little jig to show off its surprisingly limber function.

Irina giggles into her glove admiringly. Hickory stifles a cringe, which Zephen doesn't miss.

"Our son prefers playing with watercolors on the surface over fiddling with the gears and grease of our lowly world," the Kobold Lord says, looking down on his son as the fae in his court give Hickory disapproving glares.

Hickory purses his lips, holding tightly to the strap of his satchel across his chest.

Seeing Hickory like this makes me want to kick the cane right out from under the Kobold Lord. Before I can, he lifts it toward the surrounding city.

"As you can see, our Etho drives us to the very edges of innovation." Zephen takes a step toward us, his glowing eyes ablaze with a kind of mischief that makes me want to climb back into the boat. "We can hardly wait to see your own creativity put to the test in what we're sure will be the most challenging trial you've yet to survive."

Based on the dangers of the last three trials, I swallow hard. What could possibly be worse than what we've endured already?

"Until then, we'll show you to your chambers," Lady Irina says, whipping around her layered skirts as she starts back to the castle. "I wouldn't get too comfortable, though. We have a fabulous feast along with some very *special entertainment* planned in your honor."

As we follow them into the dark castle, I already know there's no way I'm going to feel settled here.

CHAPTER 46

After we find our rooms, Hickory ushers the rest of us down the hall to his personal quarters.

"Come on, there's something I've got to show you," he whispers as he looks both ways down the empty hall before putting a metal key into the bolt on his door and turning it.

Gears whine and creak as they shift and pop, unlocking the mechanism. As he pushes the door open, a rod on the wall reaches toward a lantern and flicks a match. It ignites a flame inside, bringing the room to life. At the sight, I stifle a gasp.

Hickory's room is packed from floor to ceiling. Paints and easels, books and maps, a collection of pixie dust pipes and mountains of other gears and trinkets, many of which I can't identify. There are so many colors that the entire room looks like an abstract piece of art. Still clustered near the door, the rest of us look at each other, not sure where to step first, as Hickory closes the door behind us.

"Don't be shy. Come in, come in before anyone sees. We don't have much time," Hickory says as he follows the only uncluttered path, weaving through the piles of junk, and lights a candle near his disheveled bed.

"Hickory, what is all this?" Vale asks, picking up the hem of her dress as she steps carefully.

"Oh!" He gazes at all his treasures with joy. "In the midst of drab tunnel life, this is my sanctuary." He looks at Alys. "My Vyndoria in the midst of an otherwise dreary Woodlands, if you like."

Alys' face brightens approvingly.

Spotting a pixie dust pipe on a pile of books, he swipes it up, lighting it with the nearby candle. He puts it in the crook of his mouth and gazes around again. "These are all the things I've collected throughout my travels of Faylan. I have to admit, I don't know what some of them are, but it's all quite fascinating, don't you think?"

"If you don't know what they are, then why do you have them?" Aeron asks, picking up a collection of metal pieces held together by delicate springs. As he examines one of the circular appendages with a smiling face etched into the surface, it nearly breaks off.

"Careful!" Hickory flies over a crate of paints to take the metal doll from Aeron before he can do any more harm. He cradles it in his hand as if it's the most precious thing in the world, observing its condition with his good eye. "If you knew there would come a day where you won't be able to see anything at all, then you'd probably do the same."

A pang of sadness for him distracts me, and I forget to look where I'm going. I trip over something, catching myself against the only wall that's not hidden by the stacks. It's covered in flyers, drawings, ancient maps, and scribbles so hurried, I can barely read them.

"Hickory?" I stare at the collage of clippings.

"Ah! That's what I wanted to show you." He makes his way over. "These are my theories."

"All of them?" Vale asks, intrigued.

"Yes. I've been studying the Mystics for years now. There's all kinds of theories about them, their prophecies concerning the Numa and such. At first it was just a hobby, something I found fascinating. But the more I've discovered about them, the more inconsistencies and surprises I've found. The more I've pieced together, the more I've become—"

"Obsessed?" Aeron lifts a brow.

"*Dedicated*," Hickory corrects, staying focused on the wall. "To finding the truth. I have a feeling that they were more misunderstood than we realize."

A shadow falls over his features as he runs a finger over a drawing. A dragon-winged Mystic holds a book in one hand and a ball of flame in the other.

The image makes me shudder, knowing the pain of that fire in more ways than one, but for the first time, I see something else in Hickory's obsession. A possible connection that runs deeper than theoretical curiosity. I wonder, in some way, if he sees a part of himself in the Mystic story. A faerie stuck in a world where no one understands him, not even his own already highly eccentric clan.

Blinking, his head snaps up as he shifts farther down the wall. "Now that we have the prophecy more properly translated, so many of my findings are starting to make sense." As he searches, he blows out pixie dust smoke from his pipe like a train. "Like this here!" He points to a drawing that's frayed at the edges, as if ripped from a book.

"This Mystic sketch depicts two worlds: Faylan here and the Neverworld here." He points to two clouded spheres with a decorative beam connecting them.

Alys taps me and signs. *What's that in between? A bridge?*

I shrug, relaying her guess to Hickory.

"Precisely," he says, beaming. "I think it's supposed to be some sort of passageway connecting the two worlds. After the Numa were banished to the Neverworld long ago, this bridge was somehow lost in the process. Then, I painted another vision last night."

"*Another* one?" I ask, surprised he didn't tell me before.

"Yes. I must have created it in my sleep because I woke up with my hands covered in paint, and this was lying on the floor." He hurries to one of his traveling trunks and pulls out a piece of parchment rolled up like a scroll. Flattening it on his wall of clippings, he secures it with a few pins. "At first, I thought I'd just painted the same drawing from memory, the two worlds present again here. But instead of a bridge in the middle—"

"It's a door?" Aeron asks, tilting his head as he examines it.

"Yes." Hickory nods. "This door is closed, though there's an opening for a key…" He lifts his eyebrows at us before pulling his sketchbook from his satchel. "Now, stay with me. According to Vale's translation of the prophecy, I think the last stanza is giving us the formula for creating this very key." He flips to a specific page in his notes and begins to read: "Stone and dust they must combine with every royal clan bloodline, together when the moons align. The *key* to power is the sign."

"Okay…" Vale says. "So, you're saying these elements might make up an actual key to open some kind of door to the Neverworld?"

"Theoretically, yes," Hickory confirms, puffing more clouds of pixie dust in quick succession.

"Wouldn't we want to keep that from happening?" I ask.

"Theoretically, yes," Hickory says again, though less emphatically. "But even that isn't clear. Not yet, anyway. Vale and I still have more to translate."

"Before that, can we get to the feast that was mentioned earlier?" Aeron asks. "All this theory talk is making me hungry."

"Ah yes, we better get going." Hickory motions to the door. "If we're all late, someone might get suspicious."

After making sure the hallway is clear, we exit his room one at a time. As I bring up the rear, Hickory stops me.

"I know I've been carrying the book around with me for safekeeping. I've been thinking maybe I shouldn't," Hickory whispers. "There are a slew of pickpockets in the city. Plus, I don't know if you've noticed, but most Kobolds are a curious bunch with very little regard for personal space."

He says this while standing extremely close to me. I bite down my laughter as he continues. "I'm going to hide the Mystic text somewhere in my quarters under lock and key. Even if someone went rummaging in my room, they'd have to search for hours before coming across it."

"All right. Just make sure *you* can find it in this mess, okay?" I joke.

He smiles. "Got it."

CHAPTER 47

After the feast, Lord Zephen leads us to a cavern even louder and busier than the city. As we step into the underground stadium, clouds of pixie dust smoke fill the air as cheering Kobolds line the walls, looking down at a vast maze carved into the ground below.

"No way." I smile from ear to ear, feeling the first tinge of excitement since reaching the tunnels. "I never thought I'd see it."

What is this place? Alys signs to me as we find our seats.

"It's the Labyrinth," I say, anxiously peering down into the circular maze of high stone walls.

Hickory looks at me, brows raised. "You've been here before?"

"Not personally. I know many pirates sent on missions down here who would come in disguise to bet on the games," I say. It was one of Zale and Colt's favorite pastimes. They often took their portion of the spoils and Colt's valuable explosives to use in the Kobold bets.

"How does it work?" Aeron asks.

"If you couldn't tell already, living down in the tunnels isn't exactly *exciting*. So, we've had to create our own entertainment." Hickory points to the maze. "The Labyrinth isn't a typical maze with multiple ways you can turn and get lost. That's not its danger. Instead, with one way in and one way out for each of its victims, the Labyrinth takes them through a preset path to the center of the maze, making them endure a series of challenges. Faeries must overcome each one with only their wits and resourcefulness to aid them. Kobold folk can be pretty twisted. They get quite the kick out of betting who will be the first to make it back alive."

"*Alive*?" Vale's eyes widen. "It's deadly?"

"Oh, yes. It wasn't always so lethal, but the Labyrinth has gone through some renovations over the past few years. More danger means more excitement. Which also means more Kobolds coming and even fae from other clans being allowed to attend and gamble, benefitting our struggling economy." Hickory nods to a group of Kobolds shouting something at two pucks. As one furiously writes something down in a small book, the other collects pouches of farthlings and pixie dust from the shouting crowd. The first puck must be recording their bets.

"Seems to be working well," Aeron says as he settles into his seat. The rest of us follow, preparing to enjoy the show.

"It was—" says Hickory with a sigh, his voice lowering "—until the dangers of the Labyrinth grew so great that fewer and fewer Kobolds wanted to compete. My father couldn't have that. So, these last few months he's been convincing criminals from the dust mines to take part instead. The first to make it out alive wins their freedom."

My excitement evaporates as gates below rise to reveal a handful of condemned fae approaching the maze. Some walk slowly in anxious, jittery movements. Others stumble toward their fate with vacant, dazed eyes. Probably due to the extreme dust exposure in the mines.

A few weeks ago, this probably wouldn't have fazed me. Watching the misfortune of others while winning money is most pirates' favorite form of entertainment. But my crew and I were nearly sent to the dust mines ourselves. I shiver as I picture us as the barely sane criminals below trying to win our freedom.

Then I see her.

I blink my eyes, shaking my head. My mind has to be playing tricks on me. As she lifts her tiny face to the crowd, I know it's her.

Luna.

I'm going to be sick. How did she get captured? Whit was supposed to take the crew back to Maverick. They were supposed to be safe. At least Luna grew up in the tunnels, so she doesn't seem as affected by the dust mines as the others. Still, how is little Luna going to survive this?

She scans the cheering crowd around her. Her eyes pass over me and the other heirs, then jerk back. Her eyes grow wide, focusing on me. I fully expect her features to morph into a look of pure anger, maybe even hate. But her pleading eyes only seem to say one thing: *Help me.*

My stomach lurches as my fingers curl around the railing in front of me. What can I do? I helplessly watch as Kobold henchmen strong-arm Luna closer to the maze. Staring down at her from my position as an heir, I wonder which of us has it worse—the Labyrinth or the Ethodine? At least she only has one challenge to win her freedom.

Suddenly, another terrifying thought enters my mind.

Why are we being shown this?

Hoping against hope that the fear crawling inside me won't come true, I catch Alys staring at me.

Are you okay? she signs. *You're turning white.*

I have a bad feeling, I sign back.

"Welcome to the Labyrinth," Lord Zephen announces through a horn lowered by a mechanical arm in the wall. His voice echoes off the walls, seeming to come from all directions at once. "As usual, tonight we have five criminals who will compete for their freedom."

I press into the back of my seat, holding my breath.

"And at the end of the week, the five clan heirs will enter the same maze to compete in the Test of Creativity."

The Kobold crowd explodes with cheers.

There it is. Just as I feared.

When my father originally gave me the choice of competing in the Ethodine or working in the dust mines, it didn't matter which path I chose. I might still die by the same fate.

CHAPTER 48

This is the first time we're being shown exactly what lies in store for one of our trials.

And it's torture to just watch.

At the blow of the horn, each criminal steps into the Labyrinth through a different entrance with nothing but their bare hands and their wits to defend themselves. Not only do they have to navigate an obstacle course of perilous traps, challenging them to adapt and use their surroundings to survive, but failing to overcome their trial often incurs bloody consequences.

One of the criminals tries to escape, flying up over the maze walls. He's immediately shot down, right through the chest, by an arrow-catapulting machine from above.

All the while, the Kobolds in the stands drink, cheer, and make money off of the bloodshed.

I keep my eye on Luna, who's thankfully the least injured and in the lead. She's survived fire torches, a moat of hungry crocodiles, and is now the closest to reaching the stone tower standing at the center of the maze. The first to reach the top will be proclaimed the winner.

All that stands between her and her freedom now are a series of narrow doorways with jagged guillotine blades. They lift at various intervals and drop with a slice that makes me wince.

Though her small frame has wasted away during her time in the mines, Luna is still limber and quick. She studies the movement of the blades, finding their pattern, using maneuvers she learned under my training on the Minnow to dive through each opening at just the right moment.

She has one more blade to evade.

It lifts and she leaps, but the hem of her trouser catches on something.

A nail? A screw?

I shoot to my feet even though I know there's nothing I can do. She only has a matter of seconds.

She yanks at her foot, scrambling forward on her elbows. Her ankle is still stretched over the opening.

I force myself not to look away as the blade plunges down.

Her screams are too far off to hear, swallowed by the sound of the crowd. Looking at her now bloodied stump, she shakes violently with shock. But she doesn't let this stop her. Gritting through the pain, she strips off a sleeve and wraps the wound tight. Then she releases her wings, flying with all her remaining strength onward.

As she crashes through the door at the base of the tower, I hold my breath, heart pounding.

Please let her survive.

An agonizing minute passes. Then another. Two more criminals enter the tower from separate doors. Finally, Luna emerges at the top, her voice now ringing out above the spectators who cheer or boo as money exchanges hands.

"I'm free!" she cries through bloodied teeth.

As mediks rush to her aid, I collapse back into my seat, exhausted from worrying. There's no way I could've saved her from the Labyrinth, but at least she'll be freed from this place.

I can't speak as hopefully about the five of us.

At the end of the unsettling festivities, we're allowed to exit the cavern first, leaving behind rowdy Kobolds who are still cheering and arguing over money owed. As we walk down the tunnel leading back to the city, none of us speak.

I've never been one to be squeamish, but as I picture us entering the Labyrinth in a few short days, my stomach threatens to unload everything I ate at the feast. Bringing up the rear, I stop, bracing my hand against the damp cavern wall as the others continue on. All except one.

"Quinn." Aeron stands in front of me, and I meet his eyes. They're soft with concern. "It's going to be okay. We've survived this far."

"At least we could prepare for the other trials in some way." I motion back to the Labyrinth. "How in Faylan are we supposed to prepare for that?"

Then again, maybe knowing we can't is part of the torture.

Aeron's attention shifts as raucous voices bounce off the walls behind me. A swarm of Kobolds are exiting the stadium, pouring into the tunnel after us in droves.

"We should keep moving," he says.

"I just need a minute." I spot a side tunnel ahead.

Aeron follows me just in time for the crowds of Kobolds to pass us by. I press my back against the wall, trying to breathe, feeling the space close in.

"Are you sure that's all that's bothering you?" Aeron asks, watching me. "I saw your reaction to the criminal who won. Do you know her or something?"

I study his face, eternally surprised at how well he can read me.

"Luna," I breathe her name softly, her bloodied leg and soundless scream etched in my mind. "She is… she *was* one of my crew."

He purses his lips. "I'm so sorry."

I nod in thanks, then quirk a brow. "Is that compassion for a *pirate* I hear in your voice?"

He shrugs, nodding to me. "You've already softened me toward one. I guess it was only a matter of time."

I smile to myself as he turns his attention back to the passing crowd, many of them laughing and clapping each other on the back as if the whole event hasn't fazed them in the least.

"Who knew Kobolds were so bloodthirsty?" Aeron says.

"Yeah." I try to ease my breathing. "I knew they were eccentric, but not *this* off the rails."

"Guess Hickory's pretty tame in comparison, huh?" He smirks. "Maybe I shouldn't give him such a hard time."

"Why *do* you give him such a hard time?" I ask, the heaviness in my chest progressively lifting. "What'd he ever do to you?"

Aeron hesitates. "Let's just say Hickory and I have never seen eye to eye on certain things. You're right though. Maybe I should ease up on the puck. Feeling any better?"

"Somewhat." I nod.

"Good. We'd better get going."

A high-pitched scream cuts through the side tunnel we're in, shooting toward us from the other end.

"What was that?" I squint in the darkness, stepping toward a flickering light in the distance.

"Quinn, please," Aeron pleads. "Where are you going now?"

"I thought I heard someone scream."

"Oh yeah, that's a great reason to go walking down a dark cavern," Aeron says. A train whistle sounds and we stop. "See, just a train. It wasn't a—"

Another scream. Definitely *not* a train.

"You were saying?" I ask smugly before creeping deeper into the shadows.

"You're only going to find trouble down there," Aeron calls after me.

"Well, you better follow me and do what you do best then," I shout back.

Predictably, his footsteps follow. "This pixie is going to be the end of me," he mutters.

As we draw toward the light, I slink along the inner wall. There, I find one thing I expected—the Kobie Express—and one thing I didn't.

A Sylph soldier is ordering around a group of Kobolds as they haul large sacks onto the train. The feather-winged soldier turns, a crescent-moon scar running down his cheek.

Moon Face.

"What's he doing here?" I whisper aloud, mostly to myself.

As Moon Face paces, shouting commands, he wipes his sweaty brow. He doesn't look well. His skin is darker in the dim light, but also discolored, sickly.

"Jasper, the last shipment is ready for the queen," a Kobold with a conductor's hat and a tattered, moth-eaten uniform reports. He holds out his hand. "Time to pay up."

Before Moon Face can respond, a sack topples out of the train and thuds on the ground, breaking open to reveal pounds of glittering pixie dust.

"It's just a dust trade," Aeron whispers to me, quietly shifting to leave.

I don't budge. The screaming definitely came from this direction, I know it. And if Moon Face is here, I wouldn't be surprised if he was the instigator. Besides, while dust trades might be normal enough, this is a whole trainful. It's happening far from the city, in secret. Something's up.

"This shipment is not for the queen, you imbecile." Moon Face wipes his forehead with the back of his hand again and points. "And I'm not paying you anything until you clean up that mess."

The Kobold conductor sags. Just as he turns, another bag tumbles down the steps as a faerie shoots out of the train into the air. A pixie with Kobold wings and a bloodied bandage where her right foot should be.

"Luna," I say, grasping the edge of the tunnel opening, not believing my eyes.

"What?" Aeron draws closer, his chest pressing against my back.

"How did she get loose?" shouts Moon Face. "Don't let her get away!"

Two Kobolds shoot into the air, seizing Luna, and tackle her to the ground.

"No, please!" she yells as she tries to wriggle out of their grasp. "I won! I'm free now. You have to let me go!"

As they move to gag her, she screams. The same scream I heard earlier.

My fingers prick with heat as I take a step forward.

Aeron grabs my arm. "Quinn, stop. I'm sorry, but there's nothing we can do."

The Kobold in charge turns to Moon Face again. "I guess she wasn't tied tightly enough. These things happen…"

Moon Face grabs him by the collar with one hand, lifting him like he's a little sprout. "No excuses, you hear me?" He shakes him as he growls, his voice deeper and grittier than I remember.

My eyes grow wide. This isn't the bumbling Sylph soldier I knew. What's happened to him?

"Y-yes, Jasper. Anything you say, Jasper." The conductor trembles, dangling in Moon Face's grasp until he throws him to the ground.

"That's more like it. Now show me the other cars. I want to make sure you're not trying to swindle me out of anything else," Moon Face says.

"Yes, of course." The Kobold quickly scrambles to his feet and leads Moon Face to the other side of the train.

With Moon Face out of sight and Luna being dragged back toward the train, I know this is my last chance to help her. I've got to do something.

Shrugging Aeron off, I unfurl my wings and collide into the back of the Kobold restraining Luna's right arm. We crash to the ground, the Kobold hitting his head hard on the stone floor, knocking him out.

"What was that?" I hear Moon Face grumble from a few cars down. I only have moments.

"Captain?" Luna's voice rattles.

The other Kobold holds her in front of him like a shield, sliding a jagged knife from his belt. Luna's face pales.

"It's okay, just stay calm." I put my hands up where her captor can see them, frantically thinking of my next move, when Aeron appears from the shadows behind them.

"Hey! Pick on someone your own size."

The Kobold startles, half-turning just as Aeron grabs for the knife with one hand and punches the puck with the other. I pull Luna away before she goes down with him.

"What are you doing here?" she asks, peering at me as if she's seen a ghost.

"My thoughts exactly," Moon Face growls, a handful of other Kobolds in tow as they round the train toward us, blades ready.

Aeron takes a fighting stance with the Kobold knife as I squeeze Luna's shoulders and look her dead in the face. I might not have a weapon, but I won't let them take her again.

"There isn't time to explain. Save yourself," I tell her, hoping she'll fly away while she still can.

Luna's brows knit with confusion, then narrow with a determination I've seen in her eyes before. She unfurls her wings and rises into the air as if she plans to help us attack.

"Get out of here!" I command in the captain tone I know she remembers. "That's an order."

Taking one last look at me and the oncoming rabble, she shoots into the air. She doesn't go for an escape right away like I hoped. She whips back to the train, crashing through one of the windows, glass shattering everywhere.

What in Faylan is she doing?

In the next second, a flurry of wings break free from the Express. There are more prisoners. Many more.

"This way!" Luna calls as she leads them toward the tunnel where the locomotive must have come from. There's at least a dozen other faeries right behind her.

"Go after them," Moon Face roars to the Kobolds, then turns on me with his foulest glare yet. "I'll handle this one."

Aeron steps in front of me, but I grab his arm. We only have the Kobold knife, and there's a clear shot now to escape the way we came.

"Fly!" I yell.

Whipping through the air, we reach the main tunnel where we came in from, weaving and pushing our way through the Kobold crowd.

I look back just as Moon Face emerges. His mouth twists into a snarl. He and I both know there are too many witnesses for him to do something now.

"Thanks," I whisper to Aeron. "That was close."

"*Too* close," Aeron says in a harsher tone than normal, running his hand through his midnight blue hair. "Seriously, Quinn, when are you going to start listening to me?"

He goes on, but I barely hear him. I'm just glad Luna got away.

If Luna can find her way back to the crew, then she'll have a new *Captain Shade* story to tell the mates. Maybe even Maverick will hear of it and allow me to rejoin them once I'm done with this insane competition.

Even still, I hope my crew realizes how much I did care for them. That I wouldn't have abandoned them if I'd had a choice. Assuming Luna was the only one of them held captive in this place, of course.

I glance back at Moon Face one more time. He's gone. I whip around to make sure he isn't nearby and thankfully, he's nowhere to be found. I relax a bit, ignoring the sinking feeling that I haven't seen the last of him. We created quite a mess for him back at the train. Hopefully cleaning it up keeps him busy for a while. What in Faylan was he up to? What could a Sylph soldier like him want with half-dead criminals and mounds of pixie dust?

CHAPTER 49

"How have you not found anything out yet?" I ask Vale. Our blades clash, sparks exploding in the dim, cavernous room.

It's been three days since leaving Vyndoria, and Vale still can't tell me if the poison in my system was her mother's or not. After stumbling upon Moon Face's secret deal, however, I've had doubts that it was the queen who did it.

Still, I told Aeron not to mention the incident to Vale quite yet. I need her to be motivated to finish her tests on the poison. I need to know for sure.

Sweat beads down Vale's face, nostrils flaring, her jaw set in determination. "Oh, I'm sorry," she wheezes, breathing heavily, her freckled cheeks flushed with heat. "I barely have any energy after a certain trainer works me to death every day."

She takes a fatigued swing at me.

I evade it easily.

"Well, if you learned to control your breathing, your opponent wouldn't be able to beat you because of sheer exhaustion." I bring my blade down on hers, hard, and her knees buckle. "Pace your breathing, like when you sing. Again!"

I pull back, allowing her to stand before coming at her from multiple angles.

Vale meets me each time with swift, calculated shifts. She's monitoring her breathing more with each blow, fighting smarter. Still, she's worn out.

"Good." I take a moment to admire how far I've brought her in just a few short weeks. Now if only I can get her to stop complaining so much.

Vale relaxes and lets her blade drop to the ground, hands on her knees as she breathes.

"One more thing, though," I add.

Vale looks up, and I rush toward her with my sword.

She scrambles for her blade, but not before my foot lands on it, the tip of my own weapon at her throat.

She stares at me, stunned.

"Never let your guard down, especially with your opponent's weapon still in hand." I smirk. "And never underestimate the element of surprise."

Vale gulps, my blade still hovering at her throat. "Got it."

Stepping off her weapon, I kick it up, catching it in the air, two swords in my hands. "Learn that, and I think you might be ready."

I pull back, and Vale's eyes shine with hope. "Ready? You mean we're done training?"

"Ha!" I chuckle. "I mean you're ready for the next stage."

Vale moans, struggling to stand up straight. "What else can there possibly be?"

Releasing my wings, I rise into the air.

I'd requested the queen find us an abandoned cavern with the highest ceilings she could find. We'll need all the space we can for this lesson.

"Your enemies won't always be on the ground. Time to learn to fight *and* fly." I toss Vale's sword back to her.

She catches it, surprising even herself at her coordination.

Vale's worn expression shifts into a smile as she releases her feathered wings and meets me in the air. "Now *this* I can get behind."

※

Later that evening, Lord Zephen instructs the five of us to follow Hickory to where we can prepare for our upcoming trial.

"How far is this place, exactly?" Aeron asks as we walk through the smoky streets.

On the way, we pass everything from boutiques with specialty caps and goggles to mechanics bartering with patrons over the price of metal limbs and wing enhancements. There's even a whole shop packed with miniature ticking clocks—one with an annoying wooden bird that pops out at the top and screeches, startling Alys.

"It's right outside the city." Hickory leads us around the next block. "We just have to make a quick stop on the way."

Eventually, he pauses in front of a building where it seems most of the smoke is coming from. Carts of pixie crystals are being pedaled inside. Stepping up to the large windows, we peer through to see the crystals heaved onto the moving belt of a noisy machine. They disappear in one end and come out the other as powdery dust.

Ah, so this is what a pixie dust factory looks like!

I press my fingers against the glass. Kobolds working the machine scoop the different colors of dust into pouches and labeled bottles, before pushing carts of them into a back room.

"Where are they taking the dust?" I ask as Hickory leads us around the side of the building into an empty alleyway.

"Certain amounts are usually brought to the surface to be sold and traded, though there's less and less of that happening with the crystal shortages," answers Hickory.

I look at Aeron, thinking of Luna and all the pixie dust we saw Moon Face transporting. We still need to find out what he was up to.

"Other shipments are brought to our inventors," Hickory adds.

For what kind of inventions? Alys signs for me to ask.

"Oh, all kinds," Vale pipes up in her *didn't-you-know* voice. "There are many different crystal types. Kobold inventors are constantly experimenting with combinations, often mixing them with other elements to find new uses, from powering the floating vessels in Eldore to finding new medicinal cures."

Alys looks at her healing hands, and I remember what she told me in Vyndoria. *Perhaps the Kobolds could experiment on me to figure out how to make a serum for the plague.* Though her parents don't want her to reveal her gift, I wouldn't be surprised if that's the first thing she'd do if she became queen.

Reaching a side door, Hickory looks both ways before giving the door a uniquely-patterned knock. A small window in the door opens, and a mechanical hand shoots out so quickly that I jump back. Hickory places a pouch of farthlings in the hand, which retracts, and then reappears with an unlabeled pouch of pixie dust.

Aeron crosses his arms, raising a brow. "That wasn't sketchy at all."

I shoot him a look, reminding him he promised to be nicer to Hickory.

Aeron shrugs in a half-hearted apology.

"It's for the pain in my eye, okay?" Hickory points to his misted one, tossing the pouch into his satchel. "A puck's gotta do what a puck's gotta do."

As we reach the far outskirts of the city, Hickory finally stops in front of a dusty shop with clouded windows. I would have figured it was abandoned, if not for the loud snoring coming from inside.

"Sketchy place number two?" Aeron asks.

Hickory ignores him, leading us inside.

"Nice." I shake my head at Aeron.

"Oh, come on." He laughs. "He makes it way too easy."

As we enter, the room is small with only an elderly Kobold hunched over a large wooden desk. A strange device is strapped around his balding head, and his sleeping face is pressed into a smattering of scrolls.

Hickory slides a piece of parchment across the desk.

The Kobold startles, practically falling out of his seat. A dozen or so lenses on his head device bounce on wired hinges with the movement. Seeing Hickory, he straightens.

"Sir Hickory! So glad to see my favorite customer is back," he says, beaming. "What can I help you with today?"

Based on the condition of this place, I assume Hickory is his *only* customer.

"Just this, Breckett," Hickory says warmly, pointing to the parchment he put on the desk.

"Of course, of course!" The Kobold shifts one of the lenses down, magnifying his left eye three sizes as he peers at the paper. "Ah, yes. This way."

Stepping away from his desk, he ushers us around to a series of doors. Rotating a large circular gear on one of them with a lot of grunting, he opens it wide, revealing a stairway.

"Thank you, Breckett." Hickory pats his shoulder.

"Anything for you, sir." He bows.

We follow Hickory down the stairs until they lead to a landing where a passageway opens into yet another tunnel. This tunnel is unlike any I've ever seen. Instead of stretching out in front of us, it runs vertically from floor to ceiling. Shelves upon shelves of books line the rounded walls of the large room while the tunnel stretches on for miles above us like a never ending tower.

Aeron walks forward, then stops short, shooting out his arms as Alys and I nearly crash into him. "Have your wings out and ready in this place," he warns, releasing his fin wings with a swoosh.

Alys and I look down. The floor only stretches out halfway through the room. Below, the tunnel of shelves continues into the dark abyss.

Devouring the shelves with her eyes, Vale smiles wider than I've ever seen.

Hickory catches her expression and his good eye lights up. After noticing my smirk, however, he quickly looks back at the shelves.

"Though the Sylphs love their books—" Hickory explains, "—the sky city would never be able to contain them all. Held up by only the Vine and pixie dust, Eldore has a very delicate balance. Too much weight could bring the whole city crumbling down." Hickory motions to the tunnel. "Thus, the Kobolds were commissioned to build massive libraries down here to store the extra volumes."

"Hickory…" Vale lets out an awed breath. "I knew these places existed, but I never imagined they'd be this expansive." Her eyes are glassy as she looks from the books to Hickory. "I honestly might never want to leave."

She looks at him, all smiles, and I can tell Hickory is struggling not to blush.

"Yes, well… um…" He clears his throat. "I convinced my parents to give us access to the libraries to better prepare ourselves for the trial. As you saw, I don't know if we can fully be ready. The Labyrinth isn't designed to test our brain power as much as what we can do with it: our creativity, wit, and problem-solving skills." Hickory lowers his voice to a whisper. "But, I figured with all that's here, there must be more literature about the Numa or the prophecy somewhere."

"Ingenious!" Vale exclaims. Releasing her wings, she flutters up a few stories and lands on one of the ledges.

Hickory smiles. "Why build stairs when you can fly from shelf to shelf, right? Kobolds aren't just eccentric, we're smart too."

I guess we can start here, Alys signs with a shrug. Looking a little overwhelmed at the vast amount of books, she moves to some shelves closest to us. *How much time do we have?*

"Good question," I say, before asking Hickory.

"Barely anyone comes down here unless sent for a specific volume," he says. "So we probably have a few hours until we're expected for dinner."

"Great!" Vale squeals as she flies back down to us, grabbing Aeron by the arm. "Aeron and I will take the top shelves. Come on, you won't believe what I found."

He glances at me as if I'll give him an excuse to refuse her.

I avoid his stare.

Stay focused, I command myself. *Don't encourage him.*

I'm grateful for his help with Moon Face yesterday, but being around him will only make things harder. Still, I deflate as he allows Vale to pull him along, flying up as high as they can go.

"Don't wait for us!" Vale calls back.

Hickory sighs, looking longingly after her, then puts a hand on my shoulder. "I'll help Alys look through the shelves here. If I were you, though, I might start about three stories down." He points to a cobweb-covered section below.

Pushing Aeron out of my mind, I fly to the shelf Hickory indicated and land on the ledge in front of it, wiping away the cobwebs to reveal a silver-plated label above the books.

It's engraved with a simple inscription:

The Mystics.

CHAPTER 50

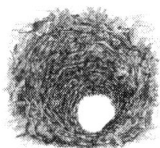

"I'm surprised you're still here." Hickory and Alys smile down at me as I sit on the dusty ledge, surrounded by a scattering of books and old maps. "You even beat Vale."

I huff.

She and Aeron fluttered out of the tunnel a short bit ago for dinner. Aeron stopped to ask if I wanted to join them, but I declined.

"Stubborn as the day is long, I'm afraid." I pore over the ragged piece of parchment in my hand again, the words starting to blur together. "Too bad I don't have Vale's Notting Potion to help this time," I mutter to myself.

"Vale's what?" Hickory asks.

"Nothing," I say quickly.

What are you studying? Alys signs before she picks up one of the texts and flips through a few of its delicate pages.

I translate her words for Hickory before responding. "Just trying to learn more about the Mystics. Hickory thought studying them might help us decode more of their prophecy."

"Speaking of…" Hickory turns to Alys. "Could I perhaps get a look at your tattoo again?"

Putting down the book in her hand, she removes her glove and rolls up her sleeve, offering her arm to him. His fingers hover just above her skin, tracing the symbol's curves in the air.

"Where did you get this again?" he asks.

Alys faces me and starts to answer in a slew of signs.

"Whoa, hold on." I stand to meet her. "I'm a beginner, remember? What was the first thing again?"

Shaking her head, Alys pulls off her other glove.

"What're you doing?" I don't like the look in her eyes.

Before I can stop her, she grabs both Hickory's and my arms with her bare hands.

Is this better? Alys speaks into my mind, her energy coursing through me.

Hickory must hear her, too, because he goes rigid and nearly topples over.

What in Faylan… A different voice echoes in my head. It sounds like Hickory, but his parted mouth hasn't moved. Shock and elation dance in his eyes.

Could I be hearing his thoughts too?

Hickory's eyes dart to me, growing bigger. *Quinn?*

Wait, did you just hear me thinking? I try to send the thought to him. He nods, and I whip around to Alys. *Did you know you could connect other fae with each other?*

Alys shrugs. *I—*

Hold on. You already knew Alys could do this? Hickory's gaze is still trained on me.

Will both of you quiet your minds for one minute! Alys barks, her eyes pinched shut as if our inner voices are giving her a headache. *No, I've never done this before, and I definitely didn't know I'd be connecting you to each other. Happy accidents all around, I guess.* Opening her eyes, she raises a brow at Hickory. *Now, do you want to know about this tattoo or not?*

Yes, please. Hickory nods emphatically, mouth pursed.

We do our best to keep our thoughts clear as Alys catches Hickory up on the basics of what she's told me. From her ability to heal and her failed attempt at saving her sister, to how new tattoos have literally grown out of the Numanic symbol on her arm every time she uses her gift.

It's something I was born with, but that's all I know, Alys finishes as she lets go, lowering her body to the ground, looking tired.

"Incredible," Hickory says with a sigh as he sits as well.

I follow suit. "Incredible, yes," I say. "It doesn't exactly help us learn more about the Numa or the Mystics, though. And not much of what I've been reading is new information to me."

What do you know so far? Alys signs.

I motion to the material littered around us. "Concerning the Numa, just that the Mystics studied them religiously. That they authored the prophecy we've been decoding, and wrote everything else in the tome we already found." I motion to another pile of books. "Besides that, they were Gwyllion magic users, able to conjure fire from their hands. They were convinced that all Gwyllions could do what they did because they believed we were descendants of dragons. I still think that's ridiculous, but if all Gwyllions really do have the potential for fire-wielding, maybe that's why I can produce it. Though I'm not sure why I'm the only freak who can."

"Unless you *are* a Mystic." Hickory smiles, still hopeful.

I sigh. "Not possible. My father is a descendant of the royal Gwyllion line. No Mystics there."

And your mother? Alys asks.

I put a hand on my boot where I've hidden the daggers my mother had commissioned. There's no way I'm walking around Tartarus unarmed with Moon Face around. Though the Numanic symbols on their hilts were my original clue to all this, I still don't like talking about them. Or my mother.

"She died when Gaius and I were very young. She was a Gwyllion commoner, though. Grew up the daughter of a local welder. Except for the fact that my father chose her as his bride, there was nothing particularly special or unusual about her."

Hickory considers the literature on the floor again. "Does anything say how the Mystics call forth and manipulate fire?"

"As far as I can tell, I should be able to just open my hand and have fire appear on command." I stretch out my palm and focus, straining as I wish it to come forward. Nothing. I throw up my hands. "I've been in this dreary tunnel with every ancient Gwyllion text under the moons, and still nothing."

"Maybe something's blocking you?" Hickory suggests.

"I don't know anymore." My body sags under the weight of all my unanswered questions.

Even more than learning about the prophecy, part of me had started to hope I would read about some special flick of the wrist or magic words I could use to keep my fire in check. To control it. If I can figure out how it manifests, then maybe I can make sure its flames never spontaneously surface again. No more singeing pain. No more inflicting agony on others. I should've known it wouldn't be that easy.

"I give up." I throw up my hands and start tossing materials onto a pile so I can put it all back and return to my room.

"You can't give up now," Hickory says with pleading eyes. "Magic isn't as hard as you think."

"Easy for you to say." I shake my head. "You've probably been teaching paints to obey your every command since you were a sprite."

"Actually, most Kobold sprouts figure out how to do that one pretty easily," he says with a shrug.

"That makes me feel heaps better, thanks." I sigh.

"Maybe we can help."

Alys nods in agreement, moving to the shelves behind me, clearing away more of the cobwebs.

Hickory picks up a scroll. "Have you looked at this one yet?"

I shake my head. They're just going to waste time uncovering what I've already found. A dead end.

Both of them mean well, but Hickory isn't going to quit. I know that he really wants me to embrace whatever mystical gift he thinks I have. But his persistence is starting to grate on me.

What if I can never do what he wants? It's too much pressure. I grew up with enough of that from my father, and I'm not going to bend to it again. If there's anything left to find, I'll figure it out myself, in my time. In my way.

"You want to help? Just go and let me focus, all right?" I snatch the scroll from Hickory and unroll it on the ground. Though I'm more angry at myself than anything, I just want to be left alone.

"Whoa. Touchy much?" Hickory frowns, and Alys slowly puts down the book in her hand. "Just one last tip. You're looking at that one upside down."

"I know that." I mutter.

I flip it over and pretend to read, waiting for them to leave. They don't. In fact, Hickory yanks the scroll from under my nose, staring at it in amazement.

"Hey!" I grab for it.

He eludes me, not taking his eyes off the page. "Where did you find this one?" he asks urgently.

"I don't know. Why?" My teeth clench, and I curl my fingers into fists. My nails prick painfully at my palms. I vow to give him one more chance before my daggers come out.

Hickory sniffs once, then twice. He glances up at me. "Quinn—"

"What?" I snap.

Alys, wide-eyed, points at my hand.

I follow their stares to where orange and red flames lick between my fingers. I uncurl them to reveal a ball of fire swirling in my palm.

"Ugh! See!" I shake my hand in the air, trying to make it go away. "I can't control it. Especially when I'm angry."

"Watch it! You could set the whole tunnel on fire!" Hickory shouts as both of them raise hands of caution. "Wait, the flames come when you're angry? No other time?"

Holding my hand steadier, I wince at the burn, as I try to remember a time the fire reared its ugly head without anger.

Aeron. At the thought of him, my cheeks burn and the fire roars bigger. I yelp as Hickory and Alys draw back.

The heat courses through my body, helplessness washing over me. "Any kind of strong emotion, I guess," I grit out, just wanting it to stop.

In all my years as a pirate, I never used to struggle with keeping the fire at bay. I've always been able to keep my emotions in check. *What's happening to me? I'm stronger than this.*

Remembering what I used to do at sea, I close my eyes and take a few deep breaths. Slowly, the fire begins to recede. A groan of relief and frustration escapes my lips. "Just another reason to hate them," I grumble.

"Hate what? Emotions?" Hickory watches the fire become a tiny flame before it flickers out, evaporating into thin air.

Alys grabs my hand, looking for burns, ready to heal. There's no sign of the flames. Just the lingering memory of pain.

She looks up curiously. *Your hand doesn't even feel hot.*

I shrug. "The flames don't permanently hurt me. Just everyone else." I can hear my father in my head, and believe his warnings against emotions now more than ever. "All my feelings ever do is cause problems."

"So you try to avoid them," Hickory concludes. "Or stuff them down?"

"Pretty much."

"That might be your problem right there," he says. "If your fire comes out by way of your emotions, maybe mastering them is the key to controlling your ability."

"That's what I've been trying to do." I shake my head. "It doesn't work."

No. Alys squeezes my fingers before grabbing Hickory's arm so we both can hear her. *I think Hickory is saying you need to learn to let go.*

Hickory nods, still wide-eyed at Alys' ability.

"Let go of what?" I have no idea what she's talking about.

She smiles. *If I blocked all the pain and emotions I feel while healing someone, I'd never be able to help them. If your gift is anything like mine, maybe you need to let yourself feel.*

Let myself feel? Has she been talking to Aeron lately?

Alys continues, *You need to learn to deal with what's inside, or that fire will always be a volcano just waiting to erupt when you least expect or want it to.* She looks at me more intently. *If you let me, I think I can help you with that.*

No! The voice inside my head shouts as I nearly jerk away from her. *I don't need to listen to this. I don't need help. I'm stronger than that. I can hold it down so the fire never comes out again.*

Alys gives my hand a squeeze. I forgot she can hear my thoughts. *Strength can take many different forms, my friend.*

Gaius' words from our last day on the shores of Greymerrow come back to me: *Sometimes strength can be weakness, and weakness can be strength. You have a different kind of strength. I know it. Someday, you will too.*

The tension in my shoulders eases as I play the words over in my mind. Could Gaius have meant what Alys is saying? Could there be strength in letting others in? A power in letting go of the choke hold I have on what I've always been told is weakness?

I guess there's only one way to find out.

I take a deep breath. "What exactly did you have in mind?"

CHAPTER 51

F*riend.*
   That's what Alys called me. Is that what we've become?

I'd called Whit a friend once. Trusting her was what got me into this mess. That, and my own recklessness.

Alys is different, isn't she? And Hickory. I've trusted them this far. Can I trust them a bit further? Part of me wants to. Still, my ideas of how to deal with my feelings and Alys' ideas are very different.

"You want to do *what*?" I ask again.

She still holds on to me and Hickory. *I told you before, when I heal someone, I can see into their memories. Especially the painful ones. I've never used it like this, especially with a fellow faerie. But if I can see your memories again, maybe I can experience them with you. Help you process through them. Maybe even help heal them.*

"Incredible." Hickory stares in awe.

"Hickory!"

"Sorry." His head drops.

Alys directs her next thoughts to him. *I have no idea what this is going to be like with just me and Quinn, let alone if I took you along too. I want you to stay nearby and keep watch. Make sure no one comes. And if anything concerning happens, break our connection by removing my hands, okay?*

Hickory reluctantly nods, obviously disappointed he'll be left out.

But this is not a game. These are my memories. My pain. I'd do anything to switch places with him right now. In fact, it's taking everything I have not to call the whole thing off and fly out of here.

Alys takes my hands firmly in hers. As the tingling of her healing energy increases, her tattoos start to glow and my body trembles.

Relax, she says, though her words waver with a bit of nervousness herself. *You don't have any physical wounds, so I think I'll have to do some searching to access your memories. Just close your eyes and focus on your breathing.*

Picturing Alys' energy swimming around my subconscious doesn't exactly help me relax. I try to concentrate on the last part of her instructions.

Close your eyes and breathe. Those are two things I can do, right? As I try, my shaking slowly subsides.

Then, I jolt.

Memories flash before my eyes, but in reverse.

Alys revealing her gift to Hickory. Me catching Moon Face in the tunnels with Luna, the train whistle sending a bolt of shock through me. The Labyrinth. Signing goodbye to Leman. Kissing Aeron, his lips pressed against mine, his ocean scent filling my senses. Alys saving me. Me saving Alys. Training with Vale. The queen's watchful eyes.

Is Alys seeing all of this too? I thought she was just going to find the painful moments. Is this part only in *my* mind?

Relax, I hear Alys say again. *Stay with me, Quinn. I think we're almost there...*

Almost where? Further back we go. Before the Ethodine. Before my time as a pirate. Even past the dreaded day I burned Gaius. Past the years of rigorous training and disappointment with my father. How far back are we going? Dizzy with the spin of images, I think I might pass out.

Finally, we stop. I'm lying on my back as a sprout's mobile rotates over me, one that usually hangs over a cradle.

A warm face with long dark curls appears above me. My breath catches.

Is she your mother? Alys' words wash over me gently.

Yes. Is this real? A memory I've long forgotten?

She's beautiful, Alys says.

She is. Her sparkling eyes peer down at me, creasing with joy as a gentle smile spreads across her face. The whole world seems to stand still; even the mobile turns in slow motion. I want to reach out to her. To touch her rosy cheek. I can barely breathe.

Another face appears. This one I recognize right away. But for the first time that I've ever seen, he grins.

Father.

He smiles at my mother first. Then at me.

He's *smiling* at *me*.

The corners of his eyes crease with happiness.

"My little warrior," he says softly, a lilt to his voice I've never heard before. I was wrong. This isn't my father. It can't be. I'm so confused. Aren't these supposed to be painful memories?

My chest tightens, something pricking at my eyes. A different kind of pain.

Both figures move out of view. I wait as the cutouts of metal arrows and dragons dangle from the mobile above.

Then I start to cry. The memory-self does, at least.

Where did my parents go, Alys? I ask, the panic of sproutling-me rising. *Why are you showing me this memory?*

I don't know. I'm not the one who led us here, Quinn, she says. *You did.*

What? Why is this memory so important?

Then I smell it.

Fire.

In a matter of moments, the nursery clouds with gray smoke, orange and red flames licking up the sides of the walls.

No, no, no!

My mother calls my father's name. Screaming for help.

My heart leaps, my eyes darting for her. My crying turns to shrieks.

She appears over me again, holding little Gaius. She reaches out. I cough through the smoke as she holds me close.

I'm short of breath, the fire growing around us as my vision blurs. The memory is drifting away.

My mother coughs, still calling out for help through the fog.

"No!" I yell.

"Quinn!" Hickory's voice cuts through the blackness as he pulls Alys and me apart.

I open my eyes, sucking in fresh air.

"What happened?" Hickory asks hurriedly.

When Alys touches my hand again, I flinch.

Quinn, I'm so sorry. I didn't mean... She strokes my arm as I reel from the memory.

"I... I think... Alys, was it my fault? Could I have possibly..."

She shakes her head. *Don't even think that. We didn't see everything. It's going to be okay, Quinn. We can—*

I pull away before she can finish, silencing her. I don't want to hear or see any more. This was supposed to help, but yet again I'm only plagued with more questions. I only feel more pain.

"No more," I say. Both of them stare at me as if I'll fall apart any minute. Maybe I will. "I'm done."

Releasing my wings, I shoot up to the main landing and back through the corridor as fast as I can.

CHAPTER 52

L anding in front of my room, I swing the door open, ready to lock myself inside. I'm not alone. Feyden is standing at the far end of the room near my bed.

"What are you—?" I try to catch my breath as I close the door behind me.

"Quinntessa," he bellows, his smile from my memory replaced by his usual scowl. "Where in Faylan have you been? I've been looking…" He narrows his eyes at my face. "What's wrong with you? What happened?" His tone lowers, yet still has a bite.

I put my hand to my face, wondering what he can see. "I, um…"

I can't get the vision of his youthful smile out of my head. The way he'd looked at my sproutling form. The way he looked at my mother. *My beautiful mother.* The image of her in the flames threatens to drag me to the floor again.

Did I cause the fire that killed her? Even if I was an innocent sprout at the time, it would at least start to explain why my father hates magic so much.

Why he hates *me* so much.

Yet, if he knew what I could do, what I *did* do all those years ago… why has he never said anything? Why has he never revealed me to the world, even after I burned Gaius too? Was he protecting me? Or protecting himself?

I close my eyes. It's all too much to process with him standing in front of me.

"Nothing. I'm fine," I say.

I hope that when I open my eyes, he'll be gone and I won't have to face him. When I don't hear movement, I look up to find him still analyzing me.

"What do you want?" Maybe my indignant tone will get him to go away. "Did you come just to yell at me some more?"

He never properly reprimanded me for failing the Trial of Life. Why? The image of him sitting by my bed in Vyndoria comes back to me. He was waiting for me to wake up. He was holding my hand. It had been him, right? Was it even real or just another poison-induced dream?

"I…" My father blinks at me before shaking his head. "I just wanted to make sure… that you weren't getting into any more trouble. You still have two more trials to complete."

Of course. It always comes back to the competition. To power.

"Right then." He moves past me toward the door. Is that all he came to say?

"Father?" The word feels strange in my mouth.

I haven't dared call him that to his face since Gaius' funeral. And definitely not with the gentle tone I just used. He never liked the term, and frankly, I decided a long time ago that he didn't deserve to be called it. After what I did to my mother—his wife—maybe I don't deserve to be called his daughter either.

He glances back, the same way he did the night of my poisoning. He waits.

I have to know.

"After the Trial of Life," I say slowly. "Did you visit me? In my room?"

He stares, unblinking, like a stone statue. "Yes."

"Why?" I ask, afraid of the answer.

His jaw shifts. "They said you were recovering. But I needed to see you for myself."

My eyes drop. He probably wanted to make sure his investment was safe. That he still had a piece in the game. Is that really all I am to him?

"When I saw your brother's body…" At his words, my eyes shoot back up. He stares at the wall. "I couldn't believe it until I saw him for myself. The plague had ravaged him, but... it was him."

I imagine my father hovering over Gaius' pale, disease-ridden body. I wonder if he shed a tear over the loss of his son. Though my father's frame remains rigid and cold, the slightest wavering taints his voice. "I needed to see you for myself," he repeats.

I swallow, though my mouth is dry. I nod, though I don't understand.

Gaius wasn't just a pawn to him. Feyden was hard on both of us, but he always favored Gaius, maybe even loved him in his own way. In this moment, my father speaks of us as if my brother and I hold the same value in his eyes. That we're equals. I lower my gaze, not knowing what to say.

He steps to the door again, then stops once more. "Stay alive, Quinntessa," he says with a firm but quiet voice. "I won't bury another."

Then he leaves, slamming the door behind him.

∼

I don't see my father for the rest of the week. Not that I'm in a hurry to see him again. Strangely, his last words are what keep me going.

Stay alive. I won't bury another.

Whenever possible, I keep to myself, mostly in my room. We all promised to keep figuring out the prophecy, but there'll be no use in any of it if we die in the next trial. I need to focus.

"You've been quiet lately," Vale says through panting breaths as our training session comes to a close. "Not that I'm complaining."

I shrug, keeping my back to her as I wipe away sweat with my sleeve and pack up my things. I've purposely kept our sessions focused and to the point. I don't feel like talking or bickering or whatever it is we do. I haven't even pestered her about how the poison testing is going.

"Here." She's next to me, holding out a small leather-bound book. "It's a book of Kobold riddles. I found it when we were in the library, and I thought it may be helpful in decoding the prophecy. Maybe even helpful for the upcoming trial." She places it on top of my bag. "I've already memorized it, so I figured I'd pass it on." Her voice isn't laced with her usual condescension. Her face is devoid of any snark or mischief.

I nod, taking the book in my hand. "You did good today," I say. And I mean it.

Her eyes crease with her smile. "Thanks. I—" she starts, but I've already turned, heading out of the cavern.

Walking back through the city toward the castle, I spot Alys heading down the same street in my direction. I dart behind a building and wait until she passes.

I've been avoiding her, too. Though I know she didn't mean to hurt me, I can barely look at her right now. Her face is a constant reminder of the painful memories she awakened. Now, I'm not only haunted by Gaius while asleep. I'm also plagued by the memory of my mother's screams while awake.

Retreating back to the safety of my room, I light a fire in the small stove and crawl into bed under a patchwork blanket, cracking open the Kobold book of riddles.

It isn't long until a knock sounds at my door. I freeze.

Hickory has come by multiple times, even going so far as to slip his latest theories, scribbled on parchment, under my door. I'm not ready to talk to him either. Maybe if I just stay really quiet, he'll think I'm out.

Another knock.

Persistent puck.

"Go away, Hickory," I warn from my bed.

"It's not Hickory," says the voice.

My pulse quickens. It's Aeron.

"Can I come in?"

"No," I say, my voice much too shrill as I leap to my feet. I cough. "I mean… I'm not feeling well. Don't want to get you sick." I inch toward the door on quiet feet.

"Is that why you've been cooped up in your room so much?" Concern rises in his voice. Considering the last time he saw me sick I was poisoned, I guess I can't blame him. "Maybe someone should check on you."

I see the gears in the door start to shift. I curse, realizing I must have forgotten to lock it earlier.

Quickly, I grab a fire poker in front of the stove and jam it into the gears. The mechanism halts and I let out a breath. "I'm fine, really."

There's a pause before he speaks again. "Quinn..."

A shudder runs through me at the sound of my name on his lips. The Nymph-like way he softens the usually harsh *Q*, like a whisper.

"I'm worried about you," he says softly. "Please don't shut me out."

I picture him on the other side, and I press my fingers to the door, yearning to open it. To tell him what I saw about my mother. What I now fear. To let him hold me like I can hear in his voice that he wants to. But even his touch can't take this pain away. Not this time.

I'm sorry, is what I mean to say. The words won't come.

Instead, I wait, holding my breath, a lump settling in my throat. I hold it there in the quiet until I hear his footsteps shift and patter away.

I swallow hard, chest thumping, resisting the urge to run after him.

It's for the best.

Right. Keep telling yourself that.

I move to return to my bed when a folded piece of parchment slips under my door.

"Hickory." I groan. "Enough of this."

I pick up the paper, ready to open the door and thrust it back out.

Instead of Hickory's hurried scrawling or line sketches, it's an architect's scaled drawing of a ship. A stunning, masterful ship that makes the Minnow pale in comparison. It looks exactly like one of the flying ships I coveted in Eldore.

Only a few words are written below the drawing in an all-too-familiar swirling penmanship:

Two more to go and she's yours.

The queen.

I crumple the paper in my hand, as if there might be someone in the shadows of my room who can see it, and rush back to my bed. Slowly unwrapping the message, I press out the creases, gazing at the beauty before me.

The queen must be pleased with Vale's progress. Provided that I follow through, it looks like she still plans on delivering my reward after all. A ship. My freedom. Even if she was the one who poisoned me before, perhaps all has been forgiven. Perhaps.

This time I fold the paper up carefully into a tight little square and hold it close.

Just a little longer and I can escape this living nightmare.

CHAPTER 53

O n the day of our trial, the stadium booms with voices, and the air is hot with the press of bodies.

As I'm guided down steep clay steps through the crowd, I pass the visiting clansfolk who, as usual, are sequestered in their separate sections, eyeing one another with disdain. My fellow competitors are already gathered at the Labyrinth's base when I reach the bottom.

Part of me regrets pulling away this past week. This could be the last time that I see any of them. Yet, the other part of me is grateful. It'll make any deaths that occur that much easier to handle. *Right?*

As each of them disappear around the curve of the maze to their designated entrances, I look back to the crowd.

The queen's eyes pass over me briefly with a nod. She knows I received her message.

Next to her, my father stares hard and intent, as if reminding me again. *Stay alive.*

I nod. *I plan to.*

"Without creativity and resourcefulness, nothing else matters," Lord Zephen says bluntly through his horn.

This snaps all the clans to attention, an unmistakable cutting blow to the other Ethos.

"Knowledge, Beauty, Life, and Strength are useless if you can't see how to use them to your advantage," he continues. "The ultimate leader must know how to take whatever is at their disposal and use it for any challenge placed before them. For our Trial of Creativity, you will display your ability to do so in the Labyrinth."

The maze comes alive as the cranking and screeching of machinery bellows from inside like a hungry animal. The crowd cheers, but I wince. The sound grates against my already-shattered nerves.

"The dangers of the Labyrinth are never the same twice, and they are not always what they appear, so you must be alert. Along the way you will face three doors. You must use your creativity and resourcefulness to open them. Do not rejoice too quickly, however, as each new section of the maze presents new dangers. Survive these trials and you will reach the center tower, where your final challenge will reside."

I look at the stone structure in the middle of the maze. This is where some of the criminal competitors never materialized. If they did, they emerged at the top, bloody and screaming.

Seeing Luna with her bloodied leg in my mind, I turn away from the maze, my heart thudding. *I can't do this.* I have to get out of here. Five smug Kobolds stalk toward me, holding pickaxes over their shoulders, ready to attack if I try to escape.

Lord Zephen continues. "Overcome the obstacles, reach the top of the tower, and you will have completed the Labyrinth. The order in which you finish will determine your ranking."

Bringing his arm down, a *boom* sounds as an explosion of glittering pixie dust shoots into the air. The crowd bursts into applause.

Lord Zephen's voice roars. "Begin!"

As I step between the looming stone walls of the Labyrinth entrance, a hazy mist covers my feet, blanketing the floor. The stretch of maze before me is a bleak gray. A damp chill runs down my neck as I step in deeper.

The sound of cheers muffles until all that's left is my ragged breathing; the maze grows deathly quiet. I look up. Some magical sound barrier must reside over the Labyrinth. I almost would've preferred to hear the crowds.

Just as Lord Zephen warned, I stay alert.

Following the twists and turns, I come to the first door. It's made of thick wooden logs with a dragon-headed gargoyle perched above it.

I look around. All that I can see through the mist is a pile of junk. Among the items are a short plank of wood, a cylindrical steel rod, a hammer, and spare leather straps like those of a belt. I pick up the plank of wood and turn it over in my hand. How am I supposed to use any of this to open a door?

Rock shifts above me, and I jump back. The gargoyle is moving! And if that isn't shocking enough, it speaks.

"I cannot talk," it begins ironically. "But I'll always reply when spoken to. Who am I?"

A riddle.

It sounds similar to the ones in the Kobold book that Vale lent me. Could answering it be the way through the door? I snort. It can't be that easy. And if so, what are *these* for? I look back to the plank in my hand and the other items on the ground.

I repeat the riddle to myself. "I cannot talk, but I'll always reply when spoken to." Immediately, I think of Alys. She can reply to me without literally speaking. Could that be it?

"Someone who's mute?" I say to the gargoyle. Even if it's wrong, what's the worst that can happen?

The ground rumbles as cranks shift in the walls and something shoots toward me. An arrow whizzes by my face, skimming my cheek. I touch my stinging skin, a thin line of blood smeared across it.

That was close.

Whoosh. Another arrow flies from the opposite direction.

I whip the plank in front of me just in time. The arrow thunks into the wood. The point just barely breaks through the surface; it'd nearly pierced my chest.

My heart pounds as I inch closer to one of the walls. A million small holes puncture its stone surface. These aren't the only arrows that are coming. I better keep thinking, fast. And in case I guess wrong again, I'll need better protection.

As I go back over the riddle, I launch myself at the pile of scraps. I use the sharp backend of the hammer to punch two holes into the wood. Though my fingers shake with adrenaline, I slip either end of a leather strap through each hole, tying them off with a tight knot. Securing the makeshift shield to my arm, I grip the steel rod in the other like a sword. Though they're far from Gwyllion weapons, they'll have to suffice.

This time I pivot in a circle, keeping my eyes on the walls as I refocus my thoughts to the riddle.

"Okay… What about a bird?" I guess, thinking of the sparrow call I used with my crew. Birds don't exactly talk, but they can respond in their own way.

Another arrow shoots toward me. Lifting the rod, I spin it in my fingers like the spokes of a wheel. The arrow zings off the metal. *Ping.* Another arrow comes from the other wall at the same angle. *Ping.*

Wrong again. I shake my head.

Suddenly, Lord Zephen's warning comes back to me: *Things are not always what they seem.*

I shouldn't think too literally. I have to get creative. I have to think like a Kobold.

Before I can shoot out another guess, two more arrows release in succession, faster this time, and I block them with my shield. *Thunk. Thunk.*

My ears twitch at the familiar sound. *There's a pattern.*

I can't always anticipate where the first arrow will release from, but based on its angle, I can predict the next. I wipe sweat from my brow before it can drip into my eyes. I don't have long to rest.

The arrows come quicker. It's like a dance as I move to evade each one. Though I'm surviving, I can't keep this up forever. I need to solve the riddle and get out of here. I can barely concentrate. Like a mirroring effect, the arrows keep coming, one side and then the other, like a call and response, echoing one another.

My mind locks back on the riddle. *I cannot talk, but I will always reply when spoken to.*

Wait. What if the danger itself is a clue to the riddle?

"You are Echo!" I yell.

The wooden door creaks open.

Yes!

The movement distracts me, and an arrow releases, driving itself into my thigh. I yelp at the shooting pain, dashing through the door, slamming it closed.

Safely on the other side, I cast my shield and rod aside and yank out the arrow with a hiss. Biting the inside of my cheek, I tear off the hem of my pant leg and wrap it tight.

As I stand on my good leg, I grab my shield and rod again. They might still be helpful with the other dangers in the maze.

Releasing my wings, I fly across the next stretch of maze, making sure not to rise above the walls and risk looking like I'm trying to escape. Blood is quickly soaking the cloth, dripping down my leg. At least I haven't lost my leg completely. I have to keep going.

After a few more turns, I see the second door. Landing gingerly before it, my stomach churns with a mix of relief and apprehension.

This one is metal, with another gargoyle stationed above it.

"You hold me without using your hands or arms. Who am I?" it says.

What in Faylan can I hold without my hands or arms? Something metaphorical perhaps?

Gears grind again, but this time, it's accompanied by the sound of rushing water. *What now?* The sound grows louder behind me, and I turn. A wave of water whips around the maze, charging my way, preparing to engulf me.

Blast! I drop my makeshift weapons, grab the door's handle, and yank hard. The wave collides with my body and thrusts me forward. My head hits the metal slab, and the water pulls me under. The waves force me deeper as my head throbs, and I'm brought back to the memory of drowning at sea.

Only this time Aeron isn't here to save me.

Aeron.

His words from last night come back to me. *"Please, don't shut me out."*

I think of him and the others. I shut them all out. Maybe I should've opened the door. I should've at least said goodbye. I picture them all struggling to endure their own challenges. If we were all together now, maybe we could have helped each other survive this, just like we did in the Woodlands.

It's then that I realize: I don't want this to be the end. I want to see them again. All of them. To apologize.

This time, I have something to live for. I have to survive.

Above me, I glimpse something floating on the surface. My wooden shield.

Though my injured leg stings with pain, I use my good leg to kick toward it. I grab on and break through to the open air, coughing up water.

"Do something!" I call out to the gargoyle.

It only repeats the riddle. "You hold me without using your hands or arms. Who am I?"

Another wave crashes over me. I clutch tightly to the shield before I'm pulled under.

Then the answer hits me. I'm *holding* my breath.

Breaking the surface again, I yell, "You are Breath!"

The door swings open and water rushes through, pulling me with it before it recedes into grated holes in the floor. Coughing, tired, and soaked to the bone, I touch my forehead. Blood trickles down my face. I wipe it away.

You're fine. Practically halfway there. Keep going.

My wings are too waterlogged to fly, so I brace against the maze walls to stabilize my woozy head and stagger around the next bend.

Breaking through the mist, I finally reach the third door. As I watch for any hint of danger, this door's gargoyle speaks with such a soft voice, I barely hear it.

"What'd you say?" I ask, wringing water from my still-dripping sleeves. "Speak louder."

The gargoyle raises its tone just a hair. "I'm so fragile, just saying my name can break me. Who am I?" It even cowers in fear as it speaks the words.

I rake my hands through my damp, tangled curls, frustration building. "These riddles are so bloody irritating!"

The gargoyle's eyes grow wide, shaking its head in warning.

"Don't you shake your head at me," I yell. "If you'd just give me some kind of hint—"

Again, the clashing of metal and grinding of gears sounds. A large panel in the floor far behind me is rising. Is the maze giving me a secret passageway out?

I should know by now, I'm never that lucky.

A low mechanical growl comes from the pit as two large glowing eyes appear in the dark. I draw back as the figure marches out into the light on two steel legs. Standing three times as tall as I am, the iron giant gnashes its sharp metal teeth. Except for the smoke billowing out of the pipes on its shoulders, it looks exactly like the giants in Eldore's murals.

The Kobolds have constructed a mechanical Numa.

It takes everything I have not to scream as the giant stumbles toward me, the ground shaking with each of its steps. Thankfully, the beast's movements are slow. Eluding it, I dart between its legs as its monstrous hands try to grab me.

If I can just get through the door. The giant is too big to follow me through.

Think, Quinn, think! With my shield and rod left behind at the last door, I have nothing left to aid me. I look at my cursed hands. Even if I wanted to use my fire, I'm too wet from the earlier flood to summon even a spark.

Before the iron Numa can turn toward me, I notice something sticking out of its back, and an idea takes hold.

Sprinting forward, I leap into the air and grab onto the nuts and bolts of its armor. Finding the loose screw I glimpsed, I clamp my fingers around it and twist furiously until it comes free.

The giant growls, trying to reach for me, smoke pumping out of its pipes in a rage.

Climbing to its shoulders, I reach around and thrust the sharp end of the screw into one of its eyes. Metal crunches. I go for the other eye, but the giant's hand seizes my waist with its metal fingers. The force nearly squeezes all the air out of me. I hear and feel a terrible crunch.

I cry out in pain and conviction. I'm not finished yet. With one hand still free, I lodge the screw into its other eye and the beast lets go of me, throwing its hands over its face.

I hit the ground hard, pain radiating through my ribs and across my back and chest. As the giant reels, I slowly force my body to stand and creep toward the gargoyle.

"I'm so fragile, just saying my name can break me…" I repeat the riddle.

The Numa's head turns, searching for the source of the sound. It might be blind, but its hearing is perfectly intact.

Hearing. I look at the gargoyle as the answer comes to me.

"You are Silence!"

That definitely gets the giant's attention.

It sprints in the direction of my voice as the door opens.

I leap through.

Thankfully, it closes behind me and the giant collides against the other side.

I take a moment to breathe. That was the third door. I just need to get to the tower, and all of this will be over.

The wall shudders. Pebbles trickle down as banging comes from the other side. The giant is trying to break through!

Pushing through the pain, I scramble further into the maze. Maneuvering through more twists and turns, I finally spot it ahead of me. *The tower.*

The tower also has a door. This one is covered in small stones, secured by three locks. *Of course.*

"Open the door!" I command the gargoyle above it, fearing the iron Numa will break free at any moment.

This gargoyle has three heads. "To open this door, you must touch the three correct stones." The first head speaks slowly, in no hurry at all. My eyes rake over the door, each stone marked with its own distinct icon.

"How do I know which ones to press?" I ask frantically as the giant's growl rumbles through the maze.

"The answer lies in these three riddles," says the same head. "The first: We've been around since the beginning of time, but we are never more than a month old."

My eyes ricochet back and forth over the stones. Once I get out of here, I never want to hear another riddle again.

No time to think about that now. Focus! What could be so old and yet so young?

Raking my eyes over the stones, I spot one with a collection of round, white circles. They almost looked like... *the moons?*

The moons are only full once a month and then start all over again. That makes sense, right? I don't have time to hesitate. I press it, and the first lock unlatches.

Thank Faylan.

"Next!" I command, feeling encouraged.

"The more of me there is, the less you see," says the second head.

I close my eyes, trying to clear my mind. Unable to see anything else, the answer hits me square in the face. "Darkness!"

I comb over the stones, spotting one that's completely black. Pressing it, the second lock unhinges with a satisfying snap.

The third head doesn't hesitate. "Feed me and I will live, but give me a drink and I will die."

That doesn't make any sense. All living things need to drink. But like each of the riddles so far, not all things are as they appear.

Water drips from my clothes, and my whole body aches as my eye stops at an icon of a flame. I look at my useless wet hands.

Of course! You can feed it with wood and kill it with water.

"Fire," I whisper.

The roar of the giant sounds again. Behind me, it barrels down the stretch of maze, stumbling in its blindness. Pressing the fire stone with all my might, the last bolt unlocks.

The door shifts open and I shoot through, slamming it closed behind me just before the iron beast reaches the threshold. It locks itself, keeping the giant out, but also keeping me in.

I let out a shuddering breath. The room I'm in now is long and dimly lit by a series of candles. At the back stairway, a shadowed figure appears, barely visible in the flickering light, wings stretched out.

Another gargoyle with a final riddle? Or perhaps one of the other competitors?

"Hello, pirate," says the shadow.

I couldn't have been more wrong.

CHAPTER 54

I t's as if all the air has been sucked out of the room.

Though the voice of the shadowed figure is garbled and distorted, I know who it is even before he steps into the candlelight. It illuminates his crescent-shaped scar.

"*You.*" I hesitate. It's Moon Face, all right. But he's taller. Stronger. Disfigured.

Fangs hang over his snarling lips, and his arms droop, elongated at his sides. Claws extend from his fingers, scraping along the ground as he stalks toward me. His skin is darker, charred-looking, and flakes of it flutter to the ground as he moves. His Sylph wings are stripped of feathers so only a leathery surface remains. They flap, creating a gust that threatens to extinguish the flickering candles around us.

Somehow, Moon Face has become a goblin.

"What happened to you?" I blink through the darkness, not believing my eyes.

"I've gone through a bit of an... enhancement. An evolution, if you will." Jasper motions to his new form with his ridiculously muscled arms.

I remember him sweating in the tunnels. The discoloring of his skin. His incredible strength with the Kobold conductor. Had he been transitioning to... *this*?

"How?" I back up against the locked door. No way out.

"It's… complicated." He takes another step toward me. "But if you know the right folk, you can get what you want."

The right folk? Does he mean the goblins? Or maybe whoever he's collecting the faeries and pixie dust for? As he draws closer, I fear the answer to another question more.

"What exactly do you want?" I stand straighter as my eyes dart around for an escape route. A weapon. *Anything.*

Moon Face lets out a guttural laugh, only a few feet away now. "Why, *you,* of course."

He reaches out and takes hold of my throat, raising me off the ground, just as he did to the Kobold conductor.

I gasp for air, grabbing at his hands. They're too strong.

No. Please. Not like this.

"You've been the bane of my existence for far too long, pirate. Terrorizing my crew, humiliating me. Giving me this scar. And now you think you can snoop around in my personal affairs and get away with it? I don't think so. They've been watching. They know you've seen too much, and I was all too pleased to volunteer to finish you off."

They? They who? I want to ask, but he squeezes harder. Spots dot my vision. I kick with all my might. Nothing fazes him.

Moon Face only laughs. "Ah, so much like your brother. He too put up a good fight."

My eyes grow wide. *Gaius?* Did Moon Face have something to do with his death?

He leans in closer. "Now it's your turn. Then I'll be going after your *friends*."

No. Even as I'm losing consciousness, something inside me snaps. Deep in my gut, a flame sparks to life.

He can do whatever he wants to me, but I can't let him hurt the others.

Before I know it, Moon Face's threats stoke a fire so savage, I can't contain it—and I don't want to. It explodes, shooting through my body. It races through my blood like a fever, burning away every lick of water left on my skin and clothes until my palms begin to smolder. Even the candles around us seem to blaze brighter.

I've been afraid of this puck for far too long.

But now? Now I'm angry.

My hands are set ablaze with fire, and I push through the blinding pain as I grab Moon Face's wrists.

He shrieks as he pulls away.

Released from his clutches, I crumple to the floor, gasping for air.

His arms flail as he tries to shake the fire away.

He isn't getting away that easily. I need to make sure he never threatens me or anyone else ever again.

With still-burning hands, I lunge forward. As I do, flames from the candles shoot into my hands. They stoke my fire into an inferno. I don't know how this is happening, but I don't have time to care.

With terror flaring in his eyes, Moon Face tries to back away, but I swipe at him again and again as the flames crawl over his skin. His terrible cries pierce my ears until I finally collapse.

Fire spreads over Moon Face's entire body. He's engulfed in flames, just like the goblin in the Woodlands. As his screams continue, all I can do is cover my ears and squeeze my eyes shut so I don't have to watch him burn.

It feels like an eternity until the room finally falls silent, descending into darkness. Moon Face is reduced to a smoldering pile of ash on the stone floor.

My breath hitches. The reality of what I've done sinks in. *I've killed Jasper.*

In place of my heat, a violent chill fills the void and courses through my bones. While part of me feels relief, justice even, the other part wants to scream.

I curse, pounding my fist against the floor. He'd known more about the goblins. About Gaius' death.

They've been watching. They know you've seen too much... he'd said.

Now he's gone, and his secrets with him. There's nothing I can do.

Every part of my body aches, and blood still streams from my leg and head. I stagger past Moon Face's remains toward a single stream of light coming from the stairway. Forcing myself to climb with great difficulty, I finally reach an upper door.

I throw it open. The shouts of the crowd hit me like a gust of wind.

I made it.

I don't care where I rank. *I survived.*

And if I heard Moon Face right, though he could have been the answer to so many questions, I might have just avenged my brother's death.

CHAPTER 55

"Quinn!" Aeron rushes toward me with the other three in tow. My legs buckle and I sag slowly to the ground. Aeron skids to his knees, pulling me into his strong arms. I let my head fall to his chest. I don't even care who sees.

The others rush in around us, Hickory fumbling as he nurses a heavy limp. He yells out into the arena for help to come, battling with the roar of the stadium as Alys and Vale gawk at the extent of my wounds.

Each of them have their own battle scars from the Labyrinth as well. Vale stares at me through a swollen eye that's already bruising. Alys holds an arm that looks like it's been yanked out of its socket.

At least they're all alive. That's what matters.

Though, there's one who didn't survive the Labyrinth in the end.

"I killed him." It's all I can say, over and over.

My skin feels coated in ice. I reach out a shaking hand to Aeron's chest. My fingers find skin. Holes rimmed in black are torn through his shirt, revealing singed muscle. The faint smell of smoke reaches my nose. *No.* I flinch back, the thought that I could have burned him too rips through me.

"Shh, it's okay. It's not as bad as it looks," Aeron assures me as I stare at the burns, telling myself they had to have come from the maze. He pulls me closer. "Quinn, you're shivering."

Aeron rubs at my arms, but it's not helping.

It's as if there's always been a dull heat inside me, simmering beneath my skin, keeping me warm—and now it's gone.

I suck in a breath, the air in my lungs winter-sharp. Even growing up in the chill of the mountains, I've never felt so cold.

So numb.

"I killed him. I killed Jasper," I say slowly, the reality setting in. Speaking his true name aloud sends tremors down my spine.

"*What?*" Aeron's brows knit. They all look at me as if I've gone insane.

Maybe I have.

Before I can say more, Kobold mediks fly in from above, pulling us apart.

The world becomes a blur of blankets and airborne stretchers as we're liberated from the tower and rushed back to the castle.

I must have blacked out, because the next thing I know, I'm waking up with a mess of heated compresses and comforters piled on top of me.

A strangled grunt of pain sounds from somewhere in the room. My head whips around to take in a small space filled with cots, a few sinks, and a series of medical mechanisms hanging from wheeled devices. I'm in an infirmary.

Hickory and Vale sit in their own cots across from me. Hickory's leg is elevated on a pillow and a healing herb patch is over Vale's swollen eye. They're watching as Kobold mediks treat Aeron's burns. He winces as they wrap his chest in bandages. Next to me, another medik sets Alys' arm in a sling.

As Kobold mediks attend to us, we're told our ranking. I came in last again, which means I'm fairly certain I have the lowest amount of points in the Ethodine so far. But that's the furthest concern from my mind. Still reeling from everything that happened in the maze, I sink lower under the blankets. I breathe in deeply, trying to collect my thoughts.

By the time the five of us are finally left alone to rest, at least I've stopped shivering. I try to fully explain to the others what happened. How Moon Face somehow became a goblin, found his way into the Labyrinth, and attempted to kill me.

Vale's bruised face twists, her expression stricken. "How in Faylan did he become a goblin?"

"You said he mentioned an evolution of some kind." Hickory sits up straighter. It's like I can see the gears turning slowly in his head until something clicks. "Does this mean all goblins were once faeries?"

"And someone sent him to kill you?" Aeron paces near his cot, refusing to lie down any longer. "What does all of it mean?"

Alys stares at me in stunned silence as the drip of a sink ticks by the seconds.

"I don't know," I say finally. I pull my blankets closer, running my fingers over the frayed edges.

If only I'd controlled myself, I could have tortured him for more information. Especially what he meant about Gaius. Maybe I'd been right in thinking Gaius' plague was a poison. Is that what my dream in Vyndoria was trying to tell me?

"He also made it sound like we're being watched," I add hesitantly, picturing Moon Face's goblin snarl.

Then I'll be going after your friends.

Another shiver shudders through me as I look around at each of their faces.

I won't put them in danger anymore.

"I think we should lay low for a while." I mean to say it firmly, but it comes out soft and unsure. I try again. "We should put this prophecy stuff aside, at least until the Ethodine is over."

"No way." Hickory throws off his blanket and shifts his injured leg over the edge of his bed. "The Moon Harvest will practically be on us by then."

"We don't even know if this Moon Harvest is the right one," I say. "It could just as well be many harvests away."

"I think Quinn is right." Aeron nods resolutely. "For now, we should just focus on the final trial."

Hickory groans. "But I was finally making a breakthrough. Remember that scroll you found in the library, Quinn? It had some of the same symbols as the tome, which has been helping me decipher it more. It looks like some of the pages might be spells of some kind."

Vale pauses in bringing a cup of water to her lips. "What kind of spells?"

Hickory jumps up on his good leg and grabs a crutch leaning by his cot. "The book is in my room. I'll show you."

He quickly hobbles out of the ward, and we wait.

Vale collapses back onto her pillow with an exhausted sigh, adjusting the patch over her eye.

I look across the room to Aeron, who's studying me as if he wants to say something. But then Alys joins me on my bed, touching my arm with an ungloved hand.

Did you use your fire? To kill him?

Yes. I pull the comforter to my chest. *Something else happened too. I'm so cold...* I swallow hard as she stares at me. *I think... my fire might be gone.*

Alys' grip tightens. My skin tingles. A low vibration of her healing energy courses through me, just enough to make the tattoos on one of her fingers glow without anyone noticing. But I'm not getting any warmer.

I can usually sense your gift when I touch you, but I don't feel it now. Alys hurriedly touches different parts of my arm as if that will help, looking more distraught every second.

I'm still numb, as if the coals that always smoldered in my gut have been doused and turned to ice.

I do sense one thing, Alys thinks to me.

What's that? I shift uncomfortably under her gaze, a sense of dread creeping in.

Fear.

I look away, not wanting her to see it in my eyes. I *am* afraid. More than I've ever been. Afraid of the trials. Of whoever is after me. Of losing anyone else.

The fire served its purpose one last time—it protected me. But its power scares me too. I can still smell Moon Face's burning flesh. I see Gaius' scars and hear my mother's screams.

If it's truly gone forever, maybe it's for the best. At least now, like Moon Face, it can never hurt anyone ever again.

Hickory rushes in from the hallway, his skin nearly as white as his hair.

"What's wrong?" I ask.

His mouth hangs open. "I can't find the tome."

"What?" Vale sits up, wincing at the quick motion. "What do you mean, you can't find it?"

"Maybe you lost it in that room of yours," Aeron sighs, not as easily frazzled. "Honestly, it's like a maze all on its own in there."

"It's called organized chaos." Hickory glares at him, gritting his teeth. "And I know exactly where I hid it. It's not there."

"Hickory," I say firmly, and he looks at me, our eyes locking. "Are you sure?"

His gaze falls to the ground. "I tore the whole room apart." He drops onto his cot in a bewildered daze. *"The tome is gone."*

EDGE
of FATES
THE GWYLLION BATTLE

CHAPTER 56

Sailing back through the dark abyss of the tunnels, the ship creaks under my feet as I stand at the bow alone. I reach for my daggers hidden under my cloak for comfort, but when my icy fingers grip the patterned hilt, I shiver.

The others have stationed themselves elsewhere on board. No secret conversations or comical insults are thrown around this time. Behind me, Vale leans quietly on the starboard railing, her feathered wings drooping as she stares aimlessly into the murky water. Hickory has his back pressed against the mast, hands clenched around his notebook, lost in thought. Alys is probably still resting in one of the cabins below because I don't see her.

A splash in the water sounds. Aeron is swimming alongside the boat, his fin-tail bobbing up and down. He must really be homesick for the sea. I don't blame him.

After a day of medicinal pixie dust treatments in the Kobold infirmary, we've been cleared for travel, sent off to Greymerrow for the final trial of the Ethodine.

As we glide out of the shadowed tunnels into the sunlit Silver Sea, the relief I'd hoped for doesn't come. Sunbeams hit my face, but they do nothing to warm my frigid bones.

It's gone.

I can feel it deep in my gut.

In the place where heat used to churn, bitter cold swirls in my stomach.

My fire is gone for good. Just like the Mystic tome.

Last night, Alys took me to a vacant room near the infirmary to filter her healing energy through my body. She urged me to try to summon the fire again and again. It was no use.

Eventually she sagged with exhaustion, and I convinced her to go back with the others to rest.

"I'll be there in a minute," I'd told her. At the sound of Hickory and Vale's endless bickering, I stopped just outside the infirmary doorway, cloaked by the hallway's shadows.

"That tome has been part of the Sylph archives for generations," Vale fumed. "I've been telling my mother it must be somewhere back at home. I knew I should've made you give it to me. Now that you've lost it, she's going to kill me."

"I didn't lose it. Someone *stole* it," Hickory asserted again, poring over his notes about the tome as if he'd find some answers there. If Vale didn't seem just as distraught about its disappearance as he was, I wondered if Hickory would've accused her of stealing it herself.

"Well then, we only have one choice now, don't we?" Aeron rolled over in his cot with a tired grumble, his back to them. "It's time we get some sleep and turn our focus to the final trial."

Amidst their squabbling, I'd stayed silent in the hallway, not wanting to incite another argument by voicing what I feared.

Could the faerie who stole the book be whoever Moon Face was working for?

The ship rocks suddenly and I grab at the railing, anchoring myself to the present again. A hawk screeches overhead, and the screams of Moon Face as he burned alive echo in my mind. The sound tears through my body, and I tuck my wings gingerly around me.

When I first thought I'd killed Jasper after my crew attacked his ship, he was just a nameless soldier in a sea storm.

At the time, I was working for Maverick, doing a job, following the Pirate Lord's orders. I did what I had to do, in order to keep my true identity hidden.

This time, it was personal. Self defense, sure. But I'd completely lost control, consumed by my fiery rage until he was a heaping pile of ash.

In an instant, I lost the one key I had to the many questions about my brother.

I tuck my wings in tighter.

It's only when the familiar beach at the base of the mountain comes into view that I feel like I can start to breathe again. Without the pomp and circumstance of a royal funeral, the scene of fishmongers casting nets and merchants preparing their sails is strangely nostalgic. Above the docks, familiar steep slopes of gray rock and craggy cliffs loom over us as low-hanging clouds cover the tall mountain peaks in mist.

Wood-burning smoke billows from the far east end of the beach, and my eyes follow it to the weather-worn shack of Finnegan's Pub, a tavern often frequented by sea-sailing visitors and local Gwyllions after a long day's work.

I lick my lips, wishing we could stop there for a pint. Maybe that would warm my frigid body.

Then I spot it.

Unlit ceremony torches and a large boulder fitted over a tomb in the mountainside.

Gaius' tomb.

A gentle gloved hand lands on my shoulder as Alys steps up beside me. She stares at it too. I'm comforted to have someone who knows the pain of losing a sibling.

It feels like just yesterday and yet a lifetime ago since I've been here last. Returning home should fill me with dread. Somehow, it ignites a small spark of hope. No matter what's happened thus far, it'll all be over soon. Then I'll finally fulfill the vow I made to my brother on this very beach.

I've nearly made it, Gaius. This is for you. I won't let your death be in vain.

After making port, Gwyllion guards guide our party up the steep mountain path. The deep roar of a dragon sounds from the high peaks above as we tread through shifting shale, up the meandering trails to Greymerrow City. As we rise in altitude and set foot in the smog-filled city, the others stifle shivers, especially Aeron in his thin chiton, his breath turning to gray mist in the air.

"You all might need some warmer clothes in these parts." I motion to a stand displaying fur and hide skin garments in the market we just entered.

No thanks, Alys signs with a shake of her head. She frowns at the animal skins and their carcasses hanging from the butcher next door. The gamey smell of smoked meat wafts toward us from the tavern at the other end of the square.

"Suit yourself. More for us." Vale runs a shivering hand over a fur coat, looking like she might snatch it up and wrap it around herself at any moment.

Aeron leans closer to me and whispers, "Do they have anything that can thaw the cold stares we're getting?"

Around us, muscled bladesmiths and weapon crafters look up from their forges with hammers and jagged blades gripped tightly in their hands. Even sprouts at their mothers' feet stop to glower at us.

"Don't worry," I sigh. "They're staring at me, not you."

Like they did when I was first captured and paraded through these streets, my folk scowl at me with stern, ash-smeared faces.

I shouldn't be surprised. Besides not being their favorite pixie to begin with, word has surely made it back here that I've been failing spectacularly in the competition. Except for the Trial of Beauty, I've come in last for every one of the challenges. And even if I'd been doing well all this time, even if I'm their only hope at the crown, I'm still the princess who deserted them to be a pirate.

Gwyllions are never quick to forgive, if they do at all.

Forgiveness is just another sign of weakness.

I feel for the folded piece of paper in my pocket. The queen's promise of my ship. I haven't come to win over the Gwyllions or even win the competition. I have one objective before I can be free and return to my own life: I must make sure Vale becomes queen.

A chorus of steady drums and heavy boots pound down the main road.

All in the vicinity turn to see Lord Feyden, followed by a unit of twenty Gwyllion guards at his back. Instead of standard patrol garb, they're outfitted with razor-sharp weapons for active combat. Even my father wears his flowing military cape, sunbeams gleaming off his polished battle armor. They march in a slow, rhythmic beat that resounds off the mountain, heading straight toward us.

The others draw back, but I stand firm as the Queen and a few of her own guards step in front of us.

"Each clan agreed to welcome the competitors in peace," she calls out above the march with her head held high, a bite to her words. "What's the meaning of this forceful display?"

Feyden halts and shoots a sharp hand into the air. His unit stops at once with a final stomp of their boots, the city square settling into silence.

"We're merely displaying our Etho," Feyden says coolly. "The strength each competitor must exhibit to become the victor of the final trial." He strides over to the nearest blacksmith, holding out his hand.

The burly faerie turns to his collection of blades and pulls out a two-handed longsword. He humbly kneels before Feyden, offering up his very best to his lord.

My father nods, gripping the leather hilt, swiping the blade hard a few times as the metal rings through the air. "Like its people, Gwyllion steel does not bend or waver. It's not enough to *appear* sharp and strong. It must be *tested*."

He walks with the sword toward the butcher's shop across the way.

The butcher steps aside as my father approaches an elk carcass hanging from a thick rope.

Feyden examines the blade one last time before thrusting it straight through the meat, the point of the blade cutting clean through to the other side.

The queen flinches, and the others wince.

I've seen this before. My father isn't finished testing the craftsmanship yet.

He yanks the blade out and swipes long slashes again and again, testing either side of the doubled-edged weapon with guttural huffs that ruffle his braided beard. Finally, he releases his dragon wings and rises in the air. Leveling his arm at the rope above, he strikes with a spin that swiftly slices the coarse material in two.

The carcass drops to the floor in a heap.

Breathing heavily, my father snaps his fingers, and two guards approach. One pays the butcher with a sizable pouch of farthlings while the other slings the heavy elk onto his back. They'll probably take it back to the fortress' kitchens for tonight's feast.

Returning to the blacksmith, Feyden wipes blood on his crimson cape and hands back the longsword.

"Fine work," says my father.

The blacksmith puffs out his chest with pride as he receives it and bows low to Feyden. With the display and my father's seal of approval, he'll sell that sword for ten times its value now.

Feyden then turns to us with flecks of splattered blood on his armor. "For your final trial, each competitor will be allowed armor and a single or paired weapon. My folk have agreed to sell you any items you desire."

He motions us to the blacksmith's display, and we move tentatively to it. As Vale studies the inscriptions on some of the swords, Aeron picks up a war hammer, turning it over, testing the grip in his hand. Alys lifts a pair of flails with spiked metal spheres that jangle on chains at the end. Hickory picks up a large battle axe and nearly buckles over with the weight, the large head of it landing back down on the table with a thud.

I move toward the throwing knives and pick up a pair. Each mirror their partner. I consider my daggers hidden at my side. Maybe I'll use those in the trial.

As I watch Vale eye a saber with an intricate swirling hilt, I reconsider. Battling with my daggers wouldn't exactly honor my brother when I plan to lose to Vale on purpose.

"You may also select a non-Gwyllion weapon, if you wish," Feyden adds. "But it must be made of non-magical material, as no magic is permitted here."

He waves his hand, and the unit recites the Gwyllion mantra in booming voices: "Magic is a crutch. Laughter is frailty. Tears are poison."

Before I realize it, I'm mouthing along with the words I know all too well.

Gwyllions are strong as steel. They do not yield.

"This will be the final stage of the Ethodine." Feyden continues, stepping closer, keeping his eyes trained on me. "Even those of you at the bottom may yet have the opportunity to rise in ranks and win."

My eyebrows raise, but I school my features, giving him a stern nod.

Though I'm not sure what he has planned, or how he thinks I could possibly secure him the crown now, I can't let my true intentions slip. Not when I'm so close to securing my freedom.

"You have one last week for final preparations." He straightens, hands folded behind his back. "So, train hard. The full rules will be explained on the day of the trial. All I can reveal is that you'll prove your strength by battling the greatest threat to your success yet." His eyes scan the five of us. "Each other."

CHAPTER 57

A s the week drags on, I work Vale tirelessly in my private training room, readying her for the final trial. In order to win, Vale will have to be skilled enough and strong enough to beat the others, and at least appear to be able to beat me.

Today, she's actually doing fairly well. Her sleeveless tunic highlights the new tone in her arms that were once thin and pale. Again and again, she matches each of my blows.

That is, until I sideswipe her with my leg, sending her to the ground.

"Cheap shot!" Her eyes flash up at me.

I laugh. "You've been doing too well. I had to throw you off somehow." Stepping closer, I offer my hand.

She smirks and grabs it. Instead of allowing me to pull her up, she yanks me down.

Taken off guard, I stumble to the stone floor as she jumps up and holds me at the point of her blade.

"Never let your guard down," she repeats my own words from Tartarus back to me. "How's that for the element of surprise?"

"Very good." I laugh harder this time. "Very *pirate* of you, in fact."

"Why, thank you." She curtsies.

"All right, let's go again," I say while getting up, brushing off my trousers. "This time, no funny business. You only have a few days left."

Vale doesn't raise her blade.

Instead, she steps up to one of the narrow windows lining the stone wall, quietly watching a hawk dip and soar over the mountains nearby.

"Before we begin again, I want you to promise me something." She turns back to me, resting the point of her sword on the ground, holding the hilt with both hands. Her eyes narrow as she lifts her chin, a muscle twitching in her jaw.

"Okay…" I say, keeping my stance ready. If this is another trick, I'm not falling for it again.

Vale takes a deep breath. "I want you to promise me that you won't let me win."

I lower my blade. "You want me to beat you?"

"Well, no, I mean—" She groans. "Why must you always make everything so difficult?"

"Me?" I exclaim. "You're the one who's not making sense. Spit it out already!"

"Fine!" Vale yells, then shakes her head. "Honestly, Quinn, with how we bicker, you're like the sister I never wanted." A smile tugs at her lips. "What I mean is, I'm going to take everything you've taught me and do my best. But I want you to do your best too. If I'm truly meant to be queen, I'll beat you and anyone else on my own. Win or lose, I want to do so fair and square."

She looks to me for a response. My mouth hangs open. I can only think of one thing. "What about your mother? What about her deal?"

"Screw her deal," Vale says firmly.

I gape again. Vale lives for her mother's approval. Who is this pixie standing before me?

"I'm so tired of worrying about what my mother thinks, always following her orders. Aren't you?" She steps toward me. "I want to offer you a new deal. One where we both find out what we're made of. Either way, you can return to being queen of the sea or you become queen of all of Faylan. Not a bad deal, if you ask me."

"Me? A *queen*?" I spurt out a laugh. Feyden did say even the lowest-ranked competitor could still have a chance at the crown during this final trial. I scoff at the idea. "Queen Quinn? Do you know how ridiculous even the name sounds?"

Vale stares at me without a hint of humor. "Quinn, I'm being serious."

"Seriously insane." I fold my arms. "Listen, we've both gone through so much to get this far, to get what we want. Even if it's cheating the system, why mess that up? Since when did you start to care so much?" I eye her suspiciously. There has to be a catch. A new game she's playing. "What do you gain if you lose?"

"My dignity." Vale's eyes drop. "If I win because you hold back, I'll never know if I'm fit to be queen."

She raises her sword. It's different from the one she usually uses. This one has a thin, double-edged blade, a golden cross-guard with gilded feathers, and the Sylphs' half sun, half moon crest etched into the pommel.

"This was my father's sword. Mother gave it to me to use for the trial," she says with a sad inflection to her voice. She shakes her head. "I can't go out there and wield his weapon of honor knowing what we're about to do."

"Vale, look—" I start to argue with her again. She takes a forceful step forward, and I resist the urge to draw back.

"You once told me that in order to win, I have to know the goal behind the swing of my blade. That a weapon is only as strong as the one who wields it."

Her eyes bore into me as I nod, impressed that she actually listened to what I said, let alone took it to heart.

"Well—" she sighs "—I think I'd rather know that my father would be pleased with me for doing the right thing instead of cheating my way to the throne. Besides myself, he's the only one I really want to make proud. Will you help me do that?"

A tightness pulls at my chest. Like Vale with her mother's expectations, I think of my father. How much do I let what he thinks affect my life, my goals, and my decisions, for better or for worse? Though I'd never admit it out loud, all I ever wanted was to be strong enough for him.

Now, the only faerie I truly want to make proud is no longer alive to see me win or lose. Still, the urge to honor Gaius above all else bubbles to the surface.

"So…" Vale takes another step toward me, holding out a hand to seal the deal. "What do you say?"

I trudge through the sand, running my fingers along the jagged mountainside as I make my way down the beach toward Gaius' tomb. Reaching the stone that separates me from where his body lies, it's as if the past five weeks never happened.

But so many things have changed. *I've* changed.

"Hello, brother." I stuff my hands into my pockets. I'm not sure what I've come to say exactly. I guess I just want to feel close to him.

Since Moon Face's death, my nightmares of Gaius have ceased. For the first time in over five weeks, I sleep soundly. As if his spirit has finally been able to move on from haunting my dreams. As if avenging his death has brought him peace.

I thought I'd feel peace too. Instead, not having the nightmares is somehow unsettling. Maybe my dreams didn't have anything to do with the Mystic prophecy after all.

Most of all, I find myself missing seeing him.

"I just wanted you to know… that I didn't let you down this time. I mean, things started out rocky. You know me." I half-smile. "If you were here, I think you'd be proud of me. I think I've even made some friends."

I kick a pebble toward the mountainside and watch it tumble to the unlit torch near the tomb. The one I ignited with my fire just before I left for the Ethodine.

My fire.

Though I've stopped shivering, my heat hasn't returned. I've tested it a few more times, trying to summon the anger that usually brings it out. Not even a spark manifested.

Looking at my hands, I see Moon Face in flames again. Gaius scorched. My mother, fighting through fire and smoke. I hear their screams and wince as Alys' words come back to me.

I do sense one thing though… fear.

I lean back against the cold stone barricading the tomb.

"I wish you were here, brother. There's so much I still don't understand, like this trial. You always knew what to do. "

I pace, focusing on the more immediate trouble.

"If I let Vale beat me, I'll be on the sea in a matter of days with a new ship and crew. That's where I belong." I try to hold on to my confidence. Instead, it drifts out to sea like the tide.

"Vale wants me to fight my hardest. She wants to have the chance to win with her own strength. I admire that, I do. But if I go back on my deal with the queen… who knows what she'll do. Or worse, if I win…" I hesitate. "I'd become queen."

Though that possibility is what I've feared the most, as I speak the words, my heart leaps in my chest.

If I were queen, what kind of queen would I be?

CHAPTER 58

I agree to Vale's deal the next day, and she trains with me more vigorously than ever. She's not the only one.

Throughout the week, I glimpse the others practicing around the fortress grounds as well. They're all drilling hard. They each have something to fight for.

Still, whether we want to admit it or not, we aren't the cutthroat competitors we started out as. Most of the others still want the crown, but *all* of us can't wait until this madness is over.

Before I know it, it's the last night before the Trial of Strength. I suggest that we sneak out of the fortress to celebrate. And I know just the place.

"*This* is the place you were so excited about?" Hickory takes a long look at Finnegan's Pub as we join Aeron and Alys on the beach outside.

Alys makes a sour face. *It looks…* she starts to sign, then pauses, and finishes with *…nice.*

I laugh. Finnegan's Pub is a complete hole in the wall, I have to admit. The sea salt from the waves have stripped the siding, there's still a hole in the roof from a brawl that happened years ago, and the sign above the door sits just as crooked as it always has. Still, it'll be perfect for tonight.

"Trust me," I say. "Only the lowest dregs of society trek out here at this time of night. It's perfect."

"How can we refuse when you've given us such masterful

disguises?" Aeron's voice drips with sarcasm as he yanks the wool cap I gave him further over his midnight blue hair, though it still peeks out at the brim. "No one will recognize us, for sure."

I roll my eyes with a smirk. "Anyone in the pub will be too drunk to care who we are."

Still, I pull my hood over my head and feel for the daggers under my cloak. If there's any trouble, I'll be ready. "Plus, the pixie ale is the best you'll find in all of Faylan," I add.

"I'll be the judge of that." Aeron rubs his hands together.

We all laugh.

"Where's Vale?" Hickory asks as we approach the doorway of the noisy tavern.

Aeron shrugs. "She said she's busy getting some last-minute training in."

I admire Vale's increased dedication since she decided to compete fairly. I glance back at the city, wondering how she's doing.

Aeron grabs my hand, shooting me a dimpled smile. "She'll catch up with us later. Don't let her delay our fun."

Inside the pub, we're assaulted by boisterous shouts and the strong scent of ale and battered fish. Bodies sweaty from the day's work fill the wooden chairs and bar stools. Many are already in heated arm wrestling matches or too busy throwing knives at a target to notice us.

An angry grunt followed by a chorus of low chuckles sounds as chairs skid back from a nearby table.

"What was going on over here?" Hickory peers at the abandoned cards and empty steins left behind.

"Looks like they were playing a little *Fury's Field*," I say. "And someone lost. Badly."

"A game?" Aeron puts a hand to his chest in feigned shock. "You mean some of you actually indulge in fun here?"

I shoot him a look. "The Gwyllion Guard always said the game's purpose is more to teach battle strategy."

Growing up around the Guard, Gaius and I learned *Fury's Field* young and played it often. I smile fondly at the memory. We'd eventually grown so good at it that the guards refused to play with us anymore.

How does it work? Alys signs as she takes a seat and the rest of us follow.

My hands itch with anticipation as I shuffle the deck and flip over a few cards. "Okay, each player starts with ten cards that either have different-sized platoons, weapons, or armor."

"Interesting..." Hickory picks up one of the cards, critiquing its crude depiction of an axe with his good eye.

"What are these?" Aeron asks, pointing to numbers at the bottom of a shield card.

"Ah, each card has a farthling coin value and an attack or defensive value." I pick up a die and roll it between my hands. "Based on rolls and trades in each round, you build up the strongest army you can and attack opponents until they're slaughtered." I pound the table joyfully. *By Faylan, I've missed this.*

The three of them look at me with concerned stares.

"Er...until they lose all their cards and are knocked out of the game," I hastily amend.

"Hmm. You know what would make this more fun?" Aeron strokes his beardless chin. "Adding cards for incantations or charms."

Yes! Or magical herbs and creatures? Alys signs, leaning in closer.

I throw up my hands. "Look, I didn't make the rules, okay?"

"This *is* a Gwyllion game." Hickory shrugs in agreement. "No magic here."

"Right." I can tell they'll need a bit more convincing. I arch an eyebrow. "I've heard it gets more fun if you have to drink each time you lose a battle."

Aeron slaps the table. "I'm in!"

The four of us drink and laugh well into the night. On our third round, Aeron's the first to get knocked out again after Alys steals his armor and Hickory throws down a weapon that pulverizes his platoons.

"Aha!" Hickory crows smugly. "I honestly thought you'd be better at this."

"Well, I would be if you all weren't ganging up on me," Aeron says, tossing his now-useless weapon cards on the table before draining the last of his ale.

"We thank you for your contribution." I smirk, scooping the cards up and distributing the spoils between the three of us remaining as he stands.

Giving up so soon? Alys signs to him, and I relay the message.

"Can't keep losing properly if I don't have something to drink, now can I?" He tips his empty mug at us before taking off to the bar.

It's possible I've had one too many drinks myself, as I somehow get knocked out of the game next. Aeron still hasn't returned, so I get up to look for him.

My head feels a bit dizzy as I stand, and I grab onto the back of my chair to steady myself, stifling a giggle. I guess I haven't had a real drink in quite a while.

Looking around, I glimpse Aeron's midnight blue hair peeking out from under his wool cap and slowly make my way over, making sure not to bump into anything. Not surprisingly, he's at the bar, hunched over another mug of ale.

"You drink enough for the both of us yet?" I ask.

I expect to face the drink-hardy-Aeron I first met aboard the Kalypso, but as I reach the bar, the stein is still filled to the brim. Now that I think about it, I don't think I've seen him drink at all since we entered the Ethodine.

He sighs, thoughtfully turning the mug in a circle. "I thought I'd need a few more drinks in me to have the courage to say something… something I've been meaning to tell you for a while now. Maybe I don't need it." He nudges the mug away, foaming ale splashing over the side.

"Is that right?" I lean on the bar, snatching the mug and taking a swig myself. Can't let a good drink go to waste. "Lay it on me."

This should be interesting.

His dimple surfaces as he points a finger at me. "See, that's the kind of thing I like about you. You never pull any punches. In fact, that's what I've been wanting to talk to you about." He turns on the stool to face me, his hands on his knees. "I like you, Quinn."

"I've grown fond of you too." I pat his shoulder absently as I lift the mug to my lips again.

"Quinn, I'm being serious," Aeron persists, trying again. "I mean, I really like you. Heck, I might even love you."

I snort, the ale practically spurting out of my nose. I wipe it on my sleeve and struggle not to laugh in his face. "You're obviously more drunk than I thought. Come on, let's get you back to your room before you hurt yourself." I take his hand and pull him off the stool toward the front door.

"No, really," Aeron insists as I drag him through the crowd.

As we reach the outskirts, he tugs me back into his chest until I'm face-to-face with his ocean eyes.

"I haven't had the nerve to tell you before, but—I think I love you. Not because I can't have you or even the alluring way you can resist my persuasive gift. In fact, I love that I *can't* control you. I love your crazy laugh." He tucks a stray curl behind my ear with a gentle chuckle. "I even love the way you bicker with me, the way you challenge me to be a better version of myself."

I blink. He sounds as sober as it gets. When I approached him at the bar, a profession of love was the last thing I expected. Recalling his soft kiss in Vyndoria, I take a step back and command the flush in my cheeks to dissipate.

"Well, I promise you, you're the only puck in Faylan who sees those as desirable traits. And need I remind the Nymph prince that he is already betrothed?"

"I don't care anymore." He shakes his head, still holding my hand gently in his. "I don't love Arista. And we both know any feelings she has for me are fabricated." He leans in close again, and my heartbeat pulses in my throat. "If *you* love me, I'll know it's not because I'm making you do it. Or anyone else. I know it would be real."

He searches my eyes, waiting for me to say something. I can barely breathe.

I let go of his hand and turn away, though my heart thuds with the desire to hear those words again. The three words I've never heard from anyone in my life. Not even my own father. Not even Gaius. Can I really believe them coming from a puck I've only known for a few short weeks? How am I supposed to know if I feel the same, let alone have the courage to say them back?

Panic chokes me, and suddenly the noise of the pub mixing with my woozy thoughts makes the room spin. Someone enters through the pub door, letting in a gust of cool salty air, and I all but dash through it.

As my feet sink into the sand, the chatter of the pub turns to muffles and I breathe in deeply.

Aeron's footsteps follow. "If you don't feel the same, it's okay, really. You don't have to say it back. I just needed to be honest with you. I can't keep playing these games. I needed you to know the truth." He pauses, a heavy silence filling the space between us. "And because I love you, there's one more truth I have to tell you."

More? I don't turn around, pretending to focus on the clouded night sky, searching for the calming anchor of silent stars. *I don't know if I can handle more.*

Aeron lets out a heavy sigh. "If I have the guts to tell you that I love you, I should have the guts to tell you where Gaius is."

I whip around.

Now he's just being cruel. How can he bring up Gaius so casually, especially right now?

"I know where Gaius is, Aeron," I try to say calmly. "He's buried just down the beach. We can go visit him tomorrow if you'd like."

"No..." Aeron steps toward me, gently taking hold of my shoulders. "That's what I'm trying to tell you, Quinn." He looks me straight in the eye. "Gaius isn't in that tomb."

My eyebrows furrow. He might be a little drunk, but he's also dead serious. His words crash over me like a bucket of cold water, sobering me immediately.

"What are you saying?" I'm either about to punch him in the face or have my world flipped upside down.

Aeron hesitates. "Gaius... is alive."

What? An icy chill runs down my spine. *He's alive?* My head spins so fast, I almost don't hear Aeron as he continues.

"I thought he was dead until recently too, though for different reasons than you might think..." He takes off his wool cap and runs a shaky hand through his hair before looking up at me. "I didn't want to tell you until I was sure, but I'm sure, Quinn. Gaius is alive. And you're so much more like him than you know."

I hold my breath as fear and conviction swirl in his eyes.

"It all started when Gaius and the rest of us first arrived in Eldore for the Ethodine's opening ceremonies. During our time there, he'd started researching all he could find about the Mystics and the Numa, just like you have. And once Hickory found out, that loon kept encouraging Gaius with all his insane theories."

Aeron glances back at the pub to make sure no one else is listening, dropping his voice. "Then Gaius went as far as to run away with a Numanic relic. That's when the queen summoned me. She assured me that he wouldn't be in any trouble, that she just needed the item back. So, I told her where I thought he might have gone."

His gaze strays to the sand, kicking at it with his foot.

"When the queen returned with her guard... she said he wouldn't let them take him alive. At the time, I believed her. She said he killed himself, Quinn. That his obsession with the Numa drove him mad. Whatever the case, the queen knew your Father would blame her for Gaius' death, threatening war again, with the rest of the clans sure to follow. She said in order to keep the peace, she needed to cover it up."

Confusion knots my stomach as I search his eyes, trying to weave together Aeron's string of stories into any kind of logic. Schemes, relics, cover-ups? Aeron is sounding less like himself and more like Hickory every minute.

"You're not making any sense." I finally say, shaking my head. "First you say he's alive and now you're saying he killed himself? You're confused. Gaius died of the plague. My father *saw* his body—"

The words die on my lips as Moon Face's confession comes back to me. *Your brother put up a good fight too.*

He never actually said he died.

Aeron lets go of me and leans on the pub wall, turning his face away.

"The queen was concerned your father would want to see Gaius' body before he was buried. I didn't want to do it, Quinn, honest. But somehow, she knew about my silver tongue and my short-term fling with Vale. She said that if I didn't help her, she'd expose my gift and claim that I used it to enchant Vale into falling for me. I told you that if my clan found out about my gift it would destroy their trust in me as their future leader, never mind the fact that I'd started a relationship with the princess of another clan. At the time, it seemed like the end of the world if the truth came out. So, I did what she asked." His eyes turn back to me, pleading, full of remorse. "I'm so sorry, Quinn, I wish I hadn't. You have to believe me."

No. Aeron can't be saying what I think he's saying. I grip his shoulders hard and give them a shake, forcing him to look me in the eye. I need to hear him say it. "Spit it out, Aeron! *What did you do?*"

Pain swims in his eyes. "The queen... she brought a body riddled with the plague back to your father and... she made me *persuade* him that it was Gaius. I'm the one who made him believe that Gaius died of the Knolls."

Dizziness threatens to knock me over again. I picture my father staring down at the plague-riddled body he was forced to believe was his dead son. Is this why Hickory warned me to stay away from Aeron? Did he suspect Aeron had something to do with Gaius' death all this time and not tell me? I turn to face the mountain, unable to look at Aeron any longer. My fists clench as I try to make sense of the revelations shooting through my mind.

"When I did it, I really believed Gaius killed himself. The queen said he was crazy. That it was his own fault," Aeron tries to explain. "I hate myself for it. Lying to your father. Lying to you. But I was trying to protect you. When I first realized you were Gaius' sister, I felt responsible for you. I vowed to myself that I would keep you safe. To make sure you survived when I thought Gaius didn't. To make up for my part in what I believed had happened. I had no idea that I'd fall in love with you. Then Vale found out that he's alive—"

I spin back around. "*Vale* knows too?" I yell, inches away from his face, my pulse pounding in my ears. "Where is he, Aeron? Where's Gaius?"

Aeron stumbles backward. "Vale didn't want to tell you yet, but she's been digging deeper into her mother's affairs while testing your poison. She overheard her talking about Gaius. Vale thinks her mother has had him all this time, maybe in the royal dungeons or something. We don't know why. We didn't want to tell you until we had a plan to get him back. I just couldn't keep lying to you. It's been eating me alive…"

I stare at his sincere face, but all I can see is Whit.

The betrayal, the lies, all of it. Bile rises in my throat.

He reaches for me. I pull away. I can't stay here another second. I'm going to be sick.

"Where are you going?" Aeron stumbles after me as I pound through the sand.

"I can't believe you waited this long to tell me!" I yell.

"Vale only found out that he's alive last week!"

"No, Aeron!" I spin around. "No matter what the truth is now, all this time you knew he didn't die from the plague. You even knew that the queen had something to do with it." I'm shaking, bitter cold rushing through my veins. "I buried my brother. I've been mourning his death. And you just… watched. I opened up to you about my dreams and suspicions, and you let me believe that I'd gone insane!"

Aeron hesitates, which only angers me more.

I storm off.

"Quinn!" Aeron pleads. I pick up my pace. "Would it really have done you any good to know what I thought was true? That Gaius killed himself? The last thing I wanted to do was break your heart all over again. Even though we know he's alive now, who knows if we can even get him back."

"*We?*" I shriek, whipping back to face him, sand kicking into the air. "*We* will not be getting him back. You've been lying to me ever since we met. I haven't kept anything from you since we were in Dryad territory." *At least, not anything this important.* I glare. "There's no *we* anymore."

"Please, Quinn." Aeron staggers closer, but I draw back and lift my chin toward the mountain.

"I need to find her," I say, my heart pounding like a platoon of Gwyllion drums.

"Who?"

"The queen." I clench my fists.

"Quinn, don't." Worry furrows Aeron's brow as he searches my expression. "It's late. She's probably already in her chambers back at the fortress, guarded by her soldiers. You'll only make things worse—"

I don't wait for him to finish. Flying off in a fury, I leave Aeron alone on the beach.

∿

Landing on the queen's balcony, I draw my daggers. My ragged breath forms white puffs in the cool air. I'm so livid, I wouldn't be surprised if it's smoke coming from my flaring nostrils.

All this time, she's had my brother rotting in some dungeon. She pretended to be kind to me, made promises I'm not sure she even intended to keep. None of that matters anymore.

I whip back the balcony curtains and two guards spring into action. Eyeing the gaps in their armor, I charge forward, driving my daggers deep into their flesh.

"Where is she?" I roar as they writhe on the floor. They only moan in response.

Another voice clears her throat.

On the other side of the candlelit room, the queen is dressed in her violet night robe, surrounded by her birds, reading a scroll in a corner chair. Unprotected and unarmed.

Perfect.

She looks up as I approach, but shows no alarm at my unannounced arrival or at the blades in my hands.

"Ah, Quinn, just who I wanted to see."

"The feeling's mutual." I point a dagger at her. "No more games, Your Highness. I know you have my brother, and I demand to have him returned. Now."

I expect her to call for help or at least look shocked. She does neither. "My dear, I have no idea what you're talking about." Standing, she walks to a crystal bottle of red wine sitting on the nearby mantel.

"You can't deny it," I practically spit, following her with my blade. "Aeron told me everything. Vale knows you have him too. Tell me where he is or I'll—"

"Or you'll *what*, exactly?" She casually pours a glass. "If you kill me, I won't be able to tell you where he is."

My stomach drops. For all my anger, the truth didn't truly hit me until she confirmed it.

"So… you do have him." I step closer, my hand shaking.

Gaius is really alive.

"My dear, you should know by now that I don't take kindly to threats or thieves, or those who persistently snoop in my business." She turns, drink in hand. "I've tried to be patient. Given you all the proper warnings. I thought for sure that after miraculously healing from my poison, you'd come to your senses."

There it is. *I was right.* She poisoned me, the witch!

Does Vale know this too? My supposed friends, keeping so many things from me.

The queen takes a sip of wine, eyeing me. "You continue to stick your nose where it doesn't belong, just like your brother. I told you to keep your distance from those who would lead you astray. Aeron. Hickory. You don't listen very well, do you, my dear? You've even corrupted my precious Vale with your ridiculous plan for a fair fight."

I gawk at her. "It wasn't my—how do you even know about that?"

Vale never would've told her, and I haven't told anyone. How does the queen always know so much?

A half-smile creeps up her face. "Oh, I have little spies everywhere."

She lifts her hand and a hawk flies in from the window, landing on the mantel. It stares back at me as the queen pets its feathers, feeding it an odd looking pellet.

The bird swallows and immediately opens its beak. Like a parrot, my voice miraculously comes from its mouth.

"What about your mother? What about her deal?" the bird says in my voice.

"Screw her deal," the creature says next, this time in Vale's timbre.

My stomach plummets. *No.*

The queen shakes her head solemnly. "If that's how you both feel about it, then you've given me no choice."

She snaps her fingers. Four more guards emerge from the shadows, blades drawn as they surround me, along with the original two guards who force themselves to stand.

"I gave you the deal of a lifetime, Quinn, and you spat in my face." Queen Gwendolyn sighs. "You could have walked away tomorrow, a free faerie with a bright future. But I'm canceling our deal, effective immediately."

Her expression turns fierce, eyes flashing. She speaks slowly and clearly so I don't miss a detail. "If you don't make sure Vale wins tomorrow, or if you tell anyone about what you *think* you know, then you'll never see your brother again."

She takes a step toward me as her guards close in.

"And I assure you, this time, he'll really be dead."

CHAPTER 59

I'm lost in a daze as the queen's guards escort me back to my room. My brother's alive. He's been out there all this time. In her clutches. And I don't even know why.

The door locks behind me and I sink to the floor. I'm right back where I started, with nothing to show for it. I risked my life entering a competition to honor a brother who never died, and now I'll lose on purpose for a freedom I can no longer have. The queen tricked me. She lied about everything. So many of them did, including my supposed friends.

One more to add to my list of betrayers.

I claw my way onto the bed, wrapping myself in the sheets, but all I do is toss and turn. I picture Gaius alone in some murky dungeon, possibly being tortured day after day, or worse. When I try to close my eyes, the fear of my nightmares possibly returning snaps me awake.

Though, how could any bad dream be worse than this reality?

Throwing off the sheets, I pace my room, trying to think of something—anything I can do.

If I run away and Vale loses to someone else tomorrow, the queen will kill my brother. If I try to tell anyone, she'll kill him. If I try to win, she'll kill him.

I want to scream. My fingers itch to destroy something before I destroy myself.

Digging my nails into the curtains draped around my bed, I drag them down with a rip. I reach for my daggers, ready to fling them at the mirror above my dresser, but the painting of my mother stares back at me. I halt.

The memory of her choking in the flames—*my* flames—seizes me by the throat. I grip the dagger hilts tighter, my fingers finding the ridged patterns where the Numanic symbol resides. Dropping the blades, they clatter to the ground as I slump to the floor.

Aeron's words from Isinglass come back to me. *"I suppose none of us are really in control of our own fate."*

Maybe he was right. Even if I can't gain my freedom, Gaius stays alive.

Before I know it, a red sun is rising and a dull hangover from the pub settles in. When the servants come for me, I'm a disheveled mess, my eyes ringed with dark circles, my room in tatters.

"By Faylan, we have a lot of work ahead of us," one of them says as the other crosses her arms with a grunt.

It doesn't matter. The queen has won. And I've lost everything.

∾

Underneath the arena, pebbles skid down the walls of my preparation room as the rumble of the crowd radiates through the stone ceiling. It isn't helping my headache, or my nerves.

My attendants can tell I'm tense. One works on my shoulders while the other sharpens my daggers.

Don't bother, I want to say. *I might as well be going out there with my bare hands.*

Before I can do anything rash, my father's voice comes from behind me.

"Quinntessa," he starts. As I stand to meet him, he corrects himself. "Quinn." With a wave of his hand, the attendants scatter, leaving us alone.

"Father." I nod, straightening my back. I'm surprised to see him, never mind to hear him use the nickname that he hates.

He takes a step closer, and I freeze. He awkwardly pats my shoulder, his last touch landing with a squeeze.

I nearly fall back into my chair. Is that the smallest hint of a smile on his face?

He reaches to his side, pulling his own sword from its sheath and holding it out to me. "Do Greymerrow proud, little warrior."

My mouth parts, pressure forming in my eyes. *Little warrior.* The name he'd called me in the memory Alys recovered. I swallow hard.

I grip the leather-bound hilt of his broadsword tentatively, admiring the craftsmanship of the double-edged Gwyllion-steel blade. Dragon icons are carved into each end of the cross guard. I swing it through the air. Perfectly balanced. Light, but deadly.

I look back at my father in awe. He's already walking down the hallway that leads up to the arena. I can't believe it. After all this time, does he really believe in me? Has the past really been forgiven?

Sucking in a breath, I move to follow. My feet are heavy with every step.

My father thinks I'll try to win today.

My stomach drops.

You may not feel the same after I lose...

As I step into the open arena, a blast of wind stings my cheeks. At least my lightweight armor and the dragon-scale garment underneath block some of the cold.

Scanning the space, I recall watching many training sessions and battle simulations that were fought here. Built on top of an extinct volcano, the sealed-up mouth of the crater forms a perfect surface for a battleground littered with pillars and other obstacles.

The elevated stone seating encircling the battlefield is packed with fae from all clans, each relegated to their own section around the stadium. They wave their clan-colored flags and banners, vying to see who will finally become their supreme ruler.

I even spot Leman and his warriors in the Dryad section to my right. He's looking at Alys, who stands below her clan with her preparation team. As she meets his gaze, her face lights up. Though she'll do her best today, I know Leman being there is already a victory for her.

Her gaze pans, landing on me. Her smile falters.

Where did you go last night? She signs the question as discreetly as she can. *Are you okay?*

Alys is the only one I might want to talk to, but now is not the time. There are faeries in the crowd that can translate our signs.

I'm fine, I lie.

Alys frowns, not convinced.

I look away. From the other clan stations around the wide open arena, Hickory's brows raise in question while Aeron's wings tense, as if he might fly over to me at any moment.

Then there's Vale. She's busy inspecting her feathered helmet before practicing the swing of her father's sword.

My fist tightens around my own father's blade. My current predicament isn't exactly her fault. Still, she lied to me too.

"As your current ruler, I welcome you all to the fifth and final trial of the Ethodine," Queen Gwendolyn calls through a horn.

My father stands next to her, both of them on a canopied platform between the Sylph and Gwyllion sections. The stadium quiets, though anticipation thrums through the air like the buzz of locusts.

"By the end of today, we will all know who is the master of the collective Ethea, and the next queen or king of Faylan," she says, and the clans cheer wildly. "Lord Feyden will now explain the rules of the Trial of Strength. May the best faerie win."

The queen offers my father her horn, but he waves it away. "Every leader must exemplify great strength in order to lead well and command respect." His voice booms across the arena, and the crowd grows still.

The five of us exchange glances. The time has come.

"Two at a time, the heirs will battle in a series of elimination rounds, with only their weapon of choice and their raw strength to aid them. No magic. Only two outcomes will end each match." His eyes land on me, and they glint in the sunlight. "Surrender or death."

I nearly drop my blade as gasps ripple through the crowd.

What? He can't be serious. It's one thing to possibly be killed by a creature, a poison, or a trap. To kill each other is—murder.

I look to the other heirs as we share the same confusion and terror. I may be livid at most of them right now, but it's not enough to want to kill them.

The Gwyllions remain stone-faced while the other sections murmur in the stands. For the other clans, I can tell surrender is just as unacceptable. The ultimate sign of weakness. Just what my father intended. To show the rest of the clans how weak they really are without their magic.

And if death is an option, it'll be that much easier for the winning heir to appoint a new figurehead for that clan. One they can more easily control. Just what the queen desires.

My father motions to a series of flags mounted vertically on a tall wooden board. Each one waves a different clan's color next to our collective points thus far.

"The order of who will battle whom will be determined by the current ranking from the previous trials, giving the higher-ranked competitors the advantage."

As the points currently stand, Alys and I are in last place. We'll face off first, our red and green flags at the bottom. The winner will then face Hickory, then Aeron, and then finally Vale, who has the most overall points.

In the previous trials, we gained more points based on how we ranked in performance. In this one, we'll only gain points if we force our opponents to surrender—or leave them lying lifeless on the arena floor.

My gut twists as my father continues.

"If an heir chooses to shame themselves in surrender, then they'll relinquish their weapon and kneel, recognizing the victor as the stronger opponent. In this case, the winner must halt in their attack, allowing the loser to live with their failure. This will continue until we have one supreme winner and ruler of Faylan."

Though my father knew my ranking before finalizing the rules of the trial, he appears thoroughly content with the arrangement. Based on the scoreboard, I'd have to beat every single one of them to get enough points to gain the crown. If he truly wants me to win, then he's not making it easy.

The queen catches my eye. She looks just as pleased, reminding me of what I truly need to do. It's my responsibility to make sure Vale wins. Gaius' life depends on it. Either way, I'll have to battle all of them to get to Vale. By then, I'll be good and tired, possibly pretty banged up, making it easier for her to beat me. But first, I have to get there.

If Vale loses to anyone else, then my brother is dead.

Maybe I should have told my father about Gaius when I had the chance. Maybe he would have believed me. Maybe he could have done something.

Too late.

CHAPTER 60

As the others clear the ring and take their seats, I take a deep breath. Alys and I slowly approach the center of the battlefield.

Alys carries a Dryad spear. The staff is nearly as tall as she is with a jagged blade on one end that's longer than her forearm. Stopping a few feet away, she grips the staff tightly, resting the base on the stone floor. She searches my face as if trying to read me and how hard I intend to fight.

I avoid her gaze, looking to the stands, tensing my muscles. Out of all of them, I want to face Alys the least.

Leman leans forward in the crowd, furrowing his brow as his eyes dart between me and his sister. I'd promised him I'd protect Alys, but I can't show weakness and risk losing Gaius again. My only option is to force her to surrender.

A gong sounds.

Alys and I circle each other.

Don't make me hurt you. I give her a hard stare, wishing she could hear my thoughts.

Instead, Alys firms her features and sprints toward me, raising her spear.

Eyes widening at her aggression, I leap back. I catch my balance on the pillar behind me and swipe at her side.

She blocks with a rapid strike, graceful and practiced, like a fierce dancer.

I knew Alys was skilled, but she's obviously gone through considerable training, perhaps with Leman himself. I'll need to slow her down.

Ducking under another stab, I dive past her, slicing the back of her calf.

The Dryads gasp as Alys lands on her knees. Her face scrunches in pain and determination as she faces me. It makes me regret what I'm about to do. Especially because with the crown, I know she could finally take control of her own life, exposing her healing gift to the world. She could use it to help so many without hope, like her sister had been.

Rising, Alys releases her wings and charges.

I'm slow to deflect the jagged blade, trying not to wound her more than I have to. I flinch as the cold steel slices my arm. The gash stings with fresh blood and cold air.

She has much to gain. I have everything to lose, I remind myself. I picture my brother in my mind, hardening my resolve. *Alys can heal herself with time, but Gaius could die today.*

Rolling my shoulders back, I charge. *Slash. Slash. Slash.* I get in multiple cuts at her arms before she can react. Every cut punches me in the gut.

She doesn't deserve this. If only I can just get her to drop her weapon.

She lifts the spear to block my next attack.

I come down hard on the staff. It slices in two.

Alys falters, but holds firmly to the half with the blade, casting the other to the side.

Blast.

I thrust a kick to her chest.

She goes down hard. I pin her down, a knee on her arm and my blade at her throat.

"This is your last chance. Drop your weapon and surrender," I say loudly so all can hear, especially the queen and my Father. They have to believe I would kill her if I have to.

Alys wriggles under my grip, not ready to give up.

My fingers find where I cut her arm before. She hisses from the touch.

I shoot my thoughts to her as quickly as I can. *I'm sorry, Alys.* I grit my teeth, hoping she can hear me. *I don't want to kill you, but I can't lose this fight. Please understand. I don't have a choice.*

Alys tenses, her deep brown eyes searching mine then softening. Her body relaxes.

Has she seen my memories again? Does she know Gaius is in trouble?

Before I can ask, Alys drops the remnant of her weapon.

"Quinntessa of the Gwyllions is the victor!" my father announces, relishing the victory.

The arena is devoid of applause. Most of the crowd doesn't seem to know how to react to a pirate nearing the crown. Fae of every clan turn to each other in soft whispers. Even my own folk only offer blank stares.

I don't care. I'm one step closer to Vale. To freeing Gaius.

Shifting off Alys, I offer my hand, and she takes it as I pull her up.

Her attendants rush in with wound wrappings. She waves them off. Still focused on me, Alys bows in a sign of respect before taking a knee.

Wiping away the wavy ringlets sticking to my forehead, I give her a small bow in return. "You fought bravely," I say.

I wish I had time to say more, to fully explain.

Alys nods, her only signal that we're okay as my father's voice rings over the stadium.

"Hickory of the Kobolds will now enter."

Of course my father gives me no time to recuperate. Still bleeding from my arm, I take my stance.

Hickory approaches the field cautiously, looking back at Alys' injuries as she passes.

I don't want to have to hurt Hickory any more than Alys. In many ways, he's become like a second brother to me.

One glance at the queen reminds me that my true brother is still in grave danger.

Why didn't Hickory tell me he'd been feeding Gaius the same obsessions that would lead him to—wherever he is? Sure, he tried to warn me about Aeron, but why not tell me of his own involvement? Why let me get wrapped up in all of this, just as Gaius had?

As I raise my sword, the reminders of his betrayal fuel my resolve to show no mercy.

Hickory tentatively grips his battle axe as it glints in the sunlight.

The gong sounds.

I lunge. He meets my blade in the air with a clang, deflecting the strike with the axe blade.

I swing again.

Another block.

Hickory doesn't go on the offensive, though he holds good form as I advance. Even with his blind eye, he counters every one of my strikes. Ready for every swing before I can even make them.

In a moment of distraction, he catches me by surprise and swings low, nicking my leg.

I stagger backward in shock. I know how great his desire is to escape the dark tunnels. Is he willing to kill me for it?

I come at him harder, slicing at every angle. My muscles are burning. I don't get in one hit.

How is he doing this? I need to try something else.

I kick at the dirt and Hickory raises his hands as dust flies into his face.

Boos sound from the Kobold section, but I'm not going in for a cheap shot.

While his eyes are closed, I dart behind a pillar, catching my breath as I observe him.

Then, I notice it. The slight twitching of his ears, listening for the sound of me.

That's it! With every shift of my foot across the ground, his sensitive hearing keeps him aware of my movements, making up for his blind spot. *Almost.*

Seeing a cluster of pebbles at my feet, I kick hard again. They scatter, sending a ripple of clattering sounds in all directions.

Hickory startles, frantically following the sounds, searching for the one that ties back to me.

I release my wings and silently leap into the air, diving to his blind side. Using the blunt end of my hilt, I strike forcefully on the back of his weapon hand.

Hickory cries out as his axe clatters to the ground, leaving him defenseless.

Kobolds stand to their feet with shouts as I grab Hickory by the scruff of the neck, the point of my sword pushing threateningly into his side.

Hickory seems more concerned with the hand that he's cradling to his chest. His fingers are swelling, one of them bent at an odd angle, and I realize—I've injured his sketching hand, which to him is probably ten times worse than what I'm about to say.

"Do you surrender?" I ask, breathing hard.

"Yes," Hickory chokes out. "I surrender." I release him and he falls to his knees, gasping.

"The Gwyllions advance again!" my father announces.

Murmurs in the stands increase. Some of my folk lean forward, watching as the gold Kobold flag is taken off the scoreboard and our red flag is raised to a higher notch.

Hickory walks off to attend to his hand, but glances back for a moment.

I look away, pressing down the guilt rushing to the surface. If needed, Alys can heal his hand as good as new—though I'm not sure any amount of her power will be able to heal our friendship.

My chest heaves, fatigue setting in as Aeron takes Hickory's place.

Two down, two to go.

As I approach him, pain and anger rises with every step. I channel it into what I have to do next. Aeron is my last obstacle before Vale. Then I can finally lose. Gaius will be safe, and this will all be over.

"I'm glad to see you're okay," Aeron whispers. His hand is on the sword sheathed at his side, but his eyes tell me he doesn't want to fight. Not like this. "When you ran off last night, I was worried you'd—"

"Save it." I take my stance. "I've heard *enough* from you."

"Competitors ready?" my father calls, giving Aeron one last chance to prepare his weapon.

Aeron hesitates, looking back at his own father.

Lord Kaito gives him a stern nod.

Aeron's sword scrapes against its sheath as he slowly unveils a sea-glass-crafted blade.

The Nymph Lord beams. His smile is fleeting, however, as Aeron lets the blade slip from his fingers, and it clatters to the stone.

"Aeron!" Kaito growls as the Nymphs explode into a chattering frenzy. His son is already lowering to the ground.

No. I whip out my blade and catch the point right below his chin.

He lifts his hands, mid-kneel.

"What are you doing?" I demand.

"I won't fight you, Quinn," he whispers.

I grit my teeth. "Yes. You will."

I catch the curious eyes of the queen and my father. It would be so much easier to let him do this. To accept his gesture and move on. But whatever he thinks he's doing won't erase what he's done. Whether he feels sorry or not, I won't let him just give me the win. He doesn't get off that easy.

Stepping back, I nod to his weapon.

He reaches for it slowly, watching me all the while.

"If what you claimed last night is true, then you *will* do this," I say, challenging the feelings he declared. If he knows me at all, then he knows that I'll never accept a pity win. "No holding back."

Without any more hesitation, I launch myself high into the air and hurtle downward with a warrior's cry.

Grasping his sword, Aeron parries and sidesteps with ease, his movements as smooth and fluid as water.

I strike again. He pushes against my blade, sending me flapping back.

Releasing his own fin-like wings, he meets me in the air, swinging again and again, though not as hard as I know he can. He doesn't want to hurt me any more than he already has.

This only makes me angrier. He still thinks I'm some helpless pixie who needs his aid. I'll show him.

I advance, pressing Aeron higher into the air. I attack with more fervor, telling myself every blow is retaliation for Gaius. For taking part in staging his death. For every time in the last five weeks that Aeron could've told me the truth, but didn't.

He takes the brunt of every hit, groaning with the effort. The air is thinner up here among the clouds, and I can hear the struggle in his breaths. But he's not giving up, and I don't have much energy left.

Changing tactics, I swing outward against Aeron's blade.

His arm flails, and I only have a second to seize the opening I've created.

Tightening both hands on my sword, I bring the hilt down on Aeron's shoulder as hard as I can. *Thud.*

My strike sends him straight to the ground, colliding with a boulder.

With the wind knocked out of him, Aeron lets go of his weapon, gasping. His team releases their wings, ready to charge the field and help him once this is over. Aeron holds up a hand to them. Slowly, he rolls onto his chest and kneels before me.

"Can I surrender now?" he manages, coughing up blood.

As he looks up at me, I steel myself for his expression. I expect to see betrayal raging in his ocean eyes like a storm, hate for me surely swirling inside.

Instead, they're soft with remorse, as if I've given him a punishment he justly deserved, and he received it gladly.

My stomach twists with the temptation to drop to my knees and forgive him right there. To ask him for forgiveness myself. But the image of Gaius half-dead in some cellar steals it away.

Forgiveness is just another sign of weakness.

I turn to my father so I can't stare into Aeron's ocean eyes anymore. I lift my sword in victory—though I feel anything but victorious.

"Lady Quinntessa advances to the final round!" my father's voice thunders.

This time, I think I hear bits of scattered applause.

Most of my folk are still silent, but many of them are standing, looking from me to the scoreboard.

A Sylph noble nervously rubs his hands together as he and his clan watch the Gwyllion flag rise to meet their purple one at the top, while the blue Nymph flag is cast to the side. Many Nymphs shake their heads, and I catch one fainting from the shock.

Even with my Gwyllion background and reputation as Captain Shade, it seems few want to believe I could actually become their queen.

"Since this is the final battle—" my father continues "—she'll be allowed five minutes to ready herself before facing Princess Vale."

I let my muscles relax, resisting the temptation to collapse. Sheathing my sword to avoid dragging it along the ground, I stagger to my attendants.

My father flies toward us.

I narrow my eyes at him as an attendant brings a chalice of water to my lips. "Why have you done this?" I gasp. "You had complete control over how the trial would run. You could have given me more of an advantage. I thought you wanted me to win."

"I'm still confident you will," he says, then leans closer. "If you are to win, our clan needs to see your skill, your dedication, and your strength." He looks up to the stands, satisfaction on his face. "And now they see it."

A soft rumble comes from the stands where my clan resides. Gwyllions are not the cheering kind, but they are warriors. They pound their feet on the stone steps, just as they did for Gaius all those years ago during the Gwyllion Guard tryouts. It starts out slow and quiet, then grows into a thundering roar as they chant.

"Quinn… Quinn… Quinn... Quinn…" My clansfolk are chanting my name. The ultimate sign that I'm not only accepted back into the clan. They truly want me to win. To rule.

A surge of emotion hits me like a crashing wave at sea. All this time, I didn't think I wanted their approval or their acceptance. Now that I have it, the pain of knowing that I'll soon lose it forever feels like it's crushing me under its powerful current.

If only they knew what was on the line.

"Father, I must tell you something." I grab at his robe.

Even if he thinks I'm crazy, this is my last chance to tell him the truth. To warn him.

He gives my hand a squeeze. "We'll have time to talk when you win."

"But—"

"Lord Feyden, I think you've given your daughter quite enough of a reprieve."

The queen is at our side, towering over us. Her eyes bore into me, daring me to reveal her. Daring me with my brother's life.

"We wouldn't want all of Faylan to think you're giving Quinn an unfair advantage, now, would we?"

My father hesitates. He searches my face for what I was about to tell him.

No. I can't risk it. For all I know, it would take a snap of the queen's fingers for one of her lackeys to snap Gaius' neck.

I pull myself together and give my father a firm nod before I brush past him to meet Vale on the field.

She has the nerve to smile. "Funny seeing you here," she says lightheartedly. To her, everything seems to be going according to plan. She still thinks we've agreed to fight fair. Maybe the fact that no one has died yet has kept her at ease.

Catching my scowl, she stops. "You all right?"

I grunt in response as I unsheathe my sword, though I might as well just throw it down right now.

"Okay…" Vale says slowly. "Do your worst. I'm ready."

I nod, and Feyden quiets the crowd. "This final duel will decide the next *queen* of Faylan. Will it be Vale of the Sylphs?"

The Sylphs cheer.

"Or Quinntessa of the Gwyllions?"

The Gwyllions stomp their feet again.

"The same rules apply," he reminds us. "The first to surrender or die loses." His gaze lingers on me meaningfully, and I force my features not to falter.

All I have to do is put on a good show, let Vale beat me up a bit, and surrender. As exhausted as I am, it shouldn't be too hard.

The gong sounds, and I remind myself that Gaius' life will be worth the humiliation.

Vale advances with forceful strikes and skilled footwork. She's truly a warrior now.

Still, I know her favored moves by heart.

I block her first few strikes, then let her get in a few slashes on my arm and side.

I hiss through the sting. Though my supposed mishaps might be faked, the pain is real. I hope that's enough for the crowd.

The murmurs begin. My father isn't falling for my act, his brows knit together as he furiously twists one of the rings around his finger.

Vale isn't falling for it either.

"What's wrong with you?" she whispers sharply as our swords collide. "You're not even trying."

"The student has surpassed the master," I snarl back. "You should be happy."

"No." Her tone is vicious. "You know the win means nothing to me unless I win it fairly. You promised."

"You keep forgetting, Vale," I spit, pushing her hard so she falters back. "I'm a pirate."

"No," she sneers venomously. "You're a coward."

My whole body shakes. It feels as if the ground beneath me is trembling too.

I rush at her.

"There's the warrior I know." She narrows her eyes, bracing herself. Her smile fades as I leap into the air and come down on her blade with all my strength.

Sparks fly.

"Careful!"

"I've had enough!" I yell and swing at her again. "Enough of this competition." Another swing. "Enough of your lying mother." Metal clashes. "And enough of you!"

Another blow knocks her to the ground.

Her sword escapes her grip, skidding away on the stone floor.

I'm too angry to stop now. I'm no longer in control.

Rage is.

I raise my sword high above her, ready to strike a final blow.

"Quinn, wait!" Aeron, Alys and Hickory are rushing the field. What are they doing?

I look down at Vale's frightened form. It isn't just my body that's trembling. Pebbles dance on the arena floor around her.

They aren't coming to stop me. They're trying to warn me.

Screams ring out at the violent tremors as cracks form beneath my feet.

A tremble in the land will quake.

I look at Aeron. Our eyes lock just before the ground gives way and I disappear under its surface.

CHAPTER 61

"Will she be all right?" I hear a deep, raspy voice ask.

"Her wing is pretty damaged," comes a much lighter tone. "She'll need to rest."

"Rest? For how long? We don't have time for this."

"Give her some time, Pylo."

My head throbs as I try to place the voices hovering around me. Dampness coats my back. *Where am I?* My eyes blink open.

At first I think I'm looking at a darkened sky, devoid of moons and stars. As my vision sharpens, I realize that I'm staring up at the towering stone ceiling of a cave. The last thing I remember is falling through the arena floor. I must be underground, deep in the mouth of the extinct volcano. But there aren't any cracks in the ceiling that I can see.

I shift to get a better look, then cry out as a sharp pain radiates through my right shoulder blade.

"I told you this was a mistake," the deep voice says from somewhere in the room.

The kind face of an elderly pixie appears above me, her dragon-like wings draped down her back. My first thought is that my clan must've found me, but this faerie is smiling from ear to ear.

Strange. Gwyllions barely ever smile.

"Oh, hush, Pylo," she scolds the other voice before turning back to me. Her gentle eyes wrinkle at the corners as she brings a cool cloth to my forehead. "Just hold still, dear. You've injured one of your wings. I'm setting it for you. Shouldn't be long." She shifts to tend to my mangled wing spread out on the ground.

I grimace, focusing on her face so I don't have to watch. "What happened? Who are you?"

Her wrinkles crease further with a chuckle. "Oh, you must excuse my manners. It's been a long time since we've had guests. My name is Leera. And my very impatient husband over there is Pylo."

Another elderly Gwyllion with a fur cloak and long white beard leans on a twisted staff close by. He nods to me, warily taking in my presence.

"You fell a long way down after the, um... earthquake," Leera says, glancing again at Pylo. "Some debris hit your wing pretty hard, I reckon. We were able to slow your fall, minimizing any further damage."

Slow my fall? "I don't understand."

"Why don't you come join your friends and we'll explain everything."

"My friends?" I ask as Leera helps me to my feet.

A small fire flickers at the other end of the large cavern. She gently guides me by the hand, but I halt when we're a few feet away.

I'm not the only one who fell from above. Vale, Aeron, Hickory, and Alys huddle around the fire with fur blankets, silently staring into the flames.

"They're not my friends," I say quietly. Though I'm relieved they're all right, I'm in no hurry to face them.

Vale catches sight of me and stands.

Too late.

"What was your problem up there?" she lashes out as I approach. "First, you don't even try, and then you come after me like you're the one who has the right to be angry. I thought..." She stops, whispering sharply, "I thought we had a deal."

"What deal?" Hickory's blanket falls to the floor as he stands. "Is that why you were so intense during the trial?" He folds his arms, and I notice the bandage wrapped around his injured hand.

Pushing down the guilt rushing up again, I thrust a finger at him. "*You* don't get to talk to me." I whip to Vale. "And neither do *you*."

They both draw back.

Hickory's eyebrows furrow. "What's wrong with you? You seemed fine last night at the pub. Where did you disappear to after—?"

"She was with me." Behind them, Aeron remains seated at the fire. His worried gaze is trained on my injured wing, his ocean eyes heavy with remorse.

"*You*." Hickory takes a threatening step toward him. "I swear, if you've been using that silver tongue of yours to mess with her head like you did with Vale—"

"Hickory!" Vale scolds.

Aeron's muscles tighten as he stands, fists clenched like he might punch him. "How dare you—I would never! How do you even know about my—"

"At least he told me the truth, Hickory," I cut in. "Something *you* should've told me a long time ago. Both of you," I add to Vale.

Hickory and Vale grow quiet, studying me as if trying to guess exactly what I know.

In the silence, Alys draws closer, inspecting my wing. I see the cuts in her clothes and the dried blood from our fight. Out of all of them, Alys deserved what I did to her the least.

I'm about to apologize when she touches my arm, her healing energy surging through me. One of the bones in my wing painfully snaps back into place.

"Alys, stop," I yelp, pulling away. I don't deserve her kindness.

"Wait. Did Alys just…?" Vale inspects the healed bone in awe.

I sigh. Though we've all been working together for a common cause, we've also been keeping so many secrets. None of us have trusted one another as much as we thought.

"She's not the only one with a gift." The elderly puck called Pylo hobbles to the fire. "If you're quite finished with your petty arguments, we must tell you why we brought you here."

"*You* brought us here?" Aeron lifts a brow, looking up and down the faerie's aged form.

Hickory's eyes widen with astonishment. "Did *you* cause the earthquake?"

Leaning on his walking stick, Pylo nods solemnly.

Hickory stares at the staff. There, engraved near the top, is the Numanic symbol. Hickory looks at me, then at Pylo. "Then you must be… forgive me, sir… but are you a Mystic?"

Pylo nods again.

Hickory looks like he's about to jump out of his skin, a million questions itching at his bobbing throat.

I'm not convinced yet. "Prove it."

Without breaking my gaze, Pylo snaps his fingers and the fire goes out.

Darkness swallows us.

Then a roaring ball of flame appears, hovering over his hand.

I gape. The Mystics are supposed to be extinct, yet here's one standing right in front of me.

"All right, enough showing off," Leera scolds. She snatches the fireball from him and throws it back to the wood pile, igniting the logs again.

Okay, make that *two* Mystics.

I gawk. I can't believe this. All this time, I haven't been alone.

Leera helps Pylo sit on one of the rocks around the fire as the flames flicker red and orange, lighting up the high walls.

"We're sorry for the way we had to get you down here," she says. "We've had no other opportunity to get all of you alone."

"Even now, we don't have much time," Pylo adds. "There's much to tell you before the clans tunnel their way down here to find you." He motions for us to sit.

Hickory obeys expectantly as Alys and Vale more tentatively take spots around the fire.

As I move to follow, Aeron gently wraps his fingers around my arm. "Are you sure we can trust them?" he whispers near my ear.

"I don't know who to trust anymore," I say, giving him a heavy stare.

His eyes drop as he lets go.

Reluctantly, my voice softens. "Right now we have no idea where we are or how to get back to the surface. We can at least hear them out."

"I promise, we're not the ones you should fear," Pylo says, as if he knows what we're saying.

I take a seat.

Aeron stays standing, slowly pacing behind us.

"There are a few left of our kind. We've been keeping a close eye on all of you throughout the Ethodine. Helping you along the way when we could."

"Helping us?" Hickory tilts his head as I recall the torches igniting on their own during the Trial of Life.

"The hooded figure in the Mystic Temple?" I ask.

"You mean the one that trapped us in that awful room?" Vale balks.

Leera bites her lip. "Technically, he led you to the plant you needed."

My eyes dart to Pylo. He's staring back at me intently.

Wait. Could he also be the hooded figure that Aeron and I encountered in Shree? I try to remember the voice that spoke into my mind about the prophecy. His touch was the first time I saw the flashes that would become my nightmares. And he knew about my brother.

If you want to learn what really happened to him, you will follow me, he'd said.

He wasn't trying to attack us that day. He was trying to *help*. If only I hadn't nearly choked him to death before he disappeared, maybe I would have learned of my brother's fate before it was too late.

"The puzzle in the temple was meant to see if you could be brought together for a single purpose," Leera continues. "While the Ethodine was designed to keep you on opposing sides, we sought to show how you could help one another."

We all exchange glances. At the time, it had done that much.

Why bring us together? Alys signs to me with curious eyes, and I relay her question. It's the same one I have myself.

Pylo stares into the flames. "As you may have guessed already, the competition is not what it seems. And neither is the queen. In fact, much of what Faylanians believe about their history has been twisted, especially about the Numa."

Vale perks up at the mention of our history as Hickory claps his hands on his thighs. "So, they *are* real...I knew it."

"Oh, the Numa are real, all right. But they're not evil as you've been led to believe. At least, not inherently." Pylo reaches out to the fire again, and with the flick of his wrist, the flames form into shapes and figures.

I lean in, mesmerized by his effortless control over the unruly element. The masterful way he uses it to create, rather than destroy.

Even Aeron draws closer as the fire shifts, depicting what Pylo describes.

"Like fae—" he begins "—the Numa have a propensity for good and evil. And though they are wingless with dully-shaped ears, they look much like us. In a way, they're our ancestors, our creators, though their true name was lost to most, long ago."

Our ancestors? Our creators? Looking at the less-ferocious images of the Numa in the flames, I have so many questions. "What's their true name?"

Pylo's eyes flick to mine. "Human," he says.

"Hu-man?" I try out the word on my tongue.

"Long before Faylan existed, the humans dreamed." The flames bend to his will again, causing the faces of the fiery figures to glow brighter. "They had visions while sleeping and awake, always filled with hope, wonder, and possibility. These dreams were powerful. So powerful, they collided in the finite space between sleep and awake—a realm we have since called *The Chasm.*"

Leera reaches out to the pit next, moving her hands in a circular rhythm. "Over time, the collision of dreams formed a kind of seed."

Sparks fly and then settle, leaving a single sphere of rolling flames hovering over simmering coals.

"A seed…" Hickory's whisper turns into an elated shout. "Are you saying that the seed that birthed our world came from Numanic dreams?"

"Hickory, hush," Vale says sharply. "Of course that's not what she's saying." She turns to Leera. "Is it?"

Leera smiles as the flaming ball opens into a developing scene of Faylan's terrain, answering Vale's question. "Dream power fell like rain from our moons, watering the seed. Eventually, that seed birthed the Sacred Vine and all that we see around us. What's been stripped from history, however, is the true reason why the rain stopped."

"Stripped from history?" Vale folds her arms, obviously not a fan of someone suggesting there's something her folk don't know.

Leera nods. "Faylan was not always a land of deficiency and conflict. It was once a place of peace and harmony. The moonrain sustained a flourishing world filled with more magic than we know today."

Out of the flaming land before us, winged fae flit about, casting sparks of magic. My fingers twitch as if wanting to join in on the display, curious to see if the fire would bend to my desires too. I sit on my hands. Even if I wanted to, the ever-sustaining chill still coursing through my body reminds me that it's no longer possible.

"At the time, every clan displayed mystical gifts that were powered by the moonstones," Leera continues. "They eventually inspired each Etho. The fae used these gifts to serve our world. Even during the first drought, the clans worked together to find the cause."

Fae of all kinds shoot out of the pit and dart toward us. A dragon-winged pixie flies around my head, frantic in her search. I put out a finger to her. She shoots her fire at it threateningly, but the flames sizzle out against my cold skin. I sigh.

Aeron is too busy swatting them away to notice, while Alys holds out her palm to one who curiously hovers over it.

"Well, obviously they were unsuccessful," Vale says shortly, examining the cluster of pixies clouded around Hickory's awe-filled face.

"Not exactly." Pylo closes his hand. The faeries look up sharply and return to the flames at once. "This was when we found the *Bridge* to the human world."

Both Leera and Pylo lift their hands, and two large spheres take form which are connected by a spiraling thread of fire.

"Yes, the Bridge! It's like a portal, right?" Hickory's good eye lights with excitement as I recall the drawings on his wall. The space between the two worlds.

Leera nods. "At the time, representatives from each clan crossed the Bridge, entering the unknown world to study the humans—keeping our wings hidden, of course."

She pulls her weathered dragon wings into the bones in her back. With her disarming smile and pointed ears hidden under her curly gray hair, I can only imagine the unaware humans welcoming her into their world with open arms.

"Soon, we learned that we could sense their dreams." Pylo's voice sinks low with warning. "Dreams that had grown dark and cold in their ever-corrupting world."

"That's when we discovered that our magic helped them," Leera adds, her face brightening. "From fueling and impassioning their dreams..." She looks at Aeron. Then to Alys. "...to even bringing dead ambitions back to life."

Aeron's eyebrows lift, his lips parting. Is Leera saying Aeron's silver tongue could be a good thing?

Something touches my arm and I turn to Alys, her bare hand on my skin. Her eyes search mine. *Remember when I used my gift to enter your memories? Do you think that—*

It could be similar to how the faeries affected the dreams of the humans? I finish her thought. *Maybe...*

Leera continues, "It was after we began helping the humans that the moonrain returned to Faylan. Quite by accident, we'd discovered our true purpose: to be the guardians of human dreams. Especially the most innocent and powerful ones, belonging to the youngest of their offspring."

The youthful, wingless figures in the fire dance around as fae bestow their gifts upon them.

I sit back. There's so much to take in. *Could all of this be true?*

"The clan lords then commissioned us to do three things." Pylo snaps his fingers as a circle of tall, winged fae form in the fiery scene. "The first, to control access to the Bridge. Thus, we forged the *Key*: a magical item that could open and close the Bridge at will."

Pylo lifts one finger, and a long item with a pointed end rises out of the flames.

If it's meant to be the Key, it's the strangest-shaped key I've ever seen. It looks more like a staff.

"The second was to chronicle our experiences in the human world, which we called the Neverworld, and the magical ways of our gifts." He lifts a second finger, and a rectangular shape appears next to the first. "So, we recorded all of our secrets in the ancient book you found in Eldore."

We turn to Hickory at once. *How are we going to tell the Mystics we lost their book?*

Pylo reaches into his fur cloak. "Thank you for this, by the way." He pulls out the very text we'd lost.

My jaw drops as Vale's mouth closes tightly, eyes wide. She nervously clasps her hands together, her gaze going from the book to Pylo's face.

"You really have been following us all this time," she says in a breathy tone.

Hickory eyes her, vindicated. "I told you I didn't lose it."

A hint of a smile plays along Leera's face. "We wrote the book in a language we created so the information couldn't easily fall into the wrong hands. Although, it seems that *someone* was smart enough to learn it." She gives Vale an impressed smile.

Despite her skepticism, Vale lowers her face, hiding a soft blush.

Pylo clears his throat, grabbing our attention again, and holds up a third finger. "Our third task was to raise a group of guardians we called the *Travelers*."

A force of flamed faeries rise in formation, standing at attention before Pylo, who sits a little taller under their gaze.

"Only the Travelers could enter the *Neverworld*. And the clan representatives who first traveled to the Neverworld were assigned to be their teachers: the Mystics."

"Wait. You mean Mystics weren't just Gwyllions?" Hickory says hurriedly, hope brimming in his eyes.

"There were originally Mystics from every clan." Pylo scans each of our faces. "But we weren't the only fae gifted with abilities like healing, persuasion, knowledge, visions... and fire." Pylo's gaze stops on me.

My stomach drops. He knows what I am. Although, is he saying that I'm not the only one?

"We were simply the ones who trained the Travelers in how to minister to the humans. Every year, the Mystics chose a new group of younglings to join their ranks."

"So... what happened to them?" Aeron still keeps his distance, though his unblinking eyes tell me he's intrigued.

Pylo closes his eyes, bracing himself for the next part. "While our gifts are ultimately meant for good, they also have a darker side."

Pylo stares deeply into the flames, and the fire dims to almost nothing.

Aeron looks around at the enclosing darkness as a chill falls over the cavern. Vale tugs one of the blankets tighter around her shoulders. Alys shivers, drawing closer to the embers in the sea of darkness.

"The Mystics did everything they could to keep the Travelers from discovering this. But one Traveler stumbled upon the truth and violently turned against our cause." A shadow casts over Pylo's face. "He only saw the flaws of the humans. Claimed that we'd become slaves to them. He wanted to use the dark parts of our abilities to turn the tide and make them slaves to us instead."

Without warning, crackling flames shoot into the air, taking the form of a gruesome, laughing face. It reaches out to us with wild flickering fingers. I inch away from their reach and from the sudden heat against my skin.

Pylo stirs the fire with a wave of his hand, and the flames settle. "We banished him and stripped him of his Traveler status, cutting him off from the Neverworld. But he wouldn't be easily stopped. Gathering a flock of followers, he used dark magic to strengthen them and incite contention between the clans. The unity of the clans weakened. They began to question us, pushing for war. We called all Travelers back from the Neverworld to help keep the peace, but…" His voice breaks at the end.

Leera places a hand on his shoulder and sighs. "When the Travelers returned, they were attacked by the Dark Traveler's army," she says softly, her cheerful demeanor fading for the first time. "With the clans distracted by their own feuds, the Travelers and most of our Mystic brethren were… killed."

We all go still.

Pylo's eyes are vacant and far-off. The fist around his staff tightens as tears glisten in his eyes, reflecting off the flickering flames.

A knot forms in my chest, imagining what it must have been like to see all their friends slaughtered before them. "But…" I lean in tentatively, knowing there must be more to the story. "…Some of you survived."

Hurried steps enter the cavern from the shadows, and we turn to find another cloaked figure. She lifts her hood to reveal a pixie not much younger than Pylo or Leera, a flame flickering in her palm. Just how many of them are left?

"Sorry to interrupt," says the pixie sternly. "A Tunneler has been detected not far from here. We think the clan lords have sent a search party for the heirs." She eyes us warily.

"Thank you, Kenna." Leera stands, and the fire quenches to smoldering coals at the wave of her hand.

"We'll have to continue this on the way." Pylo motions for us to follow with his staff. "We'll guide you to the surface. There's more you should know about the dangers that await you above."

CHAPTER 62

"This way. Keep up," Kenna says gruffly.

As we follow her down dark passages that appear to be ancient lava tubes, the three Mystics lead the way with their flaming hands. The tunnel is narrow, so we walk pressed together. Our soft footsteps and unseen scuttling creatures are the only sounds in the dark. Aeron keeps in step with me as Vale, Hickory, and Alys walk ahead.

"What do you think Pylo meant by *dangers above*?" Hickory whispers to us.

"I don't know. It seems dangerous enough already down here." Aeron warily peers up at sharply pointed stalactites hanging from the ceiling. They tremble slightly as the sound of a Tunneler boring through rock rumbles somewhere in the distance.

"Why aren't they just bringing us to the Tunneler?" Vale asks softly. "That would get us back to the surface a lot faster than this."

"They can't be seen by the clans, especially the Gwyllions," I say, not wanting to imagine what my folk would do if they knew that there were Mystics still around, never mind traveling through tunnels right under their city. "They said that they're bringing us to the surface, so don't worry."

"I'm still surprised that you're trusting them so easily," Aeron raises a brow at me. "I mean, even *I'm* starting to believe their story, but it just doesn't seem like you would."

432

I hesitate. I'm not exactly ready to tell him that it's because I have the same ability as the Mystics to call fire from my hands.

Had the same ability. My shoulders slump.

Thankfully, Hickory answers him before I have the chance. "What reason do they have to lie?" he says, still looking admiringly after them. "Hey, do you think our parents have any idea about all this?"

"No one else knows. The Dark Traveler made sure of that." Leera speaks up from the front.

Obviously, we haven't been as quiet as we thought.

"You see, when he attacked, the Gwyllion Mystics were the strongest warriors and fought the hardest. Even we were nearly defeated."

My brows raise. The Dark Traveler must have had a powerful advantage to stand against the likes of my folk. "But you *weren't* defeated," I press again, eager to hear of some last-minute victory.

"Of course we weren't." Kenna's scoff echoes through the cavern. She sounds the most like the Gwyllions who I'm used to out of the three of them.

Leera turns around sharply, and our party halts.

"We survived, yes… to our shame." She eyes Kenna, who lowers her head. "Instead of fighting until the end, we fled here to our mountains." The ache of her admission is evident in every crease of her face. Though she might be a Mystic, the Gwyllion hate of weakness still runs deep.

It's then that I realize we've stopped at what appears to be a dead end.

Vale crosses her arms. "This looks promising."

Kenna huffs, muttering something under her breath. She steps up to the wall and places her hand firmly on the limestone. The spaces between her splayed fingers glow red with heat. The wall rumbles and shifts open.

She turns back to Vale and smirks. "You were saying?"

My eyes grow wide. The opening reveals yet another dark tunnel, only this one slopes upward. I look at Aeron. "I told you."

Digging his staff into craggy divots in the ground, Pylo hobbles forward as we tentatively follow. "Though we'd failed, our hope was to preserve the Mystic way and someday rise again. When we returned to our mountains, however, we found that our chronicle of the Numa and their world had been stolen." He pulls the ancient tome he's been carrying under his arm tighter to his side.

"Our Key to the Neverworld was gone too," Leera adds.

"I bet it was the Dark Traveler." Hickory bumps Alys' arm, and she nods in agreement.

"Yes." Pylo's voice grumbles low at the mention of the name. "We knew that he had everything needed to cast the curse that he always threatened to enact."

"A curse?" Vale looks up from examining a stalagmite rising up from the floor. "What kind of curse?"

"One that could skew fae history to favor his purposes," Pylo says, huffing with the upward effort. "The humans would be remembered as vicious giants of pure evil. The Clan War would become The War against the Numa. And the Dark Traveler would be remembered as our miraculous savior. As the undisputed king, he would use his power to control the clans and enslave the humans."

Pylo picks up his pace, and Vale scurries after him.

"But it was the Sylph King who saved us from the Numa," she insists as I picture the triumphant ruler depicted in Eldore's murals.

"Ha!" Kenna laughs bitterly. "You younglings really don't know anything, do you? The only way that blithering idiot of a Sylph became king was because Pylo was smart enough to cast a counter-curse."

"Kenna, please." Pylo halts to silence her. Still, his chest seems to inflate at the compliment before quickly deflating. "Though it wasn't enough to cancel the curse entirely, it was the best I could come up with without the help of our missing tome."

Leera puts a comforting hand on her husband's shoulder. "We had hoped changing Faylan's *savior* would buy us some time to fully reverse the curse."

Pylo shakes his head. "Without the Travelers and our ability to reenter the Neverworld, we've had no way to minister to the humans. They seem to have lost their way again, their dreams corrupted."

"*That's* why the moonrain droughts have returned." Hickory nods in understanding.

"Not only that, it's the reason for our dwindling resources, and even the plague, too," Kenna adds.

"If not remedied, things will only grow worse." Pylo's lips purse.

"Thus far, it seems that the Sacred Vine that ties our world together has been fighting to stay alive." Leera stares deeply into our faces. "In fact, we believe that it has connected you five in some way. Perhaps drawing your gifts to the surface, bringing you together for this very moment." She places a hand on the vine-like tattoos on Alys' arm and looks at the spot where the Numanic tattoo resides.

I think I see a spark of hope in Pylo's eyes, but it dims as quickly as a doused flame. "If nothing is done—" he says gravely "—the Vine will fall, and Faylan will crumble."

"Just like Lord Torlon said," Aeron says.

And like you've seen in your nightmares, Alys signs to me.

"Right," I say to her. "And Hickory's painting."

He nods gravely.

"Wait, if all of Faylan's memories were changed, how come *you* remember?" Vale accuses. Not only has Pylo threatened her impeccable knowledge, but also her clan's right to the throne.

"Part of the counter-curse included a protection spell that I was able to use over the remaining Mystics," Pylo explains, leaning heavily on his staff. "Not that it did much good. After the curse was cast, we awoke to a world that we no longer recognized and that no longer recognized us."

Leera sighs. "When we tried to tell them the truth, we were rejected as worshipers of the Numa, superstitious fanatics. Our own Gwyllion brethren cast us out, banishing us into the mountain peaks."

I shake my head and look at Vale. Her eyebrows are knit together with concern and confusion.

If this is true, then our world has been so wrong about them. They rejected the one group who could save us all.

If only my folk had listened.

"What happened to this Dark Traveler figure?" Aeron asks.

"Yes." Hickory nods emphatically. "Where is he now?"

"Curses always come with a price. He didn't realize that this curse would cost him his life and he was never seen again. His minions disbanded, but in recent years some seem to have taken up his mantle and mission. Through a series of spies, we discovered that the queen herself found our text and was in search of the original Key. With both, she planned to enslave the humans and bring the rest of Faylan to their knees. For good."

"And I was helping her," Vale whispers, her face paling as she puts the pieces together. "I thought it was odd how desperate she was for me to translate the tome. I wondered what she was up to. I never imagined this…"

Alys places a gloved hand on Vale's arm as she starts to tremble.

Leera takes off her cloak and wraps it around Vale's shoulders. "We tried to find out more through a series of spies. Only one was successful. At least, in part. He found the original Key and was able to steal it before the queen could use it for herself. When he was unable to get it back to us, he passed through the Bridge, taking the Key with him so no one could follow into the Neverworld, not even us."

"That's the real reason why the queen agreed to resurrect the Ethodine," Pylo says. "To get her hands on the pieces necessary to create a new Key. From decoding the tome's pages, I believe that you already know what those elements are."

Vale quietly recites the prophecy. "*Stone and dust they must combine, with every royal clan bloodline —*"

"Wait!" Hickory cuts in. "Stone… like moonstone?"

"Yes," Pylo encourages. "The same three elements that we used to create the first Key are needed again. The moonstones, pixie dust, and blood from each clan's royal family."

"You see, it's been quite impossible for anyone to construct a new Key because of the clan divisions. But now…" Leera peers at all of us. "The queen has brought all the pieces together, just within her reach."

"Just in time for the Moon Harvest." Hickory purses his lips. "Of course. It all makes sense now."

Kenna nods. "She's also secured all the pixie dust she'll need for the ritual."

Aeron looks at me and mouths one word: *Jasper*. We saw him with a train full of pixie dust. But he'd said that shipment *wasn't* for the queen, didn't he?

Vale pulls the cloak tighter as Leera peers over at her. "If you win the Ethodine, my dear, then the queen will not only retain her control of Faylan through you. She'll also acquire the moonstones and the clan blood from the oath you've all promised to make."

Pylo turns to the rest of us. "I wish we had time to teach you more about your gifts, what you're truly capable of. For now, you must use what you have to make sure that the queen doesn't get hold of those elements. She mustn't create the new Key and enter the Neverworld, at any cost."

"Well, that settles it," Aeron says firmly. "Sorry, Vale, but Quinn has to win this last trial. We can't let those items fall into your mother's hands."

"No." My head whirls as I stand. "I can't do that." *Not with Gaius' life on the line.*

"Why not?" Hickory asks.

I exhale. "Because if Vale doesn't win, the queen will kill my brother."

Hickory blinks. "Quinn, are you sure you're all right?" he asks hesitantly. "Gaius is already dead, remember?"

"According to those two, he's not." I point at Aeron and Vale.

"*What?*" Hickory stares at them in genuine shock. If he suspected Aeron's involvement in Gaius' death, then he obviously had no idea that my brother might still be alive.

Vale spins to Aeron, refusing to meet my eyes. "You told her?"

"I had to," he says. "She deserved to know."

"None of that matters now." I slump against the tunnel wall, my head in my hands. "I should've known already. Gaius... he's been in the nightmares I told you about, maybe trying to tell me the truth this whole time. I didn't think it was important until I found out that he's alive..." My voice cracks, the words dying on my lips.

Aeron moves toward me. "Quinn, I know you don't have any reason to trust me, but we'll figure something out. If we can stop her, then we'll make her hand over Gaius."

"That's a pretty big *if*," I say. "How in Faylan are we supposed to do that?"

"What if we create the Key ourselves?" Aeron offers.

I shake my head. "We still need the moonstones and tons of pixie dust."

"We could try telling the clan leaders the truth," Hickory says. "Maybe they can stop her."

Do you really think they'd believe us? Alys signs.

"Alys is right. They didn't believe the Mystics before, and they won't believe us now. I barely believe it myself." I wave away the idea. "If the queen wasn't holding Gaius hostage, then I'd say we could just stay in hiding until after the Moon Harvest. She can't create the Key

437

without us." I groan and turn to Vale. "Are you sure you don't know where she's keeping him? If we knew, then we could just march in there and steal him back."

"Even if I knew, she'd see that coming a mile away. She's always prepared for every possibility." Vale stops and stares ahead where a small bit of light from the surface is breaking through at the end of the tunnel. "There's only one thing she won't see coming. Only one way that's sure to stop her plans."

"Oh yeah? What's that?" I cross my arms, already preparing to shoot her proposal down.

"I have an idea. Each of us would have to play a part." Her eyes scan over the others and settle on me. "And you might not like yours."

I'm about to argue again, but as I look at her, I see Whit staring back at me.

I'm doing what I've always done. What Whit always resented me for. What led to her betrayal. Thinking that I know best, refusing to listen or let anyone in.

I have a choice. I can fight Vale, or I can choose to accept her help. To dare to trust her. To trust all of them. Can I put my brother's life in their hands? My *own* life? Vale knows her mother better than any of us, and the others are looking at me as if they're ready to follow me into battle, wherever that might lead.

I unclench my tightened fists and take a step toward Vale, letting out a belabored breath. "Try me."

CHAPTER 63

"There they are!" a Gwyllion soldier calls out as the five of us stagger back into the stadium, covered in bruises and dirt.

The clan leaders fly to us in a flurry. My father reaches me first.

"Are you all right?" He extends a hand to examine my battered wing, then stops short, as if not sure how to proceed. "We haven't had an earthquake in quite some time. We were worried you'd... that the competition might be finished."

"Oh, my darling." The queen darts to Vale, cupping her face in her hands, examining every inch of her. "We flew after you when you fell, but debris shifted over the opening too quickly."

Lord Zephen puts a hand on Hickory's shoulder. "We sent a Tunneler to retrieve you. It seems you managed just fine all on your own." Zephen gives him an impressed smile.

The five of us glance at each other, keeping quiet about the details.

All that the Mystics had told us still swirls in my head. They brought us to the surface like they promised, then quickly disappeared back into the shadows once we were safe.

"In preparation for your return, the clan leaders agreed that you'd all receive treatment for any wounds and one night to recuperate," the queen says, clutching Vale to her side. "Tomorrow, Vale and Quinn will have a rematch."

Vale eyes me, giving me a subtle nod.

We have a plan. Now we just have to hope it works.

As we're guided into the city, I chew my lip. I can't help picturing all the ways that things could still go terribly wrong. If we don't play things right, there's still a chance the queen could get all she wants and I could lose my brother forever.

But Vale is right. Out of all our options, her plan is our best shot.

We have to at least try.

~

Overnight, the news about the sudden earthquake that almost put an end to all the clan heirs spreads throughout Faylan like wildfire. By morning the Gwyllion port is past capacity with even more faerie ships arriving for the final duel than the day before.

With the destruction of the stadium, my father moves the trial to a valley where the clans can watch from the surrounding mountain peaks above. As we arrive, the rocky slopes are already packed with fae, though the usual clan boundaries are forced to blend together.

I walk out to meet Vale, still nursing some pain in my right wing. I never got the chance to find Alys and let her finish healing it.

Vale and I raise the weapons of our fathers.

"Ready to lose on your own land?" Vale says loudly as we circle each other.

"Or you could just bow down and surrender now," I call back, waving my sword toward the ground with a smirk.

"I don't think so." Vale glances back at her mother. "Today, we fight to the end."

The gong strikes, and we're off.

This time, neither one of us holds back. We seem evenly matched as metal clashes again and again.

Vigorous cheers and calls for certain blows ricochet off the mountains. Even clan members who aren't Gwyllion or Sylph join the fray with gusto.

We stand toe to toe, blades slashing.

Vale falls back first.

I advance, hitting again, and again.

We find a rhythm. High, then low, then high again, we dance.

Swiping at her knees, she dodges, easily predicting my moves.

Though my father looks concerned, I try to stay focused.

"You've gotten good at this," I call out between blows. "You must have had an excellent teacher."

"She was all right." Vale smirks. "But I've come up with a few moves of my own."

She lunges forward with a move I definitely didn't teach her, spinning through the air as she slices.

I shift to dodge. A shooting pain from my unhealed wing zings through my back. I falter.

Her blade catches my face, splitting a fine line through my cheek.

The crowd gasps.

I touch the cut, smearing the blood down my face.

Vale looks just as shocked. My opening.

I charge at her, Vale blocking my strikes as she draws back.

"No. More. Playing. Around," I accent every word with a swing of my sword.

"I couldn't agree more." She finds her footing and our blades clash, locking in a standstill.

She thrusts me back, releasing her feather wings, shooting into the air.

I follow her, but my wing spasms again. I can't keep this up much longer.

Our blades meet in the open sky and I look for a weak spot.

She's not guarding her left side.

I thrust toward the inside of her free arm, making a gash.

She hisses, stunned long enough that I aim for her sword.

I hit hard, and she falls.

Her father's blade clatters to the ground just out of reach.

She stretches for it. I land, whipping my blade between her and the sword, daring her to reach for it again.

She lifts her hands, her chest heaving. I follow her with the end of my blade until she shifts to her knee.

"I surrender," she says.

The mountainsides erupt in surprise and cheers, my folk pounding the ground like a stampede.

My father stands tall, nodding to me with the smallest lift at the corners of his mouth while the queen's face grows as purple as her gown.

"Congratulations," Vale says through heaving breaths, looking up at me. "It's done. You've won."

"Not quite." I swallow hard and brace myself, knowing what I have to do next.

I bring back my sword and thrust it toward her body.

Vale gasps.

The arena goes still.

Her wide eyes don't stray from mine, not even to the blood pooling at her chest.

There's only one thing she won't see coming, Vale had said in the cavern. *Only one way that's sure to stop her plans.*

I clench my teeth, squeezing my eyes closed as I pull out my blade, now stained with Vale's blood.

My stomach lurches as she gives me a sad smile and collapses to the ground.

The queen's face goes from raging purple to ghost white. Her blood-curdling scream echoes through the valley. "Vale!"

Two Gwyllion guards seize my arms and yank my sword away.

I look at my father. His face has dropped, going from pleasure at my victory to confusion at my bloodshed. I've broken the rules that he set himself. There's nothing he can do to save me now.

The queen rushes to Vale's side as Aeron, Alys, and Hickory dart in from the crowd.

"I'm sorry, Mother," Vale tries to get out the words, blood trailing from her mouth. "I did my best."

"Shhh." Her mother holds her like a little sprout. "It's going to be okay."

"Mother," Vale persists, coughing up more blood. "I—I love you."

Then her eyes roll back into her head. Her chest stills.

Taking Vale's wrist in his hand, Aeron feels for a pulse. He turns to the queen with wide eyes. "I-I'm so sorry, Your Majesty... She's gone." He turns to me in a fury. "What did you do?"

The queen's eyes fill with tears and rage. "You'd already won. Why do this?"

I take a breath. "You took my brother so I took your daughter."

Her eyes flash.

Picking up Vale's blade, she stands and points the sword directly at me. "Guards, give her back her weapon."

"Gwendolyn, what are you doing?" my father calls.

"That's *Queen* Gwendolyn to you." She points the sword at him. "I am *still* queen. Your daughter has broken the rules of the Ethodine." She points the weapon back at me. "So, I challenge her in my daughter's stead."

The entire crowd stands still as the guards let go of me. They hand me back my weapon and back away, giving us the field.

The usually demure queen removes her robe and casts it to the ground, revealing long, toned arms. She swings her late husband's blade powerfully through the air with precision, settling into a starting stance that's not one of a pampered royal, but of a trained warrior.

Wait. Something she said weeks ago flashes through my mind.

Her father had been a Sylph guard. And her third husband, Vale's father, had been head of the militia.

I narrow my eyes. It looks like she was trained well. *But so was I.*

"No one will interfere!" the queen commands loudly, though her tear-stained glare doesn't waver from my face.

This is it. I narrow my eyes, taking my own stance. "Long live the queen."

Releasing her feathered wings, Queen Gwendolyn leaps into the air, flying toward me with a terrible cry. With all her rage, she hurtles her blade down on me.

I brace my sword against the blow. The surprising force sends tremors through my arms, nearly bringing me to the ground.

I push back with a groan, shoving her back into the air.

The effort sends pain radiating through my back again. I'm not going to last long like this.

I prepare to lunge forward, but the queen shoots down at me again savagely, her eyes wild, forcing me to the ground.

I block, dive, and duck. Her swings are so blindingly fast, I don't have a moment to retaliate.

I miss deflecting her next stab, and it jams into my already-weakened wing.

My breath hitches, and I cry out as she yanks the blade free.

She sneers.

I'm panting, sweat pooling down my face and into my eyes.

This has to end. *Now.* I can't let Vale's sacrifice be in vain.

The queen thrusts her blade again at my shoulder, but I lift my arm just in time.

She falters and I bring my arm down over hers, pinning the queen to my side.

"This is for my brother," I whisper.

Flipping my blade around, I drive the handle into her chest, knocking the wind out of her.

The queen collapses to her knees.

Before she can recover, I kick at her hand.

Her sword releases from her grasp long enough for me to catch it.

Turning her own blade against her, I corner her with weapons crossed, her neck trapped between the blades.

The guards rush in. I bring the blades closer, warning them to back off.

"Tell them!" I command the queen as the horrified crowd watches us breathlessly. "Tell them all the truth. What you did, what you've been planning, and I won't kill you."

The queen hesitates. "You wouldn't dare."

"Wouldn't I?" I inch the blades closer. "Thanks to you, I have nothing left to lose."

The razor-sharp edges graze her neck.

"Okay, okay," she relents, eyes on the swords. She starts to whisper.

"Louder!" I demand.

"The Ethodine is a sham!" she yells.

The crowd erupts in shocked murmurs.

"I was never going to let anyone but Vale win." Her voice cracks at the end. She's failed in the worst possible way.

"That's not all, is it?" I glare, tightening my fingers on the hilts. "Tell them what you were going to do with the winnings."

The queen's eyes widen, then narrow. "They finally got to you, didn't they? The Mystics—"

Before she can say anymore, I press the blades further, drawing blood.

"Wait!" she cries out. "There's an ancient item that can bring the Numa back to our world."

The crowd's murmurs grow louder.

"I needed the moonstones and blood oath to create it. With it, I could've controlled the Numa and made Faylanians bow to the Sylphs once and for all."

My jaw shifts. This isn't the exact story the Mystics told us. Does she not know the true nature of the Numa? Or were the Mystics partly mistaken? Either way, her confession is enough to dethrone her.

"Arrest her!" my father's voice booms.

Gwyllion soldiers rush to the queen. She thrashes in their grasp, trying to lunge at me, landing on her knees. "You may have stopped this plan, *pirate*, but I will destroy you for what you have taken from me today—"

"Mother," comes a soft, familiar voice as gasps flood the valley.

The queen halts, rage draining as her daughter steps into her line of sight, dried blood caked around a wound that's no longer there.

"V-Vale..." the queen stammers, shaking. "H-how?"

"It doesn't matter." Vale kneels in front of her. "I'm okay, really."

Hickory and Aeron smile as Alys replaces her glove. It worked. With the queen in her weakest and most vulnerable state, Aeron used his silver tongue, persuading her that Vale was already dead. Then, while all eyes were on me and the queen, Aeron and Hickory blocked in Alys, who was able to heal her.

Vale eyes me. *The element of surprise.*

"It's all right, Mother." Vale smiles sadly at her, glancing at the guards still holding the queen's arms. "The worst is over."

But I'm not finished yet. "I'm sorry, Vale. It isn't over quite yet." I lift my father's sword toward the queen again. "Where's my brother? If you've hurt him, so help me..."

The queen's expression goes from confusion to amusement in a matter of seconds. "The Mystics didn't tell you?"

"Tell me what?" I demand.

She coughs out a laugh. "I don't have him, my dear. I never did. After stealing something precious to me, your brother escaped my clutches into the Neverworld."

My head whirls. The Neverworld? But that would mean... Gaius was the spy the Mystics had mentioned?

"You're lying!" My blade trembles in my hand. It's another trick. It has to be. *Why wouldn't they have told me?*

The queen shrugs with a smirk. "If you don't believe me, then you should ask them." She points at the sky as screams ring out across the valley.

Shadows loom over us. Shrieking figures fill the air like a swarm of locusts, blocking out the sun. *Goblins.*

There are hundreds of them. They swoop down on the mountainsides and the battlefield around me, fangs bared and talons raised.

"Quinn!" Aeron yells and I turn.

Two goblins have him firmly by the arms as if they mean to pull him apart.

I go for him but his eyes widen at something behind me.

"Watch out!"

One of the goblins knocks my blade to the ground while another grabs me from behind. He wraps his arms so tight around my arms and chest that it's hard to breathe.

Around us, goblins patrol the sky and fill the valley, hissing with talons poised to strike anyone who makes a wrong move. They've detained all the soldiers, taking their weapons, turning them on us.

"My queen, you don't want to do this," Aeron says slowly, his words rippling through the air. He's trying to use his silver tongue on her again.

"Gag him!" the queen commands. She was too emotional to resist his gift before. Now she has her guard up. "I don't want one peep coming out of him."

Reclaiming her usual poised posture, she turns to me. "You thought you were so clever. I bet you weren't counting on my friends here."

"Gwendolyn, you traitor!" my father yells through a gang of goblins encircling the clan lords.

"What's the meaning of this?" calls Lord Kaito. He has his triton poised toward the goblin inching toward them. At least some of the folk are still armed.

"One way or another, I *will* have what I want," the queen tells them calmly. "You will put down your weapons and hand over your moonstones, or I will make sure Vale is the only heir left alive to rule."

A goblin points a Gwyllion sword inches from my neck while the one holding me squeezes harder.

"They await my command." The queen lifts a hand. "Believe me, these creatures are not as patient as I am."

"Mother, don't!" Vale calls, also restrained by a goblin.

"This is for your own good, Vale. For the good of all of Faylan. You'll see very soon."

"No, you don't understand—"

The queen waves her hand, and another goblin gags Vale.

The queen turns back to the clan lords. "Now, hand over the stones, or you can watch your legacies end here and now."

I hang my head. *I'm doomed.* My father has never given into threats easily, and he isn't going to start now.

Strangely, a peace washes over me. At least this way, the queen won't win.

When I lift my head, my father is pulling off one of the many rings on his fingers. As he does, the stone inside it glows a bright red.

The Gwyllion moonstone.

No. I watch in horror as the other leaders follow.

Lord Torlon removes the orb from the top of his staff. It lights up with a greenish hue.

Lord Kaito takes a gem from his trident. It takes on a bluish sheen.

Lord Zephen removes his goggles, pulling off a gold stone embedded in the strap.

"What're you doing? Stop!" I shout at them.

"If we don't do this, then we lose everything," my father says solemnly, refusing to look my way. I can't tell if he means losing the only heir to his throne, or losing his daughter. His unusually soft tone makes me hope it's a little of both.

My heart sinks as the goblins collect the stones and hand them to the queen.

"Very wise move." The queen motions to the goblins. "Now we fly. Bring the heirs."

"What?" my father barks, his muscles tightening. Though unarmed and outnumbered, he advances toward her. The goblins hiss at him to stand down.

"Please, you have what you need. Leave our younglings alone," Lord Torlon pleads.

"I told you, your spawn's blood is necessary to my plan," the queen shoots back. "The creation of the ancient item I require calls for royal blood from each clan heir. They'll be coming with me. And if you follow—" she warns "—I'll personally make sure they suffer slowly and painfully."

The queen and her goblin army take to the skies, dragging the five of us with them into the air.

I fight the one holding me, but with my damaged wing, I fear the drop more than the goblin.

Below us, the lords helplessly watch us go. Except for my father. He's already turned away.

Flying toward the Woodlands, I see our destination ahead.

The Sacred Vine.

CHAPTER 64

W e've failed.

How did the tables turn so quickly? We were sure we'd thought of everything. Everything except for the queen having help. And from the goblins, no less. Has she been controlling them this whole time?

The goblins' black wings must be stronger than any normal faerie's, because they don't stop until we approach our destination: the Sacred Vine. As they fly, out of the flapping of their wings wafts an overpowering scent.

A bittersweet mix of pixie dust and ash.

It comes on wings of ash and dust.

My chest tightens. *This is it.* The Mystic prophecy is finally coming to pass. I look up to the darkening sky, the moons clustering together, nearly ready for the Moon Harvest.

The end is coming.

As the flying horde lands at the base of the Vine, the fae of Shree scatter, shrieking as goblins rush the streets. Wings of all kinds take to the skies and the forest as shopkeepers barricade themselves in their stalls. No one's coming to help us.

Our captors drag the five of us to a dirt clearing near the base of the Vine, lining us up in an arc before the queen. Though Aeron is still gagged, that doesn't stop him from trying to wriggle out of the goblin's grasp, his worried eyes fixed on me. Alys is struggling too. She glares at the goblins furiously, probably remembering what they did to Tomah. She tries to remove her gloves, but her goblin captor holds her hands firmly behind her back.

Hickory helplessly watches Vale as she attempts to reason with her mother once again, her muffled pleas barely distinguishable through her gag. "Mother, please…"

The queen ignores her, inspecting the area around us and observing the moons above until she's satisfied. "Perfect. Now, we begin." She waves a hand to the remaining goblins, and they spread out.

Some of them clear branches away from the Vine's trunk, while others grab pickaxes and shovels from a nearby blacksmith stand and drive them into the earth. No longer in attack mode, their elongated arms drag along the floor, heads hanging low.

"What did she do to them?" Hickory whispers to me as we watch the goblins dig.

The creature holding him snarls as the queen approaches. "Hickory, dear. Don't be rude. Please, speak up so we can all hear you."

"I-I was just wondering…" Hickory stammers. "They're all faeries, yes? How did they end up like… this?"

His captor sustains a low growl, saliva dripping from his fangs onto Hickory's shoulder.

Hickory grimaces.

"Ah, you should know the great potential of pixie dust more than anyone." The queen places a hand on the goblin's arm, and it stills. "My private team of Sylph researchers and Kobold inventors have been experimenting with dust concoctions over the years, testing enhancement potential. Criminals and vagrants have made for perfect test subjects. Most of them have been more than willing to join the cause—well, the ones who survived."

She turns to me. "Take Jasper, for instance. He was more than eager to enter the Labyrinth, promising to kill you and bring your blood to me, or at least throw you off the scent."

An icy cold settles in my core. Moon Face had only been a distraction, working for the queen's purposes. Had the dust he collected in the tunnels been for the queen after all, or did he have other deals on the side?

"I knew I should've sent someone more capable," the queen scoffs.

"He was always much better at wrangling in test subjects who needed a bit more convincing."

I think of Luna in Tartarus, begging for her life. If I hadn't saved her, then she probably would've been turned into one of these things.

The queen lifts my chin with her finger. "It's a pity I needed you for the competition. You would have made a strong goblin."

"Don't you touch her!" Aeron's voice threatens, and I turn to see he's edged the gag out of his mouth.

The queen snatches a knife from a goblin and presses it to my neck, shooting him a daring glare. "One more word out of you, and I'll finish what Jasper couldn't."

Aeron clamps his mouth shut, frantic eyes darting to me.

The queen grins. "Everyone has a weakness. Who knew you had so many?" She draws away from me, and I struggle to lunge after her as she points the knife at Aeron. "You've been helpful in the past, my dear prince. But lately, you've been more trouble than you're worth. Things would've been so much easier if my goblins had succeeded in disposing of you in the Woodlands as planned, bringing me your blood."

I freeze, seeing a flash of the goblin going after Aeron during the lynxicorn attack. Something had been in its hand. It must've been a syringe!

She glares at the goblin restraining Aeron. "Get that gag back on, and make sure it stays this time."

The goblin quickly obeys.

I narrow my eyes. "Is that what you created them for? To do your dirty work?"

She whips back to me. "The Numa have a life source that feeds our land, a source we once served them to acquire. Without it, our world is dying. So, I sought to create an advanced breed of fae strong enough to infiltrate the Neverworld and force the Numa to serve us instead. In the end, it was samples from Knolls victims combined with pixie dust that helped us develop a formula for the perfect servants. The initial fever burned their bodies to a crisp, but if they survived, each creature became as strong as ten Gwyllions—with a weak and easily malleable mind."

The queen pets the goblin's head and it lets out a grumbling purr.

"With the numbers we've experimented on, we now have the

makings of an army of super-faeries to do our bidding. We'll soon be ready to take complete control of both the Numa and faerie world. No more threat of war or enslavement. Just complete peace under one rule."

She means *her* rule. Her eyes are wild. She's so hungry for control that she can't even see she's already begun creating her own brand of enslavement.

"All we needed was a way into the Neverworld." The queen's gaze trails back to me with a glare. "I was hunting down the original Key and finally had it within my grasp, until it was stolen by your insolent brother."

I grit my teeth, struggling against the goblin's hold.

"Thankfully, I was raised to always think through every angle, to have a plan for every possible scenario. In the event that I never gained possession of the Key, I had set a secondary plan in motion to create a new Key. I sought to collect the elements I needed peaceably, using the Ethodine to aid my cause. As long as Vale won, she would've been awarded the moonstones and the right to your blood without the mess of a war. Our world has already been through so much… But once again, a Gwyllion heir is forcing me to take drastic measures."

She snaps her fingers, and the goblins push us to the area where the others have been digging.

At first, I fear we're being dragged to our graves. Instead, a pattern of winding trenches has been dug into the ground.

It's the sign of the Numa.

Three circles, each smaller one inlaid inside the other, with the ten petals of the iconic flower stretching over them.

The key to power is the sign.

Goblins carry over baskets of pixie dust and pour it into the trenches made by each flower petal.

The queen takes the amulet from around her neck and pulls out the stone that now glows purple. The fifth and final moonstone.

The five of us are stationed on the tip of every other petal while the queen places each of our moonstones on the petal that lies opposite us. The symbol's petals have become dust-filled ditches, connecting us to our moonstones.

"It's a ritual circle." Hickory's eyes are wide as he stares at the queen. "You plan to sacrifice us?"

"In a way. Just enough blood for the ritual to be completed." The queen circles us as she speaks, motioning to the sky. "According to the Mystic tome, once the moons align, their light will illuminate the inner circle. This center circle represents the moons themselves, tying the outer circles of our two worlds together: Faylan and the Neverworld. The pixie dust will fuse your blood with the moonstones to create a new Key; one that will finally open the door to the Neverworld."

The queen motions to the Sacred Vine, where a large door etched into its base has been uncovered. The Numanic symbol is at its center. It looks just like the painting of the door that was on Hickory's wall. The Vine isn't just the root of our world. The portal to the Neverworld lives *inside* it.

She stops in front of me. "Once the door is opened, the goblins' first order of business is to find your brother and put an end to his miserable life."

Panic flares within me and I lunge again with all my might. The goblin holding me is too strong.

The queen laughs. "Tie up our guests and prepare them to make their blood oath. Be careful with Vale, but don't worry about spilling too much blood from the others."

Everything moves in slow motion.

I lock eyes with my friends as they attempt one last time to escape their captors' grasps. Alys fights the hardest, releasing her wings to try to fly away, kicking with all of her might.

Her goblin holds both her wrists with one thick hand, using the other to wrap them tightly with a rope. With its sharp talon, it cuts her arm. I watch as her blood trickles into the ditch and magically travels across the dust-filled ditches to each moonstone.

My captor spins me around and I try to fight too. I can't let this happen.

But seeing the goblin's face, I stop.

This goblin isn't a puck. She's a pixie.

Past her fangs and disfigured form, I see the stubby horns and big rounded eyes.

This goblin is Whit.

CHAPTER 65

I stare into the eyes of my former friend, unable to move. It's as if I'm staring into a mirror. One thought keeps running through my mind.

This could've been me.

If I'd become captain of the Minnow, whatever steps led Whit here would've led me to this same fate. The awful things we last said to each other sit like a pit in my stomach. Her fangs and deformities perfectly depict our bitterness toward each other. Bitterness fully nurtured, fully grown, and fully manifested.

"Whit?" I ask quietly as she binds a rope around my wrists. "Whit, it's me, Quinn."

Nothing. Whit doesn't flinch. Is she too far gone? More beast than faerie now? I can't believe that. I've got to know for sure.

"I know we didn't end on good terms, but do you really want me to bleed to death?"

Whit takes out her switchblade, the same one she used so many times on our missions, and cuts a deep gash in my arm.

I yelp as blood trickles down into the ditch.

"Okay, I deserved that," I say, wincing. "And I understand if you'd rather have me gone. But do you really want Crazy Lady over there to take over? To dictate your life like this? Are you really going to kill my brother? You're a pirate, Whit. You're not a stone-cold murderer."

Whit growls, tightening my ropes.

"Whit," I whisper one more time, hanging my head. "I understand why you resent me. Why you did what you did. I'm impossibly selfish. I never deserved you as a friend. For my part, I want you to know, no matter what happens... I'm so sorry."

For a brief moment, Whit stills. Her fangs recede, and her eyes search mine.

Then the sound of a whip cracks.

Whit howls.

A goblin stands behind her with a long cord in his hand. Whit's fangs resurface as she thrusts me closer to the ritual circle.

"The time has come!" The queen points to the sky.

This is it. In the starlit sky, the moons are clustered together, nearly aligned. Our combined blood has reached the moonstones.

I stare again at the four fae who were once my rivals.

Now, if we die, at least we'll die together as friends.

The moons glide into place, and their united beam shines down to the middle of the symbol. The moonstones glow and send light through the sea of pixie dust, back to our bodies.

A surge shoots through me, and I scream, the sound mingling with the screams of the others. It's as if hot light is filling every fiber of my body, threatening to increase until I explode.

When the blinding light and pain finally recede, I gasp for breath and gaze into the ritual circle.

There, formed by our blood and the magic of the moons and dust, stands a golden staff. It's studded with a pattern of new moonstones, each glowing with one of the five clan colors.

It looks exactly like the Sylphic Scepter depicted in the murals in Eldore.

The key to power is the sign.

No, not *is*. We must have had the translation wrong. The Key to power is found *in* the sign. The scepter. It all makes sense now.

The story of the Sylphic Scepter was twisted just like the other parts of our history. It isn't what banished the Numa to the Neverworld.

It's the Key that allowed the fae to travel to it.

"Beautiful..." The queen gazes at the scepter suspended in midair. Taking it in her hand, she runs her fingers over the engravings before heading toward the Vine. "Let's see what this can do. Bring Vale to me, and gather up the other four. They'll make strong goblins."

455

The goblins yank us away from the symbol, and my heart races.

We're going to become goblins. Gaius is going to die. Both worlds will be in ruins, and I'm out of ideas.

The others look as exhausted as I feel. Even Alys, who had begun to heal herself, hangs her head in defeat.

Something grazes my hands, cutting at the rope that binds me.

Whit's switchblade.

My eyes grow wide in confusion.

"Run," she growls softly, the words coming out strained and garbled, even worse than Moon Face's had. "I can't… escape fate. You can."

Whit is giving me an out. I could take it. It's what I always do when things get tough, and they're worse than ever now. But this time, looking at my friends, new and old—I can't.

Somewhere along the way, I started to care. I started to need them. I can't abandon them now when they need me the most.

We'll survive together, or we'll die together.

Putting a hand on Whit's arm, I smile at her. "You always forget Maverick's wise words, my friend. A pirate never retreats."

Whit smiles back, fangs and all. "Then you… need this." She hands me her switchblade.

I nod, and it's like we're back on the Minnow, knowing each other's intentions without words.

In one swift movement, Whit growls and turns on her fellow goblins who still have their hold on the others. Some goblins scatter while others launch themselves at her.

I go for Alys' binds first.

She grabs my arm. *I have an idea.*

I don't even question her. "Do it."

The queen spins around at the commotion. "What in Faylan is going on?"

Alys puts her fingers to her mouth.

My gaze connects with Vale's, and her eyes light up as Alys lets out a long whistle.

As I dart for Hickory, a large winged figure looms overhead, striking fear in the goblins around us.

"Dragon!" one of them cries as Tomah descends on the scene.

Alys mounts him, and together they attack. Tomah breathes hot gusts of fire and the goblins scatter. He lets out a booming roar.

The ground trembles.

"Another earthquake?" Hickory asks as I cut his binds.

"Not this time." I smile. "I think it's reinforcements."

Beasts of all kinds emerge from the Woodlands. They pour into the streets of Shree, bounding toward us.

"Yes!" Hickory cheers. He grabs a fallen sword and flies onto a passing horse that charges into the fray. "Let's do this!"

Aeron tries to speak through the gag as I untie his hands. Pulling it away, he beams at me. "Have I told you that I love you lately?"

I roll my eyes. I don't have time to decide if I've fully forgiven him for everything quite yet, let alone talk of love. Still, my heart races.

"Can't we maybe talk about this later?" I allow a small laugh and put my switchblade in his hand.

He returns it. "You're going to need this more than me in a minute."

"What're you talking about?"

Before he can explain, a team of goblins comes running toward us, fangs bared. I go to throw the blade but Aeron stops me—and begins to sing.

It's a wordless melody, eerie and beautiful at the same time. Immediately, the goblins stop and turn their rage on each other, as if now believing each other to be the enemy.

Aeron nods. "Feels good to put this curse of mine to good use." He grabs my shoulders.

I freeze, thinking he's about to kiss me.

He just smiles. "I'll hold these goons off and make a safe path through so you can get to Vale and stop the queen."

I nod as he points to where Vale is on the other side of the battle. Still gagged and held by the goblin at her back, she can only watch as her mother struggles to open the door with the scepter. There's still a sea of goblins separating us.

I look at the switchblade in my hand, wishing I had my fire for the first time since it disappeared.

I shrug. *It's not much, but it's better than nothing.*

Following Aeron through the battle, I slice and stab, cutting down any who dare to lunge at me.

Hickory cries out, and my head whips around.

One of them has tackled him off his horse, and his sword is too far out of reach.

The creature pins him to the ground, saliva dripping from its fangs.

I take aim and fling the switchblade into the goblin's back. It falls lifelessly to the side.

Another is quick to try and take its place. Aeron flies in, tackling the goblin to the ground. His song makes the creature go rigid as stone.

Aeron holds out a hand to help Hickory up. He takes it gladly, and I sigh with relief.

Hickory pulls the switchblade out of the other goblin's back, giving me a nod of thanks. Then his eyes fill with fear.

"Look out!" Hickory points behind me.

I whip around again.

Lifting a clawed hand, a towering goblin moves to cut me down, then freezes mid-swing. His face goes slack as he drops to the ground, an arrow lodged in his head.

War cries bellow from the streets.

For a moment, I think I might be dreaming as Leman and my father fly in with the other lords, followed by a small army of fae from every clan.

The goblins screech, flying to meet them, colliding in the sky.

Leman darts to me, shooting an arrow into a goblin's eye on the way.

"How did you find us?" I ask as he continues shooting down one goblin after another, blocking me from the battle.

A flap of wings sound behind me. I snatch an arrow from Leman's quiver and spin, lodging it into the goblin's chest just in time.

"Nice work," Leman says as I yank the arrow out and keep my back to his, ready for the next attack. "Your father called for the clans to unite right after the five of you were taken. We followed in the direction the goblins flew until the beam of moonlight confirmed your location. We're just sorry we couldn't get here sooner."

"Wait, my father did *what*?" I ask in disbelief, scanning the battle.

Feyden is cutting down the goblins with his broadsword in hand, completely in his element. He's side by side with Lord Kaito, who swings his triton, calling water from a nearby fountain to crash over the creatures as an army of Tunnelers barrel through the streets at Lord Zephen's command.

"Leman! Could use your help over here, son!" Lord Torlon calls.

I expect to see the Dryad Lord in trouble. Instead, he ducks the curled horns on his head and changes into a giant black ram, pummeling through a crowd of goblins. Lady Navi follows him, her arms shifting into green vines that wind tightly around the goblins, tossing them in the air.

Leman chuckles. "Can't let my parents have all the fun. You all right on your own?"

I cock a brow at him. "Please, I'm the Pirate Shade, Menace of the—"

"Menace of the Five Provinces. Yeah, yeah." He smiles. "You might want these back then. Your father found them in your preparation room, and asked me to give them to you."

Reaching into his belt, he takes out the twin daggers I left behind.

My chest tightens.

Gaius. All this will be for nothing if I fail to save him again.

I take the daggers. "Thank you."

Leman nods. "I'll clear you a path."

In seconds, he shifts into his wolf form and rushes back into the fight, taking down goblin after goblin between me and the Sacred Vine. Leman can't handle them all.

With my trusty daggers back in my hands, I furiously fight my way through the swarm.

On the way, I pass Alys and Tomah in the thick of things. Without a word between us, they position themselves to handle the goblins at my back.

Tomah lets out a loud roar, and soon Aeron and Hickory are fighting their way over to us too, guarding my sides.

Finally, I see Vale. She remains bound and guarded ahead, with the queen standing in front of the door in the Sacred Vine. It's still closed. *Thank Faylan.*

Lunging forward with my own battle cry, I take down the last goblins in my way. I fling a dagger at the one holding Vale and it lodges in his temple.

As he falls to the ground, Vale lifts her hands hurriedly to remove her gag.

"Quinn, wait! Don't—" she calls out. It's too late.

I throw the other dagger right at the queen.

She spins and points the scepter at the weapon. The scepter's magic flings my blade to the side.

No. I halt. I've done it again. Acted too fast and too rashly.

I have no defenses left.

The queen sneers. "You come at me with knives while I hold the most powerful weapon in the world?" She points the scepter at me.

The air crushes in around me as I'm lifted off the ground.

"Who's the strongest now?" she taunts.

I look at my friends using everything they have to fight the enemy while I hang helplessly in the air. I'm useless. Weak.

The scepter crushes harder, as if a fist is closing around me, grinding my bones.

Just as black spots form in my vision, Vale yells and leaps at her mother. They tumble to the ground together, including the scepter.

I collapse and gasp for air. I struggle to get up as the queen grabs the scepter again.

This time, she points it at Vale.

"You ungrateful girl!" she yells. "I've sacrificed so much for you. And how do you repay me?"

Now Vale is the one in the air, clawing for breath.

"Mother… please…don't…" she gasps.

"Why, Vale? Why would you turn on me?"

Vale takes in a short breath. "Everything I've done… is for your own good, Mother."

Vale's courage sets my blood ablaze, melting my icy fears.

A familiar heat that I thought I'd lost sparks.

Though it singes my chest, strength returns to my bones. I might have one weapon left.

I catch sight of Alys and Tomah fending off a goblin horde. Her voice rings in my mind. *Gift or curse, your ability does not define you. What you do with it, that's what defines you.* The heat inside me burns hotter as I recall the memories of Alys healing me, even despite the pain it inflicted on her.

Hickory is still battling with all his might. I think of him trusting me with his darkest fears and craziest theories.

Vale struggles for her last breath, and I remember her one wish: to make her father proud.

My blood boils.

In the battle, Aeron uses his song to fight. His words from earlier come back to me. *Feels good to put this curse of mine to good use.*

"No holding back." I grit my teeth. "Not anymore."

I know what I have to do. And though this move will mean losing my brother again, maybe forever—it also means saving him.

Saving everyone.

I raise my hands, and instead of letting bitterness and anger fuel me, I call forth all the good I've experienced on this journey.

Fire blazes in my hands. I hiss from the pain, and it quickly extinguishes.

What had Hickory and Alys said that night in the tunnels?

Maybe something is blocking you... You need to let go.

It isn't enough to embrace the good. I have to let go of what's holding me back.

"Let go," I command myself through clenched teeth.

In that moment, I let go of everything I can think of. My bitterness toward Whit. My hatred and disappointment with my father. My jealousy of Vale and her mother. My anger toward Aeron and Hickory and anyone who's ever lied to me. My need to prove everyone wrong and to do everything myself.

And finally, my guilt over Gaius and my mother.

It's as if I hear Gaius' voice calling me. I can feel his hand on my shoulder as the fire burns. *You can let go of me, Quinn. It's okay. I forgive you. Now you need to forgive yourself. Let go.*

"I don't want to let go. I don't want to lose you again." My eyes squeeze shut. "But I'll try!"

I shake, erupting inside until it feels like liquid fire is pooling out of my eyes, spilling out over my cheeks.

No. Not liquid fire.

My eyes shoot open.

I'm crying.

Pain like I've never felt before radiates as a flood of emotion pounds my body, thrumming through me like an unyielding wave.

Something deep inside me unlocks.

My tears turn into a battle cry as I raise my hands and extend my fingers toward the scepter. Flames shoot with precision as I scream, hot tears running down my face.

Just like Pylo and Leera's flames, my ever-growing fire takes on a distinct shape.

The monstrous form of a ferocious dragon.

It launches forward, building as it moves through the air, releasing a crackling roar.

The metal staff heats in the queen's hand. She scowls through the burn, hanging on through gritted teeth until she's forced to fling it away with a scream. Holding her damaged hand to her chest, she gapes at me in disbelief.

I'm not finished.

I keep my fire trained on the scepter, the gold heating until it burns so brightly that it lights up Shree like daytime.

"No!" the queen screams, diving for the scepter again.

Vale leaps toward her and pulls her back just in time.

In a loud burst, the scepter explodes into a cloud of a million pixie dust particles.

My flames recede. My hands fall to my sides and I sway from the exertion.

I did it.

We did it.

I collapse to the ground, welcoming the darkness.

CHAPTER 66

Come on, Quinn, a small voice calls to me in the darkness. *Come back to us.*

A surge of pain.

Light breaks into my vision, and I slowly open my eyes. Four familiar faces hover over me.

Alys is the closest, giving me a strained smile. Her tattered clothing reveals more of her tattoos, glowing like never before.

"This feels familiar," I groan.

Alys' healing continues to work its magic as she holds my arm. She isn't the only one clutching me.

"Oh, thank Faylan." Aeron says, squeezing my hand. "Don't you *ever* do that again."

The memory of my fire blazing comes back to me. *The dragon inside.*

"You mean my fire?" I ask hesitantly. I'm exposed for all to see. To judge.

"No way, that was epic!" Hickory chimes in, giving my other arm a shake.

The others give him a look.

"What? It was."

"I think what we're all trying to say is…" Vale shakes her head, patting my hand. "No more dying for a while. Okay?"

"I'll do my best." I try to laugh, though my body aches with the effort. It's all worth it. They accept me. I give a nod to the dried blood on Vale's chest. "Speaking of dying, sorry for stabbing you."

"It's all right. Thanks to this one, I'm doing just fine." Vale puts a hand on Alys' shoulder. "Besides, it was the only thing she wouldn't see coming." I follow her gaze to find the fighting has ended in the short time since I passed out, and guards are hauling her mother away. "She lied to me because she thought it would protect me. It was time that I did something just as drastic to save her."

The queen looks sorrowfully back at Vale. Then her stare turns to ice as her eyes shift to mine, promising vengeance. I look away, reminding myself that she no longer has a hold on me, or anyone else.

"What happened to the goblins?" I ask. Then I panic. "Where's Whit?"

"You mean the goblin who fought with us?" Hickory asks. "She's been willingly detained. We're going to try to help her. And to learn more about what we're dealing with."

Though relieved, I'm still confused. "And the others?"

"It was so strange." Aeron looks to the Woodlands. "Once you destroyed the Key, a loud sound echoed over Shree, like some sort of horn. The goblins took off into the forest. The queen tried to call them back, but they abandoned her."

"They just gave up?" I ask in disbelief.

"Yeah, it was weird." Hickory shrugs.

Alys' grip loosens. Her tattoos return to black, leaving dark circles under her eyes.

"Alys, are you okay?" I ask.

Alys nods. *I'll need quite the nap after all this. Honestly though, no longer having to hide or lie about my gift is more than I could ask for.*

I smile knowingly. Though I have no idea how my father, the Gwyllions, or Faylan at large will react to my forbidden Mystic fire, I resonate with Alys' relief.

My fire's a gift, not a curse.

Today I've proven it can be used for good.

I can be used for good.

And with all of our gifts put together, we are ten times stronger than if we had tried to do anything on our own.

Gaius was right. I may not be the strongest, but I have a different kind of strength.

"What happens now?" an angry voice breaks through my thoughts.

Aeron helps me stand as we watch the Nymph Lord arguing with the other clan leaders gathered nearby.

"Though we're all happy the queen is dethroned, who won the crown? My boy was next in the ranking after those two cheaters," Lord Kaito points his triton at me and Vale. "I think we all know Aeron deserves to be the faerie king."

"What? This whole competition was a scam to begin with. The queen confessed it herself," Lord Zephen challenges. "Hickory knows the most about these Numa creatures, and we all know that his painting in Isinglass warned us of a coming darkness. If anyone, *he* should be king!"

"My brothers, we have no reason to war against each other," Lord Torlon tries to reason with them. "With the Dryad's extensive knowledge of the Sacred Vine and the nature of our world, what Faylan needs now is a healer at the helm. Alys is the perfect—"

"Are you insane? She may be able to heal, but she also has the sign of the enemy imprinted on her arm." Kaito points to Alys, her Numanic tattoo showing through the cuts in her clothes. He pinches the bridge of his nose and frowns. "Well, if we can't agree, maybe we should settle it on the battlefield after all. Right, Feyden?"

My father turns around, and my once-heated body freezes solid. The Gwyllions would never let a fire-wielding Mystic rule them. Now that my secret is out, he has no reason to call me his daughter, let alone fight for my right to the crown.

Lady Navi squeezes Torlon's arm. "Does this mean we return to war?"

"Is that seriously what matters to all of you?" Aeron demands as I lean on him for support. "Our world was nearly overtaken by an army of goblins and a power-hungry sorceress. No offense, Vale."

She just motions for him to go on.

"And the only thing you all can think of is who should wear the crown?"

The clan leaders look at each other silently.

"Well, we made our blood oath to the heir *we* thought deserved to lead. So, you can all lower your weapons and bow to the new ruler of Faylan."

What? I stare at him. *We have? When? Who?*

Aeron takes my hands in his. Then he lowers to one knee and bows. My breath catches as Hickory, Vale, and Alys follow.

I shake my head violently. *No.*

Aeron's gaze goes from my face to my arms. Pulling my hands free from him, I see something else is mixed in the dirt and ash that cover them.

Four distinct hand prints encircle my arms, all dark red with drying blood.

My competitors' blood. Their blood oath.

"No," I say aloud, my voice soft but growing strong. "This is wrong. I'm not a leader. Not a good one, anyway. I don't deserve this."

"Agreed," says Lord Kaito. "You had no right to do this without our consent. To choose a vagrant—a pirate—for our highest position! It's unspeakable."

"You will not talk to my daughter that way." My father finally speaks. "Or rather, *your queen*. For what she did today for all of us, you owe her your allegiance."

I expect to see my father's lust for power lighting his eyes, motivating his words. But his eyes are soft and certain. And there's something else I've only seen in other fathers' faces.

A father's pride.

He kneels before me, and my breath hitches.

This is the moment I've always wanted from my father. For him to recognize my strength. To believe in me. Though my heart swells at the sight, it isn't what I *need* anymore.

"Wait, please. Everyone stop." I raise my hands, collecting my thoughts. This time, I speak louder for everyone in the vicinity to hear. "This was not a victory for just one faerie. It's a victory for all. It wasn't a battle of the Ethea, proving which clan is better. It showed us how powerful it is when we align our strengths together." I point toward the Woodlands. "We still have enemies out there, and our world needs us to unite, not to serve one master."

I turn to my friends. "I'm honored… and undeserving, especially after everything I've put you through. But if there must be a queen, I don't want to rule without you. So, as my first act as queen, I share the crown with each of you and ask that we create our own council where all voices are heard. We do this together, or not at all. Do you accept?"

Vale stands with a smile, and the rest follow. "I think I speak for everyone when I say, we picked the right queen." The others nod in agreement.

"We're going to need some help, of course." I look back at the clan leaders. "As I confer with my council, we'll need guidance from our elders. We'll need leaders to help us bring Faylan through this time of transition. Do you accept?"

"I do." My father is the first to respond.

"We do as well." Lord Torlon nods along with Lady Navi.

"I like your spunk, Your Majesty." Lord Zephen smiles his slanted grin next to Lady Irina. "We accept."

Lord Kaito takes a hesitant step to me. "I'm willing to comply for now." He looks deep into my eyes. "But at the first sign of trouble, my folk won't hesitate to go to war."

I nod. "Agreed."

CHAPTER 67

Gazing into the mirror, I barely recognize myself. A week after the battle in Shree, I stand in my new chambers in Eldore, dressed from head to toe in the finest silks. My makeup is dramatically done just the way I like it, the faerie crown sitting heavily on my head.

I'm no longer Pirate Shade or Princess Quinn. I am *Queen Quinntessa*, the first Gwyllion faerie queen in generations. Now I even look the part thanks to Vale, who appears in the reflection behind me.

"I know I'm a genius, but even I didn't think I could make you look this good," Vale nearly squeals. "What do you think?"

She's spent the entire day with her servants dressing me up like I'm one of her dolls. Though, I know part of her is trying to keep her mind off her mother in the dungeons below.

The dungeon I put her in. A pang of guilt, and fear of the days to come rushes through me. Though I may look the part, can I actually do it? This is much more than being captain of a ship, or even leader of a clan. Sure, I've always chased after a position of true strength, and hungered for a chance to prove my worthiness—but have I really earned this? *Can I lead an entire world?*

"Honestly?" I square my shoulders, turning my head from side to side. "I kinda feel like a fraud."

Vale's posture sags.

"Don't get me wrong, you definitely outdid yourself," I quickly reassure her. "I just can't help feeling that *you* should be wearing this crown."

Vale's smile returns as she attempts to tame my frizzy curls. "Because of you, we all wear it. You just get to be the one who carries the load." Her smile fades. "Besides, after what my mother did, I count myself lucky that I'm not down in the dungeons with her."

"You're not your mother, Vale." I squeeze her hands, and she returns the gesture. "And you're right, we now get to figure this out together."

We've spent so long being at each other's throats, who knew we were meant to be sisters?

"What will you do now?" I ask her. "Besides being part of the council, of course."

"Honestly, I don't know what I want to do yet." Vale purses her lips. "But for the first time, I'm excited to find out."

"Knock, knock," Aeron sings from the doorway, and my heart leaps. With everything that's happened, there hasn't been time for us to really talk. My hands grow hot.

"Ouch!" Vale pulls away.

"Sorry!" I fold my fingers behind me, commanding my cheeks not to burn, though I know I'm failing. Under all this makeup, I hope he can't tell. "Yes?"

He smiles. "We're ready for you."

～

Entering the great hall where we first heard the rules of the Ethodine, all five of us are back where we started.

This time, a large wooden table with five sides stands at the center. Around it are five unique chairs, each designed to represent a different clan.

One made of iron for the Gwyllions, one of sea glass for the Nymphs, a wooden one for the Dryads, another covered in feathers for the Sylphs, and the last one shimmers with a pixie dust coating for the Kobolds. It's the intricate designs etched into the table that really catch my eye.

"Hickory… your drawings," I marvel. My hand runs over his depictions of our journey through the Ethodine that are carved into the wood. He's wrapped our story around the edges so I can follow the tale as I circle the table.

Hickory beams. "I had all the pieces custom-built. I wanted to make sure that the set had a part of each of our clans. May it forever be a reminder to us, and to all of Faylan, of what we've learned and why we now rule the way we do."

I wipe a tear from my eye. "Blast, Hickory. We're not even dead yet, and you already have us memorialized." I chuckle, trying to cover the joy welling up. I'm still not used to being so emotional.

Aeron walks over to the iron chair and pulls it out. "Your throne, my queen." He dips into a dramatic bow, and I lightly punch his shoulder.

As we all sit down, reality sinks in. *We're the rulers of Faylan now.* And there's so much to be done.

Turning to Alys, I get down to business. "How's Whit's progress?"

Completely ungloved, Alys' tattoos are proudly revealed for all to see. She places a hand on my arm.

Whit is stable for now. It seems her goblin nature might be reversible, but it'll take time. She's been asking for you.

I wince. I haven't looked in on Whit since she was taken in. Though it'll be hard to see her like that, I make a mental note to go visit her soon.

After I relay Alys' report to our team, Hickory clears his throat. "Alys has also agreed to let some of the Kobolds take a look at her healing ability and see if we can find a cure for the Knolls."

Alys' eyes light up. She'll finally be able to help others with her ability, even if she wasn't able to save her sister.

I'm so happy for her, but I bite the inside of my lip as I think of my own sibling still alive, stuck somewhere in the Neverworld.

"How about the Mystics? Have we located any of them yet?" I ask. No one's seen them since our time with them underground, not even during the battle in Shree. I worry we'll never find them again. Or Gaius.

"Funny you should mention that." Hickory turns to one of the pillars. "You can come out now."

Out walks Pylo, leaning on his staff.

I shoot up and draw the sword at my side. "Stay where you are, liar!" I threaten. Apparently, this is exactly what everyone expected I'd do, as they all clamber to their feet, throwing up their hands to stop me.

"Quinn, without him we never would have been able to stop the qu... I mean, Gwendolyn," Aeron cautions me.

"Because of him, I'm no closer to finding my brother," I snarl. Pylo's hands are raised in surrender. "Why didn't you tell me he was in the Neverworld? What did you have to gain?"

"We had nothing to gain, and everything to lose," Pylo reassures me, careful not to move a muscle. "The former queen might be behind bars, but we don't think she was working alone. She may have been acting under someone else's orders. If we're right, our remaining brethren are too few and too weak to give up all of our secrets just yet. The Mystics needed to stay hidden. And, if it came down to it, we needed you to destroy the Key. We couldn't give you a reason to hesitate and have it fall into the wrong hands."

My blade falters as I remember Aeron saying the goblins seemed to be called away, abandoning the former queen in the end.

"As for Gaius, he's the one who sought us out in the beginning. He couldn't accept that you were dead when you first disappeared from Greymerrow. He searched for you, for answers. Like you, he found more than what he intended. He found us."

My anger dissipates and I lower my sword. *Gaius was looking for me?*

Pylo takes a tentative step forward. "I've been thinking more about your dreams. I believe Gaius might've been initially using dream power to try contacting us from the Neverworld. Instead, he somehow reached you. We assumed this was because of your connection as his twin. And possibly because of your mother."

Tears well up with joy and confusion. *I was right.* Gaius was trying to talk to me this whole time. I pause. "What do you know about my mother?

"Now that the immediate danger is over, we can answer more questions," he reassures me. "We can even train you—all of you—to harness the full extent of your abilities, in secret of course. When Gaius finds what he's looking for on the other side, he'll return to us."

My brows furrow at his avoidance of my question, but a more pressing one rises to the surface. "What exactly is Gaius looking for?"

Pylo hesitates, looking at Hickory, and then me. "I can't say at the moment. If he secures it, we'll not only defeat the goblins and whoever leads them now, but we'll also return the moonrain before the prophesied destruction can come to pass."

"Wait, didn't we stop that from happening already?" asks Vale.

"You kept the weapon out of evil's hands, yes. Now the moonrain must return for Faylan to be saved. We need to be patient. We must give Gaius more time."

"We might not have time," I say, and all eyes turn to me. "There's one thing I haven't told you. The dreams I've been having of Gaius… they've stopped. If what you say is true, what if they've stopped because something's happened to him?"

I'm terrified of losing him again. How can I just sit around and wait for him to come back if he's in trouble?

A hand touches my shoulder. "We'll save him, Quinn." Aeron looks at me with reassuring eyes.

"Yes," Vale says. "Along with all of Faylan. Peace between the clans is still fragile, and there's so much to do, but we'll figure this out."

Alys places her hand on my other shoulder with a nod.

"We'll do it together." Hickory smiles.

A hopeful heat wells up inside me as I look at my friends. Stretching out my hand, I conjure a ball of fire. Pointing it at the table, I light the candles at the center.

It's as if the torch at Gaius' tomb is relit all over again. Our next challenge lies ahead of us. I smile.

"Together."

EPILOGUE

GWENDOLYN

It's been a week in the dungeons. *My own dungeons.* I wrinkle my nose. It's becoming harder to distinguish which smells worse—the dingy cell or me.

The new queen obviously doesn't know what to do with me. She hasn't even deigned to grace me with her presence since I was thrown in here.

Queen Quinntessa.

I scoff at the thought of her treacherous pirate bottom on my beautiful throne. The throne where my Vale was supposed to sit.

Vale. My only love. The one I sacrificed everything for. I clench my fists, nails biting into my skin. I can't believe she betrayed her own mother to put a back-stabbing vagrant in the very position she was born to have.

"What was she thinking?" I say aloud, knowing only the rats will hear me. I sit on the creaky cot and my face falls into my hands. I go back over the details. "Everything was perfect... I had it all worked out..."

"You've always thought yourself so clever," comes a voice as smooth and oily as butter. The hair on the back of my neck stands on end, and my head snaps up.

He stands in the dim light on the other side of the bars, his hand on the hilt of the sword at his side. "All it took was one measly pirate to make all your careful planning come crashing down."

I stand from my cot. "Maverick."

I thought being in the dungeons meant the Pirate Lord wouldn't be able to get to me. Obviously, I was wrong. At least there are iron bars between us. I take a small step back and lift my chin.

"If you hadn't trained her so well, perhaps things would have gone differently. How was I supposed to know that she had the Mystic fire in her blood? If you hadn't called the goblins away at the last minute, I could've—"

"Enough!" Maverick hisses. He closes his hand into a fist, and my mouth shuts hard against my will. "You dare blame me for your shortcomings?"

I shake my head violently, eyes widening. I can't force another word out of my mouth in either defense or groveling. My throat seizes. I can barely breathe.

"You were supposed to weaken the clans, not strengthen them. I supplied all the pirates necessary to make enough goblins to keep the clans in line, and you couldn't even succeed with them by your side. Your excuses mean nothing." His eyes narrow. "You said you'd be able to create a new Key without a war, and against my better judgement, I allowed you to play your little game to do so. I even handed Quinn to you on a silver platter. I've been patient long enough, Gwendolyn. Now, come."

Though I try to fight it, my body obeys his words. My trembling legs stride forward until I'm right in front of him. My eyes grow wider as he steps closer, with only the bars and inches of air between us.

"We tried things your way," he says, a mix of sea salt and rot on his breath. "Now we do things *my* way."

LOVED THIS BOOK?

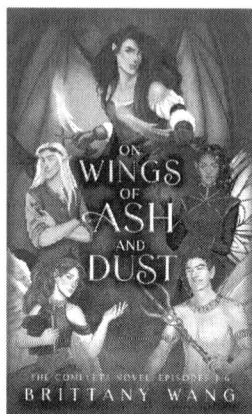

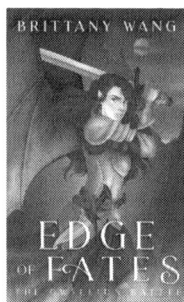

THE STORY WILL CONTINUE...

ON WINGS OF ASH AND DUST

BOOK TWO

BE THE FIRST TO KNOW WHEN IT'S COMING +
Get Behind-the-Scenes Details
The Quiz: What Faerie Clan Are You?
Faerie Clan Merch
Free Writing Resources

SIGN UP FOR MY NEWSLETTER:
www.authorbrittanywang.com/members

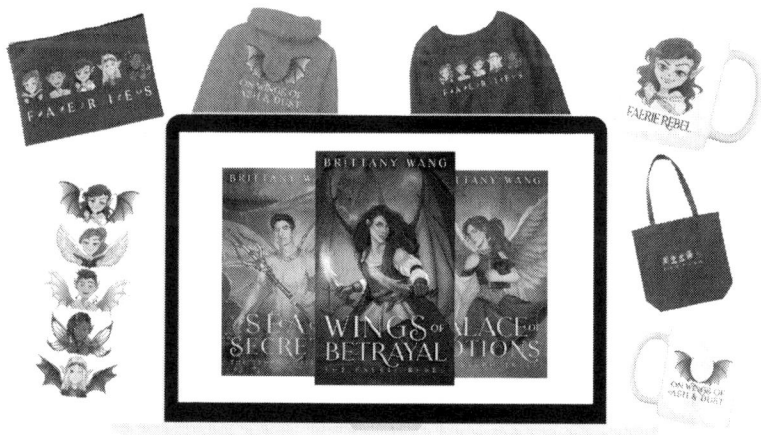

GLOSSARY

Aeron (AIR-ruhn) - heir of the Nymph clan

Alys (AL-iss) - heir to the Dryad clan

Changeling (CHANGE-ling) - a faerie who can transform into another form

Dryad (DRY-add) - a faerie with butterfly-like wings that lives in The Woodlands and values Life

Eldore (EL-door) - the Sylph's sky city in the clouds

Faylan (FAY-len) - name of the faerie world

Feyden (FAY-den) - Quinn's father, Gwyllion clan lord

Gaius (GUY-us) - first heir of the Gwyllions, Quinn's twin brother

Greymerrow (GREY-mare-oh) - the Gwyllion's city in the mountains

Gwendolyn (GWEN-dole-lin) - the Sylph Queen, Vale's mother

Gwyllion (GWILL-ee-uhn) - a faerie with dragon-like wings that lives in the mountains of Greymerrow and values Strength

Hickory (HICK-or-ee) - heir of the Kobold clan

Isinglass (EYE-sin-glass) - the Nymph's city under the sea

Kobold (KO-bold) - a faerie with bat-like wings that lives in the tunnels of Tartarus and values Creativity

Mystics (MIST-icks) - Gwyllions who were banished from Greymerrow for practicing magic

Numa (NEW-mah) - giants who were banished from Faylan

Nymph (Nimf) - a faerie with fin-like wings that lives in the sea-city of Isinglass and values Beauty

Pixie (PIX-ee) - female faerie

Pixie Dust (PIX-ee Dust) - magical dust made from pixie crystals

Puck - male faerie

Quinn, Quinntessa (Kwin-TESS-ah) - second heir of the Gwyllions. Gaius' twin sister. Pirate Alias: Captain Shade

Sprite - child-age faerie

Sprout - infant-age faerie

Sylph (Silf) - a faerie with bird-like wings that lives in the sky city of Eldore and values Knowledge

Tartarus (TAR-tar-iss) - the Kobold's underground city in the tunnels

Vagrant (VAY-grant) - a faerie who has left their clan by choice or has been banished from their clan, often for being a half-breed (meaning they are more than one faerie kind)

Vale - heir of the Sylphs

Vyndoria (Vin-DOOR-ee-ah) - the Dryad's main village in the forest

Youngling (YUNG-ling) - an adolescent-age faerie

ACKNOWLEDGMENTS

I've heard it said, "It takes a village to write a book." And boy, do I have my own "pirate crew" of amazing misfits to thank for this one!

First, I wouldn't be here without the ultimate Author of my own life-story. Thank you God for being a loving heavenly Father who blessed me with the ideas, themes, and endurance I needed to get this book out into the world!

To my incredible husband, Ben—Thank you for always believing in me when I thought I'd never finish, reading every draft (even though you hate spoilers), and cooking all kinds of delicious food to celebrate each milestone. I owe you countless hours of quality time!

Huge thanks to my extraordinary parents—Mom and Dad, you always taught me that I can do anything I set my mind to. You both are incredible examples of that and I love you so much. To my brothers, Zach and Matt—you guys are the Gaius to my Quinn. I am stronger because I have you in my life. Zach, thanks for being such a big fan of this story, even its early draft. I can't wait to see the board game you're designing based on the book! And my sister-in-law, Becci—thanks for your constant encouragement and your endless enthusiasm for the final product. It means so much!

Big shout out to friends like Zack & Cara Russell, Amanda Carlson, Gail Kay and more who constantly cheered me on in such intentional, special ways.

Then we have my writer crew!

I can't even begin to thank my wonderful friend and critique partner, Bethany Atazadeh. This whole journey started with your encouragement to get involved in the online writing community and shoot for the stars! Your love and support of me over the past 3+ years has meant more than you know. Thanks for being my friend, praying for me, helping me tackle crazy plot holes, and answering my gazillion questions about self-publishing.

With Bethany, endless love and gratitude to the other amazing ladies in my Writer Mastermind groups! Mandi Lynn, Savannah J Goins, Holly Davis & Alicia Grumley—Our friendship, weekly writer meetings, and daily marco polos have kept me going!

To my 1st round of beta readers: Ingrid Nordli, J.J. Otis, Holly Davis, Hannah Jane, Mickey Miles, Kate Fann, Abigail McCarty, Bethany Dominguez, Christine L Roland, and Paige—You all hold a special place in my heart! Thank you for your feedback and overwhelming enthusiasm for a draft I knew still needed a lot of work! And to my 2nd round, my dynamic duo: Alli Earnest and Cam Meze— Thank you for letting me test this crazy "serial" idea on you to make sure it worked. You both are wonderful and many scenes are a direct result of your brilliant suggestions!

To my editors, cover designer, and map maker—you are all full of powerful pixie dust!

Fiona McLaren—I still can't believe I found such an amazing "unicorn" of a developmental editor! Your insightful critiques took this story to the next level (especially with Aeron!) and the way you worked so intentionally with me meant the world.

Cassidy Clarke—you are a gem! Your love for this story made applying your copy and line edits the best experience. I've saved all your hysterical fangirl comments about my characters. They warm my heart so much!

Hillary Bardin, my super talented cover designer—I absolutely loved working with you! Your patience with my many requests was incredible and seeing you bring my characters to life has been a dream come true!

Cara Russell - I honestly never thought I'd see a map of my faerie world that portrays its many levels and complexities in such a creative and artistic way! Thank you so much for your attention to detail and commitment to making the map of Faylan so great!

My proofreaders CJ, Stacee, Bethany and Ben—you all went above and beyond as my final line of defense! This story sparkles because of you!

Special thank you to Sarra Cannon—your Publish & Thrive course gave me the confidence and tools to indie publish this series in 1 year! I'm eternally grateful!

My ARC Team Members—You've made marketing this story SO much fun! Your excitement and promotion of this book is a huge reason it's in so many hands now. Thank you!

My Patrons—Thank you SO much for your support over the years! It's because of you that I was able to afford these amazing editors and cover designer and I'm ecstatic to finally give you the final product! (P.S. I have something special for you on the next page!)

And of course, to you, my wonderful reader! Thank you so much for picking up this book! This story and world was created for you. I sincerely hope you enjoyed every minute of it and I can't wait to continue this adventure with you in the sequel!

THANK YOU, PATRONS!

Abby Laughlin, Alba, Alex Rodriguez, Alli Earnest, Alx LeFrey, Amanda Creek, Amanda Peters, Anna Zappia, Ashley Marie Zuck, Ashley Nicole, Athena Marie, Author Bethany Atazadeh, Author Ellie Stephenson, Bair Klos, Brendilynn, Bri Leclerc, Cam Meze, Candye Jordan, Cara Coppola, Carla Calvert, Caroline Brown, CC Gillings, Claudia McDaniel, Dani Penrose, Dania Dorat, Dar Rodriguez, Deidre Sequeira, Donna Marie Tyree, Dora Blume, Edward L Murray, Elira Barnes, Elizabeth Duivenvoorde, Elizabeth Robinson, Esther Diaz, Gabriella Slade, Gale Nienhuis, Grace for Breakfast, Hailie, Hannah Kost, Hayley Street, Holly Davis, Hudson Warm, Ingrid, J S Roberts, Janine, JJ Otis, Kallista Leigh, Kanettra, Kat Satava, Kate Drexel, Katie, Katlyn, Katrina Marie, Katy, Kenzie Dawn, Kevin Ward, Kristy Walker, Kyra Hunter, Leigh Jonsson, Leigh-An, Liz Henderson, Lori DiAnni, Lovis Geier, Mandi Lynn, Martin Marquez, Mary Wockenfuss, Mayah LaSol, Meghan Wiley, Michelle Cantwell, Morgan Lee, NoFilter Kristine, Rachel, Rhianne Roynon, Saiden, Sal Trent, Samantha Gentzel, Sam, Samantha Traunfeld, Sarah Clark, Sondae Stevens, Sophie Isabelle Daigle, Station Fiction (Marion Cécinas), Stephanie Derbas, Stephanie Van den Bos, Stormie Skyes, Susan Miner, Taci, Tayler McLendon, Teresa A Mask, Thomas McNutt, Tracy Carnes, Vanessa Marie

ABOUT THE AUTHOR

BRITTANY WANG is a fantasy fanatic whose early passion for storytelling through songwriting and theater grew into writing epic stories. When not doing writerly things, she loves traveling with her husband, eating delicious food, and getting lost in movies with magical worlds or legendary superheroes. She also loves connecting with readers and helping fellow writers through her YouTube Channel and Instagram.

Get first looks of her upcoming books and tips for writers by subscribing to her newsletter:

authorbrittanywang.com/members

instagram.com / authorbrittanywang
youtube.com / authorbrittanywang
patreon.com / authorbrittanywang

Printed in Great Britain
by Amazon